Night Glimmer

a Novel by Stephen Weagraff

FOR BETH, MY TESS

Chapter 1

Beginnings

New York City, 1912

The black cab moved slowly down the street, the driver looking for an address. It was late, the street dark with just a few gas lamps fighting the gloom. A light fog wised about the cab as it made its way down the deserted street, the only sound the steady clap of hooves striking the rough bricks.

In the late fall wind the cabman pulled his coat tighter against the chill. The neighborhood was old and the farther down the cab went the more wretched the buildings became. Finally, at the very end of the street the cab stopped at an old three story brick building.

"I believe we have arrived sir," the cabman said in hushed tones as he jumped down to let his only passenger out of the cab.

A tall man climbed out of the cab. He was well dressed, a black suit and tie, completely at odds with the dismal surroundings. His white hair was long as was his white beard. Deep set green eyes looked out from a lined face. He reached into his coat and pulled out a wallet.

"If you will, I need you to wait until I am finished. I will make it worth your while." His voice had just a hint of an accent as he handed the driver several bills.

The horse twitched and let out a long breath. She had been nervous since the cabman picked up this fare. A look of anxiety crossed the cabman's face. It was a bad neighborhood and this tall man seemed strange somehow. Still the money was good and at this hour he would never get a fare back to town.

"Of course sir, I'll be waiting," the cabman said as he took the money. With that, he climbed back onto the drivers platform and pulled his coat even tighter, his hat down against his face.

The tall man nodded and walked up the short path to the front of the building. An old brass sign attached to the brick wall read "The Bailey House for Children." He climbed up the few stone steps and stood before an enormous oak door. Grabbing the brass door knocker, he rapped twice.

At first there was no answer, but a dim light appeared in one of the upstair windows. Finally the door creaked open just a sliver. An old woman's voice croaked behind the door.

"It's the middle of the night. The children are all asleep. Come back tomorrow." As the door began to close, the tall man held it and said, "I received a message from a Mr. Campbell. He said it was quite urgent. I'm Dr. Croft, I believe he is expecting me."

"Begging your pardon, sir," the old woman answered as she opened the door, an oil lamp in one hand, "I am very sorry. Do come in."

Dr. Croft walked into the vestibule and the old woman shut the door behind them. She led him into a small parlor to the right of the door. The furniture was old but clean.

"Let me light the lamps and I'll fetch him. Please sit down." She lit two lamps and headed up stairs as the doctor took off his coat and sat down.

Sounds of movement came from upstairs and a large, rumpled man descended the stairs looking like he just got out of bed. He was balding with a large grey mustache. A potbelly filled the white shirt that he was still trying to get into his pants. As he entered the parlor, Dr. Croft stood up.

The balding man reached out his hand. "Oh Professor Croft, thank you for coming on such short notice. I'm William Campbell."

Dr. Croft smiled with a perfect smile. "Yes, of course, pleased to meet you Mr. Campbell. I came as soon as I could. Your note about this child was quite odd; very strange circumstances. Is the child still here?"

"Yes, we have him in a special nursery that we use for sick children. Given the circumstances, we didn't want the other children too close to him. The nursery is in the back next to the staff quarters."

"How long has he been here?"

"A little less than a week."

Dr. Croft thought a moment and said, "Before I examine him, I would like to talk to the staff that received him."

"That would be Maria. She has been taking care of him since he arrived. I'll have Clara go wake her."

"Clara," Campbell called. "go wake Maria and bring her to the parlor. Dr. Croft would like to speak to her."

The old woman who greeted Dr. Croft stuck her head out of one of the staff rooms then headed down another hall.

Mr Campbell asked, "Would you like some tea or sherry Dr. Croft? It must be quite cold outside."

"No, nothing for me thank you."

After a minute a dark young woman with black hair entered the parlor.

"This is Maria, Dr. Croft. She received the child."

Dr. Crofts voice was kind as he stood up, "Please Maria, have a seat. I am sorry to wake you at this hour but it's important. I would like to ask you a few questions if you don't mind."

Maria sat down, her hands folded in her lap. She looked down at the floor.

"Tell me what you remember and please, don't leave out any details." The young woman looked up and began to speak with a heavy accent.

"Five days ago a young constable brought us the baby. He left some papers and said he would be back in touch with us once they finished their investigation."

Dr Croft nodded and asked, "What did he tell you about the child?"

A pained look crossed her face. Mr. Campbell said, "It's ok Maria. You can tell Dr. Croft what you told me."

Maria nodded and spoke in a quiet voice "He said while he was down near the wharf on patrol, he heard a baby crying. He searched up and down the block and finally followed the cries into an old warehouse and on the second floor..."

She stopped and then began to cry.

"It's ok Maria, go on," Mr. Campbell said as he moved next to her and put his hand on her arm.

"He said .., He said he found the baby next to a dead man. The man was cut about his neck and the child was lying next to him, covered in blood. He grabbed the baby and searched the body but there was no wallet or identification on him. The police did not know what to do with the baby and someone in the station knew about us so he brought the baby here."

"I see," said Dr. Croft, "have you been contacted by the police again?"

"Yes," Mr. Campbell nodded, "They told us they can't identify the body. In fact given the man's features, they doubted he was the father. It's possible it could have been a kidnapping gone bad but no one has come forward. In any case, the child is now in our care as a ward of the state. This is what happens when a child is abandoned. He will be put on the list for adoption."

"I see," said Dr. Croft, "and how is the child's health?"

"He is having trouble; he doesn't easily take milk. I think he is getting weaker by the day."

"Any thing else Maria?"

"Well the cat .."

"Now Maria, Dr Croft doesn't need to hear that gossip," said Mr Campbell.

"No, No, please I need to know everything, even the smallest detail. Please go on Maria."

"It's really nothing but go on Maria, tell him," said Mr Campbell sighing.

"Well two days ago, I was changing the baby and I opened the window. I went down to the closet to get another cloth and when I came back there was a dead cat lying in the crib. Now, the rest of the staff are saying that the baby has a devil." Maria started to cry again.

Mr Campbell cut in. "I'm sorry Dr. Croft. It's just foolish nonsense. That old cat has been hanging around here for years; he is quite the pest. The children often feed him. I'm sure he was drawn to the smell of the milk and either one of the neighbors poisoned him or else the years just caught up with him. The staff here can be a bit superstitious."

Dr. Croft smiled and said, "I am sure you have taken very good care of him. The baby will be fine. Don't worry about him. William, I think she has been through enough tonight."

He looked at her again and said, "Thank you very much Maria, you've been very helpful."

"I would like to examine the child now," Dr Croft said as they all stood up.

They made their way back to the nursery.

"Can you turn up the lamps please?" asked Dr Croft.

Clara lit two lamps and their light illuminated the room. Standing next to the crib, Dr. Croft pulled down the small blue blanket. The baby woke up.

Beautiful blue eyes stared up at him. A tuff of black hair was on his head. A puzzled look passed over the doctors face.

"Now lets have a closer look at you," said Dr Croft. He placed his hand on the baby's chest. He touched his arms and feet, felt his stomach then placed his hand on the baby's head and looked down into his eyes. The baby reached up and took his finger. A frown passed across the doctor's face and he lifted his eyes like he was staring into the distance. He stood there for a few minutes.

"Is everything alright, Dr. Croft?" Mr Campbell finally asked.

"Yes, Yes, but the heartbeat is somewhat irregular. I need to fetch my bag from the cab. I'll be just a moment."

Dr. Croft made his way to the door and stepped outside. The cabman was asleep.

"You sir," Dr Croft called. "Please come down."

"Yes sir," the cabman said as he rubbed his eyes and jumped down on the street.

"Your services are no longer required this evening, you may go."

Dr. Croft pulled out his wallet and as the cabman went to take the bills, the doctor took his hand, looking straight into his eyes. The cabman's eyelids drooped for just a second then he nodded his head.

Stuffing the money in his pocket, the cabman climbed back onto the cab and slowly drove away.

The house was quiet as the doctor headed back into the nursery. As he entered, William, Maria and Clara turned towards him. As soon as he entered, Dr. Croft held up his hand. Immediately the three froze in place, their eyes closed. He moved to stand in front of them and raised both hands. He closed his eyes a moment. Reaching into their minds, he planted new memories of tonight.

Mr Campbell nodded as he spoke in hushed tones, his eyes still closed, "Yes we had visitors tonight. A young couple came long after dark. She had lost a child three years ago. He had inherited a store down south and they were moving down there. They would love to adopt the new baby. Maria liked them very much. They had great letters of recommendation. The papers would be drawn up later. Yes it was a little odd but they could take the baby tonight. They seemed so happy. They paid all the fees and left with the child."

Maria and Clara nodded their heads. Clara turned out the lamps and all of them went back to bed. Dr. Croft stepped out and retrieved his coat. He left a stack of large bills on Mr. Campbell's desk then went back into the nursery. The baby was awake, his blue eyes looking up at him. He stood there silently.

Finally, he gestured and the baby and blanket floated up and into his arms. He wrapped the baby in the blanket and said softly, "What will we do with you?"

Taking the child, he walked out the back door. In the moon light the doctors features began to alter. The white beard disappeared and the white hair was replaced with short black hair. The lines and creases around his eyes vanished. Muscles rippled along his arms. A slim, young man not more than thirty five stood where the old doctor had stood. He waited for a moment then holding the child he leapt. The darkness covered them like a glove.

After they disappeared, a darker shadow stirred in the shadow of the old building. The moon reflected for just a moment on a pale form looking out at the darkness then like them it was gone.

Miles away, a dark haired woman sat by a second story window that looked out on a large estate. She watched the moonlit garden that spread out below her, the statues glowing in the cool light. Her dark eyes never left the grounds as she waited for any movement. Finally the wind stirred and she caught sight of a dark form moving across the grass. Leaving the window, she hurried downstairs.

The house had a long glass enclosed room that opened out onto the grounds. As she entered, the young doctor came in from a side door, holding the baby wrapped in his blanket. Their eyes locked for just a minute, a look of pain crossing the distance.

She looked at the bundle he was carrying and her eyes were full of alarm, "Marcus what have you done? How could you bring that here?"

"Sophie, something quite amazing has happened. It is unbelievable. Please go call the others, we need to alter our plans" he said as he sat the baby down and removed his coat.

"Very well, Marcus," the dark haired woman said as she left.

Marcus took the child and went through several hallways. Finally he opened two doors that led into a large study paneled with rich oak. A large bookcase full of leather bound volumes filled one wall. A desk and several chairs were on one end of the room and a huge fire place was at the other. He quickly made a makeshift crib out of two chairs and laid the baby on them. He went over to the fireplace and with a wave of his hand, a fire leapt up. He checked on the baby who was fast asleep then moved back and sat by fire.

In a few minutes Sophie returned, "The others are on their way. Can I bring you anything while we wait Marcus?"

"A glass of wine would be wonderful, thank you Sophie."

In a few minutes, she returned carrying two glasses of wine. She sat the wine down and sat next to him. Marcus shook his head, "It just could't do it, Sophie. I just couldn't carry out the plan. This child is special. Go, go see for your self."

"Are you sure?"

"Yes, yes he is quite harmless now."

She nodded and went over and gently touched the baby.

A gasp escaped her. "Oh my God Marcus, how is this possible?"

Marcus shook his head. "I don't know Sophie. Perhaps Rachel can tell us when she gets here."

"What are we going to do Marcus?"

"I don't know. Please, come, sit with me a few minutes. I need to gather my thoughts before the others arrive."

She took his hand. "Of course my love, anything for you."

For a long while they just sat holding hands and looking at the flames when finally there was a knock at the door.

"I'll let them in," Sophie said as she got up and left.

She was followed back into the room by two men and two women. The first man was tall and muscular, tanned with dark eyes and dark brown hair. The other was thinner and not as tall with blond hair and green eyes. He was followed by two women, their long skirts swishing. Just like Sophie, they were immaculately dressed and very beautiful. The first had long red hair that shimmered in the firelight while the other was shorter with shoulder length blond hair.

As they entered the room, Marcus stood next to the baby.

The group stopped at the door and a short hiss escaped one of the women.

The blond haired man spoke first. "Marcus have you lost your mind, bringing that thing here." he said as he pointed at the baby. "For the love of God what have you done?"

The tall man walked directly into the room, "Marcus your compassion has got the best of you. This creature is a danger to us all. We must destroy this evil now." He moved towards the baby hands upraised as the rest of the group followed behind him.

Marcus held up his hand as he and Sophie stood between the group and the child. "Wait, wait, listen, Lucian, Julian, please hear me out. Don't act in haste as I almost did. Please just sit down and let me explain. Come I have chairs by the fire."

"It's dangerous," said Lucian the taller man pointing at the child.

"He's just a baby, we are in no danger," said Marcus.

Lucian replied, "For now but it's a vampire child, Marcus and deadly. The order will never stand for it."

"There are six of us here, Lucian, I think we can control him."

"Lucian, please, listen to him," Sophie said.

"Very well, but you know what needs to be done and if you are incapable then I will do it myself."

They all sat in front of the fireplace and Marcus began, "Let me explain what happened this evening then you'll understand why I brought the child here."

"I had every intention of destroying a monster tonight. I expected as much when I received the message from the children's home."

"When I first arrived at the home tonight, I smelled the vampire scent as soon as I entered the house. There were of course the common signs; the child was found next to a body covered in blood. There was an animal death. My first thought was that a deranged vampire had transformed an infant. I questioned the staff. The baby had been there less than a week. Frankly, I was surprised there had not been an attack of some sort. The staff instinctively knew there was something wrong with the child and had separated hime. I was all set to destroy the abomination as we agreed then cover my tracks."

Julian and Lucian nodded.

"But when I examined the baby, when I looked into his mind, I saw a miracle. I could not believe it at first but it is true. This child may be a vampire but he is also a witch."

"No, that is completely impossible," Lucian said standing to his feet shaking his head. "You must be mistaken Marcus. It's totally unnatural. You know yourself that such offspring are not possible."

"Until tonight I would have agreed with you Lucian but come see for yourself," Marcus said standing up.

They crowded around next to the chairs holding the baby. Marcus pulled the cover back and held out his hand. A light blue light flashed down and immediately a soft blue light swirled around the baby.

"See he has the sign," said Marcus.

"It's true," said Sophie. "I saw it myself."

"I don't believe it," Lucian said shaking his head.

The rest moved in closer to the child.

"Let me examine him," said Rachel quietly pulling back her long red hair.

They all stepped back and let her stand next to the baby. She laid her hands on baby's head and closed her eyes. The baby cooed and wiggled under her hands. She stood there a moment, lost in thought. Finally, Rachel opened her eyes and said, "It's true, I saw glimpses of his past. His father was a vampire but his mother was a witch. Both natures flow freely within him. I have never seen anything like it."

"But how," asked Grace, the other woman. "That should be impossible."

"If the mother was powerful enough and performed a shaping and the father was well, lets say, well behaved, it might be possible," said Sophie.

"But for what reason?" asked Grace. "What in the world would cause a witch to do such a thing?"

"Maybe she loved him," said a tall woman as she entered the room. "Not all of us are monsters."

Everyone turned as a tall, pale couple walked hand in hand towards them. Both were beautiful in the soft light. Their skin shone like alabaster as they moved catlike across the room. Marcus turned to greet them. He embraced them both and said, "Mora, Stefan I am so glad you are here. We need your counsel in this matter."

The two vampires looked at each other and laughed. Stefan was tall and lean with white shoulder length hair. Mora was slightly shorter with jet black hair. Both had blue, almost crystal eyes.

Mora said, "Is it so difficult to believe? That two immortals could fall in love. We are not as different as you think."

"Don't be so critical Mora," Stefan said.

Mora said, "Marcus we heard Sophie's call and returned as quickly as we could."

Stefan spoke, "If this is true as you say Marcus, then it truly is a miracle. Like you, I have never seen anything like it. However, the bigger question is where are the parents and why was this child abandoned? Something must be very, very wrong for two immortals to go to these lengths and then just disappear leaving their child behind."

"You are quite right Stefan. That question has been gnawing at me since I first recognized the child. Something terrible must have happened for them to abandon their infant. We have many questions that still need answers," said Marcus.

"Puzzling or not, we still have the same issue," said Lucian. "We have an infant vampire and we all know what happens to them. Once the thirst is upon him, he will quickly turn into a mindless monster. That is why they must always be destroyed. The fact that he has a witch mother has absolutely no bearing on this."

"I agree Lucian," said Grace. "Remember we discovered one of these 200 years ago in Paris. It was worse than a beast and incredibly strong. It took three of us to contain and finally destroy it. Marcus, we must move quickly now and without mercy. Humans would have no chance against such a thing. Even we could be in danger."

Marcus thought for a moment then replied, "I understand all of your concerns and I share them but I have given this a lot of thought. Some terrible tragedy has occurred here and we must determine what happened before we do anything drastic. We simply do not have all the facts and destroying the child could make us an accomplice in some terrible evil. Besides he is half witch, one of us, we can't simply destroy him."

"Marcus, you overlook the simple facts" said Julian.

Lucian said, "Say you are right Marcus, but what are we then to do? The thirst will soon be upon him and he will slip completely out of control. The transformation will happen very quickly and a great evil will be born and soon unless we act. His witch nature could in fact make matters worse. We might not be able to control him once it starts. How could we possibly allow this thing to live?"

Marcus paused then replied, "I have been thinking this through and there is one possibility; we could use his own witch nature to suspend the transformation. An enchantment could be crafted that would lock his witch nature in place and bind the vampire nature holding it in check. Both natures would be suspended, holding each in check. His immortal being would sleep and he would grow up as a normal human boy. As long as the enchantment held, his thirst and the transformation would be deferred. This would allow him to grow up naturally and understand humans as we have and when the transformation did occur, he would chose the noble path. He could learn to control his thirst just as Mora and Stefan."

He paused, "We don't know what gifts he would manifest but a vampire with a witch's abilities could be a great force for good should the need arise."

"The dark witches and Draven," said Lucian.

"Yes," said Marcus. "We wounded Draven, severely, but we all know he is gathering his strength and one day will strike. This child's twin abilities could be a great help in our struggle."

Julian spoke up, "I agree Marcus that if possible, saving this child would be the right path but how do we know the enchantment will work? How do we know he will not just become a great force for evil."

"It will take all of our strength but I am sure we can cast the proper spell. Once done, we will raise him as our own. We will watch over him and when the change begins we will help shape the transformation. He will be one of us and at the appropriate time, we will show him how to live among humans."

He paused and said, "But should we fail and he be lost to the dark path, we will be strong enough to destroy him."

Marcus stopped then looking at each of them said, "We need to make a decision, tonight. Grace is correct, we cannot put it off any longer. The transformation will start soon and once started we will be unable to stop it. But this child is here through no choice of his own. Who like me believes he is worth the chance?"

Mora and Stefan nodded yes, followed by Sophie and Rachel. Finally Grace and Julian nodded yes.

Only Lucian remained.

"I still believe this is a terrible risk Marcus. We don't know what his nature will be. The safe course would be to destroy him now while he is weak and vulnerable, that is my counsel."

The vampire Mora spoke, "I know we have had our issues in the past Lucian and I know that with good reason you greatly distrust our kind. But our coven is proof that vampire and witch can live and work together. We have to take this chance. When the time is right Stefan and I will guide him. We can help him walk the noble path but should he fall into darkness, we will be strong enough to deal with him. You need to trust us."

Stefan nodded.

Lucian thought a moment and looked deeply into the fire. Finally he spoke.

"It is still against my better judgement, but if the coven so believes then I concur; but I have your word that should the time come you all will do the right thing no matter your attachment to this child."

"Yes," they each said.

"It's decided then," said Marcus.

Everyone nodded.

"We must do the enchantment tonight. We cannot afford to waste any time. We should take him immediately down to the circle and prepare. Mora, Stefan it would be good if you could guard outside the circle, in case we are unsuccessful."

They nodded. "We will do our part, Marcus," Mora said.

Marcus picked up the child and everyone left bearing anxious faces with their task ahead.

Everyone followed the doctor towards the back of the house. A huge stone door was built into a back wall. He waved a hand and the immense weight of the door shifted and it slowly opened. He entered and carried the child down a long flight of stairs. At the bottom, he gestured with one hand and torches lit around the room. The stone room was bare except for a circle carved into the floor. Everyone except the two vampires stepped into the circle. Marcus laid the child in the center of the circle and stepping back lifted his arms and started a chant. The carved circle lit up with a bright blue light and the others joined in the chant.

It was a long and difficult night but finally the enchantment was complete and as dawn was breaking everyone left the chamber and walked up the long stairs back into the house. Everyone followed

Sophie as she carried the child into one of the sitting rooms. They all sat down exhausted with Sophie still holding the baby.

Julian was the first to speak. "I think we should move the coven. Our time here is almost over anyway. Our lack of aging is becoming apparent and a new born will make matters worse. Tongues wag and questions soon follow."

Marcus spoke, "I was thinking the very same thing Julian. Any one have a suggestion?"

Lucian chimed in, "I suggest our old estate in New Hampshire. We have not been there for a very long time. Everyone who knew us there is long gone. A young couple with a new child will not raise any questions at all."

Sophie said, "That would be perfect. It would be a wonderful place to raise a child. I would not want him growing up in the city anyway. It would be easier to watch him there."

"Good hunting as well, we would not have to travel as far," said Stefan.

"New Hampshire it is then" said Marcus. "We should start the preparations right away. Julian, we need to draw up papers and hide them tonight at the children's home just in case. We do not want to leave any loose ends. We also need to start moving some of our funds in preparation for our travels."

"Yes, that will be no problem Marcus."

Marcus sighed a moment and said, "Before everyone leaves, Sophie I know we are all very tired but could you do one reading for us, Can you try and foresee how long the enchantment will last ?"

"Of course, Marcus. I will try".

Sophie placed her hands on the baby's head and closed her eyes. She sat very still for several moments then spoke. "His future is very clouded. I cannot see him clearly. I know the binding will hold but beyond him as a child, I cannot see. It's impossible to tell."

"Thank you Sophie. I know it's been a very long night. I think everyone should go and get what rest they can. We have much work to do tomorrow."

Everyone got up and Sophie and Marcus went to the door and everyone said their goodbyes. Marcus closed the door.

Sophie smiled at him and laid her head against his chest.

"It's a miracle Marcus. We will have this beautiful baby boy to raise! I never thought that would be possible for us, after all this time."

Marcus put his arms around her and said, "Yes, he is a miracle Sophie and I'm sure you will be a wonderful mother. We will make a family for him and raise him as our own."

He kissed her head then Marcus stepped back

"Now I have work to do. There are many details I must attend to and I still have to meet Julian at his office."

Sophie nodded and said, "I need to go into the city and get some baby clothes and pack for the trip. I'll have Rachel and Grace help me. "

Marcus nodded and said, "Of course, get anything you need." He started to turn and leave.

"Marcus," she asked.

"Yes," he said turning back.

"In our rush we have forgotten something terribly important."

"Yes, what is that my dear?

"What shall we call the baby? I mean the baby needs a name."

"How could I be so foolish, Sophie. You are completely right. Now, what should we name him?"

Sophie thought a minute and said, "I would like to name him Aidan after my father. I know it was long ago and times have changed but it would mean a great deal to me."

"Of course, it's a wonderful name Sophie. Aidan it is then. Try and get some rest before you go and let the baby nap, he had a long night as well."

He leaned down and kissed her and the baby's head. Sophie smiled. and Marcus left. Sophie took the baby upstairs, singing a soft song.

Two days later as they were making their final arrangements, a message arrived for Dr Croft. It was from Mr. Campbell. He said that his services would not be required after all. The child was fine and a young couple heading down south had shown up and taken the baby on the spot. The baby was happy and with a wonderful new family.

Marcus, looking up at Sophie and the baby, smiled and nodded in agreement.

Chapter 2

Transformation

The Clayton School for Young Men
Berlin, New Hampshire
1931

It was the same dream as before. I was running through a thick forest, the moon was bright, streaming around me. I could just make out a path ahead of me that wove through the moss heavy trees.

Something or someone was behind me, a shadow that flickered from tree to tree. As I ran I took a quick glance behind me. The shadow was still there right behind the tree I had passed. I could just hear its voice echoing in the trees, calling my name, "Aidan, Aidan, stop."

I ran harder, my breath coming in great gasps. I was cold, the air misty and damp. I ran as fast as I could, seeking someway out but the forest seemed to go on forever. As I ran, I could feel the shadow getting closer. It called my name again. I turned to look but as I turned, I tripped over a root in the path and fell. My face hit the ground and I slid across the damp leaves of the forest floor.

As I turned over the moon was shining all around me. I could see him, the shadow, next to a tree just beyond the light. In the darkness, I could just see its red eyes staring at me.

He stepped out from the shadow of the tree and the moon's full light fell on him.

Thats when the screaming started because the face, that terrible face with crimson eyes and sharp teeth was mine.

I woke with a start, my bedsheets twisted in my hands. Looking around the small dorm room I saw moonlight streaming in from the window. Sam my roommate was fast asleep in the other bed, the sound of his snoring filling the room.

I got out of the bed and walked down the hall to the communal bathroom. I ran water in the sink and splashed some on my face.

Standing back, I looked into the mirror. A young angular face with bright blue eyes and black tussled hair looked back. I ran my hands through the shaggy mass and rubbed my eyes. I looked down at my watch, 4am.

Third time in two weeks with the same dream. I knew I should go back to bed, I had track practice in just a few hours. I looked down at my watch again. I could go for a walk to clear my head but I was exhausted so I went back to my room. Sam was still snoring as I laid back wishing for morning. In a few minutes I thankfully fell into a dreamless sleep.

Next thing I knew someone was shaking me. It was Sam. "Aidan, get up. You're going to be late for breakfast."

"Ok, Ok, I'm up."

"Another bad night last night?" Sam asked.

I nodded my head in silence.

"Maybe you should go to the clinic and see Dr. Marks. You look terrible Aidan."

"I'll be ok. You go on, no reason for both of us being late."

"You sure?"

"Yea, go on."

"Ok, see you at practice" he said as he bolted out the door.

When he left, I laid back down again. I was still exhausted from last night. Maybe Sam was right and I should see the doctor but right now I had to get to practice. Coach would give me hell if I missed again. I got up and dressed quickly in my gym clothes and headed downstairs. My legs felt like lead and my head was throbbing as I entered the huge cafeteria.

At breakfast I looked down at my eggs. Hunger was the last thing on my mind. My friend Robert reached over and took my toast.

"Damn Aidan you look like hell."

"Yea I know" I said looking up. Sam had already left.

"Listen I'm heading on down to the track, I'll meet you guys there," I said.

"Your funeral," he said as he dug into my eggs.

I was not looking forward to practice.

Dust from the track blew over my shoes as I leaned over with my hands on my knees trying to catch my breath.

"Aidan, you run like an old woman. What's wrong with you? Even Peterson out ran you and he is an old woman!"

"You're total ass Sammy," said a lanky young man standing next to me, leaning over as well.

"Yea, shut up, Sam," I said between gasps.

"Even my little cousin Matilda does the 100 yard faster than that," Sam said.

I just scowled at him sitting on the bench laughing at us, his bright blond hair blowing in the wind. Of course as usual Sam had the fastest time. Normally I would have come in second but not today.

"Alright, knock it off you piss ants," said a gruff voice matched by an equally gruff exterior. Coach Nelson was walking in from the center of the track scowling at his stopwatch. "Everybody have a seat," he said.

We all jumped to sit on the first row of the bleachers.

"That time was pretty awful Croft, you sick or something?" the coach asked.

"No sir, I just haven't slept too well the last few nights."

"Dreams of Elton girls keeping him up," said Peterson from the back row making an obscene sound. Everybody laughed.

"Well dreams or not, everyone one, and I mean everyone," he said looking straight at Sam and myself, "needs to get some rest. We have the big meet against Harmon day after tomorrow and I want everyone running their best. Lights out early tomorrow night, understand?"

"Yes sir," we all said.

"And speaking of the Elton ladies," he said. "The dean wants me to remind you maggots that we have the fall dance with them that same night. Everyone is going, no exceptions. We will bus you back here after the morning meet. I want you to rest, shower and be ready to go by 5:00pm sharp. No stragglers. And the dean says you are all to be on your best behavior, got that?"

We all nodded, "Yes Coach."

"Ok, practice is over. Like I said get some rest tomorrow night. Now beat it." He walked off, the ever present cigar pulled from his pocket.

We all got up to leave.

"Peterson you are such a pain," I said as we we left the track and headed back to the dorms. He made another obscene sound.

"Oh don't pay him any mind," Sam said grabbing my arm. "He's just jealous. With that big snout of his, he would be lucky to get an elephant to dance with him much less a pretty girl."

"Will too," Peterson said gruffly. "You're just an asshole Sammy."

"Asshole or not, they will be lining up to take a twirl with Samuel Tyson" Sam said as he spun around with a fake dance step.

"Yea till you trip over you own big feet," said Robert coming up behind us.

Sam made an obscene gesture not even turning around.

I laughed. "So Sam you can dish it out but can't take it" , I said as we headed through the large door that led back into the dorm. The four of us went straight up to our rooms on the third floor. Peterson and Robert had the room across from Sam and I. We had all been friends since we started at Clayton.

Once inside I headed down to the showers. I let the hot water run down my face and back, washing away last nights dream and my terrible track time. Leaving the shower, I felt better.

Back in my room with the sunlight streaming in my mood improved immediately.

Sam was already showered, sitting on his bed reading a magazine.

"Feeling better?" he asked.

"Much."

"Hey your folks coming up for the meet Saturday?" he asked as he laid back on his bed, hands behind his head.

"No, I was home three weeks ago for my birthday, remember? And we have that dance Saturday night anyway so I told them to just stay home."

"Oh yea, thats right. You turned nineteen and we all got drunk on that crap Robert brought us. The next day you were scared shitless your mom would still smell it on you. Before they got here you took what like ten showers?"

I threw my pillow at him. He grinned and ducked under it.

I got dressed and told him, "Hey I am going down to the library to study some Latin, you want to come ?"

"What and miss this view?" , he said pointing out the window. "Naw I think I'll just take a nap. Have fun with the Romans."

"Ok, I'll see you at dinner"

"I'll be there," he said.

I left the dorm and walked across the campus towards the library.

Clayton is about as far from city excitement as you can get. An all boys school on the outskirts of Berlin, New Hampshire; itself not exactly the center of the universe.

At Clayton, not much to do but study and then study some more. I guess that was the general idea. Still, I had come to love the place; the old red brick buildings and wide trees, the trimmed yards and of course all the food you could eat. I was going to miss it after graduation which was just two months away.

By that evening I was back to my old self, thoughts of the forest dream long gone and as coach instructed Sam and I got to bed early Friday.

I slept like a baby and Saturday morning we rushed down to a quick breakfast then on the bus to the track meet. Everyone was nervous although it was hard to tell whether it was the meet or the dance later tonight.

Sam of course won all of his events. I managed to win one and come in second on another one (I still beat Peterson). After our victory rally, it was back to Clayton for a quiet afternoon followed by a major logistics nightmare as we all tried to use the same bathroom to get ready for the dance.

But by 5:00pm we were all dressed in our best blue blazers, shoes all polished waiting on the bus to take us to Elton. The girls school was only about an hour away but the ride made for some sweaty palms for the freshman who Peterson ragged on the whole way.

I was not nervous but felt a little odd. Maybe I had pushed it just a little too hard at the track meet. I also a little anxious about seeing Mary again.

Mary and I had met in the fall at a similar dance we held at Clayton. We were both seniors and had really hit it off. After the dance, we had exchanged a few letters. I could still see her with her long blond hair and pretty blue sweater. The freshmen were not the only ones with sweaty palms.

I sat right next to Sam on the bus. We were about twenty minutes out from the Clayton campus when Robert motioned to Sam from his seat across from us. Robert had of course brought on a little bottle hidden under his jacket. Where he got this stuff no one knew. Sam leaned down behind the seat in front and Robert handed him the bottle. Sam took a big swig. Peterson who was in the seat behind us, leaned up and whispered, "Coach will kill you if he finds that stuff."

"Well then he's just not going to find it, is he?" Sam whispered back.

Sam motioned for me to take a drink. I thought about it but I was already feeling a little queasy. All I needed to do was puke just as I walked into the hall, so I shook my head. Sam passed the bottle back. Robert just shook his head.

Finally after a long bumpy ride we arrived at the Elton campus. Robert hid the bottle back under his jacket, then he, Sam, Peterson, and I walked into the large hall that held the dance. Elton was a lot like Clayton. Big old red brick buildings, immaculate yards. We were in a large hall that had a stage at the rear. The hall was normally used for plays and concerts but tonight they had moved all the chairs to make a dance floor. Up on the stage, a band was setting up.

Once we were all inside, the Dean of the girls school climbed up on the stage said how happy she was to see us and hoped we all had a good time. She told us to all mind our manners, to remember that there were ladies present. When she was finished, the band started to play.

There was food against one wall and a large bowl of punch. Sam and Robert looked at each other with a grin.

I headed for the punch to get a drink before Robert polluted it. It was a little too sweet but cold. I drank a whole glass and poured another one. There was an open door to the side that led out to a large porch.

"Hey guys I am going out for some air," I said hoping the fresh air would clear my head.

"Come back and get a real punch," Robert laughed. I walked out and stood on the porch listening to the music and looking out at the immaculately trimmed yards.

I heard a young woman's voice say "Penny for your thoughts."

I turned around. It was Mary. She looked beautiful in a light blue dress. She had her long blond hair pulled up.

"Mary, it's great to see you," I said taking her hand. She gave me a quick hug.

"You look beautiful."

"Thank you, you're pretty handsome yourself."

I smiled. "School going well?" I asked.

"Yes, how about you"

"Very well, preparing for exams. Latin giving me fits," I said.

"It gives everyone fits," she said.

"Well I guess I am in good company then."

She laughed. It was such a happy laugh, it put me immediately at ease.

"It's really good to see you," I said. "You too," she answered smiling.

"Would you like to dance?" I asked.

"With you, of course," she said.

I took her hand and we headed for the floor.

I saw Sam with a brunette beauty on his arm. Robert and Peterson were also on the floor.

Mary and I moved through the crowd. She was really beautiful with her bright green eyes. We danced several dances then I took her to get something to drink, avoiding the punch.

"You're a great dancer," she said to me.

"I have an inspiring partner," I said. She laughed again.

"Ready for another dance?" I asked.

"Absolutely"

We went back onto the dance floor. The music slowed down and I held her a little closer. She held her head next to mine. We swayed for a few minutes to the music.

Mary's perfume was intoxicating. I could smell it on her neck. I bent in closer and took a deep breath. She pulled me just a little closer. My lips brushed her neck. Her hand tightened on my back. Desire ran through me. I could almost taste her scent. My mouth ached. I was suddenly very, very thirsty. It would be so, so satisfying if I just...

I gagged and pulled back from her.

She looked up confused.

"I'm sorry Mary, I suddenly don't feel very well. Could we sit down a moment?"

She had a concerned look on her face. "Sure, there is a sitting area in the back, lets go sit there," she said pointing to the back of the room.

As we walked to the room I said, "I had a track meet today, I think I may have pushed myself a little too hard." As soon as we were in the room I sat down on one of the couches.

"I'll get you some water," she said.

I sat on the couch rubbing my hands together. It was getting hot in this room. The air seemed stale and thick.

Mary was gone only a few minutes when she walked back into the sitting room with a glass full of water. I drank most of it but I still felt warm. Mary noticed and put her hand on my head.

"You're burning up, Aidan. I am going to get someone to look at you."

She left and came back with one of the Elton proctors.

"Not feeling well my dear?" the proctor asked.

"Not really, it came on all of a sudden," I said. She felt my head.

"I think you may be running a fever young man, let me call over one of the Clayton chaperons," she said walking off.

Mary sat next to me holding my hand.

"It will be fine, Aidan, Maybe you just got a chill. It is a little cold in here."

"Could be. Thanks for taking care of me Mary. I am so sorry to ruin our evening."

"Oh it's alright, Aidan. You can't help it. Anyway, we'll both graduate soon and then we can see each other whenever we want," she said smiling.

"I would like that very much," I said. She squeezed my hand and smiled.

The proctor appeared with our Dean Porter right behind her. He was a tall imposing figure in a dark brown suit.

"Not feeling well, Mr Croft?" he asked.

"No, Sir. Not really. It came on all of a sudden."

He too felt my head.

"You're right," he said. "I think he's running a fever. We need to take him back to Clayton. Is that all right, Mr. Croft?"

I really did not want to leave Mary, but I didn't want to get sick in front of her either. And that strange feeling I had, that weird sort of thirst; maybe I should go back home. I could always write her and arrange another visit.

"Yes sir," I said reluctantly nodding my head.

"I am very sorry Mary, I was having such a great time." She was still holding my hand.

She squeezed my hand and leaned in and said, "Me too. Promise me we'll see each other soon." She gave me a short peck on the cheek. The proctor's face showed her disapproval but Mary didn't seem to mind.

I nodded and said, "We will. I promise." She smiled at me. Dean Porter cleared his throat.

"I guess I need to go," I said to Mary. I stood up and Dean Porter and I walked toward the door. I turned and Mary waved goodbye at me. She blew me a kiss. I smiled and waved back.

Sam and Robert came walking up. I must have been pale as a sheet.

"You alright, Aidan?" Sam asked, "You look like you've seen a ghost."

"Yea just a little too much today I think. I'll see you guys back at school. Have fun but just don't dance with Mary," I said with a guilty smile.

"She's all yours buddy. I hope you feel better," Sam said.

"Thanks Sam," I replied.

When we got to his car, Dean Porter opened the door to the passenger side. I sat down. The windows were down. Before he got in, he walked over and pulled one of the Clayton attendants aside. I heard him say, "Contact Dr. Croft at home. He left strict instructions that should his son ever run a fever he is to be contacted immediately. Send a car directly to his house. He can meet us at the school. I'll be in my office."

The ride back was terrible. I kept thinking how I had ruined Mary's night. It was so perfect until then. That weird feeling of thirst. I almost gagged again just thinking about it.

We waited in Dean Porters office. He gave me a drink of water but I could not bring myself to drink anything. After twenty minutes or so, I heard my father's voice in the hall. Dean Porter let him in.

"Hi Dad," I said.

"Hello son. Whats wrong, they told me you got sick at the dance."

"It's nothing. I felt kind of odd at the dance, I got really warm. I think I may have pushed myself a little too hard at the track meet today. I am a little sick to my stomach."

I was embarrassed to say anything about the incident with Mary.

He put his hand on my head. I felt a strange sensation like he was looking at me from the inside.

He turned to the Dean Porter. "He's running a high fever. I would like to take him home and bring him back on Monday if he is better."

"That ok with you, Aidan?" Dad asked. I nodded.

"Of course, Dr. Croft," Dean Porter replied. "Anything else we can do?"

"No, I believe you have done everything Dean Porter. Thank you very much."

Dad reached out and shook his hand.

"I hope you feel better young man," the Dean said.

"Thank you sir," I said. We walked out to my Dad's car.

My uncle Julian was in the front seat.

"Uncle Julian, what are you doing here?" I asked. He was my favorite uncle. When I was young, he taught me to play baseball and how to ride a horse. He was always telling jokes and most of the time they were really funny. I felt better that he was here.

"Rachel and I were over playing cards with your Mom and Dad so I drove up with him. I was about to take the last of his cash when they came to the house and said you were sick," he said winking.

"How you feeling?" he asked.

"Not great. Really tired and hot and my head hurts. I think I may have pushed it a little too hard at my track meet today," I said.

"Well we should get you home," he said looking at Dad, concern in his eyes.

"Aidan, why don't you just lay down in the back seat. We'll be home in a little bit," Dad said as the car passed through the gate at the front of the school.

I laid back and tried to sleep. At one point I thought I heard Dad say, "It's holding but barely. We don't have a lot of time."

Finally we were home. I was burning up, sweat running down my side. I opened my shirt. Dad came around and he and Uncle Julian started to help me into the house. I felt much weaker. Suddenly I felt nauseous.

I stopped in the yard and was sick to my stomach. Damn right on my mother's roses. I finally stopped when I had nothing else in my system. When I was finished, they grabbed my arms and helped me into the house. Out of the corner of my eye I thought I saw a brief flash of a pale white form at the side of the house then it was gone.

My mother's brother, Lucian was waiting for us.

"Help me get him to the couch," I heard Dad say to him.

They laid me down. I dozed off again.

"Aidan," Dad said.

"Yes sir," I said opening my eyes,

"Son you have a very high fever but I'm just going to treat you here at the house."

"What's wrong with me?" I asked beginning to get a little worried. My head was really hurting.

"You have a fever son but it will be alright. This kind of fever requires some special treatment. But don't worry we'll be right here with you. I just need you to relax and be calm, can you do that for me?"

Now I was really getting worried. Any time Dad told me to be calm it was usually bad.

"Yes, sir I'll try," I said."Where's Mom?"

"She's on her way. She'll be here in a few minutes," he said.

"Lets move him," Dad said looking at Julian and Lucian.

They picked me up. I felt lightheaded, the room around me swam. But instead of taking me to my room, they took me outside through the back door. The moon was just rising. The air should have been cool but all I felt was heat. We reached the garden house.

"Why are we outside?" I asked.

"I'll explain it in a minute, try to be still," Dad said.

He opened the glass door to the garden house. They carried me around some lawn equipment and laid me down in front of a dusty brick wall.

"Why are we in the garden house?" I asked. None of this was making any sense.

"I have a small exam room setup here where I can treat you. Now try and be calm, we'll be there in just a minute."

He reached down to help me up. When he touched me, it felt like thousands of volts of electricity shot through my body. My back arched and a scream ripped from my throat. I fell back on the rough floor. A burning heat enveloped me and I felt something give deep down inside of me. The burning turned to a searing pain. I had never felt pain like this before.

"It really hurts," I cried. Between my moans I heard him say, "The binding is failing. The transformation is starting. We have to get him into the circle now. We need to bind him."

Uncle Julian bent down.

His eyes were sad. "Aidan, listen son. It's possible you could have a seizure. We have to strap you to make sure you stay still. It's for your protection."

I felt something cold on my arm. They had placed a long silver chain all around me. This was all crazy. Maybe the fever was making me hallucinate.

At that moment my mother came running into the room.

She was crying. She moved to stoop down next to me. Dad caught her. "Marcus, please," she said.

He held her arm, "Sophie, Sophie, listen to me. We knew this day would come. We can't stop what's going to happen but we can shape it. But we must get him into the circle."

"Yes, Yes," I heard her say.

She bent down next to me.

"Aidan, son can you hear me?" she asked.

I opened my eyes. "Yes," I said through clinched teeth. She looked down at me.

"We love you son. Everything is going to be alright, you are going to be fine. Don't be frightened. Just do as your father says, Remember do as your father says and everything will be alright."

"I will," I said. Looking behind her, I saw that the whole family was here now.

My aunts Rachel and Grace were standing behind my Mom. To the side was my other Aunt Mora and Uncle Stefan. Why was everyone here?

With that question, another bolt of pain shot through me. I arched again, straining against the chains. I felt them give a little.

"Hold him Lucian," I heard Dad say.

I saw Uncle Lucian spread his arms. Now I really started hallucinating. Blue light like lightening flashed from his hands. The air sang around me and I felt a force holding me from all sides.

The burning was intense. It ran from deep inside of my chest out to my arms and legs. I struggled against the force that held me down and felt it quiver. A deep growl came from my burning throat.

"Marcus, he's breaking free," I heard Lucian say, his teeth gritted.

Dad leaned down and said, "Aidan, listen to me. Don't push back. I know it hurts but you have to be still until we get you into the treatment room. Please don't struggle. Let Uncle Lucian hold you"

I nodded and tried to relax. I felt the force return.

At that point, a really weird dream started. Uncle Julian touched a spot on the wall. I heard a grinding noise and part of the wall slid back. revealing a dark opening. Julian, Lucian, and Dad carried me down me down a long flight of stairs into a large room. Symbols were drawn on the floor and in the center was a large circle. They laid me in the center of it.

Suddenly, candles flared all around the room.

Dad was in the circle with me. He stood at my head and standing directly behind him just in the circle was Mom. To my left was uncle Julian and to my right was Uncle Lucian. Towards my feet were Aunt Grace and Aunt Rachel. Just out side the circle Uncle Stefan stood with Aunt Mora.

As I lay on the cold stone floor, Dad bent down to me. "Aidan, listen. I know this is all very strange but right now I need you to trust me and do as I say. Can you do that son?"

"I'll try," I said my teeth chattering.

"Good. Just close your eyes and try to be still"

I closed my eyes and tried to be calm. The burning was still there radiating out from my chest into my arms and legs.

I heard my Dad say an odd word. It was in a language I had never heard before. He said it in a kind of a sing-song way like a chant. He lifted up his hands. Everyone in the circle echoed his word and immediately a wall of blue fire flamed up along the circle behind everyone.

He moved his hands up and I felt my body leave the floor. The chains fell off of me. He chanted another word and I felt something pull away deep inside of me; something I had never noticed but I knew had been there my whole life. Suddenly that internal force released and left my body.

As it left I felt that searing fire blaze up behind it. I screamed out. The pain was blinding. I felt like my heart was on fire and waves of electricity were streaking out towards my arms and legs. Between my screams I could hear chanting, first soft and then louder. I twisted in mid-air. My heart was beating faster and faster. That deep growl sprang again from my throat.

I felt something else where that inner force had been, a deep calm center was there somewhere in the depths. It felt old somehow. In my mind I saw it, a deep stillness that connected stone and light and air. I saw the forest from my dream. The stillness was there too, between the earth and the trees. Even in the pain it was there, a calm stillness like a cold nights air or a high mountain stream. I tried to reach down into the cool but I just could't reach it.

Another bolt of electricity seemed to flow through me. I screamed again, the pain now rushing up into my head. My eyes seemed to be on fire. The shocks came in waves and waves. My heart was struggling against the shocks, fighting them. I felt like the bones in my arms and legs, my back and neck were moving and twisting and everywhere was that searing heat, the blinding pain.

It seemed like hours passed. I lost all sense of my surroundings. Far away it seemed I could still hear the chanting but it was drowned by the sound of the fire burning and twisting inside of me, the sounds of my bones and muscles like glass breaking and fusing and then against all that the sound of my beating heart.

The pain was intense. My heart struggled to beat against the heat and pain but I knew it was just a matter of time until it stopped. Slowly I felt the shocks and searing heat leave my arms, head and legs. Their twisting pain stopped. They were still now, lifeless. I couldn't move them. Slowly the heat seemed to contract into my chest. The electricity now swirling just around my heart. Its beating began to slow down.

I knew then that I was dying, my heart was really going to stop. The pain had won and I had lost. Whatever my family had tried to do had failed. The burning fire was going to win out. My last thoughts were going to be these wild hallucinations.

Finally that peaceful stillness that was there just beyond my reach seemed to rise up and embrace me. It swirled around me. I was sad that I would never see my family or friends again. I would never get to write that letter to Mary. I was tired, so very tired that I finally stopped struggling.

I felt my heart beat once, stop and then it beat one more time. Like a loud drum, I could hear it's last ring in my ears. Then it was quiet. My whole body was cold and the calm and darkness took me.

Chapter 3

A New Life

Croft Country Home

Northern New Hampshire

1931

For what seemed like an eternity, I floated in a never ending darkness. A silent, vast void. Then somewhere in that darkness I heard a tapping, a soft swooshing sound. It was pleasant to hear something after the dark, after the sound of my heart stopping. I opened my eyes. I could see; there was light. Everything was crystal clear. I had never seen like this before. I could see the tinniest of cracks in the ceiling above me. I heard the tapping sound again and turned my head.

I was in a room that had a large window. The most beautiful late afternoon light I had ever seen streamed in. The light seemed magical. Through the window I could see a forest and in the forest I could see the details of the trees, the bark on their sides, even the veins in the leaves. It was wonderful. I was awestruck with the beauty. I could have spent days just looking at the light.

Tap, Tap. My eyes tracked to see a that a butterfly was on the window. The swooshing sound was its wings moving, the tap was the sound they made as they just brushed the glass.

I must be dead, I thought. I really never gave the afterlife much thought but this was certainly beautiful. Maybe what I felt before was purgatory and this was .. heaven?

It seemed that a current flowed through my body. Not the painful bolts that I felt before but a gentle tickle. The stillness I felt before was there, all around me. I could feel an innate connection to the light streaming into the room, to the forest outside, even to the butterfly still tapping outside the window. For being dead, I had never felt more alive.

I lifted my hand so I could see it. It looked different. It was white, alabaster. Every detail showed. When the light struck it, a faint glimmer seemed to pass over it, like mother of pearl. I laid it back down to listen again.

One sound I did not hear was my heart. I put my hand to my chest. Nothing. No breathing either. It was like I was a statue. I put my hand on my face. Same nose but it seemed hard somehow now. And cold. Maybe I'm a ghost I thought.

I laid back and listened again. There were noises in the house. I heard the sound of people talking. I wondered if they were ghosts too, maybe this house was haunted but since I was one of them, I guess there was no reason to be afraid.

Footsteps. I heard a step, the sound even more gentle than the wings of the butterfly. And yet I could still hear them. It sounded like someone was coming up stairs. I could also hear a heart beat. A live person was coming up the stairs. Would they see me, would I be invisible, would I frighten them?

I thought I heard my father's voice say, "No he has a right to know. We shouldn't wait."

I lay very still.

The door knob turned. I could hear the metal plates in the knobs mechanism slide against each other. The door opened. It was my Uncle Stefan followed by my Mom and Dad.

The world suddenly snapped into place. I was in my room in our country house. The window was on the west side with our yard and the forest beyond. But the details remained. I could hear my parents hearts beating, the sound of their breath moving into and out of their chests.

"Hello Son," my Mom said. Her voice sounded like an angel's. She started to cry. I saw the tear fall from her eye, the sunlight glimmering in it. I heard it splash against her white blouse.

"You had a very long night Aidan," Dad said. I could see that his eyes were red, like he had been up too long.

But if they could see me, then I was not dead! I had escaped the fever whatever it was. I was still alive. Waves of joy flowed through me.

"Mom, Dad, I had the strangest dream," I said.

But when I tried to sit up I noticed that my skin was still pale white and my heart was somehow not beating. And my Uncle Stefan; I could not hear his heart beating either. He seemed different somehow. A feeling of shock began to overtake me. I must still be hallucinating.

In an instant, almost without moving, my parents were at my side. Uncle Stefan sat next to me on the bad.

"You ok Aidan?" Mom asked.

"Yes just feel a little odd. I guess it must be the fever. How long have I been asleep? What time is it?"

My Dad answered. "You have been out for three days Aidan. It's late afternoon. We were very worried about you. How do you feel?"

"I feel .. different. It's strange but I've never felt so good."

"That's wonderful. Everyone is downstairs. Do you think you can stand up and come down?"

I nodded and he reached down. I could feel my Uncle Stefan tense.

The second Dad touched me I felt calmer, like a wave of cool water flowed over me. For a second, I seemed to see myself through his eyes then I was back looking up at him.

He nodded and smiled and I smiled back. Uncle Stefan relaxed a little and stood up. I pulled the covers back. I had on my old undershirt and pajama bottoms. I went to get out of bed. It was like I stood up instantaneously. One second I was laying down and the next I was standing straight up. It was all so weird. Either I was still having hallucinations or Dad must have given me some drugs and I was still feeling the effects.

"Dad, I feel really weird, did you give me something last night?"

"Yes, Yes, I did. You're still feeling the effects. Lets go down stairs. and sit. You'll feel better in a bit."

Walking was equally odd. I seemed to float to the door without effort. The steps seemed to take no time. At one point I was standing with them next to the bed and in the next instant I was at the door. Uncle Stefan was right behind me, standing between me and my parents.

He seemed so different. His skin was just like mine, pale white like polished stone.

I started to ask him what was going on, why I was like him when my Dad caught my arm and said, "Come on, we'll answer all your questions downstairs."

Like me, Uncle Stefan seemed to just float. I could not hear his feet touch the ground. It was like he moved with no sound at all. When we got to the stairs, he winked at me and motioned with his head towards the stairs. Walking down the stairs was equally odd. At one second I was at the top of the stairs and at the next I was at the bottom. I seemed to just flow down them. When we got downstairs my whole family was sitting in the den just like in my dream.

They all had worried looks on their faces. Aunt Mora came up. Like Stefan she was just like me, skin pale, alabaster white and cold. Then I noticed her eyes. They were like Uncle Stefan's, blue almost crystal. I had never noticed that before.

She hugged me tight. She was very cold. "Welcome back," she whispered in my ears, Her voice was the most beautiful sound I had ever heard in my life. I was awestruck for a moment. She took my hand.

"Come now, close that dropping jaw and sit down."

I followed her to the couch. We had a large den in the country house with enough chairs for everyone. I sat down with Uncle Stefan on one side of me and Aunt Mora on the other. Mom and Dad were right across from me. Everyone else was behind them.

"You had a rough couple of days Aidan, how do you feel?" Uncle Julian asked.

"Wonderful," I replied.

"No, how do you really feel, be honest."

"Well, I think Dad must have given me some really powerful drugs because I am having the oddest sensations. I can hear things. I can hear all of your hearts beating except Uncle Stefan and Aunt Mora's. I could hear a butterfly out the window when I woke up. I can see the smallest detail. My skin's all different. At first I thought I was a ghost especially since I can't hear my heart either. Like I said, those drugs must have sent me on a real trip."

They all chuckled.

Dad nodded. "Tell me what you remember about last night," he asked.

"Oh, boy I had the strangest dream. I must have been hallucinating from the fever. I thought you carried me out to the garden house at home down into some secret room. Uncle Julian and Lucian put chains on me. I know it all sounds crazy. Then I was in this circle and all of you were chanting these weird words. I felt like I was on fire."

I thought back and got a little choked up.

"I thought I was dying, the pain was so bad. It was strange, I felt like I was burning up but cold at the same time. Then I had the strangest feeling like my heart stopped beating. It was the weirdest dream I ever had. Then I woke up here in my bed."

He paused a moment. Everyone was looking at me.

"Aidan, I am glad you are feeling better but there are some things you need to know and I think you should hear it now from me. Some of this will be hard but you need to know the truth."

He sounded really serious. "Are you and Mom getting a divorce?"

They all laughed again.

"No Aidan we are not getting a divorce. It's about what happened to you last night. I need to tell you something." He paused a second.

"You did not hallucinate what happened last night; it was not a dream. Everything you saw and felt last night was real."

"Huh, What part?"

"All of it"

Now, it was my turn to laugh. "Yea thats a good joke, Dad. Whatever you gave me sent me on one wild trip but it was not real. I mean it couldn't be real. Stuff like that doesn't happen."

"I am afraid it was real son."

I waited for them to laugh but they all had serious looks on their faces. I looked at Uncle Julian. His eyes were sad as he nodded.

"That can't be. Why would you do that, Why would you tie me up in a chain?"

"We had to Son, to protect ourselves."

"From what?" I asked

"From you," he said quietly.

"And what you feel now is true. Stefan has no heartbeat and neither does Mora. "

I shook my head. "No that can't be true. They would be dead." My voice was getting higher and I sat back harder in the seat.

"And you don't have a heartbeat either Aidan."

"No, No, that's not true. It's a trick. You gave me some drug. That can't be true." My voice was going on edge, I could feel panic about to take over. "You're tricking me or or I must still be asleep, this can't be true."

Uncle Stefan grabbed one arm and Mora grabbed the other. They were like iron vices. I pulled against them. They strained but held me tight.

"No, No. This can't be real. Tell me it's not real," I yelled. Hysteria was about to set in. I was going to lose control. The room started to spin..

My mom's hand went to her throat. There were tears in her eyes again. I looked down at the floor.

And in that moment I felt something change. It was a dryness at first then I felt a little of the fire from last night at the back of my throat. It felt like ash and I was...

"Thirsty," I shouted. They held me even tighter. I looked up.

I saw my Aunt Grace. Her features swam a little and she looked like Mary. Even from where I sat, I could hear her heart beat, the vein pulsing in her neck. Just like with Mary I wanted her ..

"Blood," I screamed.

That same growl from last night sounded deep in my throat. I struggled to free myself from the grip they had on me.

It was overpowering, the need to drink. The thirst was incredible. I would have done anything to quench it. It was like what I felt at the dance only thousands of times stronger. I needed her blood. I strained to break free, to sink my teeth into her neck.

Grace pulled back against the wall, Lucian and Rachel in front of her.

My mother cried, "Marcus do something."

"Julian, Lucian, you need to help hold him," Stefan said holding on to me with a grimace. I twisted to get away.

My uncles moved towards me. Lucian was always a frightening figure to me, very tall and extremely muscular.

"Lucian remember it's still Aidan," I heard Dad say.

As he stood directly in front of me, I was afraid he was going to strike me. Again, a growl like some animal's came from deep in my chest.

But he just stuck out his hand and I felt an even stronger grip surround me. It was just like last night in my dream.

Julian came and stood in front of me as Lucian moved to the side.

"Aidan, listen to me," he said.

"We are going to hold you. Don't struggle. We will help you but don't struggle."

He held out his hand and I felt another force grip me. I was surrounded. I could not move.

"Please, please, tell me this is not real," I said, misery in my voice.

My Dad yelled, "Sophie, you and Rachel get Grace out of here."

"But Marcus, Aidan."

"Now," he screamed.

They ran from the room as I pulled even harder against the binding.

"Hold him. I have something that should help," Dad said as he left the room.

Aunt Mora leaned over and said, "I know what you feeling right now Aidan but this will pass, I promise. I'll help you. Just don't fight us."

Her words brought some measure of calm back to me.

I could smell it before my Dad walked back into the room. Blood.

He walked in carrying two glass bottles filled with blood.

"I brought it from the university hospital." He sat the bottles down and went into the kitchen. He came back with a large glass and opened the first bottle.

The most amazing smell filled the room. It was like Mary's perfume, intoxicating. My mouth ached.

Dad poured the glass full and held it to my face.

"Drink."

I was embarrassed but so thirsty. I drank deeply from the glass. He kept lifting and I kept drinking, The thirst abated some. I finished the glass.

"More?" he asked.

I nodded. As I drank, I felt some trickle down my chin. I looked at uncle Lucian, a look of horror passed over his face.

Dad poured the rest of the blood into the glass. I finished it and the second bottle.

I felt completely alive as some new energy flowed through me. I knew I could have easily thrown off Stefan and Mora's grip and maybe even broken whatever Julian and Lucian were doing. But I was calm now, myself again. I relaxed against their grip.

"I am ok now. I won't hurt anyone," I said.

"You sure Aidan?" Stefan asked.

"Yes, I'm sure."

He nodded and Lucian and Julian dropped their hands. I felt their grip leave me. Slowly Stefan and Mora let go of my arms.

I wiped my mouth. There was blood down my hand.

I hung my head.

Mora patted my back.

"Aidan," she said.

"Yes," I said still looking down feeling embarrassed and guilty.

"Look up at me," she said. I looked up.

She pulled a cloth out of her pocket and cleaned my face and hand. It came away bloody.

"Listen to me. It's true, you are different now but you, me, Stefan, we are the same. We are just like you. We feel the thirst just like you. You will learn to control it; we will teach you. Don't be afraid."

"What's wrong with me," I asked, "What happened to me?"

Dad pulled up a chair and sat in front of me. When he did, Stefan grabbed my arm again.

"No it's ok Stefan, you won't hurt me will you Aidan?"

I shook my head, "No, no sir."

Stefan let go of my arm.

"Something wonderful has happened Aidan, something magical. There are things you don't know about yourself. Things we have kept from you. But now you need to know the truth. The world is not the way you think it is son. It's quite different, more mysterious."

He leaned back in the chair.

"Aidan when you were a baby, you were different, special. There was a part of you that went to sleep when you were a child and it slept for many years. But that part of you is now awake and you're true nature is emerging. Your senses are sharper, much keener than those of ordinary people and as you can tell you are very, very strong. The truth is and I know this is hard to believe but you were born a magical being Aidan. You're an immortal, a vampire like Stefan and Mora."

"A vampire?"

"Yes son, that's why you are so strong, why you can see what you see, hear what you hear, move as you do. It's why you need blood."

I couldn't believe it. Me, a vampire? Something out of a myth.

"It's not true, it can't be true"

"It is Son and there's more," he said.

"More?"

"You are not the only one that's different, Aidan. I know this is hard to understand, that its unbelievable to you but none of us are human. Julian and Rachel, Lucian and Grace, your mother and I. We are different just as you are different."

"You're vampires too?"

He smiled, "No Son, we are a different kind of magical beings, we're witches. What you witnessed last night was our coven at work."

"You're witches, all of you?"

"Yes son."

"All this time?"

He nodded as he put down the glass, "I'm afraid so."

He paused a minute. "When we found you as a baby, you were about to go through the transformation into a vampire. As an infant you would not have survived. But using witchcraft, we suspended the transformation to give you time to grow up so you would be older when it occurred, so you would be ready for it. But the magic could not last forever and finally time caught up with us and you went through the transformation into your true self."

He smiled and shook his head, "There's one thing more. It's amazing but true, a miracle really. You are also a witch, the same as us. This is what allowed us to save you."

"I don't understand. What do you mean?"

"I mean your are both, you are both a vampire and a witch."

I couldn't believe it. Then it dawned on me, if I was so different then something else was also true.

"So I am not your real son?"

A frown came across his face, "No, no. You will always be my son. No matter what, you will always be my son. Your mother and I love you, we raised you as our own. Nothing about that has changed or will ever change."

"But you lied to me all these years."

He stood up and starting pacing.

"Yes, we kept this from you. We did it for your own good. We wanted you to have a normal human childhood. To grow up to be the wonderful young man you are before you had to face this. So you would be ready for this day."

"So where are my real parents?"

He shook his head. "We never found them. Julian, Lucian and I, we've looked for years. We still don't know what happened. All we know is that your father was a vampire and your mother was a witch. I found you at an orphanage in New York City. A policeman on his rounds discovered you left alone and took you there. The night we found you, we cast a spell that put both your magical natures to sleep, to give you time to grow up. But it finally gave out and the transformation naturally occurred.."

"And my parents?"

He eyes were sorrowful as he shook his head again, "Nothing, no trace. We are not sure what happened but we believe there must have been some terrible tragedy that occurred. So we did all we could. We adopted you as our own, to raise you until you were ready for your true self to emerge."

"Yea, to become a freak, a bloodthirsty monster,," I said with anguish in my voice.

"No, no Aidan. Thats not true at all. You are a magical being with very special gifts. As Mora and Stefan said, you will learn to control your thirst. You are still that wonderful young man we all love. You are no monster Aidan. Trust me son, you are still yourself."

My mind was swimming.

"I don't believe any of this. How can there be witches and vampires. They don't exist."

"Oh but we do, Aidan. You'll see. Like I said, the real world is much different than you think."

I took a deep breath. I looked at Dad, at Julian, at Stefan and Mora. This was no dream. I was not hallucinating. It was real; I knew the thirst was real. I shook my head in disbelief but it had to be true.

Now I had a thousand questions.

"So what are we really, witches and vampires?"

Dad stopped pacing and sat down.

"Thats more like it," he said with a slight smile. "Curious."

I nodded just a bit.

"Let me explain best I can," he said.

"Witches and vampires are two members of an ancient race. We have lived for hundreds of thousands of years among humans but we are not human. Our beginnings are lost in far mists of time. All we know is that we are descended from an ancient, magical Elder race. We look human but we are not human. We have abilities far beyond what humans have. Here let me show you."

He held out his hand. A figurine that sat on the mantle of the fireplace floated in the air across to him. It landed on the table next to him.

I was dumbfounded.

"Witches have different gifts. Some can see into the future, some can read minds. Some can effect objects around them. Some can control the weather. All of us can change our shapes. Our abilities are responsible for most of the myths of mankind, both good and bad."

"There is a power or craft inside of us that we learn to control. We focus the power through our minds. This focus we call a shaping or a spell. One day you will learn to do it yourself."

I could not believe what I was hearing.

"What about vampires, I thought they were just a myth."

He laughed a second, "I assure you they are most certainly real. Stefan and Mora and now you are a testament to that fact. Vampires are magical beings as well but with different gifts. They don't have the same psychic powers that witches have; instead, they have enormous physical strength and speed. You heal extremely quickly. Vampires are for all intents, invulnerable. As you have found, their vision and hearing as well as their other senses are far beyond anything humans or even witches possess. They have extremely fast reflexes. They are in fact nature's greatest hunters."

Stefan smiled at me, nodding. "Wait you'll see soon enough."

"But we don't hunt humans, right? How soon until I get... get thirsty again?"

Stefan spoke, "It is true Aidan that many of our kind feed on humans. But Mora and I made a choice not to hunt humans; instead, we live on the blood of wild animals. Normally we hunt every week or so but your transformation is still in some respects underway. You will need blood again, very soon. We should hunt tonight."

I thought a minute. "During the change, I was in a lot of pain but there was also this calm feeling too. I felt connected to everything. It's still there but not as strong."

"Thats your witch nature son. That connection is the source of our power. At the heart of nature is a stillness and that stillness is our strength. When it flows through you, magic appears. It's that simple."

"And my witch powers? I don't feel anything special."

Dad answered, "That we don't know son. You are unique. Your vampire nature is very strong, it's your dominate side. It may take time for your powers to appear and even then at first they will probably just enhance or intensify your vampire abilities. But don't worry, at the right time they will appear."

At that point, Grace and Mom came back in the room.

Mom came up and hugged me.

I very gently hugged her back. She kissed me on the cheek.

"We love you Aidan. Remember, no matter what we are here for you."

"I love you too, Mom. I am very sorry I scared everyone."

I saw Grace in the doorway. She still looked frightened.

"I'm so sorry Aunt Grace. I was out of control but I'm better now. I promise I won't ever hurt you are or anyone in the family. I am so sorry."

She nodded but stayed in the doorway.

"Its alright Aidan, I understand. And you don't have to call me Aunt Grace anymore" she said with a slight smiling.

"I guess that's true of everyone isn't it?"

They all laughed.

"It's ok, come and sit by me and we'll finish answering your questions," Mom said as she took my hand and we sat down.

"So how did you all of you meet?"

"Thats a big question. It will take a few minutes to answer," Dad said.

"Oh here we go with the history lesson," Julian said rubbing his temples.

"Hush Julian and let Marcus talk," Rachel said.

"Go on Marcus."

"I was born in France in the early 1200's, a soldier in the Holy Roman Empire. Once a small village that my unit was protecting came under attack. It was a terrible battle but we saved the lives of the villagers. A few days later high in a pass that same group attacked me and a few of my men while we were out on patrol. We were totally overwhelmed and in the battle I was fatally wounded. The villagers we saved found me and carried me to their local healer who was a witch."

"To save my life he transformed me. I survived but I obviously could not return to my former life so he sent me to Ireland with some of his students. I stayed there for years but once I learned all they could teach me I grew restless and left."

"I wandered around for a many years looking for a new teacher. Then around 1280, while I was staying at an inn in Spain and I found a man there playing games of chance. He was very good and I was curious at his winnings. I discovered that he was cheating by reading the minds of the other players."

"I was not cheating," Julian said smiling.

Dad continued, "Anyway, I jointed up with that outlaw. Three years later I met your mother and Later Lucian and Grace joined us."

"And Mora and Stefan?"

Dad looked at them. "That's more complicated. To understand that part of the story there are some things you need to know first."

"Aidan not all witches are like us. We use our powers to explore, to heal, to protect. We don't use our powers to dominate others or to control them. But there are witches who use their powers for great evil. They lust for power and live off the suffering of others. They live in the shadow of dark magic."

"When our little coven was just Julian, Sophie, and myself, we looked for a teacher, someone who could help us understand and extend our powers. Along the way, we picked up another witch who had been a great friend to Julian named Titus and his mate Grace. Our small band heard rumors of a very powerful sorcerer in France so we traveled there to find him. His name was Magnus and he was indeed a very powerful witch, the most powerful I have ever seen. He had established a secret academy for witches where we could learn, practice and increase our powers. In 1310, he brought us in as students and we joined his academy."

"You should also know that in those days, witches and vampires were often at war with each other, driven by our hatred and mistrust of each other. Killings on either side were common."

"We continued our studies with Magnus and his other students for over seventy years and we all learned a great deal from him. But by accident, I discovered a terrible secret. To this day I still don't know how I missed seeing the truth for so long. After so many years of study, we found out that Magnus was not what he appeared. In secret, he practiced very dark, very evil magic. I discovered that he was raising an army, an army of magical beings."

"He was capturing and enslaving vampires as well as lesser witches, twisting them to his will. He was also breeding them from humans he captured. His dungeons were full of them, some just children. He corrupted the vampires with his dark magic, made them stronger, faster but completely under his control. The magic gave them fangs and blood red eyes. The newly made witches he turned into monsters, twisting their natures so that they would stop midway in their shifting, creating terrible creatures, half man, half wolf."

"Werewolves, he created werewolves," I said.

Dad nodded, "Yes, terrible unnatural creatures who craved human flesh."

"Magnus lusted for domination. He coveted power over humans and witches alike. When his army was strong enough, he planned to seize power and set himself up as a new Dark Lord. We discovered that many of our fellow students were plotting with him."

"When the truth came out, there was rebellion within the school. Some sided with Magnus while others fled. But many joined our cause to defeat him. Lucian and his mate Elsa as well as Titus and Grace. There was a terrible battle that lasted for several days. As we fought, we found there was a group of vampires who, enraged at what Magnus was doing to them, had joined in the fight against him. Stefan was their leader."

"In the final battle, Elsa created an opening for us to get close to Magnus but in the midst of the battle she was killed by one of Magnus's vampires."

I looked at Lucian; there was a terrible pain in his eyes.

"Finally at the end, we had our chance and our dear friend Titus, sacrificed himself to kill Magnus." Grace had tears in her eyes. Lucian put his arm around her.

"But that did not put an end to his evil. Magnus' greatest student was an older witch named Draven. Magnus had taught him the dark arts for hundreds of years. He was almost as powerful as Magnus and his first in command. But in the battle, Draven was fatally wounded. After the battle, we searched for him and found his body, but we soon made another terrible discovery. He had survived the battle."

"Wait, what do you mean, you just said you found his body?"

"That's true but magic can perform amazing deeds, Aidan and Draven was a very, very powerful sorcerer in his own right. Once Magus was gone, Draven stole a very powerful magical instrument of Magnus, what we call his Shadow."

Dad clasped his hands as he talked. "Many years before Magnus founded the academy, he discovered an artifact, a perfectly crafted crystal with incredible magical powers. It was ancient. Magnus believed it derived from the earliest age of our race. He said it was the last legacy of our Elders, their last manifestation."

He paused a minute, "The artifact was originally pure, holding great power for healing and knowledge. I believe it was constructed by our elder race as an instrument for teaching. It's the last link to our past."

"But like everything else Magnus touched, he corrupted it to his evil desires. Using his dark magic he was able to project part of his essence into the crystal gaining control of it. It became his shadow self and this Shadow held enormous dark power."

"During the battle, Draven and one of his lieutenants, another extremely powerful witch named Malek, stole the crystal and used it to perform an evil rite, a terrible, unnatural spell. They took one of the human slaves and transformed him. During the transformation,

Draven's essence left his wounded, torn body and he possessed the young body of the slave. What we found was the old husk he left behind."

"The now young Draven and Malek, along with a group of dark witches, vampires and werewolves escaped. We hunted them for weeks but found no traces of them. We do know that sometime during the conflict, Draven and Malek somehow lost the crystal artifact."

"After the main battle and the search, there were many skirmishes with the remaining dark witches. In order to survive, we formed a new coven with Stefan, Mora, Julian, Grace and Lucian. We knew we had to work together to contain the evil that Magnus had created."

"But the war had taken its toll. In addition to the witches and vampires, many humans had died or disappeared. Rumors ran wild. Enough of the truth leaked out that a great hunt for witches ensued. This fear lasted for centuries, all the result of Magnus' treachery. We had to hide, go underground and disappear. We left France and went to Italy then on to England and after many years we came to America. Rachel joined us when we got here."

"We have hidden our existence ever since then. In the modern world it has become easier since to the modern mind we couldn't possibly exist. Of course the same is true for Draven and his evil followers."

"Aidan, you need to know that the war is not over, its just gone underground. We still fight those same dark witches and destroy any of these monsters we find. After all these years, we are still searching for the artifact, the crystal that Draven lost. It holds the key to our past, to who we are. If Draven and Malek find it before we do, they will recreate what Magnus started and a great evil will be set lose on our world."

"Are there many witches left, I mean good ones like us?"

"Yes, more than you might think. Our family is our coven but there are many others. We belong to a lose group, an order of like minded covens, remnants of those who fought and continue to fight against the evil orders like those that Draven leads."

I was quiet for a while, it would take a while for all of this to sink in.

"Well what do you think, son. I know this is a lot for one day."

"All I can say is you all must be the best actors in the whole world to have kept this a secret so long."

Everyone laughed.

"It was not easy, you were such a inquisitive child," Julian said ruffling my hair. "Many, many times we had to use magic to hide things from your prying young eyes."

Stefan came up and spoke, "Enough of this history lesson. Time to live in the present. I think it's time for your first hunt."

I had been so preoccupied I had not noticed that it was getting dark outside.

Now I was nervous remembering the uncontrollable thirst, "Really that soon?"

"Yes, you need to feed Aidan, get in front of the thirst."

"I guess I am ready."

Mora snickered, "Well first, we have to change you out of those clothes. No self respecting vampire hunts in their pajamas."

Everyone laughed again.

I went upstairs and changed and when I came back down, Stefan and Mora were waiting.

The den had a vaulted ceiling and at the top was a large window. Stefan and Mora both leapt up and seemed suspended on the ceiling by the window.

I stood there with my jaw dropping. I couldn't believe the height they had jumped.

"Come on," Stefan motioned.

"I can't jump like that."

"Yes, its easier than it looks," Mora said.

I looked up and holding my breath jumped and gracefully landed by the window. Somehow I just stuck to the ceiling.

"We'll be back," Mora said.

I waved to everyone below and we jumped into the darkness.

I used to be somewhat afraid of the dark, especially being out in the woods at night. But hunting in the dark as a vampire was the most exhilarating feeling of my life. We flew towards the forest. In seconds we were deep into it. In a blur, we ran for what seemed to be miles and miles. Finally Stefan stopped and climbed straight up a tree barely touching the bark as he sailed upward. Mora shot up right after him. It was amazing, I was not even breathing hard. What would Sam think if he could see me now!

I climbed up next. I could just touch the side of the tree and it held me. Hand over hand, foot over foot, in a blur I flew up the side and sat right next to them on a big limb. We were far north and there was still some snow on the ground but I didn't feel cold at all.

"Don't worry, you'll never be cold again," Mora said.

Stefan looked out. He pointed at a shadow several hundred yards away.

"There," he said.

As I looked out I saw a shadow move. It was a large animal of some sort. Then I caught the sent of a human. I turned and far away, high up on a ridge was a small house. The human scent came from there. I turned towards it.

"No, not that one. Remember we don't hunt humans. Think about your friends, Aidan, you would not want to hunt one of them would you?"

"No," I said horrified.

"Well that human is someone's friend, someone's child."

"Yes I know," I said ashamed.

"Its alright, Aidan, just focus on the animal."

She pointed again.

I could see. It was a huge grizzly bear.

"But its a big grizzly," I said. "I can't possibly bring that down."

"Oh yes you can," Mora said.

"What do I do?" I asked.

"Just run up to it. Your instincts will take over. Don't worry you won't get hurt."

"You have to be kidding me, that bear is at least nine feet high," I said.

"Just run up there. Trust me," Stefan said.

I climbed back down the tree (upside down this time. It was really amazing).

As Stefan instructed, I ran right up to the bear. It stood up and growled. It was at least nine feet tall. As I ran at it, it swung its giant paw and hit me square in the chest. I flew backwards into a tree. I struck it very hard and fell to the ground.

I heard peals of laughter come from the tree that held Stefan and Mora. They were doubled over laughing. "Go on, try again," Stefan said pointing with one hand while holding his side with the other.

The enraged bear came at me. An overwhelming power overtook me and I jumped right into his charge. I leapt up and over him as he charged. I was so fast, I easily dodged his claws.

I growled again and jumped for his head, sinking my teeth into his neck. The thick muscle separated and hot blood sprayed into my mouth. I drank and drank. The bear fell over but I stayed locked to him. Finally he was still.

I looked up. Stefan and Mora were standing right next to me. Mora gestured that I had something on my mouth. I wiped the blood away.

"Don't mind her. You did well Aidan," Stefan said, patting me on the back, "But there's something I need to show you. The carcass is drained but there's only a single wound at the neck. A hunter might become suspicious. We have to make this look like a different kill."

With that he took his hand and cut several large slices in the back and arms.

"Now it looks like a normal kill. Also this will attract the forest scavengers. We must always cover our tracks Aidan."

I nodded.

"Any questions?"

"It isn't the same as what I had at the house, not as pure or clean."

Stefan nodded, "You're right Aidan, It's different; it's not human blood. It will never taste the same but you'll get used to it. It'll be enough."

"Want to go again?" he asked

"Oh yes."

Finally as dawn was approaching, I sat high on a rocky bluff that overlooked the forest, its dark trees spread out in front of me. Somewhere deep down I could still feel that stillness but it seemed to have retreated to a far away place.

"How you doing, kiddo?" Mora asked sitting down next to me.

"I don't know. Three days ago I was a nineteen year old student who's biggest worry was finding someone who would dance with me. Now I am this vampire, witch thing that I can't even begin to understand. Other than that, I guess I'm great. Hunting is fun though."

She laughed. "Yes it can be quite overwhelming. But it can be a fulfilling life Aidan. I have lived it for over 900 years. It is difficult at first, especially learning to live with the thirst but you will learn and be happy. Stefan and I will always be here for you."

"Thank you Mora, You don't know what it means to have you and Stefan with me, to know that I'm not alone in this."

"We're your family Aidan. Don't forget that."

"I know."

I just sat for a moment then said, "One odd thing happened tonight on the last bear I took down. I could almost sense what he was going to do right before he did it."

She nodded, "That's witchcraft at work. You are getting glimpses of the future. Like Marcus said, your powers will at first just enhance your vampire nature. That means they will probably be ones that help you hunt or fight. It will be interesting to see what develops."

"Any other burning questions?" she asked.

I remembered Dracula from English class.

"Just one, don't we have to sleep underground in coffins or something before the sun comes up? Won't the direct sun burn us?"

"Don't worry Aidan that's just a myth. Now your skin is very pale and your eyes are like blue crystal so in bright sunlight you could look different from humans. They might become suspicious. So we usually stay away from humans when the sun is bright. But it can't hurt you."

I nodded and sat for several minutes.

"My old friends, I can't go back can I?" I asked, thinking about Sam and Robert but mostly about Mary. How I left things with her.

"No, its far too dangerous for them and for you," Mora said. "It will take a while before you are ready to be around humans again. Besides, they would see that you are different now and wouldn't understand. Given what you know, would you really want to go back?" she asked.

"No, I guess not," I answered.

"Then there is the rule," she said.

"What rule?" I asked.

"We only have one rule but it's absolute. It's what keeps us and them safe. Humans can never know the truth about us. You can never tell them. Believe me, it would only bring them misery. We would be forced to deal with them and that is never good for them or us."

I understood now.

"Its going to be a lonely, isn't it?"

She thought a minute, looking out.

"Afraid so but you have us, and the witches and all the bear you can take," she said poking me in the side. I laughed but then stopped as I looked out. The sun was just beginning to come up.

Yea, it's going to be lonely, I thought as the first rays of a new day touched my now stone white face.

Chapter 4

The Killing Machine

San Francisco

Today

I felt his fear as I chased him across the rooftop. He floated like a shadow in front of me, our only light the glow of the street lamps below us. It was a silent chase, just the sound of our shoes against the roof gravel. He ran to the end of the roof and leapt across the alley separating the buildings, jumping twenty feet to the next rooftop. I jumped right after him, my black coat streaming behind me. My boots hit the roof with a slight crunch and I was after him again.

The chase started, just as Rachel had foreseen, with the vampire attacking a young man. He dragged his victim into the dark shadows of a old warehouse. We found them far in the back against a dirty graffiti lined wall. The light from a second story window the only thing breaking the gloom. On a dusty concrete floor a young man not more than seventeen was struggling against his captor. The vampire's pale hand was held tight against the young mans mouth. Julian and I had interrupted him just as he was about to start feeding. He stopped when I approached. When he looked up I saw his red eyes and fangs, definitely one of Magnus' spawn. When he saw me, he assumed I was trying to take his prey. "This one is mine," he hissed. Julian stepped out of the shadow next to me and said, "Not tonight."

The vampire stood up dropping his young victim. Once released, the young man screamed, "Help me," terror in his eyes. The vampire backhanded him, flinging him twenty feet against the side wall. He crumpled down on the concrete floor. Julian ran over to the young victim. Thinking we were both distracted, the vampire jumped straight up the wall and climbed out of the window.

"Aidan, wait," Julian said but it was too late.

Now the predator was going to be the prey.

Anticipation welled up in me as we ran across the rooftops. Two shadows flowing from building to building. He stopped once and pulled a huge AC unit off the roof and threw it at me. I dogged it easily. He hissed and took off again.

I chased him for three more blocks. Finally I was close enough and when he jumped to the next building, I sailed over him, grabbing his collar as I flew over. We landed together on the next roof top. In a blur we twisted and turned, each trying to gain a hold on the other. He snapped at me; I dogged his fangs by a hair. Each time he attacked, I anticipated his move and pulled out of his way. We twisted again but I was faster and stronger. I threw him up against the back wall of the building. He got up and lunged towards me. He struck me across the face and as I fell back he reached for me. I grabbed him by both arms and threw both of us back against the wall, pinning him.

"Why do you protect them, you young fool. They are nothing but food for us," he hissed, fangs inches from my face.

"Not for you," I said.

"You don't have the strength," he said between clinched teeth. He twisted again to loosen my grip.

"Oh but you are so wrong." I grabbed his face and twisted, exposing his neck. I bit down hard and felt a crunch. He struggled as I fed lifting him off the ground. I held him like vise and twisted harder. When he was drained, I made one final twist and felt his neck snap. His now limp head fell to the side as I dropped the body.

Julian in his jaguar form leapt silently onto the roof. He padded over to me and transformed back into his human form. "So yet another of Magnus' creations."

"Yes," I said smiling, "But it wasn't much of a fight."

Julian shook his head, "Sometimes I think all you love is the hunt Aidan. The only time I see you smile these days is during the chase."

"It is what I do," I said.

I hesitated a moment, uncertainty in my voice, "He asked me a question, Julian. He asked me why we fight, why we protect them. I didn't have an answer to give him."

"You know why, Aidan. They are pure evil. Its our duty to fight them. Its been that way since the beginning. You know the cruelty they inflict on their victims."

Julian came and stood next to me. He knelt down. checking the pockets of the dead vampire. Nothing. "We need to take care of the body," he said holding out his hand. Witch fire flamed in his palm, its blue light glowing in the darkness. He placed the flame on the chest of the dead vampire and within seconds the body was ash.

As the wind blew the ash away, I walked to the edge of the roof. "And the boy?" I asked.

Julian stood up and walked behind me, "He's fine, just stunned and terrified. We arrived just in time. A few seconds later and it would have been too late. I calmed him and gave him a new memory of tonight. He thinks he went to the movies then got lost on the way out. I sent him walking into the crowd. In a few minutes he'll come out of the trance and go on with his life as if nothing happened. He won't remember a thing."

I stood passively looking down off the roof at the crowd below. "Do they really ever come out of their trance?" I asked.

"You're quite somber tonight, Aidan."

He walked up next to me, "Thats how you see them now, isn't it, like sleepwalkers? You seem to have lost any lasting connection with them"

I motioned with my head to the people on the street below.

"They go on with their inconsequential, short lives, oblivious to the real world, our world. It's as if they are asleep. We are a myth to them and now they are a myth to me. I protect them but I don't feel for them. Since I don't feed on them, I have no interest in their petty lives whatsoever. They are like shadows to me, lost in their dreams. Except for the hunt, I'm not sure why I do any of this anymore."

"Their lives are important even if they are not as long as ours. Remember, once you too were a seventeen year old boy. Don't count them off so easily," Julian said placing his hand on my shoulder. "Come on, lets go home." He transformed and jumped from the roof. I followed him.

As we crossed the Golden Gate bridge, the lights of the city shining in the darkness, I knew Julian was right about one thing. I did live for the hunt. Now, it was the only time I felt alive, when I was truly myself. Besides the hunt, the only thing that concerned me was my coven and its safety. I had no real interest in the affairs of humans. It was true, I was a shadow to them and they were a shadow to me, insubstantial and untouchable.

We drove on, my mood still dark. We turned off of the highway down a road that bordered Muir Woods. After several more turns in the dark, we went down a long private drive. We passed a wall then drove through a gate. We drove on through deep forest and finally arrived back home.

Nestled in the woods far away from human eyes, home was a huge old stone mansion. Several wings were attached to the central house. The moon light cast long shadows on the old stone work. With its light stone and high windows it had a faint medieval look to it. We drove up the driveway and passed the giant oak front door. I parked in the garage.

As we got out Julian said, "You were very quiet on the drive back Aidan, you seem especially troubled by tonight."

"Don't worry Julian, I'm fine, just a little lost in my thoughts," I replied.

"Don't let them be too dark Aidan. You must see the good in what we do," he said smiling putting his arm around me.

"I see the good, Julian and I believe it. I just sometimes feel like a stranger looking in," I replied as we walked back in the house.

Even though the house looked dark from the outside, it was bright on the inside. Most of the family was traveling but Rachel, Lucian and Mora were still home. Stefan was out on an errand for my father.

They were all waiting in the main study. It was one of my favorite rooms in the house. A long line of books went down one wall and a roaring fireplace covered the end. On the other side a long set of windows looked out over the pool and gardens. Rachel hugged Julian as we came in.

"Did you get there in time, was the young man safe?" Rachel asked me.

"Yes, we were in time. The young human is safe. Just as you saw it was one of Magnus' vampires. I killed him and Julian disposed of the body. He will not threaten the humans again," I said.

"Excellent work Aidan. You too, Rachel," Lucian said.

"This is the second one in two months Julian. We seem to be getting more of our share recently," Mora said.

"I don't know, perhaps there is some deeper cause but it still seems very random.," Julian said. "Aidan took care of him all by himself. Everything was done by the time I got there. We didn't find anything on him. I suspect he was just passing through. We saw no evidence of others."

"Our Aidan is very strong," Mora said holding my arm. I smiled and pulled off my jacket, "Its been a long night. I think I'll go on to my room. Good night everyone."

"Of course, get some rest," Lucian said. Everyone else said good night and I left the study. They were still talking as I walked up the long flight of stairs. When I got to my room, I pulled off my jacket and clothes and put on a pair of sweats and undershirt.

As on most nights, I went to my desk and pulled out a small box, a gift from my father. Inside were five bright crystals, each a different color. Witches used them for training. I pulled out the green crystal and sat it on the desk. The aim of the exercise was to clear you mind and levitate the crystal.

I had attempted this exercise so many times I had lost count and each time it ended with the same result. I tried to clear my mind. Thoughts of the young victim swam in my mind. These were replaced by thoughts of the vampire. His question haunted me. Why did I protect them? Why did I kill my own kind to protect them? I know that my father, Julian, and the others believed that they were evil, totally corrupted by Magnus. From what I had seen, this appeared to be true. But still they were my kind.

Years ago I learned to control my thirst for human blood. I no longer craved it. I came to accept what I was and to leave my old life behind. But I could sympathize with the others of my kind, ruled as they were by their thirst. Never free from it, enslaved to its demands.

Yes, I had control but it came at a great price. I kept a barrier between me and anything human. I avoided them when I could and I ignored them when I couldn't. It was true what I told Julian, humans had become like shadows to me, almost invisible. But that made the question even more burning for me; why did I protect them? What were they to me? And why did I kill my own kind for them?

I tried again to clear my thoughts. The images of tonight receded. Far, far way I could just sense the stillness, that connection that was the craft, the source of a witch's power. I reached out my hand toward the green crystal. I willed it to move, to hover. For a brief second, I felt a small glimmer of the power. I tried to channel it, to have it move the crystal. I took a deep breath and just as I thought it might actually flow, that once out of a thousand times, the craft would appear, the image of the young human floated into my mind. The fleeting connection faded and the stillness was replaced by frustration then by rage. In my anger, I reached over and took the crystal between my thumb and finger and crushed it. As it cracked it sang, the sound filling my room. I am sure the rest of the house heard it as the magic flowed from the crystal. I didn't care. I threw the crushed crystal on the desk and got up. I put on headphones and sat in my chair. I let the sounds of a Mahler symphony take me.

Next morning, I found myself out on the porch as the sun came up. I often sat here in the early morning. It was very peaceful, the tranquility of the garden helped me forget the turmoil of last night. But as was her nature Rachel, all smiles, came almost bouncing out the door. Tranquility evaporated like the morning dew.

"You seem mighty happy this morning Rachel," I said as she came out, "Hex some small mammal or something?"

I loved to tease her.

"Oh, hush Aidan. Nothing you say is going to ruin my mood today. And I have great news. Julian wanted to tell you himself but I just couldn't wait. He had a grand idea last night. He said you needed to be cheered up, that you had been working much too hard, acting way too gloomy."

Oh man what did I get myself into I thought. Anything that got Rachel this excited had to be awful.

"Ok, so whats the big idea," I asked apprehensive at what she was going to say.

"As soon as Stefan comes back were all going to Canada to hunt then after that we're going to take a trip to New York! I can't believe it. New York! Its been over a year since I've been back. Its going to be such fun. We all need a break."

Hunting in Canada could be exciting, especially if Mora and Stefan went along. I started to say something when Julian came out the door.

"I see Rachel couldn't wait and spilled the beans."

"Seems so," I replied.

"I think you could use some time off Aidan. We all could. You've been very grim of late. It will be fun, all of us together. We haven't done this in a very long time, much too long by my account."

Rachel chimed in, "And we can buy you some new clothes in New York. We've got to get you out of that dark grunge look you are wearing all the time. Yes that's exactly what you need to get you out of this funk. Some new clothes. And a hair cut, you really need a haircut. That mop of yours has got to be cut back. It's hanging down your neck as it is. And shows, we can go to some broadway shows. It will be fantastic."

"Julian, please," I said holding up my hands. Not shopping, anything but shopping with Rachel.

"Actually I think that would be a wonderful idea for Rachel to take you shopping. You're beginning to look a little too, whats the word, Gothic. You'll have a good time Aidan. School's out, there no reason not to go."

"Besides, if you don't go I won't get the pleasure of kicking your skinny butt hunting," Mora said as she came outside.

"So, I see now the whole family is ganging up on me, is that it?" I said smiling.

"See you feel better all ready," Rachel said.

"Well I do like hunting in Canada and I suppose a show in New York would be nice," I said.

Rachel ran up to me and put her arms around me, "Thank you Aidan, we are going to have such fun. Mora come on and help me pack!," she said as she let go of me and ran back inside.

"Go on," I said to Mora. "You and Julian got this ball rolling so you are going to have to do your part."

"Alright smarty, but you should get to packing too. Stefan will be back soon and I am sure Rachel will not want to miss a minute."

"Yes ma'am," I said smiling. She swatted me on the way out.

"We'll if everyone else is packing I guess I should start too," Julian said. "You coming in?"

"I'll be there in a minute," I said.

I sat in the peaceful sun for a few minutes. The whole yard was awash in morning light now. The pool was beautiful, smooth like a mirror. Of course, leave it to Julian to come up with some new scheme to distract me. But it would be good to get away. I must have shook everyone up with the crystal last night. No one said anything but I could tell they were worried about me.

I went upstairs, read for a while then started packing. Jeans, shirts, a couple of sweaters, overcoat, boots, everything I needed. When all you wear is black it's pretty easy. If Rachel gave me any grief I would simply reminder her that I was a creature of the night after all.

Stefan arrived back around noon and of course Rachel immediately won him over to her cause. He packed (quickly with Rachel hovering) and we left around one. We drove and parked at the airport and boarded a chartered jet. Julian as usual took care of everything. Our standard cover for these trips was nature photography.

Both Rachel and Mora were very good photographers, the house full of their artwork. Rachel even had some placed in a gallery. We loaded all our gear and the plane took off for British Columbia. The flight was quick and uneventful. When the pilot found out we were going into the back country without any firearms, he suggested we take his gun, said we had to watch out for wolves. Julian convinced him that we would be alright. Two jeeps were waiting for us at the small airport. The pilot reminded us that he would be back in three days to pick us up. We packed the jeeps with our gear and Julian, Rachel, and Mora left in one jeep; Stefan and I in the other.

We headed due east on an old two lane road. It was about four hours drive to the cabin. After an hour or so, the forest began to get thicker and the sun began to dip. As we got into the foothills the road began to get steeper. For the first part of the trip, Stefan and I just took in the scenery. It was beautiful with thick forest and high mountains in the distance. Fall was ripe in its full colors. There was some traffic at the beginning but after two hours our jeeps were the only vehicles on the road.

"Quiet tonight, Aidan," Stefan said.

"Sorry just enjoying the scenery. I forget how beautiful it is up here. It's been way too long since we've been back."

"Reminds me of many happy days," Stefan said. I nodded.

"The last few weeks you've been keeping to yourself, Aidan. You seem troubled. Mora and I worry about you. We heard the crystal last night. It still bothers you doesn't it, the witchcraft?"

I nodded again, looking out the window. "Yea, sometimes; it's very frustrating. It seems so close I can almost touch it, but I can never quite reach it."

"Is our life so terrible for you? I know that for some of our kind the weight of the years becomes almost intolerable, a burden so heavy that often our kind feel cursed."

"No, No, Stefan. Its not like that at all. I don't feel cursed. I am happy with my life. I have you and Mora and the rest of the family. I am content. Its just that sometimes I feel like a part of me is missing. It's like I have a memory that I can't quite bring into focus, something I have forgotten, something essential to me. I guess at some level I believe that the craft would somehow make me whole."

He nodded as the trees flew past. Stefan was not a man of many words. The sun was setting now. The jeep jumped some as the road began to get bumpy. He turned on the lights. We drove in silence a few minutes.

"I do question sometimes why we go out of our way for the humans. The dark one I killed the other night. He asked me why I protected them and I didn't have an adequate answer. I think sometimes I do it only for the hunt. That's what Julian fears, that the hunt has become the center of my life, my sole reason for living."

"Was he right?" Stefan asked.

"Maybe. I feel most alive, most myself when I am hunting. That's what worries me the most. I don't want to become a monster, who lives only on the fear of others, especially my own kind. Once Rachel called me a killing machine. I sometimes think that she was right."

Stefan was quiet a moment then spoke.

"We are natural predators Aidan. So its natural for you to feel alive when you are hunting. It's who we are. But we are also beings with a heart and soul and that part of us desires to do good. I know you Aidan and I know that part of you is just as strong if not stronger than your other side. Trust that part of you. It doesn't have to be in conflict with your aggressive nature. Your many talents can serve that higher path Aidan. They don't have to drive you to darkness. You can be whole Aidan, whether the craft appears or not. You should never feel guilty about who you are or your nature if you are true to yourself."

I smiled, "You're quite the philosopher tonight Stefan."

He laughed. "Old habits die hard."

I asked him, "What do you feel about them, the humans. I mean once I desired nothing more than to feed on them and now its like I care nothing for them. I have no interest or concern for them at all. Their short lives seem so meaningless to me."

Stefan sighed a moment then spoke again.

"You know Aidan, unlike you, I lived on them for centuries. I've been a vampire for over a thousand years. It was our way and in some respects it's still what comes most natural to us. But when I experienced the evil that Magnus inflicted and met Marcus and his struggle for good, I knew I had to make a decision, that in one way or another my life was going to be different. When I discovered the depths of Magnus' evil, it made me reflect on both my past and my future. I knew that then that it was either the noble path for me, to join the struggle with Marcus or to become blind to the evil that Magnus represented and in that way become a servant to it. I chose to take the noble path. Like you I did not want to be a monster. I have not always agreed with Marcus or Julian or Lucian for that matter but one thing I have learned from them is that the noble path is the same for witch, vampire, or human. Our lot in life doesn't matter, it's what we do with it that matters."

"I once thought of humans as nothing more than food and sport. I was only interested in their blood. But now I know they are not that different from us. They have the same choices; to follow the noble path or the dark path. I protect them because it is the right thing to do. I care for them because they are on the same path as we are. I know they love the same way I love and care for Mora and for you. So for me it's very clear."

Darkness had finally fallen and we still had many miles. I was silent for a long time.

"I know that what you say is the truth Stefan. My mind understands it but my heart is still cold and empty, especially when it comes to them. I don't hate them or desire them, I just feel nothing for them."

"Its understandable, Aidan. You are still very young in this life. You haven't even crossed the century mark yet. You still have many things to learn, to experience. But its important to take time to enjoy life, the simple gifts that life brings. Real happiness and joy is to be found there. That's when you will be whole."

"Thank you Stefan. Thats more comforting than anything else."

"Besides," I said, "We are going to have a wonderful time here in this beautiful place. I feel better already. I guess Julian was right."

"Julian is a very wise man, take it from me but don't tell him I said that."

I laughed, "Your secret is safe with me."

Stephen Weagraff

We drove on and by midnight we arrived at the hunting lodge. It was a primitive stone cabin, very cold and very, very old. It had three small rooms but a large fireplace. Huge wooden beams crossed the ceiling. There was no running water and no electricity, just an old hand pump in the back. Lucian had built it many years ago. It was so remote and so old that no one knew it was here.

Julian went inside and lit some old oil lamps. I started a fire for he and Rachel. It would get even colder tonight. Of course that didn't matter to Stefan, Mora, and I but I wanted Julian and Rachel to be comfortable.

Once we were unpacked the hunt was on. The moon was bright and we wasted no time. Julian skipped his usual jaguar form and took the same form as Rachel, a large grey wolf.

Game was everywhere, grizzly and moose for Stefan, Mora, and I with deer and elk for Julian and Rachel. Dawn was just breaking as we headed back to the cabin. We all cleaned up using the hand pump in the back and went inside. Everyone rested for a bit then at midday we went for a long hike. Rachel and Mora took some amazing photos. Late in the afternoon we went on another hunt.

Mora, Stefan and I stayed with the big game but Julian and Rachel went for fish in the nearby river. It was fun watching them try to paw the fish out. They succeeded sometimes. At one point, they changed back to their human form and just walked along the shore. Of course, Rachel pushed Julian in and just as he fell, he pulled her in. They came to the surface laughing. The rest of us then had to join in.

The next night we skipped the hunt and instead just sat around a big campfire. Rachel and Julian tried to tell some scary stories but given the crowd there was not much point to it.

The next morning, early before the sun was up we set out for our last hunt. Again Rachel and Julian took wolf form. We left the cabin and headed deep into the forest. At one point, a wolf pack followed us for a bit. Julian and Rachel approached them but I think our scent scared them off. For a while I just watched Julian and Rachel. They worked in perfect harmony. They found a deer scent and chased it for over a mile. They were so perfect for each other. As I sat in a high tree,

I wondered if I would ever find someone to be with, to be as happy as Rachel and Julian.

Following the hunt was another hike with more pictures. For our last hike, we climbed a large peak where the views were spectacular. Finally it was back for our last night. Julian of course had brought a deck of cards and we played until well into the night, no cheating allowed. He won anyway.

Early the next morning it was time to clean up and leave. It had been a wonderful three days. I felt at peace here. I knew that if things ever got too much to handle, I could always come here and just lose myself in this wild and free wilderness.

We cleaned up our gear, packed the Jeeps, locked up the cabin and drove back to the little airport. As we waited for our plane, Rachel and Mora compared photos. The plane was right on time. The pilot asked us about our trip and Julian and Rachel smiled as they said we had no issues with the wolves.. By evening we were on our way to Chicago then on to New York.

We landed about ten o'clock. Rachel of course was exuberant. A car picked us up and we drove straight to the St. Regis. We checked in and everyone wanted to clean up after three days in the forest. I met Stefan and Mora in the lobby and in a few minutes Julian and Rachel came down. Stefan of course had on his black suit, Mora a beautiful blue jacket and pants, Julian a jacket and slacks. Rachel was dressed to the nines with a silver dress and heels. Her short red hair shimmering in the lights. I had my standard black jeans, shirt, leather jacket, and boots.

Rachel took one look and shook her head, "First thing tomorrow we are fixing that getup," she said. I tried my line about creatures of darkness but she just held up her hand, turned and flagged down a cab. Julian just shrugged his shoulders. Mora had a smug smile on her face. Thankfully they got in the first cab. Stefan, Mora, and I took the second. We drove straight to the Blue Note for some Jazz. The music was great. After that it was a mid-town restaurant. Julian and Rachel ate while we picked and pretended. Then it was clubs. Julian and Rachel hit the dance floor and finally so did Stefan and Mora. I just watched from the bar, some drink that I would throw away in my hand. A pretty human smiled at me from the bar. I smiled but turned away. Stefan motioned and I took his place on the floor. Mora was a great dancer. Finally by two am, we all had enough and it was back to the Regis.

The next morning it was the shopping crusade. Armed and ready I met Rachel and Mora in the lobby. Julian and Stefan were going to a museum. I whined to go but I was out numbered. We were going to meet them later for dinner and afterwards a show. After Rachel grabbed a quick coffee and roll, we were off. It was a whirl of shops and boutiques. I felt like some doll they were dressing but I went along. Rachel brought out slacks and suits, then sweaters and sport coats. I ended up with 2 suits, several shirts, some new ties, new shoes, and two jackets.

"Now for a haircut," she said. Bags in hand, we headed out. Rachel flagged down a cab and he took us to some fancy salon that smelled of evergreen and hot oil. While the girls did God knows what, I was washed, cut, clipped, and shaped. So much for the creature of the night, more like the creature of the Sunday brunch I thought. At long last my ordeal was over and we headed back to the hotel.

I changed into one of my new suites and met everyone down stairs. Mora and Rachel were even more beautiful than last night. "Wow," Rachel said as I stood up, "Better, much better." Mora nodded. I finally smiled, took her arm and we headed for our car. We headed straight for dinner, then it was off to our show.

Rachel of course had planned everything. We picked up our tickets and took our seats to Wicked. Rachel had ordered them as soon as we knew we were leaving. It was very entertaining although at one point I laughed when I shouldn't have and Julian elbowed me. Witches were so complicated. We teased Rachel during intermission about turning green. All in all it was a wonderful time. The girls were singing as we left the theater and headed down towards the water front. We went to a restaurant for some dessert for Julian and Rachel.

After their dinner, the weather was perfect so we decided to take a walk. We were just a few blocks down from the restaurant when I noticed a man in a large coat and hat behind us. We turned down a street and he turned with us. Strange. This happened twice more, each time we made a turn he made the same one always staying the same distance behind us.

I walked up next to Julian and whispered, "We are being followed. A man in an overcoat and hat is about 100 yards behind us. Should we try and lose him or split up?" I asked. "No," Julian said, "lets go down a little farther and see if he follows us. We can let him catch up and when he's close I'll read his mind and see whats going on."

We walked another two blocks. The area thinned out and we were alone. We turned into an alley. The man continued to follow us moving closer this time. Just as he was about to pass, I stepped out in front of him. "Can I help you," I asked. His face was hidden by his hat. He was of medium height and slender build. The man stopped and pulled his hat back. He was ancient, with long white hair, a beard and a haggard face. He looked over and addressed Julian.

"Hello young man," he said.

"I am sorry, do I know you sir?" Julian asked.

"You did in France, many years ago Julian," the man answered. With that his features began to turn every so slightly. His hair got thicker. The white beard disappeared. The thick wrinkles around his eyes disappeared. His hair turned a dark brown.

A much younger man stood in front of us, a mischievous grin on his face. Julian looked closer and his eyes lit up with surprise. "Jakob, is that you?" Julian asked. The man smiled, "Yes Julian it's Jakob." Julian smiled ear to ear and embraced the man. "I can't believe it after all these years, to see you again."

Julian turned and said to all of us, "This is my old friend, Jakob. We knew him from long ago in France. He was a great friend to Marcus and I."

Julian paused, pain in his eyes, "Jakob, I thought you were dead, we looked for you for weeks after the battle. What happened to you."

"No I escaped that very first night," he said.

His grin disappeared and in hushed tones he said, "Julian, its extremely important that I talk to you. There is much you don't know and we don't have much time." He looked nervously around, "It's not safe out here in the open. I know a place we can speak in private." He grabbed Julian by the arm and started for the main street out of the alley. We were about 20 feet from the entrance when the man suddenly stopped and put his hand to his neck, a look of puzzlement on his face. He took another step and pulled his hand away, blood on his palm. He stumbled down on the alley floor.

"Jakob," Julian screamed and knelt next to him. Jakob pulled something from his neck, a small dart. "Malek," Jakob said.

Julian looked around. "We have to get him out of here." As he reached to pick him up, Jakob gasped for air.

"It's poisoned with dark magic," he said. He pulled Julian down to him.

"I am sorry Julian," he said, tears in his eyes. "I should have found you and told you the truth long ago. Now there is no time and I must hurry. Malek is close." He gasped again and took Julian's hand.

"Tell Marcus I am sorry." His eyes began to close. Julian took his hand in both of his, "Everything is forgiven, old friend, it was long, long ago. Any evil from those days has been long forgotten. But now we have to get you out of here," Julian said.

Jakob shook his head, "I have run out of time. You have to stop him Julian before it's too late," his voice failing. He reached into his pocket and pushed something into Julian's hand, it was an old scrap of parchment. It looked to have been torn out of a book. His voice grew faint. He pulled Julian closer and spoke in his ear. His head fell back.

"Forgive me," he said again. His eyes closed. I heard the sound of another blade whiz by. It embedded itself in the alley floor. We all looked up. Two men stood above the alley. I looked down at Julian. He had tears in his eyes, "Go, Go ," he said to Stefan and I. Stefan said, "Mora stay with them, there may be others." She nodded. Rachel knelt down next to Julian.

The two men took off. Stefan and I ran and scaled the building. They were already running when we got to the top. We took after them. They were fast, far too fast for humans. They were a blur in front of us. They jumped and sailed to the next building. We did the same.. They got to the end of the next building and jumped off, heading down a back street. I jumped down the three floors and I heard Stefan land right behind me. We followed them down the street. They were heading towards the water. They ducked down a line of warehouses and then I saw them scaling one of the old buildings right next to the docks. We climbed after them.

When we got to the top, we saw that the two men were standing at the end of the roof. Three men stood between them. They were shorter than the two we chased and were dressed in very expensive suits and overcoats. One was dark featured with a dark goatee. The other two were clean shaven with short blond hair. They all looked like businessmen. We were about 40 feet from them when the darker man raised his hand. "Far enough" he said.

"So Stefan, we meet again after all these years.," the darker man said.

"Malek, you always were Draven's lap dog. Where is your master, I would like to pay my regards to him," Stefan said.

"Pity that Mora is not with you, a reunion with her would be quite delightful," the dark man said. I noticed the two men we had chased. They were very tall, just under seven feet. Malek raised one hand. Their features blurred and their faces began to change, red eyes now looked down at us, fangs descended from their top teeth.

"Like the new models?" Malek asked, "we have made several improvements. I think you will find them quite formable."

At that point Stefan pulled back to lunge. The two blond men standing next to Malek held out their hands. I felt a grip surround me. Stefan stopped in his tracks. The blond men smiled. We both began to push against the force. As we each took a step forward, the smiles left their faces. I felt their grip increase. Their faces took on a grimace as we took a couple of more steps, straining against their force. One more step and we would break their spell.

"Stefan you always were such a bore," Malek said. He lifted his arm and a bolt of lightening flew from his fingers striking Stefan directly in his chest. He flew off the roof and sailed out into the river.

At that point I started to run towards them, crouched and ready for a fight. Rage engulfed me. I wanted to tear them limb from limb. Both men now focused their power on me. It was like pushing against a solid wall. I paused and focused then took a step forward. At that point, Malek held out his hand. My forward momentum was stopped dead in its tracks. I felt my feet leave he ground as I was left suspended in mid-air, about two feet off of the roof.

"So you must be another of Marcus' pets," Malek said.

"I am sure he has convinced you to join him on on his noble path of light, fighting against the powers of darkness. I'll bet your little coven is quite warm and snuggly."

His face took on a sneer. "Pathetic, the only thing you are struggling against is your own true nature. Like the others, you are afraid of who you really are, deluding yourselves in this foolish crusade to protect the humans."

"When I get down from here, I'll show you pathetic," I said struggling against the force that held me, my feet moving toward the roof. He laughed, "You really shouldn't speak unless spoken to," he said. He nodded to the other men. I felt a new force tighten around my neck. I struggled but could not move. "Now that's better," Malek said. "Marcus should really teach you to have better manners in front of your superiors."

"I am not going to kill you quite yet. Instead, I have a small favor. I want you to take a message to Marcus. Tell him that soon we will have the Shadow and then my master will show you all the true nature of the craft. I am going to enjoy watching Marcus and your whole brood of weaklings writhe like worms in the flame. But before I send you back to him, I am going to give you a small taste of what the craft is really like."

He smiled in anticipation. He held out both his hands and I was surrounded by witch lightening. Blue bolts of electricity surrounded me. I would have cried out, but their combined grip was unshakable.

The pain was intense. I couldn't move. I struggled to reach the roof, I could almost touch it. Finally, Malek dropped his hands and the lightening and pain vanished.

"You are very strong, I'll give you that young one. And you do have some fight in you. I feel your rage and lust; it's unfortunate its so misdirected. It will be a waste killing you. But until then, remember my small favor."

He raised his hands again and I felt a bolt of lightening hit me in the chest. I flew out and over the water, crashing into the river.

When I came up, I saw Stefan in front of me. He swam over to me. "You alright?" he asked. shaking the water from his hair. "Fine, just singed a little." We swam forward and pulled ourselves up on the dock. I looked up. Malek and the others were gone.

"That stung," I said. Stefan nodded smiling, "It's been years since I felt witch lightning," he said. I looked down at both of us. "Well we're a mess," I said. My new suit was ruined. It was totally soaked and a large spot was burned into the chest. Stefan looked at me, "Rachel is going to be furious with you."

We dried the best we could then ran back to the alley. Jakob's body was already gone. "I freed him with witch flame. He is at peace now," Julian said wiping at the edges of his eyes. We filled them in on the events including what Malek said.

Julian had a look of disgust on his face. He spat on the ground. "Malek was always a braggart. Vicious too, loved to play mind games on people. Still we can't discount what he said." At some point, Rachel noticed my suit. "Aidan you ruined your new suit," she said. I nodded, "I guess these clothes are just not made for my lifestyle."

Stefan laughed.

"I am very sorry about your friend," I said to Julian. He nodded with a sad look on his face and said, "He was a great friend to me, almost like a brother. We shared many, many happy times together. Its tragic how this all ended."

I was curious about what Jakob had said. "What did he say at the end, Julian, I couldn't understand what he meant," I asked.

Julian answered, "It was nonsense, just rambling. I think he was terrified of Malek. He said find the twins and that we all are in grave danger. Then he said that only together will it be strong enough. He mumbled about a key then whispered a phrase in German. Like I said he was rambling at the end."

"Who are the twins?" I asked.

"I have no idea. I've never known a set of twins that were witches. Perhaps Marcus knows what he's talking about. I think he might have been hallucinating, I'm sure there were powerful drugs in the dart. In any event, there's nothing else we can do here. We need to call Marcus and head home."

We walked out of the alley and hailed two cabs and went immediately back to the hotel, packed and took the first flight back to San Francisco.

It was a long flight, Julian sat withdrawn and silent. Nothing seemed to shake him out of it. Even Rachel couldn't couldn't get him to talk. It was odd this sudden appearance of his old friend. And Malek, the very thought of him made me angry. I wanted nothing more than to get my hands around his neck. We finally landed and our gloomy group headed home.

When we arrived, everyone congregated in our large family room. Julian, Stefan and I recounted the events. Julian paced in front of the large screen TV as he talked. "Typical Malek boasting. He was a vicious coward from the beginning. But Jakob, I still can't believe he was involved with this."

"Nor can I," Dad said. "And the document fragment he gave you?"

"I can't make any sense of the fragment. It seems to be in code and I don't understand the diagrams. I've never seen them before."

"Did he say anything about how to read the text?"

"No by the end he was rambling nonsense. I think he may have been hallucinating from the drugs in the dart. He said we had to stop him before it was too late, that we had to find the twins. He said that we are all in danger and that only together will it be strong enough. Then he mumbled something about an old book in German which I didn't understand."

"I'm very fearful Marcus. Jakob was distraught, overcome by fear. Draven is planning something terrible. I'm sure of it and I am afraid that once events start we will be unable to stop them. Malek must be close and the thought that he would find the Shadow terrified Jakob. That's why he took the risk to find us, to warn us that we were all in danger."

Dad just nodded, deep in thought.

I asked Dad, "Do you know what he meant by the twins?"

"I have no idea. I don't remember any twins at the academy, much less any that Jakob knew. Perhaps he met them after he fled the academy or maybe it was just the drugs in the dart. I am sure they were very powerful to bring down a witch like Jakob."

Dad rubbed his eyes, "Jakob was right. We must double our efforts to find the Shadow. If he was right its just a matter of time until Malek finds it. I still believe it's here in San Francisco just as Rachel saw in her vision. I think thats why we have seen more of Draven's creatures here over the last few months. It's essential that we find it before they do."

We spent the next day going over all our old clues about the Shadow. Years earlier while we were all still living back East, Rachel had a vision about the Shadow. She had seen a man taking it into a building near the San Francisco waterfront. While she recognized the landmarks, she never saw the man's face.

That's when we moved out here. We finally tracked down the building and checked its history but everything had been dead ends.

We went back through the documents to insure we had not missed anything. Lucian and Dad reviewed the fragment Julian received but they could find no way to translate it. Next day, Stefan and I went back to the place Rachel had seen in her vision. Again nothing but dead ends so we were no closer to discovering its location. It was very frustrating for everyone, especially Julian.

The next day it was very tense around the house. I was actually happy that my new term at the university was starting.

Chapter 5

Something Unexpected

University of California

San Francisco

I opened the door as quietly as possible and moved to the back of the auditorium, as far back in the shadows as possible. It was a sparse class, as most night classes are. Then again, I would not have expected a crowd for any Medieval history course. I would probably have this whole section of seats to myself which was fine; less chance of humans.

I quietly slipped into the last row. The professor had already started and I was almost ten minutes late. I had just opened my notebook when I heard a noise to my left. Someone arriving even later than I had just slipped in the door. Like me she did not want to draw any attention, so she moved quickly to the last row and motioned for me to shift over.

I moved over about eight seats in and as I sat down the seat let out a very loud creak. Everyone in the class turned around. Even the professor stopped talking. The late student pulled her pink hood back and sat in the seat I had been been in, a look of total consternation on her face. It was clear she did not enjoy the attention. She was very pretty with thick tussled hair that fell to the back of her neck. It was a light brown with shiny hints of red. Bright green eyes and a full mouth. She was slender, like a dancer. In fact, she moved like a dancer, very poised as she came in.

"If you two in the back are finished with your musical chairs, I'd like to continue the lecture, if thats ok," the professor said.

"I'm sorry, sir," she said. She shot me a look of pure contempt.

"Sorry, Professor Brown," I said.

She pulled a laptop computer out her backpack and started taking notes as the professor continued his lecture.

At one point she turned ever so slightly and looked at me. At that moment something completely unexpected happened. I felt thirst. It was a raw almost primitive emotion completely at odds with my carefully crafted control.

It had been almost eighty years since I had felt any thirst around a human. For years I had been surrounded by literally thousands of humans and not one of them had the slightest effect on me. But somehow this young woman had torn through my carefully built defenses. I was astounded; it was something I simply couldn't understand. As I thought about it, I was puzzled at first and then I was irritated that she could have such an effect on me. I looked around for the exit but after the noise incident, there was no easy way for me to leave so I tried my best to ignore her.

As soon as class was over, I quickly slipped out the other side of the aisle. On my way out, I noticed she went down front and met three other girls. I looked down and checked my watch. Great; class had let out early. Stefan was going to meet me after class but I had at least twenty minutes to kill so I headed to the lounge next door to the auditorium.

I heard the young woman and the other girls talking as they came out of the door. I knew I probably should just leave and have Stefan pick me up somewhere else but it would be hard to get out without them seeing me. Climbing the wall and going over the ceiling really wasn't an option. I heard them speaking again; they were right outside lounge. Now I was stuck until they left. Normally, I paid no attention to the endless chatter of humans but while I was here and not going anywhere I figured I'd just listen.

"So why were you late tonight, Tess?" one of the girls asked.

So her name was Tess.

"I got held up at work, again," she replied.

"Well you and that cute guy certainly made a spectacle of yourselves," one of the other girls laughed.

"Yea, who is that guy," Tess said.

"I don't know but he's definitely fine, those beautiful blue eyes. Could use some time in the sun though. A little pale for my tastes," a second girl said.

The last girl answered. I recognized the voice from a class I had last semester. "I know who he is. His name is Aidan Croft. Yea he's cute but he's also really strange. Hangs out with some other pale, really blond guy and some dark haired girl. There's something weird about them, they never talk to anyone, stay to themselves. I heard they were in some cult or something."

"Well, this could be interesting," Tess said.

"What do you mean, Tess," the first one said.

"I have a paper to do for Sociology on modern non-traditional social groups. I was going to try and talk the gothic kid next door into it, but these guys would be perfect. It's exactly what the professor is looking for."

The girl from last semester spoke up. "He'll never do it, I tell you they're all off the ranch. It's like they are on some other another planet."

"Oh leave that to me. This is getting better all the time, I feel an A coming on as we speak. Listen, we have a partner project coming up for this class don't we?"

"Yea so what?" the first girl asked.

"Well I'll ask him to be my partner then while we are doing this one, I can slowly move him over into the other one."

"Don't you think that's a little devious, Tess ?" the second girl asked.

"No, not really and besides he is kind of cute," Tess laughed.

"Oh sister you are wasting your time. I tell you they are totally weird," the last one said.

"Well I think its a great plan," Tess said.

With that, they walked out of the door. It was odd, I was almost sorry to hear them leave. It was funny, I hadn't followed a human conversation this close in years. I was laughing at my self when Stefan finally walked in.

"What's so funny," he asked. "And why are you still inside?"

"You know I don't know," I said chuckling as we left and drove home.

Two evenings later, I had the same class. I sat in the same back row but the third seat in. I could't believe it but I was just a little curious. It would be interesting to see what she would do. Then just like clockwork, she came in. This time instead of asking me to shift over, she came and set in the chair right next to me.

"Hi," she said. Under normal circumstances, at least for me, I would never have even noticed her but sitting next to her I had to admit that she was quite beautiful, stunning actually.

"Hello," I replied.

"Tess Michaels," she said putting her bag down.

"Aidan Croft. Pleased to meet you," I said getting out my notebook.

"Hey listen, sorry about the other night, I didn't mean to embarrass you," she said. Her eyes were very bright, her voice rich almost musical. I had to focus on what she said.

"It's fine, don't think anything of it. I am the one that squeaked the chair," I replied with a slight smile.

It was her turn to smile. When she did, it was as if her whole face lit up.

"Well you wouldn't have if I didn't make you move over. I feel like we got off to a bad start."

"No harm done," I said.

"So, you like the class so far?" she asked.

"Yes, it's interesting. I had one of Professor Brown's classes last term. He was very good, seems to really know his material."

At that point, the class started.

"Well we should be quiet, don't want to make another spectacle of ourselves," she said. She smiled just a little as she sat back for class.

A couple of times I glanced over and saw that she was tapping her finger on the table. She seemed a little nervous. When I caught her eye, she smiled again. And once again I had a tremor of thirst. It was beginning to aggravate me, I was immune to humans, how could she possibly be having this effect on me?

At the end of class, I said, "It was a pleasure to meet you Tess" as I started to get up and leave as quickly as I could.

"Aidan," she asked stopping my departure. She put her hand on my arm.

I had not been touched by a human in many, many years. It startled me just a second. I looked down at her hand then up at her. "Yes," I finally said.

"Listen, since you had this professor last term, would you be my project partner? I've never had Professor Brown before and I could use some help. I really need a good grade in this class." Her eyes sparkled as she smiled. I was completely captivated by them.

Ah so she was a little devious. In the past I would have avoided this kind of protracted human interaction like the plague and in this case it would absolutely be the best thing to do; just brush her off and leave. But curiosity got the better of me. I knew better but I was just powerless to say no. It was like the words just blurted out on their own without any volition on my part.

"It would be my great pleasure," I replied.

"Great!," she said smiling.

Her eyes sparkled again. I was enchanted by them. almost like in a spell.

"Aidan," she said.

"Yes, I'm sorry did you say something else?" I asked. I was so distracted I didn't hear what she said. How did that happen?

She smiled again and said "I said when would you you like to get together and discuss the assignment?"

"Oh, Uh, how about after class next week?" I replied trying to regain my composure. I couldn't seem to make a complete thought.

"Perfect, I'll see you then," she said. She smiled again and once more, I felt the beginning rise of thirst. Speechless, I left quickly through the back exit. She grabbed her bag and headed up to the front.

As I was leaving I heard her say, "See I told you."

She was cunning. I could respect that trait. There was more to her than meets the eye.

I headed home but couldn't seem to get her out of my mind. Again there was this twinge of thirst but now it had been replaced by an almost overwhelming curiosity. I couldn't remember ever being so distracted. I had never met a human quite like her before. I couldn't figure out how she was having this effect on me and truth was it was more than just a little annoying. I could hear a pin drop on the other side of the auditorium but still I didn't hear her question. That shouldn't be possible, not for me.

That night after I got home, Stefan and I headed downtown. A gristly murder had been reported and given what happened in New York, Dad wanted to make sure it did not have an "unnatural cause"; his code word for a witch or vampire killing. "Hey let's take the Porsche," I said. Stefan smiled and threw me the keys. In fifteen minutes we were heading south out of Muir Woods towards San Francisco. In no time we were flying towards downtown.

Once in town, I parked the car several blocks over from the attack and we got out. Stefan of course wore his usual black suit and I had my leather jacket and black jeans so we disappeared right into the shadows. When it was clear, we climbed the nearest building and jumped from roof to roof until we were right over the crime scene. Several policemen and a couple of detectives were standing around the body. Even from the roof we could see details as if we were standing next to them.

It was a young woman. From appearances she had been beaten then strangled. Other than a small cut over one eye, there were no wounds on the body, Stefan sniffed the air. No vampire scent.

"Not one of our kind," he said, "False alarm, lets head back home."

As we walked back to the car, I stopped a minute looking down the street. Far down a couple walked, hand in hand.

"You ever miss humans, Stefan?" I asked.

"That's an odd question Aidan, we see humans all the time."

"No I mean, do you miss spending time with them, talking to them?"

"Did you like get up this morning and forget you were a vampire or something?" he said smiling.

I laughed, "No, I just wondered."

He looked off in the distance a minute and replied, "Well to answer your question, yes sometimes, sometimes I miss their laughter. They can be very happy, especially when they laugh."

"Yea me too," I said.

"They can be so innocent at times. Unfortunately, we usually see them like that," he said pointing over his shoulder, "Tragic." He shook his head. "Enough of this doom and gloom, what do you say we take a real drive up the Pacific Coast, and this time no holding back?"

"You're on. First one there drives," I said as I flew towards the car.

Next day, Tess sat down front with her friends. I heard her voice laughing. It was like music to me. Just as the other night there was a slight rise of thirst in her presence but tonight but there was something else I couldn't quite place. Then it dawned on me, I was nervous, I just couldn't believe it. It was hard to admit but I was anxious to see her again, a human girl!

I watched the clock as class progressed. Time seemed to slow down. It was almost surreal.

Finally the class was over and she came up to where I was sitting. "Still a good time to meet?" Tess asked me as everyone started to leave the room.

Her eyes were just as brilliant but this time I was not going to get lost in them.

"Yes it is. Where would you suggest we work?"

"How about the big student lounge over near the A building?"

"That sounds fine," I answered.

We gathered our bags and headed out towards the lounge.

I tried to make small talk to distract myself.

"You take many evening classes?" I asked.

"Yes, some. I work a lot during the day so its convenient. How about you?"

"Yes, same thing. I have very busy days."

Odd, I felt bad deceiving her so I added, "I also find them much less crowded."

"I guess thats true. Usually have a little older crowd as well," she said.

"Can't argue with that," I said with a slight smile.

We went into the A lounge and walked all the way to the back.

We both pulled our laptops out and as she sat down I said, "Throw me your power cord. There's two outlets here."

"Thanks."

"My pleasure," I said as I plugged in both cords and sat down.

I noticed she had a mac exactly like mine.

"Like your Mac?" I asked.

"Love it. Couldn't live without it."

"Me too," I said as both chimed during boot up.

I felt a little guilty, just sitting with her, having her all to myself. Of course she had no idea of the inner battle I was having. One part of me wanted to just sit and talk like we were old friends. But another wanted nothing more than to bite and drink deeply. What if I lost control? I was fine now but what could happen later?

I had to get my mind off of my inner turmoil so I focused on the project.

"Ok, so we have a couple of choices," I said looking at the course syllabus project list. "It looks like we can either detail the root causes of the Inquisition or discuss the rise of the feudal land system. I am sorry but this was all that was left."

"That's ok. I think the Inquisition would be more interesting. I'm sure I would have burned with the best of the witches had I been there. So lets do that one."

I laughed again to myself and shook my head. If she only knew.

"Something wrong?" she asked.

"No not at all, it sounds like you have a strong passion there," I said.

"No, it just the Inquisition has always fascinated me," she said arranging her notebooks. "It shows what can happen to people that are different, that don't fit in. I guess I've always had some sympathy for them."

Funny, we've something in common, feeling different.

"So you don't feel like you fit in?" I asked as I logged into my mac.

"Sometimes," she said with a mischievous grin.

"Well, the inquisition it is then," I said.

Reading the class syllabus she said, "Looks like we need a powerpoint, a class presentation and a ten page paper. Which do you want to do first?"

I thought a minute. "Why don't we do an outline first then work on the powerpoint. We can circle back and fill in the paper. That worked pretty well for me in my last class with Dr. Brown," I said.

"Perfect," she said.

She got out a legal pad and dug right in. "Why don't we list the main dates to give us a range then we can look at the root causes before and the results after. That way we can frame everything then put in the details."

I liked the way she thought. I nodded, "That sounds great."

We listed the main dates and we each started looking for root causes. I could tell that this part of history fascinated her. She was flipping through our textbook and also doing web searches. About every ten minutes she chimed, "Found another one" and she would write furiously on the legal pad. At one point we both went to write on the pad and our hands brushed.

"Excuse me," I said a little embarrassed.

She smiled, her green eyes completely captivating. "It's ok. Uh are you cold in here? Your hands are like ice."

I thought fast, "Yea, it is a little cold in here. I think its the air vents."

She put her pen down and rubbed her eyes. "It is a little cold in here. I need some coffee," she said getting up. "Can I get you anything? Maybe some coffee will warm you up. You thirsty?"

I laughed again and she looked a me with a puzzled look.

"Did I say something funny?"

"No, you just reminded me of something else. Sorry, I don't really drink coffee, I'm warmer now anyway."

"Ok," she said as she got up. I watched her walk up to the counter.

She came back with a coffee and a large donut. She sat down, broke a big piece off and took a bite. I just watched her eat. It was fascinating.

"What, you never seen someone eat a donut before? Want some?" she asked her words a little garbled from the donut. As she held the donut out, a big piece fell on her shirt. She looked down then looked up at me and I looked at her then we both laughed. Finally she wiped her mouth and said,"Sorry about that. I usually have better table manners."

She was completely enchanting.

"It's fine, I am a little messy when I eat too," I said with a slight smile.

We worked for about an hour and a half and by the end we had a decent outline.

"Why don't I take the first three sections and you take the next three," she asked.

"Thats great," I said.

We divided up the pages of the outline.

"Want to meet Tuesday and put the stuff together? What's your email so I can send you a draft?" she asked.

Email. Should I give her my email? This could get complicated. In the coven we strictly guard our secrecy. I compromised and gave her a generic one that I used for public sites. She wrote it next to her notes.

"I'll try and get you something by tomorrow evening. I have a couple of hours in the morning," she said.

"That would be wonderful."

She paused a minute and said,"Hey, you want to grab something else to eat? I could still go for something. I skipped lunch today and donuts are not exactly dinner."

I looked into her eyes. She was very beautiful. I could get lost in them. The thirst rose again. I had to make an excuse and get out of here. I looked at my watch.

"I am sorry Tess but I have somewhere else I need to be. Perhaps another time?" I said. "Sure thats ok, some other time," Tess replied. A tinge of regret in her voice. I could see a faint look of disappointment in her eyes.

"See you Tuesday," I said grabbing my laptop and bag. "Tuesday it is," she said packing up. I really needed to get out of here before I changed my mind. The thirst was rising and I bolted for the door.

The next day I checked my email before I left. There was one from Tess. It read:

Hey Aidan,

Here is a rough draft. Hope you like the picture.

See you Tuesday.

T

I opened the attachment. The presentation was very good. Right at the beginning was a picture of a small kitten carrying a rather large donut in its mouth. It was being followed by a Great Dane. The caption read, "Cute beats muscle every time."

It was quite funny. I wrote back:

Tess,

Excellent Presentation. I know exactly how the dog felt !

I will have my draft ready by Tuesday.

See you then, Aidan

I hit send. Later I received one back that said, "Great! looking forward to Tuesday."

Julian stopped by my room. "What's so funny? I heard you laughing earlier," he asked.

"No, just doing some school work," I answered which was the truth. Thank God that witches could not read vampire minds.

Tuesday came. I felt both happy and anxious about seeing Tess again. It was also irritating, this sense of not being in control and I was very, very much used to being completely in control. But it was also exhilarating in a strange sort of way. The thirst was subdued, almost gone but it had been replaced by an almost insatiable curiosity. I couldn't explain it and that made it all the more exasperating.

The weather was perfect so I took the bike. On my way to class I passed a donut store that was open in the evenings. Oh what the hell I thought. I did a U turn on the bike and parked. I had absolutely no idea what a donut tasted like or what was good. A young man was standing in line as I walked in. He had on dark jeans and wore dreadlocks. I got in line behind him.

"Whats good?" I asked him.

"They're all good," he said not even looking back.

"Whats your favorite?" I asked.

He turned around. A young bearded face looked back at me.

"Oh man the chocolate glazed. Can never go wrong with chocolate glazed."

"How many would you eat?" I asked.

He looked at me funny and said, "All of them."

I smiled feeling slightly foolish, "No I mean how many at one time. I am not a big donut fan and I'm buying them for somebody else."

"Girl friend?" he asked.

Before I could think my traitorous mouth blurted out, "Yes, no, well maybe, sort of."

I caught myself. What a completely unplanned and unexpected answer. It was like someone else said the words.

He nodded his head, "Ah just getting started, want to make a good impression. Well what you need is two eclairs, chocolate on the outside, white filling in the middle. They're awesome but I'd also get one of those pink ones with the the little red sprinkles. They're lady killers. That way you have some for now and some for later. My lady goes wild over them, works like magic every time."

Magic, I could use a little magic.

"Thank you," I said still confused over my answer.

"No problem. Good luck with your lady friend."

"You too," I mumbled.

He ordered his chocolate glazed and turned to leave.

"That your bike," he asked pointing at my motorcycle.

"Yes, yes it is," I said.

"Sweet ride. Taking her on it?"

"Don't know, should I?" I said. Again it was like someone else was talking and I was just watching the words come out of my mouth.

"Gotta do that too man. Between the donuts and that sweet ride, you will be in the love house for sure."

I smiled, "We'll see."

"Keep it loose brother," he said going out winking at me.

I ordered what the donut expert suggested and drove straight to class.

She was late. Class was well underway. I thought for a minute she had ditched me or something had happened to her. I was anxious about her. Where was she, why was she late? My anxiety was annoying. Why the hell was I so anxious about her?

After about fifteen minutes she finally showed up. She quietly tiptoed in and sat next to me.

"Sorry," she whispered. "I got stuck at work again."

"It's ok, I'm glad you made it," I whispered back smiling. I can't believe I said that, I thought to myself.

She smiled, really smiled then winked at me.

And with that the world stopped. I couldn't think straight. I just sat there for a second in a fog. Finally I turned back to the lecture.

As soon as class was over, we picked up our bags.

"Back to the lounge?" I asked.

"Lead the charge," she said and we headed over.

Once we sat down and got our bags out, I told her, "I have something for you."

"What," she asked with an inquisitive look on her face. One eyebrow went up.

I pulled the box of donuts out of my bag.

She laughed out loud as I opened the box.

"Oh my God, Aidan. These look delicious," she exclaimed.

"An expert told me they were the best," I said smiling.

"Well it sounds like he knows his stuff. These are my favorite."

"Really?" I asked

"I never lie about sweets. I going to get some coffee, you want any thing to drink?" she asked.

"No, I am fine," I said.

She came back with a large coffee and a knife. She picked out an eclair and cut it in half. "No way I can eat that whole thing," she said. She put one half in front of me. She took a bite of hers. I just looked at mine feeling a little stupid.

"Aren't you going to eat your half?" she asked.

I didn't know what to say. I fumbled a minute and said "No" with a faint frown. I had to think of something quick.

"I have a confession. I actually bought four but I ate two at the shop. I don't think I could eat another one," I lied. Again, it felt wrong somehow deceiving her though I never had that problem with other humans.

"We'll then I'm not the only one with a guilty conscience," she said with another wink.

She took another bite.

"Ah," she said. She really enjoyed it.

I noticed a little bit of filling was left on the side of her mouth.

"Uh, you have a little," I said. She looked at me funny so I grabbed a napkin and carefully wiped it off. She smiled. Again that smile and beautiful eyes.

"Thank you," she said. "I just seem to make a fool of myself when I am eating in front of you," she said.

"No I think its enchanting," I said. She laughed.

"Now that is a new one. I've never been told I was enchanting before, especially after making such a mess of myself."

She took a sip of coffee and finished her eclair. It was fascinating watching her eat. She absolutely loved her food. I had been a long since I had eaten anything so it was a little like being a food voyeur .

"That was awesome," she said. "Sure you don't want the other half?".

"Glad you enjoyed it. No, please take the rest home. I really couldn't take another one."

"Really," she said.

"Absolutely," I replied.

"I'll have it for breakfast but I'll have to hide it from my brother. He loves them too. I will share the one with sprinkles with my nephew," she said.

"I hope he likes it," i said.

She wiped her hands and pulling her notes together said, "Ok Mr. Donut, lets see what you got."

"Alright," I said pulling up my powerpoint.

After about two hours or so of merging stuff together and adding in some additional info and final links at the end, the powerpoint presentation was done.

"We'll that's done," she said a note of satisfaction in her voice.

"It looks quite professional," I said. She started packing up.

"You hungry now?" she asked.

Her question startled me a minute. The thirst was rising just a bit. I almost panicked but then remembered what I said the last time we met about dinner so I asked, "Want some dinner?"

"I'd love to," she said.

I was completely at a loss of where to go. "You know I have never really eaten around here before, have any suggestions?"

"There is a little French place down the street that's pretty good."

"I have my bike, want to ride over?"

"That would be fun," she said "just let me drop off my stuff at my car."

We took our bags and put them in her car. "My bikes over there," I said.

"Thats a nice ride," she said.

"Thanks," I said.

I handed her my helmet and we got on the bike. She said in my ear, "Just go straight then take the first left. It's four blocks down on the right."

The bike started. I took it really slow. I didn't want to frighten her.

Once at the restaurant, we sat down in the back. The server came up. Tess ordered a salad with some grilled fish.

"Gotta pay for that eclair," she said smiling.

"You know, I had a late lunch and I am still full from those eclairs," I said. "I'll just have a glass of water," I told the server. "You sure," the waitress asked. "Yes, just water for me," I said. She left the table.

"Aidan, really, we didn't have to come just for me,"Tess said. She seemed a little embarrassed.

"Now I couldn't have you going home hungry," I said trying to set her at ease. "You would just be tempted to eat another eclair."

"You're probably right," she laughed finally.

"Besides it's nice to talk about something other than Doctor Brown's project," I said.

"So why medieval history?" I asked trying to change the subject from food.

"I don't know, I guess I just love old things," she said.

I laughed. She was full of surprises.

"Whats so funny ?" she said taking out a bread stick.

"I don't know, I like history too," I said doing a quick recover.

"No really why the class?" I continued.

"I'm a history major so its required. How about you?" she asked.

"Archeology but I am getting a minor in History."

"So what are you planning to do with a Archeology major," she asked.

In this light her eyes were a deep green like the forest. I almost forgot the question.

"Do field work first then later maybe teach," I finally said.

"How about you, going to teach History or something?"

"No, I really want to go on to Law school one day," she said.

"That's wonderful Tess. Seeing how you've put the presentation together I think you would make an outstanding lawyer."

"Thats very nice of you to say, Mr Croft," she said teasing me a little.

"Especially if you were litigating defective eclairs," I teased her back.

She laughed and pretended to throw a bread stick at me.

Her laugh was like music, it lightened the whole room.

At that point they brought her salad. "You sure you don't want to order something else?" Tess asked.

"No really I am full from those eclairs," I said, "But you go on and eat."

"So tell me about your family, you said you had a brother," I asked.

Finishing her bite she said, "Yes, actually I have two older brothers. My parents and my oldest brother live in LA. My Dads a doctor there. So is my older brother. My other brother, Nick just got out of the Army a few months ago. He is about to start medical school. I live with him and his wife Karen and my three year old nephew, Austin."

"That must be nice, staying with family," I said.

"It is most of the time. They moved here after Nick got out of the service. I was already living here but I moved in with them to help out with the rent. I mean Dad helps us a lot but living together saves us both a load of money. I'll move out when he finishes school. The house does get a little crazy sometimes. Thank God, its a two story so I basically have the upstairs to myself."

"That was considerate of you," I said.

"We'll he is family and I would do anything for family," she said.

"Believe me I understand," I said.

"So a lawyer in a family of doctors. You must be the rebel in the family."

"How'd you know?" she teased.

"Just a lucky guess."

"So Mr. Donut, whats your story?" she asked taking another bite.

I laughed a moment and took a breath trying to decide what to say. This was going to be a little tricky.

"You know it's not really that much different," I said. "I am very close to my family too. My parents live north of here, up by Muir Woods. I have a place near them. I have several aunts and uncles here too They're all in business together," I said taking a very small sip of water.

"What do they do?" she asked.

"They have an import, export business," I said. "I work there on the weekends and over the summer."

"By the way where do you work?" I asked remembering she was often late.

"I teach a couple of classes and I work at a shop," she said.

"What do you teach?" I asked curious. She was full of surprises.

"I teach some yoga classes at the Y and I also teach a Karate class," she said.

"Really, a karate class?" I asked a slight note of disbelief in my voice.

"Yes, is that hard to believe?"

"No, just unexpected." She was so different from anyone I had every met.

"I teach at a martial arts school a couple of days a week. Like I said I grew up with two older brothers and they were really into martial arts. So was my Dad. He was in the army too and he wanted me to be able to protect myself. So it was just part of growing up."

"Are you an expert," I asked.

"I got my black belt when I was 16. Come by sometime and I'll show you the mat," she smiled teasing me back.

"That's a bet," I said laughing. She laughed too.

"So what kind of shop?" I asked. I hopped I was not prying but it was fascinating discovering more about her.

"Oh it's an old antique shop. Mostly just jewelry and small stuff, some books too. Owner is a nice old man. I work there part time a couple of afternoons a week. I told you I like old stuff. That's why I am late sometimes. I have to close up at the end of the day and sometimes I just can't get that last customer out. Sometimes the karate classes run late as well. I try to time them just right but you never know whats going to happen."

The waitress came by to check on us.

"You know when I first met you, I thought you were a dancer. You move like a dancer."

"Really? I did have lessons as a kid. That's the way we got my mom to go along with the karate lessons. The dance stuff didn't stick but the karate did."

She took a bite of the fish. "You sure you don't want some, it's very good."

"No I'm ok," I said.

"So you like living in the city?" I asked.

"I love San Francisco. My parents told me I would hate the weather but I really like it here. There is always something to do, lots of parks and recreation, theater. I like it much better than LA. It feels like home now. How about you, you like the city?"

"Yes, there's always something interesting going on. We've been here for years now and I never grow tired of it. It's full of surprises .. like you.," I said.

She blushed just a little.

"You're quite charming Mr. Croft."

Now it was my turn to blush.

We talked more about our favorite locations while she finished eating.

"Want anything else?" I asked.

"No I'm fine. I already had my dessert," she said smiling.

I motioned for the waitress to come by with the check.

"Hey thanks again for dinner, you didn't have to do that," she said.

"Least I could do after I polluted you with that eclair."

She laughed again.

We left the restaurant and walked back to my bike. She went to put on the helmet but she was tugging at the back of her shirt.

"Aidan, my necklace is caught on the back of my hair, can you get it lose for me?" she asked turning around.

"Alright," I said.

I leaned in to look at the clasp. I smelled her perfume and then her scent. As I leaned closer I could hear her heart beat then there was a surge of thirst. I hesitated just a moment then I pulled back. We were alone, no one was around. This was dangerous, I should get her back to school.

"You doing ok back there?" she asked.

I quickly untangled her necklace and I closed my eyes just a second.

"Yes, it's undone," I said. She turned around.

I noticed my hands were clenched. I unclenched them but my face must have betrayed my anxiety, She looked worried.

"Something wrong, Aidan?" she asked.

"No, No, Its ok. I think maybe those eclairs are extracting their revenge. If you are ready we can go," I said. I handed her the helmet. We got on the bike. I noticed she held on just a little tighter. I drove us back to school. The wind in my face calmed me. By the time we were back to school, my control was back.

"I had a good time tonight. Thanks for going.," I said.

"I did too," she said. "Thanks again for dinner."

"My pleasure," I said.

"Meet Tuesday again after class?" she asked handing me my bag.

"That would be wonderful."

I reached in my bag and pulled out the box. "Enjoy your sweets."

She smiled taking the box. "I will. Thanks again Aidan. See you Tuesday," she said.

"Bye" I said and she drove off. I got back on the bike and headed home.

I didn't know quite what to do. This was spinning out of control. I wanted to get to know her, to spend time with her. But I knew that another part of me, smaller, deeper, darker wanted nothing but her blood.

I was miserable. When she was with me I was happy but worried about my control. But when she was gone I couldn't get her out of my mind. I was afraid of what I could do to her but I feared never seeing her again.

The thirst was under control but why was it there to begin with? Why was I so curious about her. She was just a human. In one way it hurt my pride that a human could have this effect on me but in another way I was happy that it did. I feared the loss of control more than anything.

I didn't know what to do. But one thing I did know was that I would have to be very careful. Under no circumstance could I let my control slip even for an instance. Maybe it would be better to break everything off now. But I just couldn't bear the thought of not seeing her again. I was angry at myself for getting into this situation but in a strange way grateful. It just wasn't like me at all. Humans were not supposed to have this kind of power. It just didn't make any sense.

When I got back to the house, Mora was in the front room watching TV. "You were out late," she said. "Yes I'm still working on this school project," I said.

"Sounds like a big project," she said.

"Yes it is. I am going on upstairs," I said glumly.

She turned around to look at me, "All you alright?" she asked sensing tension in my voice.

"Yes just a little frustrated with this project," I said.

"Anything I can do?"

"No. It's something I have to work on myself"

"Ok, see you in the morning."

"Goodnight," I said.

I got to my room, unpacked my bag and laptop. and sat in my chair.

I tried to enter into the vampire rest state, not sleeping but immobile, completely still. Normally I entered into the trance smoothly with no hesitation. But tonight I was restless. I tried to clear my mind but all I could think about was Tess. I tried several times. Finally, I just sat on the floor and after a while I felt my body relax and I lost myself in the trance.

About 2am I heard Rachel screaming, "Everyone come down stairs, now!"

Chapter 6

Fork in the Road

San Francisco

I rushed down to the first floor almost tripping Stefan on the way down. Julian was already there. as Rachel was pacing back and forth.

Lucian was right behind us followed by my father who said, "Rachel what is it."

She was looking up at the wall, her eyes staring into the distance. "A vision of death. A young woman is going to be attacked. It's one of our kind."

"Where?" I asked,

"Near Jackson Square on Pacific," she said looking blankly in the distance. "Hurry, we don't have much time."

Dad stood up and said, "Julian, Rachel and I will take one car. Stefan, you, Mora, and Aidan take the other. The rest of you wait here and watch for news. Call us if you hear anything. We need to catch this thing before it strikes and find out who's behind this."

We grabbed our jackets and headed for the cars. In just a few minutes we were heading down the highway. When we were several blocks from the Square, we slowed and pulled into a vacant lot. I could see Rachel in the other car. She closed her eyes and said something to Julian. They left the lot and we followed. Julian pulled over and stopped on a side street. We parked behind them and got out of the car.

Rachel closed her eyes a second, opened them said, "This way, hurry." We ran down two blocks. She stopped, turned right, then ran down an alley. She stopped suddenly and coming up behind her I saw we were too late. A body was lying at the end of the alley next to a dumpster.

It was the remains of a young woman. She had been brutally attacked, bites around her neck and shoulders. There were long gashes down one arm. Stefan leaned down. He pulled up a long brown hair and holding it up, sniffed.

"Werewolf," he said. "Left here five maybe ten minutes or so. It might have felt us coming."

My Father moved away from the body. He held out his right hand. A small blue flame appeared in the center of his palm. He dropped it on the ground near the woman's body and the flame slowly encircled it. Near the woman's head, large, clawed footprints appeared glowing blue. He waved his hand and the flame left the body and followed the footprints.

More prints glowed on the ground heading farther down the alley. Stefan and I fanned out following the glowing footprints. They twisted down two more alleys and suddenly changed. The huge, claw prints were replaced by human footprints. The smaller human prints went on a few more steps then stopped. I looked behind us, The glowing tracks were slowing fading. After a few seconds, Dad and the others ran up. He knelt down by the now fading prints.

"He shape shifted back to human form here."

A main street was ahead. Several people waked by in front of the alley. "He must have slipped out into the crowd. We've lost him," Dad said shaking his head.

We heard sirens and the sounds were getting closer.

"We should split up and head back home," Julian said.

Lucian, Mom, and Grace were waiting for us. "Definitely a werewolf," Stefan said as we all sat down. "Victim was a young woman, long gashes like claw marks down one arm with large bites on the neck and torso. I also found a hair with the scent. It was definitely one of them."

Dad said, "We'll go back tomorrow night and canvass the area. Its possible the creature was just passing through although its a little unusual for them to hunt right in the middle of the city like this. Lucian lets go and check to see if there have been any other unusual murders either south or north. We might be able to figure out which way it's traveling."

Lucian nodded and the two of them left to go do some research. The rest of us went back up stairs.

The next morning all the local news were reporting the brutal murder. For the next three nights all seven of us went back into the city. We staked out places within a three mile radius of the attack but none of us saw any trace of it. Rachel was unable to see it in any vision. Father and Lucian found one report ten days earlier of a particularly brutal murder about two hours south. His conclusion was it must have just been passing through on its way north.

Tuesday came and as much as I didn't want to admit it I was looking forward to seeing Tess. After the events of the past few days, spending time with her would be a welcome change. Class passed quickly and afterwards we tweaked the presentation and worked more on the paper. The final argument that Tess crafted in the paper was excellent. We wrapped up for the night.

"Hey by the way," she said packing up. "You know Friday is a school holiday and I have the weekend off. Some friends and I are going up to Tahoe to snow board this weekend. How would you like to come? My friend Jesse's parents have a huge condo right on the slopes. I've been a couple of times. Its really fun." There was a slight tone of expectation in her voice. Her heart was beating faster.

I was not expecting this at all. She was full of surprises. Now I had to make a decision and the road would fork here.

I could refuse and just let things fade. Finish the project and then never see her again. I knew that would be the wise course, the safe course for her and for me. No entanglements. I would let this happy dream I was living just fade away.

But I also knew that wasn't what I wanted. I didn't want the dream to end. So in the end, I didn't really have a choice. I was entangled.

Besides, so far I had the thirst under control. Once again, curiosity got the best of me. But I had to check one thing. There would be a lot of humans around. "Let me check something," I said pretending to look at my calendar. Instead, I did a quick check on my iPhone for the weather this weekend in Tahoe. Overcast, no direct sun. That would be perfect.

"Yes, I would love to go. It sounds like a lot of fun. But I have to warn you, I'm not really much of a skier. I did a little when I was a child but I have never been on a snow board before."

"That's perfect. Don't worry about not having been on a board before. I'll teach you everything you need to know. You'll get the hang of it in no time."

She was beaming. Her beautiful eyes flashed. I could hear her heart beating slightly faster. I t was odd but making her happy made me happy.

"You want me to pick you up on Friday?" she asked,

It would be better if I had an option to leave on my own.

"How about I drive, I have a large car," I suggested.

"That would work," she said nodding. "mine's not the best anyway. It's a little small."

"So what's your address?" I asked her.

"How about I just email it to you," she said.

"Wonderful," I said. "What time should I pick you up on Friday?"

"How does nine o'clock work? Then we'll drive over and meet everyone else at Jesse's."

"Sounds great. Thanks Tess.," I said.

We started walking back to our cars. Right down from where Tess parked, I saw three forms standing. It was Stefan, Mora, and Rachel. Rachel sometimes took a class here as well and Stefan and Mora must have stopped by to pick her up.

Great, no getting out of this one I thought.

"Hey, Tess there's some people I want you to meet," I said walking towards Stefan's car.

When we got to the lot, they each looked Tess over then looked at me with a puzzled look.

"Tess, this is my ah cousin Mora, her boyfriend Stefan and my cousin Rachel."

"Guys this is Tess, she's in my history class. We're doing a project together."

Mora said, "Nice to meet you, Tess."

Stefan sort of bowed his head and said, "Pleased to meet you."

Rachel shook her hand and said. "Pleased to meet you Tess. My cousin treating you right on this project, doing his fair share?"

"Oh Yes, he's gone out of his way to be helpful. He's quite the gentleman, charming really."

Oh God, I thought to myself. I'll never hear the end of this.

"Well just don't let him charm you into doing all the work."

"Oh I won't," Tess said laughing.

"You enjoying your class," Rachel asked.

"Yes, it's quite interesting. How about you. What class are you here for?" Tess replied.

"Anthropology."

"Awesome, is it interesting?"

"Yes, it is. Human history is so, intriguing," Rachel said with a slight smile.

I looked at her with a frown.

Rachel said, "Well we have to go, so we will leave you two to your project. Nice to meet you Tess. See you later, .. cousin."

"It was a pleasure to meet you Tess," Mora said.

Stefan just nodded again.

We walked off back towards's Tess's car.

I waved as they drove off.

"Charming am I," I asked teasing her a little.

"I was just being nice," she said with a smile then she asked, "By the way, is there anyone in your family that doesn't look like they just stepped out of a fashion magazine?"

I laughed, "I never thought about it but Rachel might think she belongs in a magazine."

"Well, I thought they were very nice, especially Rachel," Tess said.

"Rachel can be quite annoying but she has her good points and yes Mora is very kind and Stefan, well Stefan is a little shy and doesn't say much," I said.

"Well like I said I thought they were very nice. Thanks for introducing me," she replied.

"No problem. So I'll see you on Friday?" I asked.

"Friday. It will be a blast," she said.

We said goodnight and I headed home.

Stefan, Mora, and I hunted Thursday night. I wanted to be ready for the trip the next day.

"So who was that human you were with the other night Aidan. She is very beautiful ," Mora asked.

"Just someone in my class. Like I said we have a project to do. I do have to keep up appearances."

"Oh leave him alone Mora. I am sure everything is quite harmless, right Aidan."

"Absolutely," I said with a slight twinge of guilt.

We had a great hunt. I made sure I was very full just in case.

Dawn was just breaking on Friday when we got back to the house. Everyone else had plans. Mom, Dad, Rachel and Julian were going up to visit some vineyards. Would be gone until Sunday. Stefan and Mora had some play they wanted to attend and then were driving down the coast. So I said I thought I would go for a long drive up into the mountains. Maybe do a little more hunting. Mora was a little surprised but didn't press the issue. I told everyone that I would be back on Sunday. I took the keys to the Range Rover. No one objected.

I packed my bag, retrieved my winter coat and gloves and packed the Rover. I drove to the address that Tess had emailed me. It was down in Potrero Hill. The house was a nice old victorian style two story that bordered a park. I parked the car, walked up the brick drive to the front door and rang the bell.

A young woman in an apron answered the door. A very young boy was behind her, holding her leg. "Yes," she said.

"Hello, I'm Aidan Croft. Is Tess here?"

Since I had on my gloves, I shook her hand.

She just stood there a minute looking a little dazed then said, "Oh yes, please come in. I am Tess's sister in law Karen. Sorry to keep you at the door."

I walked in. It was a beautiful home, small but tastefully decorated. I could see a room in the back with lots of toys.

"Please have a seat," she said motioning towards the living room. I went in and sat down. The young human followed me with a book.

"Poo," he said.

I looked up at Karen confused

"He wants you to read him the book. This is Austin, Tess's nephew. The book is Winnie the Pooh, his favorite. He does this to everyone, don't let him bother you."

"No it's quite alright, no bother at all. Come sit by me Austin. How old are you?"

"Three," he said with a grin holding up his fingers.

"You are a big boy," I said.

He climbed up next to me and I started to read. Until I met Tess, never in my life would I have thought I would be reading a story to a three year old human. It was almost surreal.

"I'll go and check on Tess," Karen said as she went up stairs.

I could hear her as she talked to Tess.

"Oh my God Tess he looks like he just walked out of a magazine. Where did you meet him? I mean those eyes. I was speechless at the door. He probably thinks I'm a moron or something," Karen said.

"He is cute isn't he. I met him at school and no I'm sure he doesn't think your a moron. What do you think of this outfit for the car."

"Oh, it looks great on you," Karen said.

"Ok, just let me finish getting ready. My bag is all packed. Go down stairs and keep him company and don't drool. I'll be down in just a minute."

"I'll do my best," she said with a slight laugh.

Karen came back down stairs. I was deep in the hundred acre wood with all of Pooh's friends.

"He likes you," Karen said.

"Yes, were having a good time, aren't we Austin," I asked.

"Good time," he said laughing.

Karen smiled.

"Can I get you something to drink," she asked.

"No, I'm fine."

"Pooh," Austin said.

Karen picked him up. "Austin, go get some of your toys and show them to Aidan," she said putting him down.

He ran over to the other room.

"He must keep you busy," I said.

"Oh yes, that he does," she said.

"But he is a really good boy and we have a lot of fun. He adores Tess."

Austin returned with a large yellow stuffed bird.

"Big Bird," he said.

"Yes," I said. "Very Yellow."

Austin ran back in the other room.

I heard Tess coming down the stairs. I stood up. She looked absolutely stunning. She had on a blue sweater with a white coat, jeans and boots. My turn to be dazed.

"You look beautiful," I said.

"Thanks.," she said smiling.

"You're not too bad your self," she said with a slight wink towards Karen.

"Ready to go," she asked.

"Yea as soon as Austin shows me this last toy." It was some kind of dinosaur.

"Barney," he said.

"Hello Barney," I said. He laughed.

"He'll do this all day. You guys should get going," Karen said.

Tess kissed Austin and hugged Karen and said, "I'll see you on Sunday."

I heard Karen whisper into Tess's ear, "I want all the details."

Then she said, "OK, you guys have fun. Pleasure to meet you Aidan, come back anytime."

"Thank you, I will," I said.

We walked out the door. She and Austin blew kisses at us as we left.

"Wow, this is a nice car," Tess said getting in.

"Yea, it's fun to drive too," I said. "So where are we going to pick up your friends?"

"Actually we're going up on our own. Nicole, Max, Jesse and Sharon got off work early so they decided to go up last night. They wanted an early start this morning. Everybody else is driving up later this evening. So its just going to be the two of us if that's ok."

"Great. Better this way, I'll have you all to myself," I said.

She blushed just a little.

We both got in, buckled up and put on our sunglasses.

I put the address she gave me into the GPS and we were off.

After a few minutes she said, "So, lets see what you have on your iPhone to listen to."

As she scanned the entries, her nose wrinkled up. I could tell she was not impressed by my Mahler and Vivaldi.

"Oh that's just some old stuff. Maybe we should use yours instead," I said.

"Well if you insist."

She plugged in her iPhone and in a few seconds music filled the Rover.

At first I heard strings. They were flowing, melodic. It was a beautiful arrangement but I could't place the composer. I thought she was just toying with me by putting on a classical song when the singing started.

It was a delightful song.

"What is this?" I asked.

"Your kidding right?"

"No but it sounds wonderful," I said.

"Its Secrets by OneRepublic.," she said smiling.

"I can't believe you've never heard this song Aidan. You really need to get out more."

I laughed. "I guess I do. See you are teaching me new stuff and we haven't even gotten to the slopes yet."

She smiled and we just listened to the music for a while.

"Austin seems like a great kid. He must be fun to have around," I said trying to break the ice.

"Yea, he is a lot of fun but he gives his Mom fits sometimes. He's very stubborn."

109

"Like his Dad," I asked.

"More like his Aunt," she said laughing.

"I'd never guess," I said smiling.

"He was such a surprise. For a long time they couldn't have children and suddenly one day Karen was pregnant. It was a little touch and go for a while but everything turned out well. He is a great kid. My folks come up all the time from LA to see him."

"So tell me about growing up in LA ," I asked.

"Well it's definitely not like it is in the movies. It was really very ordinary. Nothing exciting. We had a nice house in the suburbs. By the time I came around, Dad was already well into his practice. It was good place to grow up and we were all close."

"So whats your favorite memory?"

"Wow thats a hard one"

She thought a moment. "One time when I was about ten we all went to the beach. We used to go often, my Mom loves the water. Anyway we went to the amusement park and then the beach. We stayed out and watched the stars and and then we had a fire. I remember my older brother took his guitar and we all sang some songs. It was fun having us all together."

"You miss your parents?"

"Sometimes, but we get together often. We Skype a couple of times a week and every couple of months I either go down for a long weekend or they come up here to see us so it all works out. How about you, you go down to LA often?"

"Sometimes. My Father and Uncle do some business down there on occasion and I usually go along."

"You like the beach?"

Now that was an odd question to answer. What could I really say.

"Not really. I'm more of a mountains guy myself."

"But you don't ski."

"No, I like to hike and camp but I never really did much skiing."

"Well maybe I can make a convert out of you"

"Maybe so," I said.

The rest of the drive was quite interesting. We covered topics from school to politics to why the American Revolution really happened. History was definitely her passion. The time flew by and next thing I knew we were in Tahoe.

Tess gave me final directions to the condo and we pulled in. I grabbed our bags and Tess knocked on the door. Two of her friends came out. One I recognized from class.

"Jesse, Sharon this is Aidan. Aidan these are my friends Jesse and Sharon"

Jesse was of medium height and light brown hair. Sharon was the girl from class. She was taller with black hair.

"Pleased to meet you. Thanks very much for inviting me," I said.

"No problem, glad you could come. We were about to run to the store. You guys want anything?" Jesse asked.

"No, I am not particular. Can I give you some money for groceries?" I asked.

"No No, I got it," Jesse said.

"Tess you want anything?"

"Just no donuts," she said. We both laughed. The other girls had a questioning look on their faces.

"Inside joke.," she said, "It doesn't matter just get whatever. I am sure it will be fine. Thanks Jesse," Tess said.

Tess and I walked into the condo. It was a multi-story home with a giant den and kitchen on the first floor. The den had a beautiful view of the slopes and a huge fireplace on one side.

Tess said, "There are three stories and six bedrooms. The guys are all bunking on the top floor and the girls are on the second. Your room is the second on the right after you get off the stairs."

She went to grab her bag but I said, "I got it, just tell me what room."

We climbed up the first flight. Tess's room was on the left. It was tastefully decorated and had a balcony. The forest came almost up to the side on the left and on the right she had a great view of the mountains. I put her bag down on the bed.

"Thanks," she said. "Why don't we meet back down stairs in ten minutes and we'll get our lift tickets and equipment."

"Ok, I'll be right down," I said as I took my bags up to my room. It was small with a window that looked out at the forest. It reminded me of my trip to Canada. I dropped my bag on the single bed, not that I would be needing it.

I put on my really warm jacket, again for appearances and my gloves and hat and headed down to the first floor. Tess was already there. "Ready for some fun?" she asked.

"Absolutely," I replied.

We walked down to the main plaza. The air was crisp and clean. Even overcast the mountains were beautiful. It reminded me again of how much I missed the forest. I would have to plan another hunt in Canada soon.

Tess saw me looking out. "Penny for your thoughts," she said.

"Its just so beautiful here. You forget how beautiful the mountains can be, even in winter."

"Well you will have a spectacular view when we get up there," she said pointing up to the top of the lift.

"Can't wait," I said.

We bought our tickets and headed out to the equipment rental shop. It was a large shop with skis and snow boards lining the walls. At this point, I had no idea what to do with a snow board.

"Come on, I'll show you," Tess said.

A young man obviously bored to death sat behind the counter. He yawned and said, "You know what board you want?"

Tess told him exactly along what boot size and helmet. "How about you," he asked.

"He's a first timer," Tess said.

"Oh," he said with a certain lack of enthusiasm as he came from behind the counter. He measured me up and checked out my shoes. He was not exactly fast as lightening but in twenty minutes, I had boots, a board, and a helmet.

Once we got outside, Tess said, "So, we can either go over on the bunny slope and you can practice or we can take a lift up to the green area and I could show you a few things. Thats a little crazy but it depends on how adventurous you are."

"Let's do crazy," I said.

"I was hoping you would say that," she said rubbing her hands together, "I think I'm going to get some revenge for all that donut crap."

I laughed and we headed for the lift.

She showed me how to strap into the boot and we got in line for the lift. The ride up was quick. "When you get to the top, just stand up and push off the chair. It's ok if you fall. Everyone does it."

I nodded and when we got to the top, Tess lifted the bar. I jumped down and glided over to the the edge of the hill where everyone was waiting to go down.

"You've never done this before ?" Tess asked with a slight look of disbelief on her face.

I think she was a little disappointed that I didn't fall.

"No, but it's like skiing. I guess I'll live."

"Well we'll see about that," she laughed.

"Ok, we are going to slip onto the board and just try to go down this hill.," she said. "See what the other people are doing, you go side to side using the edge of the board. Just do what they're doing. I'll go down first and wait about midway down by that small tree. When I'm there, you come down. I'll check to see how you are doing."

"I'll give it a shot," I said.

She took off down the hill. It was a small grade with a bank on the left side. She stopped about halfway down the hill. I clipped in and started down the hill. I followed her tracks exactly.

"Not bad, not bad at all. How did it feel?" she said as I came up to her.

"Feels great. Can we try something with a little more slope?" I asked.

"You are looking for crazy. Ok, come on."

We took a lift up to a blue run. We clipped back in and Tess said, "You go down first and I'll follow you."

She had a big smile on her face. Waiting for my big crash no doubt.

This course was much steeper so I could generate some speed. I flew down the center. I noticed a steep rise on the side. I went up the bank, flew in the air, did a flip and landed again in the center. It was exhilarating. I did that several more times down the hill. I stopped about half way down and looked back.

Tess waved and shot straight down the slope stopping about 3 feet in front of me. "Ok, you big liar, you've been putting me on. You flew down that slope like a pro. What, did you grow up on a ski slope or something?"

"No really, its my first time on a snowboard but I did ski as a kid remember so I guess all of that stuff I learned paid off. But you're right, this is amazing."

She looked unconvinced but motioned down and we took off down the rest of the hill.

It was great fun. We went down the rest of the slope next to each other. It was great just she and I. At one point I whipped by her and she got sprayed with snow. She laughed and hit me with a snow ball right in the head. I chased her down the hill.

She was laughing as stopped at the bottom. "All right Mr Beginner I think you've graduated the easy stuff. Let's try you out on a black course. Maybe we'll get a face plant out of you yet."

I nodded and we found yet another higher lift. The black ones were even more fun. I could sail even higher in the air with more flips and turns. We flew down the mountain together.

When we got to the bottom of the mountain, I told her, "This is wonderful Tess, thanks so much for inviting me."

Tess said. "Well we worked really hard on that paper, so I think we deserve a little fun. But I still can't believe this is your first time Aidan, you ride that board like a pro." At that point her phone rang. It was her friends. They were up at the top of the mountain. Tess told them to wait, we'd be there in just a few minutes. We found another lift and when we got to the top they were waiting right outside the lodge.

"Hey guys, this is Aidan," Tess said. There were three guys and three girls.

"Aidan this is Max, Shawn, Nicole, and Peter. You've have met Jesse and Sharon."

"Hi everyone, thanks for inviting me," I said.

"Great to have another guy," Max said. "The girls had us outnumbered."

"We were about to grab some lunch, come on let's get inside," Shawn said.

The lodge was huge with a large vaulted ceiling. Giant wooden beams crossed the roof. It was warm so everyone opened their coats.

This was going to be one of those awkward situations. being around humans. I knew I had to appear to eat something.

Years ago, Stefan had taught me a trick for when you were in these kinds of circumstances. You order something that comes all together with a sauce. Then you either tear it or move it around on your plate. If there is more than one plate even easier. No one pays any attention, they only see what they expect.

We all got in line and I looked at the menu. Perfect, there was a beef stew and bread. I picked up an empty cup. There was a machine dispensing drinks. I filled the glass half way.

As everyone ate, I pulled the bread apart and pushed parts into the beef stew. As everyone else ate, I moved the food around. I brought a few pieces to my mouth but quickly put them down and I pretended to drink the half full soda.

"So Aidan, how did you and Tess meet?" Peter asked. He was tall with wavy blond hair. I felt some tension in his voice. His heart was beating a little faster than normal and there was a slight tinge of tension in his voice. Tess had an odd look on her face. Then it hit me; he and Tess used to be in a relationship. Last thing I needed was some silly confrontation with a human male.

"Ah, we met at the University. We both have a history class together. Sharon is in the same class."

"Yea, Doc brown. You had him once didn't you Peter?" Sharon asked.

Stephen Weagraff

"Yes, the man can drone on and on". He made a impression of Dr. Brown that had everyone in stitches. With that, the tension seemed to disappear.

After a little more chatter and everyone was finished, I quietly cleaned my plate in the trash and left it with the others. No one noticed a thing. We all headed back down the mountain. Everyone seemed to really enjoy themselves. I toned it down a little so as not to invite too many questions. Still I got several stares as I did a few more acrobatics. Tess just rolled her eyes. At one point I faked a fall. I made sure Tess saw me go straight down on my face.

She came right over.

"You alright," she asked. I could hear the concern in her voice.

"Yes," I said smiling, "Guess I turned too sharp."

"Everybody does that sooner or later, don't feel bad. Anything hurt?"

"No, just my pride," I said. "I'm fine."

"Well at least I got to see one face plant," she said teasing.

I pretended to grab her ankle but she flew down the hill.

We made several more runs until we started to lose the light. I could have gone all night but I could see fatigue starting to set in everyone else.

"Lets do one more run and call it a day," Max said. Everyone nodded and off we went.

The sun was setting as we walked back to the condo. It was beautiful with the sun reflecting off the mountains. Everything was bathed in its golden glow. Tess really looked beautiful with the sun in her hair.

We got back, showered, changed and headed into town for dinner. It was Italian, another good choice. I ordered spaghetti and meatballs. I cut up the meatballs and just moved the pasta around.

Tess's friends were very amusing especially Nicole. She told a story about one of her cousins that had everyone almost in tears it was so funny. All of Tess's friends were warm and open. They talked about movies they had seen, vacations they had taken. I enjoyed just listening to them talk. It was a side to humans I had forgotten.

At the end, we paid our bill and went back to the condo. Everyone piled into the den to watch a movie. The fire was blazing in the fireplace. Tess snuggled up next to me. I put my arm around her. About midway through the movie, I could see everyone getting tired. I pretended to yawn. Finally Shawn said, "man I'm beat. I am heading upstairs."

Nicole and Peter said, "we're going to the hot tub, anyone want to join us?"

Tess looked a me. This was one I couldn't fake. "I am beat too, I think I might have over done it a little," I said. "I think I'll turn in."

Tess smiled and said, "Yea you were superman out there today. You're going to be sore in the morning."

"Probably. Good Night Tess, Good night everyone." I headed up to my room. I laid on the bed listening to the house. After about an hour, the movie ended and everyone went to their rooms. I heard Peter and Nicole come in, they had a room to themselves. Soon the house was quiet. I heard snoring from Shawn's room and remembered Sam, my friend from long ago. I closed my eyes and just listened, remembering a simpler, happier time. Being with Tess was bringing back a life I had long forgotten.

I locked my door and at half past midnight, I quietly slipped out my window and flew over into the trees. I climbed up one that was outside of Tess's room. She and Jesse were sharing a room, twin beds, Tess's closest to the window.

"He's really nice Tess even if he is drop dead gorgeous."

"Really I hadn't noticed," she said laughing. Then said, "He's really interesting to talk to and he's funny. A little odd about somethings but I like being with him."

"What do you mean, odd?"

"I don't know just little things. Songs, movies that you would think he would know but doesn't, his taste in music. Sometimes his speech is I don't know, strange, like he grew up somewhere foreign. I know this sounds funny but he's a real gentleman."

"Not many of those around anymore," Jesse said.

They were quiet then Jesse said, "One thing I can say he's damn good on the snow."

"That's another thing. He told me he had never been on a snow board before."

"I don't know Tess, that's a little hard to believe. He did some tricks out there today that even really experienced guys won't do. Maybe he's a natural Tess or maybe he just didn't want to brag. He could just be shy."

"Yea maybe. There's just something about him. I know's he different but I can tell deep down, he's a good person Jesse. I like him."

"Well he seems to like you too. You going to keep seeing him?"

"Oh, absolutely," Tess said laughing.

"By the way, I thought Peter was going to bust a gut," Jesse said. Tess laughed, "Yea, me too but he and Nicole are doing great so everything worked out."

They talked for a bit more then turned out the light. Tess was asleep in a few minutes. As the moon streamed in, I watched her sleep.

I couldn't explain my attraction to her. At first, it was thirst that changed to curiosity. But now it was more than simple curiosity. Tess was so different from any human I had ever met. The more I got to know her, the more I wanted to know. It was so unlike me.

For decades humans were just something I overlooked but now here I was fascinated by her every word. I hated to admit it but I liked her, I liked being with her. She was funny and she was so alive; she lived every minute. I had forgotten what it was like to be that way. One thing I did know, I had to be very careful. I sat there for the next few hours just watching her. I knew I would never let anything harm her, especially me.

Before dawn, I slipped back into my room. By seven I heard the house beginning to stir. I changed my clothes and when I heard Jesse in the kitchen, I went down stairs.

"Good morning, Jesse," I said as she made coffee.

"Oh hey, Aidan good morning. Coffee will be ready in a minute. How did you sleep?"

"Very well thank you," I said.

I heard Tess coming down the stairs. She had on some grey sweats and her sweater. Even in that, she looked beautiful to me.

"Good Morning', she said.

"Good Morning, Tess," I said.

"So how does superman feel today"

"Superman is sore in places he didn't know he had," I lied. I limped just a little for effect.

"Well serves you right," she said winking at me.

She walked over and poured herself a cup of coffee as Jesse laid out some boxes of cereal.

"Coffee," Jesse asked.

"No I'm fine," I said.

Slowly everyone came down stairs. By 8:30 everyone was ready to go.

I couldn't wait to get up on the slopes. We retrieved our gear and headed for the lift.

"How you feel this morning," Max asked.

"Sore," I said.

"Yea me too, I don't get up here much and when I do I tend to over do it. Tonight you should soak, it really helps."

"Thanks, maybe I'll give it a try," I said.

We got to the top and everyone took off down the hill. I did a few flips and turns. Nothing too fancy; I didn't want to draw any more attention, especially given what Jesse had said. If I wanted, I could have flown over the trees but that really would have blown their minds.

On our second run after a particularly long jump that did cause a few stares, I figured I needed to perform another fall, what Tess called a face plant. I waited until Tess was pretty close and down I went right on my face. I slid a bit and rolled over and unclipped. Again she boarded right over next to me.

"Everything ok?" she yelled.

"My ankle is a little sore," I said.

She unclipped and came over.

When she was close, I threw a small snow ball at her hitting her on the head.

"Oh, you are going to regret that," she said. She grabbed a big snow ball that she sent flying directly at my head. I could have easily dodged it but I let it hit me. We exchanged a few back and forth then she came over and pushed a a handful right in my face. I tackled her and we both fell into the snow laughing. We rolled around in the snow and finally we stopped with her underneath me. She smiled at me and I brushed the snow off her hair. I smiled back at her. Just at that moment Jesse came by and yelled "Come on you guys let's get to the bottom."

"We better go," Tess said and we got up and got back on our boards and headed down. The rest of the day was just as wonderful. I didn't want it to end but finally we did our last run and everyone headed back to the condo.

That night, after dinner, Tess and I walked out on the back patio and down onto the snow. It was very cold but she was bundled up, gloves and coat. She reached down and threw another snow ball at me. I threw one back. She tried to push some down my shirt. We laughed and tussled a minute. We extracted ourselves and as we walked down the hill, I reached over and held her hand while we walked. The path turned and went behind a small clump of trees.

The moon was bright and she looked so beautiful. I had never seen anything as beautiful as she was in that moonlight. Her eyes were gleaming and her face almost glowed. I was awestruck.

We stopped next to the trees. There was something I had to know, I had to know if I could control myself with her. At the first sign of danger, I was ready to fade back and leave.

She looked up and I bent down and kissed her lightly. She kissed me back. Her lips were were warm and soft. I held her tighter and kiss became deeper.

I felt the first slight stirrings of thirst.

Please, please I thought, let me keep control. Her heart was beating faster. I could hear the blood sing in her veins. The thirst started to surge and I was about to step back, to make an excuse and leave before I lost control. There was no way I could let any harm come to her.

But at that moment, before I stepped back as I held her, a miracle happened. The stillness that was buried deep, that had been unreachable to me for years and years, flowed up out of the earth and swirled around us. The thirst vanished and we were surrounded by stillness.

Immediately, the world seemed more alive than ever. I felt that same innate connection to the earth, the forest, the moonlight and then most clearly to Tess. In that calm moment, the world seemed perfect. I felt the craft, the power, flowing through me. It was like an electric current flowed through us. I felt I was a part of the forest and the mountains and even the people around me. It seemed to swirl around us pulling us together. The thirst, the craving was completely gone. Then as quickly as it came, the stillness seemed to flow back into the earth. As it flowed away it took the thirst with it. I was whole, at peace for the first time in a very, very long time. I held her just a moment longer, happy and content.

She opened her eyes, smiling and said, "Wow, that was some first kiss."

"Yea," I said.

She smiled and I bent down and kissed her again.

This time she noticed my lips were cold. She pulled back and took off her glove, reaching up to my face, her happy expression turning to concern.

"Aidan, you're face is cold out here. We need to get you inside. Come on." She grabbed my hand and we headed inside.

"Here come and sit by the fire," she said sitting down and patting the spot next to her.

"Tess, its ok, I'm fine," I said.

Just as I got to the fire, a tone went off on my phone. I pulled it out. It was a text from Stefan:

"Another incident. Party's over. Come home."

"Oh No," I said looking up at Tess.

"Whats wrong," Tess asked.

"It's from my cousin. There's been an accident. I have to go home."

"What happened?" she asked.

"I'm not sure but they said I needed to come home right away. I'll call once I'm in the car. It must be serious or my cousin would not have sent it."

"I'll come with you," Tess said standing up.

"No it's ok Tess. Really, stay and finish your weekend. I am going straight to my Dad's. Can one of you give her a ride back?" I asked.

"Yea, she can ride back with me," Jesse said.

"Thanks Jesse," I said.

"Let me pack, I'll be right back." I ran upstairs.

I packed my shirts and clothes and my second pair of shoes. I looked around for my keys. I saw that they had fallen on the floor. I reached out my hand and just as I started to bend down to pick them up, I felt the craft flow and my keys floated up into my hand. I was dumbfounded. I shook my head in disbelief.

From down stairs, I heard Tess, "You alright up there Aidan?"

"Yea, I'm coming right down."

I put the keys down on the desk a second time. I opened my hand but this time there was no flow. The craft had left as quickly as it had came. I reached down and picked them up and ran back down stairs.

When I got back down, Max said, "I'll take your equipment back Aidan. Don't worry about it."

"Thanks very much Max," I said.

"No problem," he said.

"Thanks again everyone, sorry I have to go. I really had a great time," I said.

"Come back anytime Aidan, I mean it and I hope everything is ok," said Jesse.

"Thanks Jesse, Bye everyone," I said and I headed for the door.

"I'll walk you out," said Tess.

I got to the car and put my bags in the back seat.

"I hope everything is ok at home."

"I am sure it will be alright," I said. "But I need to be there especially for my parents."

"Ok, call me as soon as you know something. Drive safe."

"I will. I had a wonderful time Tess, thanks for inviting me. Sorry I have to go."

"Me too," she said with a smile.

"I'll call you tomorrow. How about that?"

"Ok"

I kissed her quickly again and left.

I needed some time to think. For the first time since the change, I felt happy, whole. And the appearance of the craft after all these years; I still didn't believe it. Somehow, in some way I didn't understand, Tess was at the center of it. I was sure of it. In someway she opened a part of me that I thought was long lost.

Two weeks ago, I passed through the human world like a ghost. It was like they didn't exist. And now a human was at the center of my world. I needed someone to talk to and fast.

Chapter 7

Decision

San Francisco

As soon as I was on the highway, I called Stefan.

"I am on the highway now. I should be there in a few hours. What happened?"

"Another attack, a gay couple in North Beach. Bad, really bad. Two young men. First one was completely decapitated. Bite marks, claw marks, same as before."

"Was it the same werewolf?"

"I think so. The scent was very similar. Unfortunately, Rachel didn't see anything. We heard about it on the news so we couldn't do any cleanup. I am sure the police are going nuts. If we have another one, they'll think its a serial killer and the whole city will lock down. Your Dad is frantic. We need to find this thing and fast."

"Where is everyone?"

"Mora and I are still in the city with Julian and Rachel. We've been combing the area but nothing so far. Your Dad and everyone else went home. Why don't you just come down here and we will do a wider sweep."

"Ok, I'll meet you down in North Beach. I'll call when I am closer."

"Ok. Bye"

This was bad. Either one of these things had taken up residence here in the city or there were multiple ones moving through. Either way we had to find it. Dad would not stop until this thing was dead.

I thought about calling Tess but I am not sure what I would say to her. I needed to think before I talked to her again. I put on some music and let the miles roll by. I was hoping it would clear my mind but it just reminded me of Tess.

I met Stefan and Rachel on a side street. Mora was still out patrolling. We made several more passes through the area and at one point Rachel thought she had something but when we got into the alley there was nothing there. About three am we decided to go home.

It was too late to call Tess. I would have to talk to her in the morning.

When we arrived, Rachel was exhausted and went straight up stairs. Stefan and Mora started to go to but I stopped Mora. "Mora can I speak to you a minute?" I asked.

"Sure," she said. "I'll be up in a bit," she told Stefan. He went on up.

"Lets take a walk," I said.

We walked outside and in minutes we were deep in the forest. There was a stone outcropping high on one of the hills. I often went there to think so I took Mora there. I climbed up the rock face and sat with my feet dangling over the side. She climbed up and sat next to me. The forest was dark all around us.

"So whats on your mind, Aidan. It must be important for us to climb all the way up here," she asked with a slight smile.

"I am not sure where to start."

"I've known there was something going on with you for several weeks now. You seemed almost too happy and now tonight it's like you have your tail between your legs. So go on, tell me."

"I've been spending time with a human, a human girl."

"I see. The girl we met at the school that night, the pretty one?"

"Yes," I nodded

"You're struggling with thirst?"

"No. Yes, at first, but now it's different."

"How's it different?"

I couldn't decide what to say.

"So go on, just start at the beginning," she said. The wind began to blow through the trees.

I let out a long breath.

"For a long time now, I think I've just been going through the motions, passing through life and at some point, I reached a compromise with myself. I've been very careful about my thirst. You know that. I've always taken the safe and controlled course. I did my best to stay away and ignore humans. I kept my passion in check so I could always be in control. But I've come t see that this compromise left me numb. I felt like my two natures were locked in a struggle. Neither one winning, neither one losing. It was a stalemate and I couldn't move forward or back. I was just stuck in this grey, featureless fog."

"I've know for a while now that something was wrong with me, Mora. I've come to doubt myself. First there was the dark one that I fought who challenged why I fought for humans at all, then when Stefan and I fought the dark witches in New York, Malek told me that I was fearful of who I really was. And you now something; he was right, I was afraid of myself, of my passions, of my inner demons, of what real feelings could lead to. I've buried them so deep that I forgot who I was."

"But then I met Tess. At first, it was simple thirst. I wanted her. I couldn't control myself, my passion just seemed to overflow. I know I was lying to myself but I wanted her. That passion was the spark. Try as I might, I couldn't stay away from her. But then the thirst turned to curiosity. She was interesting and funny, Now the curiosity has turned to something else. I want to be with her, to know her. I think I'm falling in love with her Mora and I think she feels the same way about me."

"Now the world is bright again, not grey. I'm happy in a way I've not been since the change. Don't get me wrong, I love you and Stefan and the rest of the family but there was always something missing and now in some unexpected but amazing way, I feel whole again. Like I am myself again. And I owe it all to Tess."

"I want to be with her but I can't be with her. I can't tell her anything and I am terrified she is going to find out the truth. I'm in love with her and I don't know what to do. Help me Mora, I don't know what to do"

She sat closer to me and took my hand.

"I can't tell you what to do Aidan. You'll have to figure that out yourself. But I can tell you something that happened to me years ago and it might help you. I've never told anyone this, not even Stefan."

"A few years after my change, many years before I met Stefan, I met a young man. I was living in France at the time. His name was Jean. In those days, at the beginning, I fed on humans and one night while searching for prey, I saw him. He was a young actor and was walking home late at night from the theater. He turned in an alley and I followed him. I was about to take him when two men jumped out. They were going to attack me."

She laughed.

"He of course ran to my rescue and fought them off. He was very handsome and like you, I became curious. I just could not bring myself to take him after his noble act. I thanked him for saving me and he asked to see me again so I agreed to meet him after his next performance. A few nights later I went to his theater to watch him perform. I sat in the back and I couldn't take my eyes off of him, I was completely enchanted. I met him after the performance and we talked and laughed long into the night. He was so full of life. I saw him several more times and one thing led to another and we became lovers."

"It was blissful at first. It was like someone opened a window and let warm light into a dark room. I loved him and he loved me. We were happy. I had not felt that way about anyone since my change."

"He knew there was something different. My skin was always cool to his touch even when it was warm outside and I didn't go out in the direct light. But he either didn't care or he was so blinded by love that it didn't matter."

"One night, I slipped out while he was asleep to feed. I didn't realize it but he followed me. He thought I was cheating on him with another man. I had slipped into a house where an old bachelor lived. I had just started feeding when Jean burst in, screaming in a jealous rage. He thought he was going to catch me in the arms of another man. Instead, he saw me there with blood on my mouth, a dead man in my arms."

"He understood then. He ran in absolute terror back to our apartment. I found him there crouched in a corner. I think he thought I was going to kill him. I tried to talk to him but he just backed away. I pleaded that I loved him, that I wanted to be with him but he was so overcome with fear all he wanted was to escape. I even offered to make him like me, an immortal if he would stay with me. But he just cried and screamed. I was so afraid he would die of fright that I let him leave. After all these years, I can still hear the sounds of his screams."

She closed her eyes a minute, pausing. I could tell that it still troubled her after all these years.

She opened her eyes and looked out at the forest. "He left the city that night and I heard later that he joined a monastery."

She turned and looked at me. "I was beside myself with grief. Nothing would console me. I lost him because of what I was. I grieved for him for years. I thought of ending my tragic life but as you know that is very difficult for our kind. Time passed and the pain and remorse disappeared. Many years later, I saw him again. He was older but still very handsome. He was waiting outside a cafe and as I watched from the shadows a young woman arrived. It was his wife and she had their children with her. He kissed her and took his children into his arms. He was happy, content and that's when I realized something"

"While we look the same, Aidan, while we look human, we are not human. Not anymore. We are different from them. Our life is different from theirs. And after the change there is no going back. That's what I was doing with Jean. I was trying to go back to live the human life I lost. But it's a fools dream Aidan. Sooner or later they will discover the truth and then you will lose them one way or another. I realized then that it was better for Jean, for him to live a happy human life with a human woman."

"When I came to that realization, I came to accept what I was. Many years later, I met Stefan and all that happiness that I thought I had lost and would never find again, found me. That warm light came again into my dark room. You will find happiness Aidan but the path you are on is a very difficult one. I am glad she makes you happy because I know you have been very unhappy for a long time. What you said about your life is true. I know it's grey because I have been there. I also know what its like to be in love, to feel the warmth of love's passion. It's possible that things could turn out different than what happened to Jean and I; the world is a different place today but she is still human and thats not going to change."

"Be yourself Aidan. If it is with Tess then so be it, but be yourself. If you love her do whats best for her. That is the only way you are going to find true happiness."

We both sat there a few minutes. It was not what I really wanted to hear but now I had a decision to make.

"Thank you Mora. I don't know what I would do without you and Stefan."

She put her head on my shoulder. "You always have us Aidan. I know sometimes it's not enough, but you always have us."

We went back home. Mora kissed me on the cheek and said, "Don't worry or be afraid Aidan. Be yourself, it will work out in one form or another, it will work out. Believe in yourself. I do."

"Thanks again Mora." She hugged me and nodded and went upstairs.

I went back to my room. The sun would be up soon and I had a very hard decision to make.

At noon I called Tess. She and Jesse were in the car coming back. "Hi you," she said, "How is everything?"

"It's ok, one of my uncles had a small accident but he is alright now."

"Oh, that's wonderful Aidan, I was really worried."

"Yea, me too. But he is much better now. Sorry about having to leave, I really wanted to stay."

"Yea, Jesse says she missed you." I heard laughter in the background.

"Well tell her I missed her too. So what did everyone do after I left?"

"Oh the guys all talked us into watching some stupid werewolf movie. It was terrible. I went upstairs after half of it. It gave me nightmares."

"That's no way to spend your last night."

"Well that's what you get when you let guys plan an evening."

"Speaking of evening, How would you like to have dinner tonight?" I asked.

"I would love that."

"How about I pick you up at 6:30"

"Sure, I'll see you then."

I've never had an afternoon go by so slow. The hours seemed to crawl. Rachel could find nothing in her vision so there was no search tonight. Finally it was time to get ready. I put on my best black jeans, a blue shirt and my black jacket. I took the Audi TT and was off.

Tess looked beautiful when I picked her up.

"Nice car," she said., "How many cars do you have Aidan?"

"A few. We kind of share them in the family but this one is actually mine," I answered as I opened her door.

I took her to a nice Italian restaurant near Jackson Square. We made small talk. I asked her about the rest of her trip. They had make a few runs that morning. No one could believe that I had never snow boarded before. We talked about class. Finally dinner was over and there was an awkward silence.

"Everything ok?" she asked.

"Yes," I said glumly.

"You hardly said anything at dinner, what is it, I can tell something is bothering you Aidan."

I looked off for a moment, "It's just things are really complicated for me right now Tess."

"What do you mean?"

"Us, you and me, it's complicated."

"I don't understand, you didn't seem this way yesterday. Is there someone else?"

"No, no, nothing like that."

"Are you gay?"

"No," I said shaking my head.

"Then how complicated can it be?"

I looked around. This was not the place to say what I had to say. I hated what I was about to do, extract myself and disappear. Mora had been right and this was what I had to do. I loved Tess and I wanted her safe and she would never have that with me. Tess deserved a human life not darkened by my shadow and if that meant that I had to disappear, then that's what would happen. I just had to lie a little and let her down easy. I had to be strong enough to let her go.

"How about a walk?" I asked.

"Sure," she said a tone of exasperation in her voice.

I paid the check and we walked over to the park. There was a long line of trees with an alley right across the street. It was dark with a few street lights. We walked in silence for a minute.

"You know my store is only a couple of blocks from here. I come here sometimes for lunch," Tess said.

"Its a nice area."

"Yea, but I know we didn't come here to sight see. So explain why things are so complicated Aidan," she said a hint of anger in her voice. Her body was tense. I think she suspected what was coming. She kept some distance between us.

"Ok, let's just walk and talk" I said.

As we started to walk, I put my hand in my pocket. That's when I noticed my phone was missing. I was so distracted, I had left it in my jacket in the car. We were only about half a block away from the car. I needed it in case Stefan called me.

"Hell, Tess, I left my phone. Stay right here, I'll be right back."

She nodded and waited. I could tell she was very angry. Her heart was pounding. This was not going to be easy. I had just got to the car when I heard footsteps. A man stepped out of the alley right in front of Tess. I could hear him speaking to her.

"Excuse me miss," he said.

She held up her hand and said, "No, no thank you," Tess said stepping back. She must have thought he was panhandling.

There was something not right about the man. I forgot about the phone and walked as quickly as I could back to her. The man was of medium height, dressed in old jeans and a stained blue shirt. He was wearing old tennis shoes. As he saw me come up behind her, he looked up at me.

"Buzz off fang boy, this one is mine," he said to me. That's when I noticed the smell, like an old wet dog. Fear gripped me. It was him, he was the werewolf! Tess was in terrible danger. I had to get her out of here, put her in a cab and circle back and deal with this thing.

"She's with me. We don't want any trouble. Let's go Tess."

"What is she, tonight's dessert? I told you I saw her first."

"Aidan, this guy is giving me the creeps, let's get out of here" she said as she started to turn.

He reached out and grabbed her arm. At that point, Tess swung into action. She grabbed his wrist, pulled down and kicked him square between the legs. He let go of her with a grunt and bent over.

"You shouldn't have done that miss," he said looking up.

He stepped back and looking straight at me said, "First, I'm going to kill you then I am going to have my way with her. I'm really going to enjoy this."

His body began to blur and he got taller, a lot taller. A long mane of hair bristled from his head. His chest expanded, ripping his shirt. His arms lengthened and swelled and thick black hair sprouted along them. Muscles rippled under his fur. His face twisted and his nose and mouth extended into a short snout; long fangs grew behind his lips. His hands turned into long claws. His ears were pointed and curled up along his head. His eyes became slits and turned red. The shape shifting took only seconds and when it was done a seven foot werewolf stood in front of us.

A look of horror and disbelief passed over Tess's face.

I grabbed Tess and tossed her over my shoulder. I stepped back and then leap into the air. As I jumped, I heard Tess hit the ground hard behind me. The werewolf growled and jumped. We hit each other in midair and fell back to the ground. We twisted and leapt again into the air, each of us trying to gain advantage.

I felt his claws tear into my shoulder. He threw me against a wall then turned toward Tess. I jumped and twisted in the air again. Rage engulfed me, anger that he would threaten her. I felt strength surge in me. I grabbed him again and threw us both against the wall. I pinned him and grabbed his head. Thirst surged through me mixing with the rage. I pulled his head to the side and when his neck was exposed, I sank my teeth into it,

Blood sprayed into my mouth. As I held him in my grip, I drank deep. Finally his struggles ceased and I let him fall. The creature transformed and a man's dead form lay on the ground.

"Aidan," I heard Tess say.

I turned around and saw it in her eyes, the look of complete horror. She was shaking her head as if to make the sight go away. Then I understood. I put my hand to my mouth. Blood was dripping down my chin. I looked back up and she fainted.

I wiped my mouth and hands on what was left of the dead creatures shirt and I jumped to Tess.

Oh God, Please, please don't let her be hurt, I thought,

I picked her up. She had a small cut on the back of her head. When I pulled my hand back her blood was all over it. The smell of her blood was overpowering. I closed my eyes and felt tthe thirst surge. For just a moment, I hesitated then regained my control. I could feel the stillness and the thirst disappeared.

I listened and I could hear her heart, she was still breathing but I needed to get her to the hospital. I tore my shirt and applied it to the cut for a minute. The bleeding seemed to stop.

But the creature's body, I needed to get rid of the body. I had torn open his neck and we couldn't afford to have an autopsy. With everything going on it would lead to too many questions . It would wind up in the paper and Tess might find out. I laid Tess down and pulled the creature's body into the alley. I checked his pockets. There was nothing but a door key. I took the key and set the body over to the side next to the wall. Only one way to dispose of it, I needed witch fire. That's the only way to destroy a witches body. I had to try.

I bent down over the body and held out my hand. Nothing.

Please, I thought, just this once let it work. I cleared my mind. Nothing. I starting to panic, I had to get her to the hospital. I exhaled and tried again. Nothing.

Then, I thought of Tess. I had to do this for her. I took a deep breath and focused. I felt it then, the connection. I looked down. A small blue flame danced in the palm of my hand. I dropped it on the body and immediately the creature was engulfed by it. It didn't flame, it just seemed to flow over and into it. Then it faded and nothing was left but gray ash. A wind blew through the alley and then there was nothing.

I ran back, grabbed Tess and sprinted to the car. I got her strapped in and headed as fast as I could to the hospital. I put my jacket on to hide my torn shirt. I was flying down the road when she came to.

"Aidan," she said.

"I'm here," I said.

Her eyes opened, they were a little groggy then a look of fright appeared. "I saw a thing, a monster." Her eyes darted around. For a second she didn't know where she was. I had to get her calmed down.

"Tess, listen, you hit your head. You're in the car. I'm taking you to the hospital."

She touched the back of her head. "Ouch," she said.

"But the monster."

I had to make something up, fast.

"Tess, listen, a man came out of the alley when I went back to get my phone. He had a big dog, a really big German Shepard. The dog jumped on you and knocked you down. You fell down a step and hit the back of your head."

She shook her head, "I don't understand. What happened?

She blinked her eyes, "I thought you were breaking up with me and then this weird guy shows up. I didn't see any dog. What I saw was that weird man turn into a monster and then you were fighting with it. You had blood on your face."

She reached up and touched my face with a slight dazed look in her eyes. I reached up and took her hand.

"Tess, listen, didn't you say you had watched a scary movie last night? Some werewolf movie? I think you're mixing them up. You really hit your head hard. Please just lay still, I'll have you to the hospital in just a minute."

I saw the emergency room sign just a head. I pulled into the hospital and parked. I picked her up and sprinted into the ER.

When I got there a nurse took one look at her head and took her right back in a wheelchair. She told me to wait in the lobby.

In a few minutes a young man came out and asked me some questions. I explained the dog and that she had fallen down a step and hit her head then fainted. He took everything down. I paid them with my credit card and they told me to wait in a waiting room.

As I came in, I saw the room was full of humans. A lot of very anxious families. Some men paced, other family members sat trying to console each other. I could tell they were were all frightened of what could happen to their loved ones. I found a seat in the back.

I sat there for a long time just watching them.

It was then that I realized something. Humans were not really that different from us. Sure there were physical differences, some fundamental but sitting here, watching them, I realized that these people were just like me; worried about someone they loved. Those lives meant as much to them as Tess meant to me. I understood what Mora said, but I knew that my situation was not the same as hers.

I knew then what I had to do. Up to this point, I had tried to do everything by myself, make every decision. But that really wasn't fair. I never gave Tess a chance with the truth. Everything had been built on a lie and I was still lying to her. I knew now that that had to stop. She deserved to know the truth regardless of the circumstances or the outcome. She deserved a choice. I owed her that.

It was an anxious time. I paced, waiting like everyone else. I strained to hear what was going on but there were too many noises. For all my abilities, I was as powerless as rest of the people in this room. In this terrible regard, we were all the same.

Finally they called me back into a small examining room. Tess sat on the table. A older woman doctor was standing next to her.

"How you feeling?" I asked as I entered the room.

"Better, my head's a little sore," Tess said.

"Are you the boyfriend?" the doctor asked.

"Yes, yes I am," I said looking at Tess.

The doctor finished writing in her chart and said, "She's had a rough night young man. She took a bad fall. There is a small cut on the back of her head and her back is bruised. The cut wasn't big enough to stitch and there's no sign of a concussion so you can take her home but someone needs to watch her for the next twenty four hours. If she gets sick to her stomach or gets dizzy or has any problems seeing or hearing you need to bring her right back. Make sure she gets plenty of rest and drinks plenty of fluids. She may have a slight headache for a day or so. You can give her Tylenol but nothing stronger. If she gets a really bad headache or has any other symptoms, you bring her back here, understand. Now, these same instructions are on the discharge papers. You two have any questions?"

"No, I don't," I said nodding.

She looked at Tess, "How about you Tess, any questions?"

"No, none for you," she said, looking at me.

"Then you two are free to go. Watch her, boyfriend."

"I will, I promise. Thank you very much, Doctor Bates."

"See that you do. Remember bring her back if there are any problems. Take care Tess."

The doctor walked out of the room.

I picked up her discharge papers and we headed to the car.

"I am so sorry about all this Tess."

As soon as we were outside Tess said in a hushed tone, "I'm fine. But my memory is groggy. I don't remember any dog jumping on me. What I remember is a guy turned into some weird animal right in front of me and next thing I know you are fighting with that thing. I saw you jump like twenty feet in the air then wrestle that thing. to the ground. That's what I remember. It's crazy but that's what I remember. I didn't tell them that or they would lock me up for sure."

"Tess, listen, the doctor said you hit your head really hard. You fell off a step backwards!You're bound to be groggy. I think your mind is mixing up the movie you saw last night. Let me get you home and let you get some rest. Let's do what the doctor says, ok?"

"I promise tomorrow I'l come pick you up and we can finish this whole conversation. Doctors orders remember."

"Well what about this complication stuff." I could tell she was getting angry again.

"That was just talk Tess. I was just rambling. Can we talk about that tomorrow? I'm very worried about you and I feel responsible for what happened. I really want you to rest. Here let me put on some of my old music and you can just relax a bit while I drive you home. No more talking."

"Ok, first you're superman on the slopes and now you're that doctor on ER. A girl just can't catch a break with you."

"Not when it comes to your health."

"Ok, lets hear your stuff but I am not sleeping."

I selected a symphony from Brahms. She was asleep in under a minute.

"Hey sleepyhead, we're here," I said as we pulled up to her house. I helped her get out of the car and walked her to the door.

"I'm home," Tess said as we walked in the house.

Karen came out from the kitchen. "You just missed Nick," she said. When she saw Tess she said, "Tess what's wrong?"

"She took a bad fall tonight. We just spent several hours in the ER."

"What, what happened," she asked.

Before Tess had a chance to say anything I said, "We were taking a walk and I had to go back to the car. While I was gone, a guy walking a dog came from nowhere. The dog jumped on her and she fell down a step. She hit her head pretty hard. The doctor says she's fine but she needs to rest and be watched for the next twenty four hours. I think we should get her up to her room."

"If I can get a word in here, I would like to sit on the couch," Tess said.

I got her to the couch. She sat down and I handed Karen her discharge papers.

"I could stay and watch her," I said.

"Whoa there cowboy, that won't be necessary," Tess said.

"Tess, really I feel terrible," I said.

Karen said, "If you want to stay Aidan, its no problem but really I can watch her. Nick will be home in a little while and Austin is asleep so if you have to go really it's ok."

I needed to get back and tell Dad and the others what happened but I really wanted to stay.

"Tess do you want me to stay, it's no problem."

She shook her head, "No it's alright, Aidan. You go on home. I'll be fine. Its just a little scratch. Karen is here with me," she said. "I am going upstairs to change."

I started to help her. "I can do it myself, thank you."

I could tell she was still angry with me.

"Alright, if you're sure, I'll call you first thing in the morning."

"I'm sure. I'll talk to you in the morning."

As Karen walked me to the door I said, "Karen, I know she says she is alright but she took a very bad fall. If she needs anything or has any trouble, call me on my cell."

I wrote the number down for her.

"Thanks Aidan. If she has any problems at all, I'll call you, I promise."

I nodded and she let me out. I got back in my car and drove straight home.

Dad was in the study when I got there.

As I walked up to his desk, he was deep in thought staring at the fragment that Julian brought back from Jakob. Dad looked up as I walked in. He could tell I was upset.

"What's wrong Son?"

"Dad, I have something I need to tell you. I have some news I think everyone should hear. It's about the werewolf"

I took off my jacket. He saw my torn shirt.

"Oh my god Aidan. What happened, are you alright?" he asked getting up.

"Yes but I saw him tonight."

Dad nodded, "You sit down. I'll get Julian and the others."

I sat down and when everyone was in the study, I started.

"I was downtown tonight when I was attacked by the werewolf."

"What, Aidan are you hurt?" Mom asked.

"No, I have a small scratch on my left shoulder but I'm fine."

"Let me have a look," Dad said.

I took off my shirt. There was a dark blue stain on it. He examined my shoulder.

"Yes, definitely the werewolf, same claw marks but it's just a scratch. So what happened."

I pulled my shirt back on.

"I was down near Jackson Square when he appeared out of nowhere. He attacked me, must have thought I was a threat. We fought and I killed him."

"Where's the body?" Dad asked.

"I didn't have time to hide it so I had to get rid of it."

"How did you do that ?"

"I burned it"

"You burned it?" he asked.

"Yes I burned it with witch fire."

"You generated witch fire? How?"

"I don't know. I guess being in a real bind gave me some inspiration. It just happened."

I needed to get him off this subject. "I found something on him however."

"We'll talk about this witch flame later but what did you find?"

"I found a key."

I pulled the key out of my pocket and handed it to him.

"Its a hotel room key."

He examined it. "No name or address, just a number 315. Was this everything he had?"

I nodded.

Dad asked, "Sophie, can you determine anything from this?"

Mom took the key in her hand and shut her eyes.

"Its a old room, dark on the west side of a building. There is a bar across the street. The sign says George's bar and grill."

Her eyes snapped open but she was looking into the distance. She had a quick intake of breath like she was startled. "In the room, it's dark, dank. Pain, something terrible happened in that room. I sense tremendous fear. They have to get away, they have to run. But they're bound. It's coming for them." Her hands shook around the key.

"Sophie, Sophie," Dad said. She continued to stair, her hand trembling even more. Dad slowly reached over and took the key from her.

She blinked her eyes.

"It's ok Sophie," he said as he took her hand. He handed the key to Julian.

"I am sorry. Thats it, thats all I see." She shook her head, "Some terrible nightmare happened in that room." She laid back against the couch.

I felt the hair raise on the back of my neck thinking about what could have happened to Tess.

Dad walked over to the computer and did a search for George's bar and grill in San Francisco. Believe it or not there were two. One was in Oakland but the other was up in North Beach on the way to Jackson Square.

"Julian, I want you, Aidan, and Stefan to go check out this room first thing in the morning. I don't want to draw too much attention tonight. Aidan lets go upstairs and see to that shoulder. Grace we probably need your help."

The three of us went upstairs. Grace had a small study that overlooked the gardens. The room was full of jars, old scrolls and books. Dad and I sat on a small couch. She pulled several jars down and mixed the contents of them in a bowl with water. She made a paste and put it on my shoulder. As she rubbed it she chanted a low chant. A warmth spread around the cut and the shoulder immediately felt better. When she stopped she placed a bandage on it.

"This will do better if you get some rest tonight."

"Thank you Grace," I said. "You always fix me up."

"Your welcome, Aidan," she said smiling as she put up the jars.

Dad put his arm around my neck and said, "Listen to Grace. Try and get some rest son."

"I will. Good night Dad, Grace." I went to my room and put on some music and tried to rest but I couldn't get the thought of Tess being attacked out of my mind. I was furious with myself for putting her in danger.

Early the next morning, Julian, Stefan and I headed back downtown. We parked a couple of blocks over from the address and walked over. The building was an old hotel. Just like Mom said, George's Bar and Grill was across the street. We went in and took the stairs to the third floor. Room 315 was at the end near the fire escape. The hall was empty so we let ourselves in.

It was a shabby room, dark brown curtains drawn shut. Julian turned on the one dim light and we searched the room. There was nothing in the closet and the drawers in the beat up old chest were empty as well. A wooden chair was sitting in the center of the room.

As we continued to look, Julian found a wallet in the top drawer of a scratched up desk. He opened the wallet and pulled a card out. He threw the rest of the wallet to Stefan.

Looking at the card Julian shook his head, "I can't believe it."

He showed me a Massachusetts license with a Boston address. The name read Paul Atkins.

"Is this the man, the man that attacked you?" Julian asked me.

The picture was the same as the man who attacked Tess.

"Yes that's him," I nodded.

Julian said, "I recognize him. The name is all wrong but I recognize the face. When I knew him his name was Tomas. He was a novice witch at the academy, disappeared right before the revolt. I always wondered what happened to him. He came from a fine family. More of Draven's treachery at work."

Stefan pulled the rest of the wallet's contents out and placed them on the desk. There was several thousand dollars in cash and a couple of credit cards all in the same name. There was also a room key for the Ritz hotel.

Stefan stepped over and examined the wooden chair.

"There's a blood stain" he said pointing to one of the arms of the chair. He bent down on the floor and pulled up a long brown hair. He sniffed it.

"Werewolf," he said.

Stefan got up and said, "It doesn't look like he was staying here. No clothes, no travel bags. He was using this room for something. Let's take it all back home, maybe Sophie can get something out of it. How about the Ritz, we need to figure out the room number."

Julian said, "Leave that to me. All we need to do is go to the desk but lets go home first. Marcus will want to see all of this." He put the wallet in his pocket and we locked up and left.

"This is a bad sign," Dad said as he examined the license. He handed the license to Mom. She held it for a minute and handing it back said, "He's looking for something or someone. It's very misty."

Lucian said, "He was definitely using that room for some evil purpose. We need to get into his hotel room at the Ritz and see what else he has."

"I agree," Marcus said. "Tomas was here for a reason. He would not have come into our backyard without a plan. Julian you and Lucian take Rachel and see what you can find in that room. Take Aidan and Stefan in case there are any more of them."

We immediately headed down to the Ritz. The rest of us waited in the bar right off the lobby while Julian walked up to the counter.

"I'm supposed to meet a colleague in the bar and I'm running very late. I think he may have gone back to his room. Could you call him for me please?"

The clerk said, "Of course sir. What's the guests name ?"

"Atkins, Paul Atkins," Julian said.

He looked up the name and placed a call. He waited for several seconds then hung up the phone. "There is no answer sir, He may have stepped out. Would you like to leave a message."

"No, no thank you. I am sure he will be back in touch with me later. Thank you for your time."

"My pleasure sir. Have a pleasant day."

"You too," Julian said.

We all walked out of the lobby.

"It's room 1535," Julian said having read the clerks mind. We took an elevator to the eight floor and quickly crossed down to 1535.

It was a beautiful suite. There were expensive clothes in the closet, a laptop on the desk. I went straight to the laptop. "It's password protected.," I said. There was also a set of maps of San Francisco printed out on the desk. Stefan went through the desk drawer. It was empty except for an envelope. He handed it to Julian.

Julian opened it and took out a small key. "Looks like a safety deposit key, but its unmarked except for a serial number."

"He was very careful, wasn't he," Lucian said.

We checked the rest of the room but there was no other evidence.

"Aidan how about the laptop?" Julian asked.

"It might be secured. If we tamper with it we could destroy all the data. I think we need an expert."

"Lucian, if Sophie can't read anything on the key how long to track it to the correct bank?"

Lucian thought a minute, "I know someone who could help us. Probably a day or two before we can identify the serial number."

Julian nodded and said, "It's clear that this is all part of some larger plan. He's here looking for someone. We'll take the key home to Sophie in case she can do a reading. Lucian go on and talk to your bank contact. I'll contact my expert and see what he can do about the laptop. I don't think there is anything else here."

When we got back outside I said, "I've got some something at school to take care of, I'll see everyone back home later." I had taken the Audi down this morning so I could go straight to see Tess.

I called Tess as soon as I got in the car.

"How are you feeling, you sleep ok?" I asked.

"I'm fine, had a little headache but I feel much better today. Thank you for taking care of me last night. I guess my imagination got the best of me."

"Hey it was the least I could do. Listen, I know it's a little earlier than we planned but would you like to go out for lunch?"

"Sure," there was still a tinge of anger in her voice. She was still upset about last night.

"I am already downtown, I'll be there in about twenty minutes. That ok?"

"Yea, let me grab a quick shower and I'll be ready. Karen is here, she can let you in."

"Wonderful, I'll see you in twenty minutes."

Karen met me at the door, "Come on in, Austin is asleep and Tess is still upstairs."

"How is she doing?" I asked.

"She's fine. I think she's had worse knocks at that karate place she works, not that she has a hard head or anything."

We both laughed.

She yelled from upstairs, "I heard that."

She yelled again, "Aidan, I'll be down in a minute."

Karen asked, "So how is your Uncle. I heard he was sick."

"He is much better now. Thank you."

I heard Tess coming down the stairs.

"So this is big surprise, I thought I wasn't going to see you until tonight."

"Well I was free this morning and I figured why wait. Besides I was worried about you. You ready to go?"

"Wow, you must be hungry. Let me grab my coat."

I took her to an nice place for lunch but she ordered breakfast instead, an omelet and coffee. So I ordered eggs which I just moved around. Tess must have been starving because she finished everything.

"Feeling better now," I asked.

"Yes, that was a great omelet,"she said.

"I'm glad you liked it. How about a drive?"

"Where do you want to go?"

"It's a surprise."

"Ok," she said with a little hesitation in her voice. "Last surprise place you took me didn't run out so well."

"I promise this will be better," I said.

We drove north out of the city on highway 101. I knew there was an old park that had a great view of the north woods. We stopped there and climbed a small hill. At the top was a terrace that overlooked the forest. I knew it would be deserted this time of day. We sat on a bench partially hidden in the trees that overlooked the forest. We could talk in private here.

"Great view. How did you find this place?"

"I found it once just taking a drive. I agree, it's very scenic."

She stopped a moment, her mouth drawn tight, "So, I know you didn't bring me up here just to see the view. Is this more about what we were talking about last night about how I'm complicating things for you?"

She paused a minute and looked out at the forest a look of sadness in her eyes. It broke my heart to see that in her eyes.

"There's someone else isn't there?"

I shook my head.

"Then you're married."

"No it's nothing like that, Tess."

"So what is it like Aidan?"

There was an edge to her voice. I knew I had hurt her feelings last night, talking about complexity.

"I want to talk about last night."

"You mean the incident with the dog? Don't worry about that. It wasn't your fault. You shouldn't feel bad about that. I mean you took care of me, took me to the hospital. I think you were very sweet to me."

"What do you remember about last night?"

She rubbed her head, "It's a little fuzzy. A big dog came out and knocked me down. I fell and hit my head."

"Is that what you really remember? That's not what you said last night."

"I hit my head Aidan, I wasn't really thinking straight. I think my imagination got the best of me. We watched that stupid movie after you left the condo and I think my imagination just put the wrong pieces together. You told me this yourself, in the car."

"What if I told you it wasn't your imagination."

"What do you mean?"

"I mean what if your memory of last night was true."

"What are you saying, that a man turned into a monster right in front of me? That's crazy; it was just that stupid movie I watched."

"Tell me what you do remember, Tess. Not what everyone told you to remember but what your really remember."

"This is nuts Aidan."

"Please just humor me, it's important."

She thought a minute looking off in the distance, "It's all mixed up but what I remember is a man came out of the alley. He tried to grab me and I kicked him in the nuts. Then I saw him turn into some kind of a monster. You pushed me out of the way. Next thing I know I am in your car. But it can't be real. It's something with the head trauma."

"Tess, what if I told you that it happened just as you remember it."

Tess stood up. "Then I'd say you were more nuts than me, that I'm not the only one who hit their head. Did you bring all the way up here to just make fun of me, to play some kind of sick joke? Is this how you want to break up with me? If so then I am ready to go. You can take me back home now."

"Tess, I am not playing a joke nor am I crazy. I am trying to get you to remember something. Please sit down. What do you remember about me?"

She sat back down and took a deep breath. "I felt you fling me backwards out of the way of that monster. I saw you jump like twenty feet in the air, fighting with that thing."

I could tell she was struggling with the memory.

"That's what I remember," she said.

I stood up. I would have to show her.

"I am very sorry Tess but there's no other way."

With that I jumped and turned a backwards somersault and landed about twenty five feet up in a tree. I flew from tree to tree, then climbed down head first and flipped back to the ground. next to the tree.

"Is that what you remember?" I asked her again.

She sat with her mouth open, disbelief in her face. She was in shock.

"Tess can you hear me?"

"Yes," she said starting to shake a little. A tear rolled down her cheek. I jumped and was immediately sitting next to her.

"Tess, it's ok. Just breathe, I'm right here. Nothing is going to happen to you, just breathe."

She took several deep breaths and wiped the tear from her eye.

"Aidan, you just jumped like thirty feet in the air and you climbed down that tree head first. I see it but I don't believe it. How did you do that?"

"Forget about how I did it, It's not important. What is important is that you remember last night. I only did it to prove to you that it was true Tess. That what you saw really happened."

"But that means that monster was real. It can't be." She started to cry again.

I put my arm around her, "Yes, Tess, but it's dead now. I killed it. You don't have to be afraid. It can't hurt you now. Nothing is ever going to hurt you now."

"But how did you do that?"

I pulled away from her and I took her hand in mine. "You know Tess, you already know, you just have to put the pieces together. Just remember what happened at the end of the fight. The last thing you saw."

Her eyes were distant as she was remembering. "You fought with it and you held it down. You were really strong."

I put my other hand on top of hers. She looked at my hand.

"Aidan, your hands feel cool. You alright?"

"Yes, Tess just remember."

She took her hands back.

She touched my face "So is your face, just like the other night on the slopes."

I nodded. "Yes Tess just remember what happened at the end of the fight, what happened to the monster."

She looked off into the distance. her mind reaching. "I remember at the end. You jumped just like you did now and the two of you struggled. Then you bit that thing on the neck. You killed him."

She paused a second remembering. I could see she was putting the facts together. Her eyes got big, opened wide.

"What you did on the slopes, the way you fought."

Her eyes narrowed as she remembered the end, "You had that things blood all over your mouth."

There was a sharp intake of breath and she put her hand to her mouth, "But that means."

She shook her head,"No, it can't be, it's not possible."

I nodded slowly.

"But that would make you..."

She stopped.

"Go on," I said.

"It can't be," she said shaking her head. She was trembling.

I was struggling. I didn't want to lose her but I had to tell her. She had to know.

"You're right Tess. You know. I could kill it because I am a vampire," I whispered.

I looked away a minute, then back at her, "Yes, Tess. That's what I brought you up here to tell you. I need you to know the truth about what happened, about me."

"But its not possible," she said shaking her head. Another tear spilled from her eyes.

"Yes it is, Tess. I am sorry but the world is not like you think. In the real world there are werewolves and vampires. We are real Tess. I am real."

She looked away for a minute.

"I see it but I don't believe it." she whispered.

After a moment she continued, pain still in her eyes "I don't understand Aidan. If this is true, why me? What could I possibly be to you? Food, some kind of game? If you wanted to hurt me, you've had many chances before. I don't understand." She wiped a tear from her eye.

I took her hand. It was warm against my cold skin.

"Tess, before I answer, I want you to know that I can alter things so that you don't remember any of this. About last night, all you will remember is being attacked by a big dog. And for this morning you'll believe that we had a big fight and that you broke up with me. Then I'll disappear, vanish. You'll never see me again and all of this will be like a bad dream. If you decide that's what you want, I can make it that way. It will be like I never existed and you can go back to living the life you had before all of this. No monsters, no vampires, no fear. It's important to me that you have this choice, a choice to forget all this and go back to your life."

I paused a second, not wanting to admit what I was about to say, "And that is probably the best choice, the wise choice. But before you decide, I want you to know something."

I paused a minute. It was painful to say.

"It's true, Tess. Last night, I was going to break things off with you."

"I thought I knew what was best for you. I was going make that decision on my own, to give you back the life you had before my darkness entered it. I thought I had that power. But when you got hurt I realized something. Waiting there, not knowing what was going to happen, I realized that I really didn't have any power at all. I was helpless; my fate in someone else's hand. I realized I didn't have the power to make a decision for you."

I stopped a second. Then with pain in my voice I said, "I'm just so tired of all the lies. I decided then that I was not going to lie to you anymore and that I was going to let you make your own decision come what may."

I stopped and smiled, "But to answer the first question you asked, that's easy. I am with you, here, now because I'm in love with you, Tess. I never believed that I could ever feel that way. Before I met you, I lived in a dark, grey world. A shadow living in a world of shadows. Then I met you, and it was like a window opened and warm light streamed into that cold, dark room."

"Now that I am with you, the world is bright and or the first time in my life, I'm happy Tess. Really happy. Life without you now would be unbearable. I love you Tess, I could never hurt you. I might have saved you from a monster but you saved me from an even greater monster, you saved me from myself."

"So it was very simple for me. I decided that if I really loved you, I couldn't lie to you. I owe you this choice and once made, you really can't go back. It's either with me as I really am, with everything that that means or all of this goes away and you go back to the life you had. I wanted you to know the truth and be able to make up your own mind. I owe you that much for all the happiness you have brought me, even for this short time."

She sat for a few minutes and wiped her eyes again.

She put her hands on top of mine and looked straight into my eyes.

"I love you too Aidan. I've known since we started that silly project. That's when I made my decision. I don't want a normal human life if it's a life without you. What's normal anyway in a world where werewolves exist? It's simple for me too, the only life I want is a life with you. All of this, who you are, your past; it doesn't matter. I don't care. I only know I want to be with you. I love you Aidan no matter what you are."

I took her in my arms and kissing her again felt more joy than I had ever known.

Chapter 8

Light in a Dark Room

Pacific Coast Highway

The drive back to the city was magical. The Pacific Coast never seemed so spectacular and Tess never seemed as beautiful as she did today.

"You know I have a thousand questions now," Tess said.

"I'm sure you do," I said as we drove south.

"You don't feed on people do you? Everyone else is safe, right?" There was just a hint of anxiety in her voice.

"No Tess, I don't feed on humans, only wild animals. Sometimes, I use donated human blood."

"You mean like from the blood bank?"

"Yea, something like that only it's more discreet, mainly from hospital and clinic supply companies. So no human is ever harmed."

"Is it difficult, being around people?" I could tell she was thinking about her family and friends.

"Not anymore, not for a long time but you were different. I have to admit that when I first met you, it was almost overpowering. That was odd because I had not felt that way in a long, long time about a human. I normally pay humans no attention at all."

"So I was driving you out of your mind from the beginning?"

I looked over at her smiling, "Yes, it started that way."

"Good, I'm glad because I felt the same way the first time I saw you too. So I guess we are even."

I laughed.

"And now?" she asked.

I promised her the truth.

"I'd be lying if I didn't admit that somewhere the thirst is still there but its more like background noise now. I just have to be prudent."

"So by prudent, you mean we have to be, careful?"

"What do you mean careful?"

"I mean you know, physically. Careful."

She leaned over and took my hand.

"Ah, I don't know. This is completely uncharted territory for me. We might have to do some, controlled experiments."

"We'll that's one science class I wouldn't mind taking."

We laughed again. It was amazing just holding her hand, to have her next to me. Knowing that she loved me for me.

She was silent for a second then said, "So how old are you, really?"

"I'm nineteen."

Her face took on a slight frown. "Hell Aidan you are younger than me! I just turned twenty one. Now I feel like I'm robbing the cradle. But that not the age I was really asking about."

I smiled slightly. "I know, I was just avoiding the question. Do you really want to know?"

"Of course."

Here it goes.

I clinched my eyes a little, "I was born in 1912 in New York City."

"Wait, that makes you almost a 100 years old."

"Well you said you liked old things."

"I do but then I wasn't quite expecting you."

"Is it a problem?"

"Not unless its a problem for you. I've always had a thing for older men so whats a few more decades?"

I laughed again.

She thought a minute, "So your cousins, the ones I met. They're not your real cousins are they?"

I shook my head, "No, no they're not."

"They're vampires too?"

"Yes, Stefan and Mora are both vampires."

"Are they good vampires?"

I smiled again. They would laugh hearing that question.

"Yes, they are good vampires. They're like me, they don't feed on humans."

"So what is Rachel, some kind of vampire groupie?"

I almost choked and this time I really did laugh.

"She better not ever hear you call her that. But no Rachel's not, what did you say a groupie."

I laughed again just thinking about it. I just couldn't stop. I thought for a minute I would have to pull over.

"You ok, Aidan?" Tess asked.

"Yes," I said trying not to laugh again.

"It's just that is the funnest thing I have heard in a long, long time."

"Glad I could amuse you."

Everything she said was just so unexpected.

Finally when I had composed myself I said, "You should know however that Rachel's not human either."

"What? What do you mean? She's not a werewolf is she?"

"No"

I almost started laughing again. It was a shame I could't tell Rachel or Julian any of this.

"No she's a witch."

"Wait, are you telling me that not only are there real werewolves and vampires, there are also real witches?"

"Yes, Rachel along with everyone else in my family are witches. Tess, vampires and witches have lived among humans for thousands of years. You don't believe in us so you don't see us. But we are here just the same."

"So what are you going to tell me next, that you have a leprechaun in your basement?"

"Not that I know of," I said teasing her.

We passed a turn that lead off the highway. "Tess, you must be starving, lets stop and get you something else to eat."

"Aidan, you don't eat so whats the point? Now I feel bad, eating in front of you."

"Don't. At least now I don't have to pretend. Anyway Stefan, Mora, and I are hunting day after tomorrow. So what will it be, your wish is my command."

"Can we go somewhere on the water?"

"Sure."

I got off the highway and looked for a place near the ocean. We found a great little restaurant and got a table on the terrace at the back. We pretty much had the place to ourselves. It had a great view of the ocean, you could feel the spray from the water.

Tess ordered a shrimp salad.

"So how often do you have to hunt?"

"About once a week"

"Where do you go?"

"Deep in the forest. Sometimes we take a quick trip to Alaska or Canada. Bigger game there."

"Whats it like?"

I thought a minute. "Hard to describe. Ever been hiking or camping?"

"Yea, used to go all the time with my folks. I love the outdoors."

"It's like hiking but much better. On the hunt you are part of nature, part of nature's wildness. Not just viewing nature from the outside but being nature inside. Like I said its hard to describe."

"Sounds like Thoreau."

"Very good. So you didn't sleep through English I see."

"No believe me, I paid attention."

She stopped like she didn't know how to ask her next question. "I have another question," she said hesitantly.

"I am yours all afternoon, ask away," I said.

"So how did it happen, how did you become a vampire? Is it like in the movies?"

"Not exactly and my situation is a little weird."

"What, this other stuff wasn't weird?"

I smiled again. "Alright I'll give you that but my case is very different from other vampires."

"In what way"

"I was born this way."

"What do you mean?"

"Yes, I was born this way. My father was a vampire but my mother was a witch. So I was born like this."

"So what you're half witch and half vampire. How is that possible?"

"It's something of a mystery even to us. Our kind are not born; they're created. Witches too. We are transformed from humans. But somehow I was different. My Father found me at an orphanage when I was a baby so I never met my parents. We don't know what happened to them. Mom and Dad adopted me into our coven, our family. They used powerful magic to suspend the transformation until I was nineteen. Until then I was human, just like everybody else."

"How does it work, I mean how does a human get transformed?"

"For vampires part of the myth you see in the movies is correct, you have to be bitten and the vampire has to stop feeding. It's difficult though, most vampires can't control the feeding once it starts. After the bite and the human is drained, the vampire has to share some of his blood. Vampire blood carries an agent that triggers and controls the transformation. If the human survives and has the right physical makeup, the transformation takes about three days. Most humans however don't survive the transformation. In almost every instance, if the vampire doesn't kill them the transformation does. That's why vampires are very, very rare."

"So tell me about Rachel and the other witches. How are they different from you."

"They are different. Where vampires have extreme physical powers, witches have mental and psychic abilities. They can read minds and effect peoples perceptions. They can levitate objects around them. Some have other gifts. Rachel can sometimes see the future and things happening at a distance. My Mom can touch an object and see its history or people that have been involved with it. Grace can heal things and make things grow. Lucian has this extraordinary levitation power. I once saw him levitate a truck."

"Every witch can shape shift. They usually have a specific animal they transform into called their familiar. In fact they have to. Thats how they feed. Just like we have to feed on blood they have to spend time in their familiar form. Julian is a real master at it. His mind reading capabilities are also better than anyone else's. My Dad is the most powerful of them all. He has almost all of these powers."

"So are witches made the same way vampires are by bitting?"

"No, not exactly. Sometimes witches spontaneously transform. Thats what happened with Rachel. But witches can also be created from humans if they have what Dad calls the spark. These humans need a push to go into transformation. It starts with a bite from a witch in their animal form. That's where the werewolf myth comes from, being bitten by an animal turns you into one."

She raised one eyebrow, "You're not reading my mind now are you?"

"No my powers of witchcraft never developed. What gifts I have just enhance my vampire abilities. Because of that, I am faster and stronger than other vampires. Thats how I was able to kill the werewolf."

"We'll that's a relief, I wouldn't like it if you could read my thoughts. It would be embarrassing."

"Don't worry your secrets are safe."

"And werewolves, are they the same?"

"No. Werewolves are really witches that have been corrupted by dark magic. They don't transform into normal wolves; instead, they transform into this half human, half wolf beast like you saw the other night. They are pure evil."

I could tell the wheels were turning in her head.

"So how did all of this get started, I mean where do witches and vampires come from?"

"We don't really know. Stefan and Dad argue about this all the time. Dad thinks that vampires and witches are really the same species; that we all had a common ancestor. He thinks that vampires evolved to enhance their physical abilities to better their capabilities as predators while witches evolved their mental and psychic abilities to make them better hunters and trackers. Stefan thinks it's all a bunch of bunk."

About that time they brought Tess's salad.

She just looked down at the salad.

"Go on," I said, "it doesn't bother me at all. In fact I kind of like to watch you. Since I don't eat anymore, its the next best thing. So enjoy every bite."

"Ok." She started right in. "Um, Um," she said teasing me waving the fork back and forth."

"Ok, Ok, you don't have to rub it in," I said laughing. "You have any more questions."

"Only one, my head is spinning."

"Ok last one"

"Why school, why are you in school? I mean surely you finished school long ago."

"Interesting question. Couple of reasons. First, I like college, I like learning new things. It also provides good cover. We have to fit in and appear normal and attending school does that for us. But the main reason is we are looking for something."

"What do you mean you're looking for something" she said taking another bite.

"This is going to be a bit of a story but hear me out. You'll like it, it's all about old stuff and history. "

"In the 11th century a very powerful sorcerer named Magnus founded a school for witches. Dad, Mom, Lucian, Julian, and Grace were all students there. After they had been there for sometime, they discovered that Magnus was actually a dark witch, a very evil sorcerer. He had a lust for power and domination. They learned that Magnus was enslaving vampires and transforming humans into werewolves to build an army. Long and short, there was a terrible war between the witches. Other vampires came into the fighting including Stefan and Mora."

"During the battle Magnus was killed along with Lucian's wife and many of my Dad's friends. Some of the dark witches were killed but many others escaped. For protection, Stefan and Mora joined my fathers coven. That's how my family formed. The aftermath of that battle caused a wave of witch hunts across Europe as the civil and church authorities tried to get to the bottom of what happened, why so many people disappeared. That's the real reason for the inquisition and witch trials. Of course you will never hear that in class. The werewolf that attacked us was one of Magnus's dark creations."

"Now to what we are looking for. Many centuries before he founded the school, Magnus found an artifact, a crystal of enormous power. It was constructed by ancient witches as a great healing and teaching instrument. But Magnus used his dark powers to corrupt it. He inserted part of his dark power, his essence into the artifact and used it to extend and increase his powers."

"At the end of the battle after Magnus was destroyed, the coven looked for this crystal, this Shadow but it had disappeared. We don't know who took it. Our coven has been looking for it ever since. You have to remember that the war is still underway between those that followed Magnus with dark magic and those like us that oppose them. We fight and kill any of these monsters we find. It would be a terrible if one of the dark witches found the Shadow. It would give them enormous power for evil so its essential that we find it first."

"So as college students we have access to all kinds of research and materials that help us in the search. So I am a student at the university and so is Rachel. In fact, my Dad's a professor there, teaches some Psychology classes on occasion. "

Tess put down her fork, "This is all just blowing my mind Aidan. I mean this morning the worst thing I was thinking of was that we were going to have a fight and breakup. Instead, I find out that there is an entirely different world out there, it's just incredible."

She stopped eating. "You know I probably would have died if you had not been with me last night. I never said thanks so thank you. I'm also thankful you gave me a choice in the matter. I don't care how crazy this other world is as long as I am with you."

She picked up her fork. "Not that anyone would ever believe such a tale anyway. They'd just lock me up."

She took another bite of shrimp and smiled. "You know thinking back, kicking a seven foot werewolf in the crotch was probably not the smartest thing to do."

Now it was my turn to laugh. "I would say probably not."

The waiter came up and asked us if we needed anything else.

Tess said, "No I've had quite enough for one day thank you" and she winked at me. I paid the check and we left.

As we drove back south, we passed a sign for a carnival.

"Hey pull off, lets check out the carnival. We have a few hours," Tess said.

"I haven't been to a fair since I was a child.," I said.

"Then you are in for a treat," she said.

I pulled off, parked in a grassy area and we bought some tickets.

It was unlike any fair I had been to. First there were no animals. But there were rides, lots and lots of rides. There were games of chance that I did remember as well as all kinds of food. There was a large crowd milling about. Everyone appeared to be having a good time. That part was not all that different from what I remember as a human.

"Lets ride the roller coaster," Tess said, grabbing my hand and pulling me along. I had never been on one before so I wasn't sure what to expect.

We bought two tickets and got on the metal monstrosity. Tess sat right next to me as we strapped in. As the car road the track up a large incline, Tess grabbed my hand. Just as we crested the top, Tess reached over and gave me a big kiss. As the car fell down the hill, she laughed and then started to scream. As the ride progressed, she alternated between laughing and screaming. At one point as we got to the top of a particularly long drop I yelled, "Why do you do this if it scares you so much?"

"Because its so fun!," she yelled back.

We road it three times. She seemed to scream and laugh louder each time. After the third time, she held on to my arm as we walked off the ride.

"That was awesome," she said. "I feel much better now."

"Lets ride the bumper cars," she said grabbing my hand again. It was quite an experience. Tess was quite aggressive, randomly attacking any car that came close to her. I had a great time just watching her. Several times she gave my car quite a bump, laughing harder each time. After that it was a ferris wheel. Tess snuggled up against me when the wind started up.

After the rides it was games of chance. The poor vendors didn't have a chance. Within an hour, I had a stuffed monkey, a rabbit, a fuzzy clown, and a giant Winnie the Pooh. I held back some so as not to draw too much attention but Austin was going to be ecstatic.

After the games, it was popcorn and a hot dog for Tess and we were ready to go. It was amazing watching her at the fair. She was so intense, completely engaged in what ever she was doing, living life to the fullest. Until today, I had only felt that during hunting. It was wonderful having someone to share all this with. We struggled with the animals back to the car, Tess holding onto my arm. I loaded the stuffed animals into the trunk and back seat.

"Aidan, today was just incredible."

I nodded, "I can't remember when I've had so much fun."

"But I have to tell you though this morning was the strangest I've ever had."

"I'm sorry but I didn't know any other way to tell you but I'm glad you made the decision you did. I never knew life could be like this."

"I am too." She reached over and took my hand.

It was getting dark when we got back to Tess's house. I grabbed the animals and we went in the house. This time Nick was home and Tess introduced us as we walked in.

"Nick this is my friend, Aidan. Aidan this is my brother Nick."

Nick was tall with dark wavy hair. Austin looked just like him. I could see the resemblance with Tess as well. He had an easy smile.I had my gloves on so I could shake his hand. I put my hand out in the midst of all the animals. "Pleased to meet you Nick," I said.

"Me too Aidan. Here let me help you with these."

As he took a few of them Nick said, "Tess has told us a lots of good things about you, it's great to finally meet you."

"Thanks. She said nice things about you too."

"Well that's a first," he said smiling at her.

She threw the monkey at him. As it hit the floor, Nick and I and I put the others next to it.

"Wow thats a lot of stuffed animals, where did you get all these?" he asked.

"We stopped at a carnival on the way back, seems Aidan is quite the shot," Tess said winking at me.

"I hope Austin likes them," I said.

"Oh, he'll love them," Nick said.

"You want a beer or a soda?" he asked.

"Thanks but I need to get back. Next time. It was a real pleasure to meet you," I said.

"You too, Aidan, You're always welcome here, Come back anytime and thanks again for the toys."

"My pleasure," I said.

"I'll walk you out," Tess said.

She walked with me to the car. She put her arms around me.

"You know it was a magical day," she said kissing me.

"Magical, I like that," I said kissing her back.

"So tomorrow is our big presentation. You want me to come down and pick you up?" I asked.

"I would love that but I am working in the afternoon. I could meet you before class. Want to meet at the lounge ?"

"Alright, I'll meet you there."

I kissed her again and she went inside. In the background I could hear Austin playing with the toys. I could also hear Karen and Tess laughing at him. Her laugh was like sunshine.

Next evening, I waited for her in the lounge. I brought her some flowers. She showed up about ten minutes later.

"These are for you," I said.

"You got me flowers !"

"In my day, thats what we did."

"There're beautiful Aidan, I've never had a man give me flowers before."

"Beautiful flowers for a beautiful lady," I said.

She reached over and hugged me. "Much better than donuts," she said smiling,

"You doing alright? I know that was a lot to take in yesterday."

"I feel fine, quit worrying. I'm made of pretty tough material."

"Thats what Karen said. How was your afternoon?"

"It was fine, a couple of classes at the Y. I remember what the doctor said, to take it easy."

"How's your head?"

"A little sore but fine."

"You want anything before class?"

"No, I'm a little nervous about the presentation."

"Why it's perfect? You're going to be fantastic."

"I hope so"

We talked a few more minutes and left for class. Instead of sitting in the back, we sat with her friends in the front. Sharon was there. At one point I saw her wink at Tess. She just smiled. Then it was our turn to present.

The presentation went flawless. Tess did an incredible job. I let her do most of the talking, she was so engaging with people. Afterwards, everyone wanted to go out and celebrate so we went to a bar down the street.

Peter and Nicole were there along with Jesse and Max. Shawn and Sharon came in right behind us. Peter went to the bar and came back with a pitcher of beer. He started pouring glasses. He started to hand me one. Tess grabbed it and said, "No, he's driving." Then she winked at me.

Sharon said, "Tess you did a great job tonight. I think you and Aidan's presentation was the best in the class."

"Well we worked hard on it," she said. "Here's to being over," she said with a toast.

We laughed and talked about class. Everyone had a great time. This was a whole side to humans I had completely forgotten. I finally felt like I fit in. At one point Tess looked over and smiled at me. She could tell I was having a good time. This time I winked at her. Sharon caught us and just shook her head. We laughed together. After a couple of hours, it was time to go. I was actually sad to be leaving.

On the way back to the car, I asked her, "You know you never asked me about that other project."

"What other project?" she asked.

"The one for Sociology, the one you were going to trick me into."

"You fink, you were eavesdropping on me," she said hitting me on the arm.

"Hey, I only said I couldn't read minds. There's nothing wrong with my hearing."

"So you heard everything that night?"

"I did, its what sparked my interest in you. You really were quite devious."

"We'll it worked didn't it ?"

"I guess it did," I said smiling.

"I mean after we got to know each other, I felt bad about deceiving you so I just asked Nick to help me. Although on the scale of deceit, I think your's tops mine by like a thousand percent."

"Thats fair but it worked didn't it," I said smiling.

"I guess it did, I guess it did," she said.

I dropped her off at home and parked my car three blocks over. I silently slipped into her room through the window and sat on her bed. After a few minutes she came in wearing her pajamas and a pink hoodie. I put my finger to my mouth to signal her to be quiet. She came over and sat next to me.

"What are you doing here, how did you get in?" she whispered.

I gestured at the window with my head. "I didn't want the day to end. Can I stay a bit?" I whispered back.

"Of course," she said.

I laid back on her bed, she put her head on my chest.

"I could get used to this," she said.

"Me too." I stroked her hair.

"You're so bright Tess, you did a great job tonight. You have a wonderful future ahead of you."

She raised up, "And here I thought all you were interested in was my body," she teased.

"We'll there is that', I said with a smile.

"Well, now that's you're here, lets try one of those science experiments," she said smiling back.

"But your brother and Karen are downstairs," I whispered.

"Listen the way Austin keeps them going they're either doing exactly what we're doing, we'll maybe not exactly what were doing, but close or they are passed out from sheer exhaustion. Besides don't you have this like silence ability."

"Yes I do" I said reaching over for her. I kissed her lightly at first and the kisses became more passionate. She put her hand on my neck and pulled me closer.

I kissed her a little harder. She pulled me down next to her.

"I'm not too cold am I?" I asked.

She pulled off her hoodie. Underneath she had a tank top on. "No, I'm hot enough for both of us," she said pulling me closer. Very gently, I put my arms around her, my face next to her neck. I could hear her heart beat.

There was the first stirring of thirst. She turned around and kissed me harder. Her heart was beating faster as was her breath. I was holding her tighter. I noticed she flinched just a little under my grasp. The thirst was there but I ignored it. It grew just a little then suddenly the inner calm surfaced. I felt the connection flow between us. The thirst disappeared. I softened my hold on her. I put my hand around her neck and I kissed her lightly again.

I looked up. One of her earrings was floating above her night stand.

I pulled back and raised up on one arm.

"Whats wrong," she asked. "Is it," she showed me her teeth.

"No its not that at all," I said laughing, "It's there a little but like I said, just background noise."

"Then what is it?" she asked.

I laid back on the bed, she leaned on my chest.

"I love you Tess, and I want you but we have to be very careful. I am very, very strong and I could easily hurt you without realizing it. Besides, I haven't met the rest of your family yet. I know to you its 2010 but to me in away it's still 1931. Back then there was an order to these things. We just need to go slow, until I'm sure."

"I can do slow, I might not be happy about it but I can do slow."

"Then there is this one other thing," I said.

"What's that," she asked.

I pointed to her earring, it was spinning in mid-air.

She raised up from my chest and looked over, amazement in her eyes.

"Are you doing that?" she asked.

"Unless you are," I said smiling.

"Very funny. I thought you said your witch powers were suspended or something."

"They have been ever since the change but now they seem to be surfacing."

"Wow this is amazing Aidan. Has this happened before?" She seemed mesmerized by the floating earring.

"Once before up at the slopes. After we kissed the first time, my keys levitated."

Her earring dropped. The noise startled her.

"It just seems to happen on its own. I can't control it. See."

I held my hand out. Nothing happened.

She sat up on the bed.

"You mean after we are together like this, your powers just start working."

"It appears that way. Like you said, its magical," I said holding out my hand again.

"I'd say. I mean I wanted to rev your engine but this is just incredible."

"Well I could use a little more revving," I said.

She smiled and reached down and kissed me again.

After a few minutes she laid her head on my shoulder.

"I'm glad you came back."

"Me too"

I just held her for a while. She almost nodded off.

She woke herself and said, "It might be awkward if we both fall asleep like this."

"Don't worry Tess, I won't sleep. I just want to stay a little longer and then I'll go."

"OK," she said as she snuggled up against me. I held her like this for a long time.

"I love you Aidan," she said.

"I love you Tess, sweet dreams. I'll be right here."

I held her for a while longer and then slipped out the window.

I stood outside for just a minute. I could hear the soft rise and fall of her breathing. The only thing I wanted in the whole world was to make her happy.

Thats how it went for a couple of weeks. Tess worked during the day and we saw each other at night. I would slip down and see her in the evening. Sometimes I would take her to dinner, sometimes we would just hang out at school. We spent the weekends just driving around. My excuse to the family was research and school work. Life had seemed to have settled down to an almost perfect rhythm. That was until Julian called us all together one morning.

His contact had finally traced the safety deposit box key we had found in the werewolf's room. It was from a bank in San Bruno near the International Airport. Julian and I left to meet Lucian there.

It was a small regional bank branch. We waited about twenty minutes for the bank to open at nine. Once it was open we walked in. A clerk sat behind the desk. Julian, Lucian, and I waited at the front. The clerk motioned towards us and we sat down at the desk.

"How may I help you gentlemen today," she asked.

"We have a safety deposit box and we need to retrieve some items."

"Of course, I'll need to see the key and some identification."

Lucian pulled the key out. Julian looked at the clerk reaching into her mind.

She said, "That's right I already saw your identification. I'll show you to the vault."

She got up and we followed her into the vault. There was no one else there. We found the box and she put in her key.

"Please just stand there in the corner, thank you," Julian said to the clerk. She walked over to the corner.

Lucian inserted the key and pulled the box out. Inside was money, a lot of money, close to a hundred thousand dollars. The only other item was a small black leather bound book written in Latin.

"We need to get this back to Marcus," Lucian said.

Julian nodded.

We placed the money in Julian's bag along with the book and put the box back into the wall of the safe. Julian took both keys out and handed both of them to the clerk. He reached into her mind again, her face blank. She nodded and said, "The deposit box is free now. The owner came this morning and retrieved everything and closed out the account. I'll wait here then come out in five minutes and I finish all the paperwork."

Julian nodded and we walked out of the bank and got into our car. We drove home as quickly as we could. We found Dad in his study.

"This was all that was in the box except cash," Lucian said as he handed the small book to him.

Dad inspected the journal. "Dad translated as he read the first page. It's just a short description of medicinal plants." He turned a few of the pages and said, "There's a few spells. It looks like a simple set of notes that a new witch would keep."

He turned to the back. The last set of pages were in a different handwriting and were just a long series of numbers with some diagrams.

There's a page torn out, third from the end," he said.

"I didn't notice that," Julian said.

Dad went over to the desk. He pulled out the torn paper that Jakob had given Julian. It was a perfect match. It was torn out right in the middle of the codes and diagrams. Julian shook his head.

"Why would Jakob have a torn page from a beginners notebook?" he asked.

"I have no idea," Julian said shaking his head.

"I'll need to study this a while, my latin is a little rusty," Dad said. "Lets get back together this evening, I should have something by then. Julian any word on the laptop?"

"As we suspected, most of the data was encrypted. It will be a few more days before they'll be able to recover the files. They will contact me as soon as its finished."

"Wonderful, soon we should be able to piece together what Tomas was doing here."

I called Tess once I was in the car. "Hey you free for lunch," I asked.

"I will be in about an hour. I have one more class. Want to pick me up at the Y? I know a great place over in Sausalito. You'll at least be able to enjoy the view even if you can't enjoy the food."

"The only view I am interested in is you," I said.

"Now Mr. Croft I think you will just sweep me off my feet," she said in a fake southern accent. We both laughed.

"Ok I'll pick you up in about an hour," I said.

Tess finished her class right on time. As we crossed the bridge, she gave me directions to the restaurant. As she said the view was spectacular. She ate then we walked down along the waterfront. We stood for a long while just looking out at the water, my arms around her, her head on my chest. A few tourists walked by snapping pictures of the bay.

I bend down and kissed her ear. She laughed and turned around. We shared a long kiss then found a quiet spot and sat on a bench.

"So what was it like, the transformation?"

"I see, its going to be more questions."

"I've had a little time to think besides, I am a history major if you remember."

I looked out at the water. Finally I rubbed my hands together and said, "It was difficult, very painful."

"What did you do afterward? How did you learn to control, you know?"

"Thats a long story."

"Its nice here, we have plenty of time. I would like to know."

"Some of it's not very pretty Tess," I said looking away.

"That's ok, I want to know everything about you."

"I'll tell you what. I'll tell you my story then you have to promise to tell yours."

"I am sure mine's not as interesting as yours but it's a deal."

I paused a minute deciding where to start.

"After the transformation, Stefan, Mora and I slipped into Canada, far out into the wilderness where there were no people. They said it was better that way, to get used to feeding on animals without the temptation of humans blood."

"We were in the forest for almost six months. It was very hard at first, the thirst was uncontrollable. You have no idea how powerful it can be. No human addiction even comes close. But over time I learned to hunt, to be silent, to use my speed and strength and after a while things seemed to settle down. I felt more myself; that I was in control instead of the thirst. When Stefan thought I was ready, I came back to live with my family. They had moved by then, farther west."

"I tried my best to fit in but I had a hard time with all the humans around; they seemed to be everywhere. I felt confined being in town. I was restless and wanted nothing more than to go back into the forest and lose myself there. But Stefan said to give it time, that I would get used to it but as the months passed it got harder not easier. The thirst was a constant temptation. So one day, when everyone was out of the house, I left a note and slipped away. I wanted to be on my own for a while and go back to Canada. I hopped the first train heading north."

"This was in the early 30's so men moving around looking for work was not uncommon. I moved though the midwest feeding on cattle and livestock as I went. I got shot at once by a farmer when he heard me in his barn. I had just moved into Michigan when things changed dramatically for me. I had not fed for almost two weeks and I was very thirsty. It was late in the afternoon when I walked into a small town. As

I passed down the main street, I heard a group of men talking on a corner. A convict had escaped from a local penitentiary. A few months before, he had murdered a whole family during a robbery, not just the adults but the children as well. Brutal murders. They were mounting a search so I followed them. The convict had escaped into a deep forest near the town. While the men were still forming their search party, I flew into the forest."

"I was going to capture and turn him in, hoping that one of the local farmers would put me up and I could feed on one of his animals. Locating the convict was easy, I just followed his scent. When I found him, he was running through the forest. There was a river ahead and if he made it he would be free, the town's people would never catch him. I was moving overhead from tree to tree and I swooped down and took him. He fought back and in the struggle he hit his hand against the tree. It was a deep cut and it began to bleed profusely. The smell was overwhelming and next thing I knew, I was feeding. I just couldn't stop. It had been two weeks and I was desperate. It seemed it took only seconds. I carried his body and threw it in the river."

"I was terrified at what I had done but I also felt powerful, strong. The feeling was almost overwhelming. Part of me felt terribly guilty at taking a human life but another part rationalized the act because the man was a murderer. I convinced myself that I had avenged the family he had murdered."

"I left that town but I found another and so I began to hunt serial killers, murderers. They were easy to find. Times were very hard then and men were desperate. It sent many over the edge into madness. I forgot all about Canada. I still fed on animals but when I was able to hunt down a murderer, I did."

"I was terrified the whole time that Stefan would find me. I knew they were looking for me but I couldn't go back, not hunting humans the way I did. I knew if they found me, Stefan, Mora, and Lucian would kill me. I hate to say it but part of me wanted them to find me because I was becoming the very thing I hated the most, a monster living on the blood of humans."

"But one night another event occurred, one that changed me forever. I had not fed in almost three weeks. I had been through several towns and couldn't find any cattle and there were no criminals about. I even tried to steal blood from a small hospital but there was none to be found. I was desperate when one evening I saw a young woman leave what I thought was a brothel. She was young and full of life. I followed her, I couldn't help my self, her scent was intoxicating. A man dropped her off at a small house right outside of town. There was a small grove of trees near by and I waited in the shadows. The moon was very full that night. After all the lights went out and it was the deep of night, I crept up the side of the house and into an open window. I followed her scent to a room at the end of a hall and I slowly opened the door. The moon was streaming in from her window and I saw her fast asleep. I knew it would be so easy to take her. I could slip her out the window and into the woods, feed, and then hide the body. I would be long gone before anyone found her."

I stopped a moment. Tess's eyes were very tense.

"Standing there, I hesitated because I knew I was about to cross a line. I would become the very thing that my family fought against. But I was thirsty, so very thirsty. I started into her room to steal her away when I heard a sound behind me. I turned and there at the doorway to another room stood a small boy. He had almost white hair like Stefan. He must have been about four years old, just a little older than Austin. He was standing there rubbing his eyes."

"Is my mommy alright?" he asked me. "I heard a noise and I'm thirsty so I was going to her room."

"Yes she is fine, she is sleeping. I'll get you a drink," I said.

"I took him into the small kitchen and got him a drink of water. When he finished I took him back to his bed. The moon was very bright and it reflected on my pale face. "Are you an angel?" he asked me as he reached up and touched my face.

"Yes, I'm an angel tonight," I said. I kissed him on the head and tucked him in. He fell back fast asleep, the sleep of the innocent. I closed his door and the door to his mother's room and I slipped back out the same window I came in."

Tess had tears in her eyes.

"That night I knew I could never take a human life again, no matter what their crimes. I was not going to become a monster. Just then like magic a large buck stepped out of the trees. I fed and waited in the forest until daybreak. At dawn I went back into town. Later that day, I saw the same woman and found out that it was her sister that worked at the brothel. She had been there trying to get her to leave and come back home. That night, I found a southbound train and went home. When I got there, I confessed everything."

"It was hard at first living among humans but with Stefan and Mora's help I learned to control my thirst. I got to the point where I didn't give humans a second thought. My control was perfect. Time passed and the world moved on and so did I. My thirst for humans disappeared and with it any interest I had in them."

"That was until I met you. You were so different, so alive. When I met you it was like stepping out of a dark room into sunlight. You woke me from a dark dream Tess and I was drawn to you like no human I had ever met."

Another tear fell down her cheek.

"It must have been awful for you Aidan, so alone. I can't imagine it."

"Yes I was very lonely for a very long time." But I smiled and added, "but now I have you and my family, so I have everything I want."

"Were there any happy times?" she asked.

"Yea, there were some happy times. One in fact was sort of funny. I was reminded of it when you asked me if I ever got down to LA."

"Once a couple of years ago, Rachel got this great idea to move to LA. She said we needed a break, that San Francisco was too gloomy. So she convinced Julian, Stefan, Mora, and I to go along. The rest of the coven had no interest at all. So we moved down and rented two condos. Then Rachel had this notion that if we all got a tan we could fit in better, you know the spray on ones they do in a salon. I even got brown contact lenses to fit the part."

"Anyway, one night we went out and found this tanning place. Stefan, Mora, and I tried to pass off as albinos. When the attendant took us back, the stuff would simply not stick to our skins. It just turned green and sort of pooled on us. We looked monstrous, especially Stefan, he looked like some kind of a zombie. So when the attendant came back he completely freaked out. He was running around, screaming at us in Spanish. We had to restrain him and Julian had to clear his memory. We cleaned up best we could, but Stefan was so bad we had to wrap him head to foot in one of Rachel's coats. After that we closed down the condos and moved right back home. It took two weeks for that gunk to come off."

Tess laughed, "That is funny. I just can't image Stefan looking like that."

"Oh, he was none too pleased I'll tell you."

"Ok, you heard my saga now it's your turn," I told her as we walked back towards the car.

"Well mine is not nearly as exciting as yours and some you already know. I grew up in LA, funny coincidence. I told you my Dad's a doctor, an anesthesiologist. My Mom is a realtor. We had a typical, normal California family. I generally got along with my two older brothers. I guess there was some benefit to being the youngest and the only girl."

"I was never really popular in school. I was something of a tomboy so I didn't really fit in. I had decent grades but was not first in my class. I ran track and did martial arts. I didn't date that much. I think the karate put most guys off, along with having two older brothers. Anyway, after Nick left for the service, I felt like I was sort of in the way. It was weird being the only kid at home. I really wanted to be on my own, with my own rules. So when I graduated from high school I came up here. I stayed here well over a year by myself. It was lonely at first but I made some friends. Then when Nick and Karen moved here, I jumped at the chance to be with family again. Its weird, you know I couldn't wait to get away from them at the beginning now I can't imagine being without them."

"Thats funny. You know I ran track too, that is before the change."

"Really?"

"Yes, really"

"Were you fast ?"

"Not as fast as now but I was fast enough for 1930."

"Maybe we can go for a run sometimes, you can try to keep up," she said with a smile.

We both laughed and I put my arm around her and we walked to where I had parked. I drove her back to the Y.

As we sat in the parking lot I said, "Tess I am sorry if I disturbed you with my past. Maybe it was better if you didn't hear all that."

She leaned over and kissed me, "There's nothing about you I don't want to know. You're everything to me Aidan."

She got out of the car and before she shut the door she said, "Yea and maybe tomorrow night we could do another science experiment." She winked at me.

"That's a date," I said and she drove off.

Next day I was just finishing up some work when my phone rang. It was Tess.

"Hey I was just thinking of you," I said.

"Well that's always good to hear," she said. "Ah listen, about tonight. I forgot that it's Karen and Nick's anniversary. I promised I would babysit Austin. So can we go tomorrow night instead?"

"Sure," I said.

"You going to be there by yourself?" I asked.

"Yea, I do it all the time, why do you ask?" she said.

"How about some company?"

"You mean you want to come and help me babysit?"

"Sure. At least this way I get to see you tonight."

"You sure, I mean it is babysitting."

"I can't think of a better way to spend my evening. I mean I can think of something I'd rather do with you."

I paused thinking, "Wait, I mean, that didn't come out right."

I was getting tongue tied and embarrassed.

Tess was laughing on the other end of the phone.

"I know what you mean, Aidan don't worry. I think about it too, probably too much. Anyway just come by. I am sure Austin will be thrilled as will Karen."

I was glad to change the subject.

"What time should I be there?"

"They are leaving about 6. But they won't be back until tomorrow afternoon. I told them to just take the whole night. They really haven't had much time to themselves since Austin came along."

"You really are quite the romantic," I said.

"No just really happy for them. They are so perfect together."

"Well let Karen know I will be the perfect gentleman."

"Party pooper," she said laughing.

"Ok, see you at 6. Should I stop and get you two something to eat."

"Really, you don't have to do that Aidan," she said.

"It's no problem, it would be my pleasure."

"Well he almost never gets them but I am sure Austin would love a Happy Meal. Karen is really funny about what he eats."

"What's a Happy Meal?" I had some totally different vision pop in my head.

"It's a kids meal from McDonalds."

"Oh, ok and what would you like?"

"I like their salads, they are pretty good. You sure this is no bother?"

"None at all, I'll pick them up and see you in a few hours."

I had never been to a McDonald's before. It was a very efficient operation. Within minutes I had the food and was on my way. Very different from any restaurants I remembered as a child.

I arrived at Tess's house at 5:50. Nick and Karen were just about to leave.

"You look beautiful," I said to Karen carrying in dinner. "You are a very lucky man Nick."

Karen blushed and Nick said smiling, "Don't I know it. Hey, thanks for watching the little monster."

"Happy to do it. I was a little monster myself once," I said with a slight grin.

Tess just shook her head and took the bags. "It was also nice of you to bring dinner," she said.

Austin yelled, "Happy Meal, Happy Meal," and started running around.

"Ok, you love birds need to hit the road," Tess said.

"Don't worry, everything will fine here. We're just going to watch some movies and I'll leave around midnight," I said.

Karen said, "Don't worry about it Aidan. It's ok leave when you're ready."

Tess just rolled her eyes.

Karen picked up Austin, "Now you be a good boy for Aunt Tess and Aidan."

"Good Boy," he said.

Karen handed him to Tess

"Have fun," I said to Nick.

"You too," he said then they were off after another round of hugs.

Once they were gone Tess said, "So let's feed the little monster first," as we headed into the kitchen.

I just sat and watched Austin as he devoured the happy meal. I was fascinated just watching him; I had never spent any time around human children. He was totally engaged with his food. Once he was finished, there was food everywhere. He had fried potatoes in his lap, and a line of ketchup was on his shirt. There was also a ring of ketchup around his mouth.

"Don't even go there," Tess said wiping his mouth.

She finished her salad as Austin played with some sort of toy that was in with his meal.

After dinner it was time to clean up. I reached down to start picking up the fried potatoes that had not either fallen into his lap or his mouth.

"Aidan really you don't need to do that," Tess said as she cleaned him up.

"No it's ok, part of the experience," I said as I picked them up.

Finally he was clean as was the floor and we went into the family room.

"Pooh," Austin said and the next hour was spent with Austin and I playing hide and seek with various stuffed animals. I hid behind the couch and would lift one up. He would scream with delight then it was the next toy. After that Tess put on some of her favorite music and she and Austin danced in the middle of the room.

"He loves doing this," Tess said as they moved around the room.

She motioned and I came over and we all danced, Tess holding Austin and me holding Tess.

At one point I reached over and kissed her.

Austin patted my face and said, "Silly."

I grabbed him, gently, and flew him around the room. I started to climb up the wall and ceiling with him when Tess said, "Uh, probably not a good idea. He's going to want me to do that and no can do."

I nodded and settled for more airplane rides around the room.

Tess finally stopped us and I put him down. She said. "Ok, Austin, time for bath."

"No," Austin said rather emphatically and ran behind the couch. Tess spent the next five minutes trying to chase him down. They were both laughing by the end. Finally she caught him and took in the back to give him a bath.

After the bath it was a bed time story. I sat on his bed and read him a strange story about a cat with a hat. Finally Tess kissed him goodnight and we went back into the family room.

"I never realized they were so active," I said as we sat down.

"That he is, and as you can see, he can be quite a handful". She smiled a second , "You know you were really great with him tonight, thanks for coming over."

"My pleasure, it was fun," I said, "Although the ketchup was kind of gross."

"Hah," she said. Her voice softened and she said, "You know watching you tonight, you would make a great father."

"Thanks. He is a good kid, it was very easy."

"Do you ever think about it ?"

"Think about what?" I asked picking up the last of the toys.

"Having a family, being a father. Not that I am suggesting anything, just curious."

"Me, not really. I guess I never had any reason to. Remember we don't reproduce in that fashion."

"You mean it's not possible?"

I shook my head, "Not between vampires. It's hard enough to control things as an adult. Even if it were possible, a vampire child is destroyed on sight. That's why children are never transformed. They turn into uncontrollable monsters."

"I see," Tess said nodding. "But then what happened with you?"

I shrugged my shoulders, "I don't know, it's a mystery. Even my Father doesn't know what happened. So I guess it's possible, I am living proof of that. We just don't understand it."

The subject was a little uncomfortable for me so I turned the tables on her, "How about you, you every think about it? Having a family?"

"Me, no way. I was always too busy. But being around Karen and Austin, I see how special it is. So maybe one day."

"Well I guess we are alike in that way."

She snuggled up against me and we put on a movie. About midnight the movie ended and Tess checked on Austin. He was sound asleep.

"Maybe I should go," I asked her. "It's after midnight."

She took my hand. "Stay awhile," she said. "I know, I know about the gentleman thing. Just stay with me."

I smiled, "Anything for you," I said.

So we went upstairs and after a while, Tess fell asleep in my arms.

It was wonderful, just holding her. She was so peaceful. I wanted nothing more than to be here, to keep her safe and close to me.

I spent the night just looking at her. She was so beautiful, the most beautiful thing in the world. It was peaceful, just lying here with her. As dawn was breaking, she stirred and opened her eyes. They still had sleep in them.

"Good Morning, beautiful," I said as I stroked her hair.

She smiled, her head on the pillow and said, "Good morning, Aidan."

They were the most wonderful words I had every heard.

"I could get used to this," I said.

"Me too."

I kissed her quickly and whispered, "I probably should go."

She nodded but then put her hand on my neck and drawing me to her, kissed me deeply.

She put her forehead against mine and said, "Am I still dreaming? Sometimes I can't believe you're real," she said.

I smiled, "I'm real and I'll be with you forever," I said.

She kissed me again, got up and stretched.

"Time to fix Austin's breakfast."

"Need some help?"

"Sure, might as well get the whole effect."

We went down stairs and she put on some coffee and we fixed Austin some cereal. She mixed the ingredients and as she stirred, I rubbed her shoulders.

"That's nice," she said "But if you keep doing that, I'll never get going this morning."

"Now who's the party pooper?"

She smiled and we sat the table. She went in and brought Austin out. His hair was sticking straight up. He was rubbing his eyes. She took him into the bathroom and when they were done, the three of us sat down. Austin dug right into his breakfast and Tess took a bite of toast and a sip of coffee. She reached over and took my hand.

"You don't have to stay Aidan. I am sure you have things to do today. Besides, Nick and Karen will be here in a couple of hours. After that I have to go into work."

"Sure you don't need any help ?"

"No you have done enough already. Besides, if you distract me anymore, I won't get my paper finished this morning."

I feigned disappointment but smiling said, "Well if you insist."

She walked me to the door. We shared a long kiss and I said, "I'll call you later."

I left and headed home. I spent the day finishing up one of my papers. I checked in on Dad a couple of times but he just smiled and waved me away. He wanted to concentrate on the journal.

I called Tess before she went to work.

That evening, Mora, Stefan and I watched a movie. It was late, almost midnight when Dad called us all together. We all sat in the main study. He lit the fireplace and we all sat around him.

"Even though my Latin is not what it used to be, I was able to translate most of the text. The front is a simple set of notes about medicinal plants followed by a few spells. The last pages however are very different. I think they were written by Jakob."

"Parts at the very end are still in some sort of code but from the parts I could read it was Jakob and another witch named Arius who stole Magnus's Shadow. Arius was one of Magnus's star pupils, a rival to Draven. That night when Draven used it to transfer his essence into the young slave, Arius was so terrified at this act of dark magic that he knew he had to do something to stop him. During the chaos of the fighting, Jakob and Arius stole the crystal and left that very night for the coast. Julian, that's why we never found Jakob."

"The journal says that they believed it was their sacred duty to protect the crystal and keep it safe from Draven. It says that they had found the perfect hiding place. The last line I can read says that only the true seeker can read what follows. After that there are several pages of numbers and diagrams. The torn page that was given to Julian was in the middle of these codes."

"Can you read the codes at all?" I asked,

"No I don't recognize any of them."

"Any idea how Tomas got the journal," asked Lucian

Marcus shook his head, "No but I have an even stronger belief now that the Shadow is here in San Francisco, that Rachel's vision was correct. Rachel, I think the person you saw in your vision was Arius himself; your vision limited because of his protective spell. Malek boasted that they were close to finding it. Tomas was here looking for it. It was no random act that he was here nor the presence of the dark vampires we have seen."

He opened the book almost to the end.

"I found one odd reference towards the end before the codes. It says the seeker must find the way to see. After that is a drawing of Janus, the roman god with two faces. In the margin in a different handwriting there is a note in English and at the bottom is an address. I think Tomas might have written it. It a street address and says LA. It did a google search and there is such an address just north of LA."

"It will take another day or so for the laptop work to be complete. We should go down there and check out the reference," Julian said.

"I agree," Marcus said, "Lucian and I have a few items to close at the office in the morning but we can leave as soon as we are done."

Everyone else went upstairs. I walked out back to call Tess. I would have to change our plans for tomorrow. I looked at my watch, it was late, I hoped she was still up.

"Hi, I hoped you'd call tonight," Tess said when she answered her phone.

"Sorry to call so late. Were you asleep?"

"No, just finishing some reading. I was about to go to bed but I am really glad you called."

"Well I missed hearing your voice and I wanted to say goodnight. I don't want to keep you up but there is one thing. I have to go out of town tomorrow. We have to make a fast trip down to LA. So I need to postpone our date. I'm really sorry."

"Darn, I had such a great time today, I was really looking forward to it, must be something important."

"It is. Normally I would just let them go without me, but Dad needs us all there."

"It's not dangerous is it, could I tag along?" she asked a faint hint of concern in her voice.

I had to steer very clear of that, I was not ready to explain Tess to them yet and there was no way I was going to let her anywhere near Draven's creatures. I also didn't want her to worry.

"It's probably best if you stay put. It's not dangerous but you never know. I would feel better with you safe at home. Anyway it'll be boring ride and I am sure you have better things to do. We just have a few things to check out. I'll call you when we are heading back."

I paused a second thinking, "I tell you what, I'll pick you up day after tomorrow and we'll spend the whole afternoon and evening together, I promise."

"Ok, I'll call Jesse tomorrow, there's a movie she had been bugging me to go see. I guess it's true what they say about absence makes the heart grow fonder."

"I hope so. I'll talk to you tomorrow. Sleep well."

"You too. Love you."

"Love you too."

I hug up the phone. I didn't know how much longer I could keep this all secret. I would be glad when this Shadow business was over and we could all go back to just living, especially now that I had a real life.

Chapter 9

Things are not as they seem

Croft Home, Muir Woods

We met down stairs just after noon as soon as Dad and Lucian were back. Rachel, Julian and I took the Range Rover and Lucian, Mora, Stefan, and Dad took his Mercedes. We had been gone about an hour when I turned on my iPhone music and one of Tess's songs came on. I had forgotten that she had loaded up some of her music earlier. The sound of "Hey, Soul Sister" blasted out of the speakers. It was one of the songs that she and Austin danced to. I laughed to myself remembering how silly she acted dancing to it. Just thinking about her made me smile.

Rachel reached over and turned off the music.

"Ok. So, what's going on, Aidan," Rachel asked.

"What do you mean?" I said puzzled.

"Since when do listen to a song like that. And smile while listening. You have been very, I don't know, buoyant these last few weeks. You're smiling all the time and I think I even heard you singing the other day. Where's your usual dark, brooding self."

"Yea, I noticed it too, especially the bad singing," Julian said laughing.

"Hush Julian, I'm being serious. So whats really going on Aidan?" Rachel asked.

I had to be careful here. I wasn't ready to spill the beans just yet.

"I don't know, I haven't noticed anything different. Doesn't a man have the right to be a little happy once in a while? I've been getting out of the house more and I really like my classes this term. I'm just having some fun. I think I was just in a rut, spending too much time at home. The trip to Canada and New York really helped. So, what are you the happiness police now?"

"No its just you seem different. And you have been gone a lot recently," she said.

"Like I said, I haven't noticed anything. Maybe today I just like your company," I said smiling.

"Oh yea, Right," Rachel said. I turned back on the music.

I hummed a few bars then broke out in a really bad rendition of the song. Julian jumped in and finally so did Rachel. We were all laughing as we sailed down the highway.

We arrived just as the sun was going down. The address was a modern building in the center of an industrial park. We stopped a block down the street.

"You sure this is it?" Julian asked.

"Yes this is the address," I said.

Dad said, "the note said the top floor."

Stefan pointed, "Security cameras on the corners. It looks like this place is really locked down."

Julian said, "Let's leave the cars here and see if there is a back entrance."

We walked around an adjacent building and checked out the target building. The back was just as fortified. There were more cameras, one on each corner. There was an unguarded door however.

"Well this is just as bad," Julian said.

I looked up. On the west side was an adjacent building, that was very close to our target. A large tree grew next to it.

"I have an idea," I said taking off.

"Aidan wait," I heard Dad say but I was already running. I sprinted over to the adjacent building. There were no cameras or security on this one. On the other side was a fire escape. First, I broke off a large limb from the tree, then I climbed up the fire escape and ran over the roof. The target building was about 40 feet away. I got a running start and sailed over landing on the roof of the target building behind the cameras. I placed the limb right in front of the back camera. I motioned for the others to come over. Now that the camera was blocked, Stefan and Mora scaled it easily.

Dad looked up then looked down at a small vine that was growing at the base of the building. He motioned with his hand and the vine started to grow. It expanded and grew all the way to the top of the building. Dad, Rachel, then Julian climbed up the vine.

When she got to the top Rachel said, "glad I didn't wear a skirt."

"Me too," I said smirking.

"Speak for yourself," said Julian.

Stefan found an entrance on the roof to the building. Luckily it was not wired.

"I don't think they expected a roof entrance," he said.

Dad nodded.

Julian waved his hand over the deadbolt on the door and it slid back with a click. He opened the door and we all went in. We walked down the stairs and opened a door that led to a hallway. At the end of the hall, the room opened up.

It was a huge room, very open. Cubicles covered about three fourths of the space. There were offices at the other end. At one side of the offices was a door with a large steel cage in front of it. Bars held the cage in place. The room appeared to be some sort of a financial or trading house.

I looked, no security cameras in the room.

"I bet that's it," I said pointing to the caged door.

"You think," said Rachel.

We made our way through the cubes and over to the barred door.

"Steel," Julian said.

"No problem," I said nodding to Stefan.

We each grabbed a bar and pulled. It was immobile at first but I gave a big jerk and the first one broke loose. Stefan not to be outdone pulled harder and finally the second one gave way. We swung open the cage. The door itself was not locked. Just as we were about to go in, we heard a noise at the back. The elevator was opening.

When the doors opened, five men in dark business suits got out. Two were extremely tall, stooping to get out of the elevator. As soon as they stepped into the room, they saw us and at that point all hell broke loose.

The man on the far right dropped down on all fours and transformed into a werewolf. The features on men to the far left swam just a second, fangs grew from their upper teeth and their eyes turned blood red. The two vampires and werewolf launched themselves immediately towards us.

Stefan, Mora and I ran towards them. The last two other men stepped forward. Blue witch lighting flew by us. I looked back. Dad and Julian returned fire with their own bolts. Blue and purple light lit up the room. The strong smell of ozone was everywhere. The two streams met in the center of the room and the blast knocked Stefan, Mora and I to the ground. The werewolf and vampire sailed over several of the office cubes and hit the ground.

"Go," I heard Dad say. Rachel and Julian moved to the left and he and Lucian moved to the right. Stefan, Mora and I stood up again.

One of the witches motioned and a file cabinet flew towards Julian. Lucian lifted his hands, a slight smile on his face. The file cabinet stopped in mid air then flew back towards the witch. He ducked as it flew over his head. It shattered a glass wall behind him.

The other man moved forward. The lifted his hand and multiple pieces of glass raised off the floor. He waved his arms forward and the glass sailed out like missiles towards us.

Rachel stepped forward and held out her hands. A shimmering wall of blue surrounded us. The glass seemed to hit a barrier in the middle of the room and fell back hitting the ground. Dad launched another bolt of witch lightening. It hit one of the men in the chest, flinging him backwards. The other one, knelt behind a desk and shot a bolt out, hitting Lucian. Out of the corner of my eye, I saw the werewolf. He was about to spring on Lucian. I jumped and caught him in midair. We fell to the ground. As I struggled with the werewolf, I saw Stefan wrestling with the first vampire, Mora and the other one were circling each other. They moved so fast they were almost a blur, moving front to back, each trying to pin the other for a fatal bite.

Bolts of witch lightening and various metal objects whizzed through through the air as I fought with the werewolf. His fangs reached within an inch of my face as I turned to throw him off. His claws tried to scrape down my back but I held back his arms. His fetid breath was right in my face.

Finally I lifted him up and threw him across the room. He hit a desk and I flew over and held him down. He struggled to get up. I pulled back and hit him right between the eyes. His body went limp and his human form slid off the desk.

I looked up. Rachel was next to the gated door. Stefan and Mora were still fighting with the dark vampires and the other two witches were still flinging bolts. Lucian sent a huge metal desk flying all the way across the room. It hit both of them.

Dad yelled, "Aidan you and Rachel get the artifact."

I sprinted in a blur over to Rachel.

When I got there I heard Rachel yell, "Aidan look out."

I turned around. As I spun about, I saw that Mora had a look of horror on her face.

A torn, metal shaft was flying across the room right towards my chest. Without thinking I held my hands out. I felt the craft flow around me. and touch the flying metal. The shaft slowed, quivered then stopped, suspended off the ground. I dropped my hands and let out a long breath. The metal shaft fell to the ground as I felt the craft flow away.

I turned and looked at Rachel, "Did you do that?" I asked.

"No I think you did," she said, shock in her eyes.

That lasted only a second until a another round of flying glass came towards us.

She yelled, "I'll hold them off, go get whatever the hell we're looking for."

I ran through the gate. There were boxes and metal trays stacked around the room. I didn't see anything special until I noticed a metal case behind another cage. The case had a Janus face stamped on it. I tore open the cage and pulled out the case. Inside was a red, cloth bag. I opened the bag and inside was a small, six inch rectangular mirror with a silver border, etched with some sort of symbols. I put it back in the bag and put everything back in the box and ran out.

"Got it," I yelled.

Stefan saw I had the box. He lifted the other vampire and threw him back into the wall behind the two men who were just standing up.

Mora kicked the one she was fighting and he sailed back with the other one. Dad nodded at Lucian. The two of them launched streams of witch lightening. The bolts hit the two witches directly in the chest and they flew back.

The room was a shambles. Chairs had holes burned through them. Metal objects like staplers and printers were now melted puddles. Glass was everywhere. Smoke curled up from several of the desks and chairs. The smell of ozone still filled the room.

"Wow, you really made a mess in here Aidan," Julian said looking around.

In the back the men were getting up. One of them looked at Dad then he held out his hand. A wave of flame, bright yellow and red burst across the desks. As we made our way back to the hall, I saw them pick up the still unconscious werewolf and run out, the room covered in flames.

We made our way back quickly back to the car. No one was seriously injured. Rachel had a small scrape and Lucian had a burn mark from where the bolt had caught him. When we got to the cars, I gave the case to Dad. "It has a mirror in it."

He examined the front and nodded then turned towards the car.

Out of the corner of my eye, I thought I saw a pale shape go into the shadow of the trees. I asked Stefan,"Did you see that ?"

"What," he asked.

"A form, I saw a shape move into the shadows."

Stefan looked at the trees.

"No, you must be mistaken, Aidan. There's nothing there."

"Funny, I could have sworn I saw something there."

I almost followed it into the shadow.

Mora put her hand on my arm. Alarms were beginning to go off and the police would be here in minutes. "There's nothing there, Aidan. Come on, we have to go."

It was a long drive home. Rachel and Julian fell asleep in the back. On the way back, Stefan, and Mora drove with us. At first I couldn't get the evening events off my mind. The sudden appearance of my witchcraft and then it's disappearance. Then the shape I saw. It was unnerving. Stefan could see that I was bothered.

"Don't fret too much about tonight Aidan. We will figure out the mirror."

"No its not that, its just the witchcraft. I seem to be having short glimpses of power but then it fades. I have no control."

"Now I am not an expert in these things. Frankly I find all of most of these witch issues disturbing. Present company excluded of course. But I think things will settle in time. If it bothers you, talk to your father or Julian. I am sure they can help."

I wanted to talk to them but I knew they would begin to question me about how it started and that would lead them to Tess and I wasn't ready for that.

"Maybe," was all I said.

The sun was just coming up as we made it back to San Francisco. Everyone else went inside. I walked around the back and called Tess. She was just leaving for the Y.

"You sound tired," she said.

"I am but I am still coming down to pick you up for lunch," I said.

We met that afternoon and just walked downtown. She did a little shopping. It was nice to relax and have a normal day after the events of yesterday. We went out and saw a movie and I took her to dinner. I dropped her back at home and told her I'd call later.

Dad was still reviewing the materials when I got home.
He looked up when Lucian also walked in behind me.
"Did you find out anything about the mirror?" I asked.
He picked up the mirror.
"No but I recognize its use. It's a far seeing mirror. Years ago, witches would sometimes use these to see events at a distance or to find hidden objects. I examined it but there's nothing special in the inscription. There is some enchantment about it however. Something is hidden here, I can sense it. But it's blocked by a powerful spell. I've been working all morning to break it with no progress. But the journal

was right you need a way to see and," he held up the mirror, "it's a way to see."

At that point, Julian came in. "I have good news, I just heard from our friends working on the laptop. They have made a major breakthrough and should have the files from the laptop ready tomorrow. I have a rather large sum of money I need to gather, cash only of course," Julian said. "Any headway on the rest of this stuff?"

"No I was just telling Aidan that without the spell to unlock the mirror, its useless to us." He looked down at his watch. "There's not much more we can do tonight. I hope the results from the laptop give us more clues. Everyone should get some rest. We will have a lot of work to do tomorrow."

Julian got his call at one the next afternoon. Dad, Stefan, Julian, Lucian and I drove down to retrieve the laptop. We drove through the heart of Silicon Valley passing one high tech firm after another. Finally, we stopped at a nondescript office tower and took the elevator to the fifth floor. We walked down a hall to a door that read Stone Consulting. We went in and the receptionist took us into a conference room. Julian waited outside. In a few minutes a man carrying a briefcase met him outside the room. Julian handed him a large envelope. The man handed him a the laptop case and some printouts. They shook hands and he left. Julian came in.

"It took quite a bit of work but they were able to recover and decrypt most of the files. They lost a few of the old ones but many of the more recent ones were salvaged. He made print outs of them."

He placed the printouts on the table. Several were black and white photographs.

"Oh my God, Julian look at this," Dad said when he saw one of the photos. He pushed it to the center of the table. The picture showed a long table with a white cloth on it. Various pieces of jewelry were spread out on it. A date was marked on the lower right corner that read June 1925. Julian nodded and pointed to a piece second on the left. "That's it, that's the Shadow. I remember those gold swirls. There's something a little different about it but its generally what I remember."

He was pointing to a circular pendant. In the center was a dark crystal, surrounded by swirls of silver and gold. Five stones that made a pentagram were embedded on the pendant's edge, circling the center crystal. A loop of silver connected the pendant to a chain. Faint symbols seemed to float in the center crystal.

A typed document was stacked next to the photographs. It was a list of names and business addresses. Dad read over the list rubbing his chin.

"Something is odd here," he said.

"Whats that?" Julian asked.

"I recognize that first name, Mary Whitehall, Whitehall and associates. Wasn't the first victim's name Mary?"

Lucian checked his notes. "Yes Marcus, you're right that's her. Mary Whitehall. She owned an antique shop."

"Where was the business in relation to where her body was found."

Lucian did a search with Google maps on his laptop. "It was within two blocks."

"And the next name on the list?" Julian asked.

"Jamison and Tyler, Antique Jewelry," Lucian answered. He checked again.

"Those were the two next victims. Their office was just three blocks away."

A third printout contained a map of downtown with several addresses circled.

Dad leaned back and said, "Now we know what Tomas was doing. He was systematically going from dealer to dealer, looking for any clues. He must have thought these people either had the Shadow or had information about it. He was using the first room to torture them for information and when he was finished he killed them. Did we find any emails or other communications he sent out?"

Julian answered, "The last email was over a month ago stating that he had leads but nothing specific. He said he would send details when he had something. It appears he was working alone."

"Did we trace the email account ?" Marcus asked.

"Someone in France is all we know."

"How about his cell phone?"

"He received a call just before the email but nothing after."

"Draven probably has agents all up and down the west coast looking," Julian said.

"Who is the next name on the list?, Julian asked.

"It says T Michaels, Exquisite Antiques," Dad answered.

I looked up from the map. "What, what did you say?" I asked.

"It says T Michaels, Exquisite Antiques."

"Let me see that," I said.

I checked the printout. The address was near Jackson Square. Oh God, it had to be a coincidence.

"Does this mean anything to you, Aidan?" Dad asked with an inquisitive tone.

I started to gather my things, "I think I've driven by there once before. I'll go and check the address, see if there is a T Michaels employed there. Maybe I can find out if Tomas had been there," I said.

"I'll come with you," Stefan said.

"No its ok Stefan, I have to swing by school later. I'll just meet everyone at home. I'll let you know what I find. Perhaps the rest of you should split up the rest of the list and check them as well. It looks like he was doing a pretty wide sweep."

"That's a good idea," Stefan said.

As they were splitting up the list, I said goodbye and dashed out to my car, grateful that I had drove myself this morning.

As soon as I got in the car, I called Tess.

"Hey Aidan, how's your day going?" she asked.

"Fine Tess, listen I have a quick question, whats the name of the antique store where you work?"

"Exquisite Antiques. Its over near Jackson Square. You remember, we went to dinner near there that night. Why do you ask?"

My heart sank. The attack by the werewolf that night was no accident. He was stalking her! He wasn't interested in me, he was looking for her! I tried to remain calm, I didn't want to alarm her.

"You don't work today do you?"

"Yes but not at the store. I am at the Y, my class is about to start."

"Just stay there Tess, I will explain when your class is over. Just don't leave."

"What's up Aidan, why do I have to stay here?" I could hear the tension in her voice.

"Just trust me Tess, I'll explain everything when I get there, just stay put alright?"

"Ok. see you when class is over," she said concern in her voice.

When she hung up I hit the accelerator.

I had only one option now, I had to come clean with the family. They had to know everything. Thats the only way we could protect Tess.

They would have to understand.

I hope she could.

Chapter 10

The Coven

YMCA, San Francisco

I made it to the Y in record time. I waited in the lobby until Tess was finished. It was a frantic few minutes for me. Finally she walked out in grey tights, a towel around her neck. I was so happy to see her, I ran up and and took her in my arms.

"Wow, what's that all about?" she asked.

"I'm just glad to see you," I said releasing her.

"So whats all this talk about me staying put at the Y. Whats going on?" she asked.

I looked around, "Its a little crowded her, lets take a drive."

"Uh, I don't think so. Aidan, I'm all sweaty and my hair is a mess. I need to take a shower and get dressed. I am not too keen on you seeing me like this, much less driving around in your car."

"Ok, but hurry we really need to talk," I said.

"Give me ten minutes," she said with a frown. She gave me a quick kiss on the cheek and headed back through the door. I almost followed her, to watch outside but that would have created a scene. Instead, I sat as close to the door as possible. I could hear her walking and just make out her heart beat. This was one time I wished I could project like Rachel.

Right at ten minutes, she came out of the door. Black jeans and a tight blue blouse. I would have fallen in love all over again. "You look, fantastic," I said. "You're just saying that because I rushed," she said. "Besides, my hair is still damp. If I get your car wet, it's all your fault."

"I am sure it will be fine," I said. We got in the car and I drove us over to a cafe she liked. We went in, sat in the far back and ordered two coffees. I just looked out the window for a minute as I tried to figure out the best way to tell her.

"Just spill it, Aidan," she said. "You know you might be this magical being but I can read you like a book. Whatever it is just spit it out, I'm a big girl."

I smiled, "No getting anything past you is there?" I asked.

I took a deep breath, "Ok, let me ask you a question. The man that attacked us, did you ever see him before that night," I asked.

"I think I would have remembered a seven foot werewolf," she said smiling taking a sip of coffee.

"I am serious Tess, did you ever see him before?"

"No, not that I remember. Of course, I didn't get a real good look at him. It was dark that night. So, no I don't think I ever saw him before."

"Did he or someone that looked like him ever come into your store?"

She thought a minute. "You know now that you mention it, I do remember a man that looked sort of like him. Same build but this guy was really well dressed, expensive suit and tie. I remember he came in but I was with another customer. I told him to wait, that I would be right with him. I remember he seemed a little nervous. After another customer came in, he took one of my cards and left. I guess its possible it was him."

"The man in the store, did he say what he was after?"

She shook her head, "No, all he said was that he had a question about some jewelry. I didn't think anything about it. What does this all mean?"

I paused a second gathering my thoughts. "Tess we were not the first people this monster attacked. We think he was involved in two murders over the last couple of weeks. The first one was a woman, the second a gay couple. We thought at first the attacks were simply random, that he was just passing through the city. But the night of our attack, I found a key on him. We tracked the key back to where he was staying and we found a list. These three victims were on that list. One thing they had in common was that they worked at or owned an antique store. The third name on that list was T Michaels."

Her face turned to ash. "Oh my God, Aidan. That means he was stalking me. He was waiting for us that night." A tear formed in the corner of her eye. I moved over and put my arm around her. I gave her a napkin and she wiped her eyes.

"Why me, what would he possibly have wanted with me?" she asked.

"Remember when I told you about why I went to school, that we were looking for something, that artifact I mentioned?"

"Yes vaguely," she said nodding.

"The evil sorcerer that my coven killed, he had lots of apprentices that escaped. They are also looking for this artifact. We know now both from a vision that Rachel had and from information we retrieved from our attacker, that the artifact is still here in San Francisco or was until very recently. We think that the werewolf was systematically looking for it, going from dealer to dealer."

"Aidan, if you had not been with me that night, if I had never met you, I would be" I interrupted her, "Don't think about that Tess. You are safe now and I'll never let anything happen to you."

"Oh God, Aidan, Karen and Nick and Austin, if he somehow followed me home." She looked like she was about to bolt from her chair.

I took her hand, "Tess, I don't think they are in any danger. Neither your home address nor home phone number was on your card. None of the information we found mentioned it. I think he only knew you from the store. You never used your first name only your first initial. He was canvassing several of the stores at one time. Several were marked on his map. So, I don't think he followed you home. But to be sure, I don't think you should stay home or go to work for a while."

"What do you mean? Am I still in danger from these people?"

"Probably not but I would feel better if you would come home with me for a few days. We didn't find any evidence of communications that mentioned you by name. So your information trail probably ended with him. But to be sure, I want you safe at my house. My family and I can watch you until we get to the bottom of this. I assume Julian and my father would like to ask you some questions too, if thats ok. But I absolutely don't want you to go back to the store. Will that be a problem?"

"No actually the store is closed. The owner is traveling in Europe. He left a few days ago and will be over there for awhile. He usually closes the store every year about this time. As far as going to your house, I guess that's ok but but what do I say to your family? What will they think about me, a human in their house?" she asked.

"Don't worry, I'm sure as soon as they meet you, you will capture their hearts just like you captured mine."

"Well I don't know about that but one thing I know is that before I meet your family I need a proper shower, do my hair, and put on some decent clothes."

"I think you look perfect but how about this. I'll take you back to the Y so you can pick up your car and I'll follow you home. You can shower, pack then we'll head up to my house."

"That will work," she said. "How about the Y, should I keep my classes?"

"No," I shook my head. "I know I am being overly protective but I just want you to stay with me. Please Tess, just do it for me."

"Alright, I'll let the Y know that I have to go out of town for a few days. There are a few other girls who can cover my classes. I'll let the dojo know too."

We both sat for a few minutes. She finished her coffee. She put her cup down and said, "I just can't believe this Aidan, that I was involved in this, this conflict all along but didn't know it. It's like there is this complete other world out there that I was walking blind in. All I know is its a good thing I tricked you that first night into doing that paper otherwise I would be just another statistic, some unsolved crime. I still can't believe it."

I took both her hands in mine. "Tess, we are together now and nothing is going to separate us. I am going to be with you every minute until we figure this out. You are my whole world now Tess. Nothing is going to happen to you, I promise."

She nodded and held my hand as we walked out of the cafe. As we got back into my car I asked her, "By the way, what are you going to tell Nick and Karen, just so I have the story straight?"

"I am going to tell them that you and I are going up to meet your parents. That we will be gone for a few days. That's the truth. I just don't want them to worry."

"You can be a little devious," I said.

"Only with the ones I love," she said.

She picked up her car at the Y and told them she would be gone a few days. I followed her home. She packed a quick bag and got ready while I played with Austin. When she came down stairs, I stood up, staring up at her. She looked absolutely beautiful. She had on a light blue sweater, black jacket slacks and heels.

"You look stunning," I said.

"Only one chance to make a first impression. Besides I've seen some of your family, I just want to fit in."

"Wow, you look awesome, sis," Nick said. Karen nodded too, "You look perfect Tess."

"Thanks," she said handing me her bag. She hugged Nick then Karen. She almost had tears in her eyes. Karen with a frown on her face said, "Everything alright, Tess?"

Tess smiled, "Yes it's just a big day. I'm ok. I'll call you tonight. Don't worry."

"Alright call me"

She leaned down and kissed Austin goodbye. "I see you in a few days, Austin. OK?"

"OK," he said giving her a big hug.

"I'll take good care of her," I said. "I am sure you will," Nick said. He gave her another big hug. "Have a good time, but don't forget to call," he said. "I will," she said. She waved goodbye as we headed out.

"I am going to miss them," she said as we headed towards downtown.

It was a clear, late afternoon as we crossed the Golden Gate Bridge. The city gleamed behind us. Looking over, I could tell that Tess was nervous. She was not her normal talkative self. She just looked out the window at the bay. Her heart rate was up and she was drumming her fingers on the door. I reached over and took her hand. She looked around. He eyes were worried.

"Tess, it's going to be fine. Don't worry."

"What about Mora ? I don't think she thought very much of me when I first met her."

"She is just trying to protect me. She doesn't want to see me hurt. Let me handle Mora." I smiled, "her bark is worse than her bite."

"Easy for you to say, you won't be the only human there."

I smiled. "Believe me, you don't worry about that. It will be fine. There is no safer place you could be than with Stefan and Mora. They are the most noble and caring people once you get to know them. It's true, they can be a little cold at first but give them a little time, especially Mora. Next to you, she is probably the best friend I have in the world. They took care of me all this time. They will come to love you just as I have. Just be patient."

"I'll try," she said. Then silence enveloped her.

We drove for a while and finally turned off at our exit. We were in the forest in no time. The drive seemed to take forever and the gloom and darkness of the forest made Tess even more nervous. We passed the gate and finally made the turn. The house was directly ahead.

"You live there?" she asked when she saw the house.

"Yes, my father had it built in the late forties." I smiled and said, "Remember, my family has had generations to invest and being able to predict the future helps as well. But don't let it put you off, it's just a house."

We pulled into the garage and got out. "When we get inside, let me do the talking."

"No argument from me," Tess said, taking my hand.

She stopped a minute as if remembering something. "They're not going to be reading my mind are they?" she asked a worried look on her face.

"Why, you have something to hide?" I teased her a little, trying to get her to relax.

"No but," I stopped her.

"'I'm just kidding. No, they won't be reading your mind. It's considered bad manners to do that. Its only done in very specific circumstances or with your consent. They would never do it without asking. It would be like listening in on someone's phone conversation."

"Don't scare me like that. I'm nervous enough," she said slapping my shoulder.

"Don't worry. I told you it will be fine. Maybe a little rocky at first, but it will turn out great. You'll see."

We walked through the garage and headed into the main foyer. Mom was coming down the stairs as we came in.

"Aidan, I am glad you are home. I felt a presence," she stopped half way down when she saw Tess.

"Mom can you call Dad and the others, there is someone I need you all to meet."

She looked at Tess, "Of course dear. Please come in and sit down young lady. I'll gather the others." She turned and went back upstairs.

I took Tess into our large living room.

Tess looked out of the windows and into the garden.

"Your house is beautiful Aidan. I love the garden."

"And not a broomstick in sight," I joked taking her jacket.

She frowned. "You're terrible," she said.

I sensed them immediately but a noise at our backs made Tess turn.

My father, Julian, Mora, Stefan, Mom, and Rachel were at the entrance.

Rachel immediately understood. She smiled at me then came right in and hugged Tess. "Hello Tess, its good to see you again," she said.

"Good to see you again Rachel," Tess said smiling, relived that she had one smiling face in the group.

Mora looked at me. I nodded. She nodded back and came over to Tess.

"I am pleased to see you again Tess," Mora said holding out her hand. Tess shook it.

"Thank you Mora. Its a pleasure to see you again," she said.

"Ah yes Tess, we met at the University. You are as lovely as you were that day," Julian said taking her hand and kissing it.

"Thank you Julian. Its good to see you again.," she said a little embarrassed.

Stefan reached out his hand. Tess looked at me. I nodded. She nervously took it. He smiled and said,"Its a pleasure to see you again Tess." He stepped back.

"Its good to see you again Stefan," she said.

Holding out his hand Dad said, "Well it seems we are the only ones yet to make your acquaintance young lady."

"I'm sorry. Mom, Dad this is my friend Tess."

Dad said, "Tess, welcome to our home, any friend of Aidan's is always welcome here." He shook her hand.

Mom said, "Hello Tess, pleased to meet you. Sorry about the stairs, I wasn't expecting company."

"Its quite all right. Thank you very much Mr. and Mrs Croft. You have a beautiful home."

"Thank you Tess, please come and sit down."

"Tess, come sit by me," Rachel said sitting on the couch. Tess went over and sat down.

I remained standing. I was a little nervous and paced a second before I spoke.

"I have a few things to say and I am sure you will have some questions but let me start at the beginning and cover the most important item first. Tess and I met at the university. We became friends and now we are in love with each other. We have been seeing each other for a while now. We want your blessing. There are also a few items I have not been completely truthful about and I need to set somethings right."

"I see," my Father said sitting a bit tighter in his chair.

"First, I need to explain what happened the night the werewolf attacked."

Dad interrupted me a frown on his face holding up his hand. "Aidan, please we don't want to scare this young woman with such talk."

"Dad you have to just trust me, let me finish. Don't jump to conclusions."

I could tell he was not happy but he nodded. Julian was scowling but quiet.

"I was not alone the night the werewolf attacked. Tess was with me. She knows about everything."

Julian leaned forward shaking his head, "Aidan you know the rule, this can't be condoned. You know what we have to do, that we cannot afford the risk to your or her. The consequences could be disastrous."

I held up my hand, "Please, hear me out Julian."

"It's true, my judgement may have been somewhat clouded when it comes to Tess. But I am in love with her, she is everything to me now. She saved me from darkness, living in the shadows. I'm happy now, happier than I have every been and I will be with her for as long as she will have me."

I looked at Mora. "She put the pieces together herself. Once she figured out the truth, I gave her a choice to either be with me as I truly am or to have her memories changed, to forget everything. But she chose me, creature that I am. She loves me and I love her and we need all of you to support us. I don't care about rules or consequences, I only care about Tess."

I paused a second, "But there is more. You see, Tess was already involved in this whole affair., already linked to our fates. We just didn't know it."

"What do you mean Aidan, I don't understand.," Dad asked me.

"Tess is T Michaels, the third name on the list. The werewolf was not stalking me that night, he was after her."

"What," Julian said looking at Tess.

"Yes, Tess works at an antique store. We were attacked very close to it. She was going to be his next victim. None of this was an accident. So you see, Tess was involved from the very beginning."

"So please, I ask you, trust me in this. I know its unusual but I need her, we all need her. She may have information vital to our cause. I brought her here to be safe with us, to be protected by us but if you can't accept and support my decision, we will leave and go it on our own. I'll keep her safe myself. I won't live without her."

Tess stood up and came over next to me. She took my hand.

"I know I am a stranger here, a human in your house. I know things I am not supposed to know, have seen things I'm not supposed to see. I also know you all love Aidan and want what's best for him. That you are worried about him, about us. I am the first to admit that this is a very unusual circumstance and I am very much in the dark about all of this."

She paused a minute, "But I want you to know that I'm in love with him, that I love him more than anyone. I would never do anything to harm him or put any of you in danger. I will do anything to help you in this conflict you have. I don't know if there is anything I can do, but I'll try my best. All I ask is that you let me be with Aidan. I don't care about our differences or the magic. All I want is Aidan, he is all the magic I need."

The room was silent for a minute.

Dad spoke, "Tess I understand your feelings in this matter, truly I do. But it's very dangerous. Dangerous for you and for us. Our way has always been to provide safety and comfort for the humans that discover us by using our talents to make them forget, to allow them to go on with their normal human lives untroubled by the world of witchcraft. This has always been the safe and best course. That is my counsel here."

Julian turned to me and said, "Aidan I must agree with your father. I know how you feel but this is too risky. She is very, very vulnerable."

He looked at Tess. "Tess, let me work my spell. I promise, you will be in no danger. I have done this many, many times in the past. You'll wake up and not remember anything and you can go on with your life as if nothing every happened. It would be best this way, best for you and best for Aidan. This is why we have our rule, to protect everyone involved."

I said. "Dad, Julian I understand your concern and I have thought long and hard about this. I love Tess and I would never put her in any danger. I believe I can protect her better with her full knowledge. I know we are different but she has a right to make her own choice in this matter. We all have that right, magical being or not and I will support her decision come what may."

Dad said, "But Aidan, the simple fact is that she is human and vulnerable in our world."

I was getting angry now.

"Do you think I can't protect her or is your real fear that I can't protect her from myself? Is that what you're really afraid of, that I will harm her, that I won't be able to control the thirst? Is that it? If so, then you really don't know me at all. If that really is your issue then maybe it's best for Tess and I to go."

I started to turn for the door but Dad put his hand up "Aidan wait. That's not what I am saying. We don't want you to go. Now, I would be lying if I didn't say that part of my concern is the thirst. Your vampire nature is very strong Aidan. But I also know your control is very strong, we all know that. But I am more fearful of the other parts of our world. You have seen the evil that Malek and Draven have let loose. She herself has seen it."

At that point Tess said, "Dr Croft, Julian, I appreciate your concern but I love Aidan and he loves me. Being with him is all that matters to me. I know he would never hurt me, he only wants to protect me and we will face whatever dangers occur, together. I understand the danger is real. Believe me after the werewolf I understand the danger. But I think these dangers are the same whether I know about you or not. I was blind to your world before and maybe ignorance was bliss but I would rather face these dangers with a full understanding rather than stumbling blindly around them. Aidan and I will face them together. Please, please do not take this away from us."

At that point, Rachel got up and put her arm around Tess.

"Julian, Marcus, are you blind? Can't you see? We need to face the truth. It's impossible to separate them now. We would just lose them both. It would be wrong to deny them. I for one am happy she is here." Rachel smiled and pulled Tess closer.

Mora came and stood by me and took my hand.

"When this affair first started, Aidan came to me and asked my advice. Yes, I know, I kept it from you, even you Stefan. I told him that I didn't think it would work, that humans could never understand us, that Tess would flee when she found out the truth."

She looked over at Tess. "But it seems I have underestimated her. I think we all have. I know the rule, but I say in this instance, screw the rule. It's clear they love each other and I have never seen Aidan as happy as he has been these last few weeks. It's hard for us, especially our kind."

She smiled at Stefan,"So who am I to deny Aidan what Stefan and I have? Or what you and Rachel have Julian, our you and Sophie, Marcus. Aidan deserves to be happy and I know that Tess makes him happy." She put her arm around me and looked at Tess.

"Tess I was fearful when I first met you, I was afraid of what this would do to Aidan. Even then I could see the light in his eye. But now that I see you two together, see what joy you have brought him, I am happy you are together. There's no doubt that it will be hard but you've saved Aidan for all of us and I will do everything to protect you and him, from anyone." Stefan nodded his head and looked at Marcus and Julian.

"I too have seen a change in Aidan. He is like the boy I remember, the young man I think we have all missed for sometime now. I am not happy that Mora kept this from us but I agree with her, its time to let the old ways go. Tess I am grateful for what you have done for him and we will protect you from any that would cause you harm."

Mom went over , sat and took Dad's hand. "Marcus, they are in love, it's plain to see and Aidan needs us now more than ever. We need to set aside our concerns and embrace this with joy."

She had tears in her eyes when she spoke to Tess.

"Tess for many years I have worried about Aidan, worried as only a mother can. I feared more than anything else that we would lose him to darkness. But I can see now with you a true light in him that I have not seen in a very, very long time. I want to say thank you and tell you that you are welcome here no matter what."

The room was quiet then Julian spoke. "Tess as you said this is highly unusual, a human with Aidan." He laughed a minute, "But then everything about Aidan has been unusual."

Everyone laughed a bit at that.

"But I have been known to be a rascal myself and I have certainly bent some rules in my time. Perhaps I jumped to conclusions too quickly. It seems in this as in many things Rachel was ahead of me."

Rachel smiled at him as he continued, "and while I think there will be many difficulties ahead, it's also clear that you two belong together so who am I to stand in your way."

Dad stood up, "Danger or not, I have also seen the changes in Aidan these past few weeks. I've seen a side to him that frankly I was afraid we would never see again. He is more alive than I have seen him in years, thanks it seems to you Tess."

He looked a little stern at me, "Of course we would have preferred to find out sooner but given the circumstances I think I understand."

"Tess ours is a hard life, it's difficult and dangerous. Given what has occurred, I think you understand that. We have been a closed circle for many, many years. All we had was each other and perhaps we've grown too closed, too cautious. But life has a way of circumventing caution, providing joy from the most unanticipated places."

Dad smiled and said, "It's clear that Aidan loves you and that you love him and you have made your choice. As Mora said, who am I to deny the two of you what Sophie and I have just because you are different from us. Aidan is a part of our family and now that you are with him, you are a part as well. Welcome to our coven Tess." He put his arms around both of us, gave Tess a kiss on the cheek then stepped back.

I didn't know what to say, "See Tess I told you their bark is worse than their bite."

With that everyone laughed and the tension in the room disappeared.

Tess said, "Thank you all, I see now where Aidan gets his good qualities."

"And good looks," said Julian. Everyone laughed again.

Dad spoke again, "Tess there are questions we would like to ask and I am sure you have some yourself but before we do that lets go into the kitchen and get something to eat, you must be starved after this inquisition."

Mom took Tess by the arm and everyone went into the kitchen. Tess looked at me with a question in her eyes, "Go on, eat," I said. "We are used to this. Mora, Stefan and I will hunt later."

"Ok," said said taking some fruit and cheese. Everyone went back into the family room and sat down.

"So Tess," Mom said, "You must tell us how you met Aidan."

Tess looked over at me. "It's a pretty normal boy meets girl story. Aidan and I are in the same history class. I came in late one night and sat next to him. When I found out he had the professor last term, I asked him to partner with me for a class project. And being the gentleman that he is, he agreed. He is quite charming and then one thing led to another."

"What Aidan, this Aidan, charming?" Rachel said fake disbelief on her face.

Tess smiled, "Yes he can be quite charming."

"Julian, you sure she doesn't have a spell on her?" Rachel said with a grin.

"Oh you two, stop," Mom said shaking her head.

"And what was the subject of this project, if I may ask ?" Mom said.

"The inquisition," Tess said with a slight smile

"We'll that must have prepared you for tonight," Julian said laughing.

Everyone laughed again, "I guess it did," Tess said.

Rachel said, "We were not too hard on you, were we Tess?"

"No of course not, you were all very warm and accepting, thank you," said Tess smiling. "I just wasn't sure what to expect."

"Well we are very glad you are here Tess," Mom said.

"So am I Mrs Croft, thank you," said Tess.

Everyone finished their food and I stood up. "I think it's best if Tess stays here for a few days, until we get to the bottom of this."

"I agree completely," Dad said nodding. "Sophie we should put her in the room next to Aidan upstairs."

Rachel said, "Come on, it's right down from our room. I'll help you unpack."

Tess looked at me. I said, "Go on she won't bite, not you anyway."

Rachel stuck her tongue out at me then grabbed Tess's arm and they headed out to the car to get Tess's bag.

"She is lovely, Aidan. She has a good spirit about her, not afraid to speak her mind," Dad said once they were upstairs.

"Thats very true," I said smiling.

My face took on a somber look, "Dad I know I should have told you sooner, I just didn't know how to break it to you. I was not sure how everyone would react."

"I know, I understand son," he said.

"You don't think she is in any immediate danger, do you ?" I asked.

"No, we didn't find any other evidence about her in Tomas's affairs. I think they were very confident in his abilities. They probably don't even know he's dead. I'm sure the trail to Tess ended with him. But they will find out soon enough and replace him."

He came over and put his hand on my shoulder, "From what you told us, she is a very lucky girl. This could have turned out much differently if you had not been there."

"I know," I said, "It haunts me, knowing what could have happened. I guess we were both lucky."

"The craft, Aidan," Dad said. "It can direct us at times even when we don't see it. Perhaps the craft led you to her, son. I find it hard to believe that this was a simple coincidence."

"She is safe with us Aidan," Stefan said. "We will all watch after her. No harm will come to her, I promise."

"I would like to ask her some questions about her store when she's up to it," Dad said.

"Sure, I know she wants to help."

I could hear she and Rachel talking upstairs. "Let she and Rachel spend some time together. How about later this evening?"

"Whenever she's ready," Dad said.

"Lets go on up," Julian said smiling. "We don't want to keep you two love birds apart for too long."

I smiled and we went upstairs to the third floor and knocked on the door to the Tess's room. Tess and Rachel were lying on the bed chatting away. They got up when we came in.

"Aidan I can't believe this room. It's amazing," she said. It was a large room, very well furnished with its own balcony that looked over the gardens.

"Would you like a tour of the rest of the house?"

"Absolutely," she said.

Went went back down stairs. I showed her the family room, the library, and the other rooms on the first floor. She was especially interested in the exercise room. "I know where I'll be in the morning," she said.

I showed her the home theater room. "Wow now that's a huge screen," she said.

"Thursdays are movie nights. We all take turns picking the movie. It's my turn, but if you're good , I'll let you choose," I said adding with a smile, "and you can choose anything but a monster movie."

"I'm always good," she said with a mischievous smile.

"Don't I know it," I said with a wink back.

We were back to the stairs. "Well that's it for the first floor. Second floor is all offices and third floor is bedrooms," I said.

"There is one more thing I do want you to see," I said.

"Upstairs?" she asked.

"No out in the garden."

I took her hand and we walked into the garden.

"This is beautiful," Tess said as we walked through the flowers and plants. I pointed to the glass building in the corner. "That's the greenhouse. Grace and Mom grow all kinds of medicinal plants in there."

"By the way where is she and its Lucas, right ?"

"It's Lucian. He can be a little intimidating at first. Call him Lucas you might end up floating in a tree or thinking you're a parrot for a hour."

When she got an odd look on her face, I smiled and said, "Sorry, that's a joke. Actually Lucian not bad once you get to know him. He is traveling on business today and Grace is out getting supplies."

We walked on around the garden and she stopped at one of the rose beds. "I love roses," she said stopping to smell one of the large blooms. "We had a small rose garden growing up, I would help my Mom with them." She took another deep smell.

When she let the bloom go, one of the thorns scratched her finger. A small spot of blood welled up.

"Ouch," she said.

I stared at her hand just a second then as I looked up, I caught her eye. She saw me staring.

"Oh God, I'm sorry Aidan," she said.

I let out a long breath.

"It's fine don't worry. Come on, let's go to the greenhouse and clean that cut." I put my hand over her finger and we walked over to the greenhouse. I opened the door and she stepped in.

"It smells good in here," she said.

"Like I said, Mom and Grace grow some amazing plants in here. Come on there's a sink in the back."

When we got to the sink, I let her hand go and went to turn on the water. There was blood in my palm where I had held the scratch. I looked down at it. I calmly took her hand and my hand and let the cold, clean water run over them.

"Is everything ok?" she asked.

The smell was intoxicating but I had the thirst under control.

"It's all going to be perfect," I said.

"Just let me get some soap to disinfect it."

"Its fine, really Aidan"

"There is no way I am letting you go home with an infection. I promised your brother I would take care of you, so let me clean it."

"Ok, if you insist," she said holding out her hand.

I washed the spot good with the soap and dried it with a paper towel.

The scratch was almost gone.

"Let me put a bandaid on it," I said. In the cabinet was a first aid kit.

"Aidan really you don't have to do this, its just a scratch."

"Can you just hold still?"

"Alright"

I put on the bandaid.

"See completely fixed, can we go now?" she asked.

"Yes but we're going to have Grace check it later," I said.

We walked around several more beds that held all sorts of exotic plants. Tess stopped at each one. Finally we reached the end.

Tess reached up and gave me a quick kiss.

"Thank you, you take such good care of me," she said.

"Hey, thats what I'm here for," I said as we left the greenhouse.

We walked down several more paths Tess stopping at each bed and finally we got to the end of the garden. After that it was just deep forest. A large stone fence separated the forest from the garden.

"This is what I wanted you to see," I said.

"It's a big stone wall Aidan. You wanted me to see a big stone wall? I gotta tell you it's not doing much for me," she said with that funny I don't believe you look in her eye.

"No what I had in mind would make your heart race a little more," I said.

"Oh, I'm not sure you could make my heart race," she said teasing, a slight smile on her lips.

"Oh we'll just see about that," I said picking her up in my arms. I jumped with her onto the top of the wall then flew directly into the forest.

"Oh my God Aidan," she screamed as I jumped onto a large tree.

"Heart racing now?" I asked her.

"Oh yes.," she laughed.

"Just hold on, I've got you. Close your eyes if you get too scared."

"I'm too scared to close my eyes!," she yelled.

"Better than a roller coaster?" I asked jumping again. "Way better," she said putting her arms around my neck. I jumped from tree to tree. Finally we came to the stone outcropping, the cliff wall rising above us. It was the same place I brought Mora. I scaled straight up.

Her heart was pounding when we got to the top. I put her down and she looked all around us. The deep forest spread out below us and far beyond you could see the Pacific, an ocean of green followed by an ocean of blue.

Tess walked around the top of the outcropping. It was circular area with soft grass, at the back where the outcropping met the rest of the cliff, a tangle of vines grew covered with blue flowers. Next to them was a growth of ferns their green blades stark against the white stone. She lightly touched the blue blossoms. I sat down with my feet dangling over the side of the rock. It was a vertical, sheer rock face all the way to the bottom. She walked back over by me.

"This view is fantastic, definitely heart pounding," she said.

Looking up I took her hand and said, "Come, sit by me. I promise you won't fall."

"Are you sure?" she said peeking down.

"I am sure, You'll be safe, I promise."

She sat next to me still holding my hand.

"This is one of my favorite places. I come here a lot to think, to get away and be alone. I've spent a lot of time here over the years. It's spectacular at night with the stars and the forest. When the wind blows it seems like the sky is whispering to you."

"It certainly is beautiful and I can definitely see how it would be hard to be alone at your house, to have time to yourself with such a big family," she said.

"I don't know, you can be alone in the middle of a crowd. Sometimes, sitting here at night I thought that I would always be alone, that I'd never find someone like you."

She put her head on my shoulder.

"I am glad we came here. Thanks for sharing this with me," she said.

"I'm glad you're here too," I said.

We laid back and just watched the sun move towards the ocean. The wind picked up and it was like we had the world to ourselves. Tess laid her head on my chest and looked out as the wind moved the trees. After a while, when the sun was starting to set, Tess sat up and said, "Hey it's getting a little chilly, I didn't bring a jacket when we left."

"I'm sorry Tess, I completely forgot," I said.

I felt terrible. I was so caught up in the moment, I forgot she would get cold up here.

"Here take my shirt, it'll keep you warm."

"You sure, won't you get cold ?"

"No, I never get cold. Part of the package," I said pulling the shirt over my head. I handed it to her.

"Ooh muscles," she said laughing pulling the shirt over her head.

"Come on lets get you warmed up," I said. I turned her around and rubbed her back and arms.

She turned and pulled my face down to hers and kissed me, a long kiss.

"Now I'm warmed up," she said with a smile.

I looked up. The western sky was a riot of color, the sunset staining it with red and orange. Long shadows were falling in the forest.

She turned around, "It's really beautiful here Aidan."

"Not as beautiful as you."

She smiled a big smile and kissed me again.

She looked out one more time and said, "I'd love to stay all evening but we probably should be getting back. I know your Dad has some questions for me and I really want to help if I can. Let's just do the superman thing and get back."

I picked her up.

"Ready Miss Lane?" I asked.

She smiled again and gave me a quick kiss. She took a deep breath and we were off back to the house. She didn't yell quite as much gong back.

When we got to the stone fence, I sailed over it with one bound and flew to the end of the house. When we got there, I put Tess down right in front of the door. She took off my shirt and handed it to me.

"That was awesome Aidan. The view was spectacular. Maybe we can go back tomorrow? I can see why you love it so much."

"That would be great Tess. You know I could get used to having you here.," I said with a smile putting my arm around her.

"I love being here. It's nothing at all like I imaged."

She put her arm around my waist. "Lets go find your Dad."

We found Dad in his office on the second floor.

"So Tess, did you kids have a good afternoon?" he asked looking up as we came in.

"It was wonderful, Aidan took me to see quite an impressive view in the forest."

"Oh his old hiding place. He would slip out and head up there when there was too much going on around here. Be gone for hours at a time. It is an impressive view but tough to get to. He must have given you a hand."

"That's one way to put it," Tess laughed.

She stopped with a more cautious tone, "Dr. Croft, I was serious when I said that I wanted to help you. I would be happy to answer any questions. I'm not sure I can help with anything but I am certainly willing to try."

"That's very kind of you Tess. But please call me Marcus," Dad said with a smile.

But his smile faded. "I'm just sorry you had to get involved in such a dark business. I would much rather you two were out having a good time. But if you're sure, I would like to ask you a few questions. Let me get Julian and I'll meet you both in the library."

I took Tess up to her room to change a minute then we headed back down stairs.

"Want anything to eat," I asked as we passed the kitchen. "We might have a donut somewhere around here," I said laughing.

"Shh, someone might hear you," Tess said in a whisper swatting at me. "And no, I'm fine. Maybe I'll grab something later."

"Somebody say donut," Julian asked coming around the corner.

Tess just rolled her eyes, "No, Aidan is just teasing me. I think he has some secret desire for donuts."

"Well I have some secret desire for donuts.," Julian said.

"Come on, you can look for donuts later," Rachel said taking his arm as we all went into the library.

Dad was standing at the end. He waved his hand and a fire leapt up in the fireplace. Tess's eyes were as big as saucers when she saw it. She just stared at the fire. Dad noticed her intent look. "Sorry Tess, it looked like you were cold. Shall I put it out?"

"No, No its wonderful. It's just I am still getting used to how things work around here. I've only seen stuff like this in the movies."

"Well we'll try and not spring anything else on you," Dad said.

"Please everyone come in and sit down."

Just as we sat, Mora and Stefan walked in. "Come on in and have a seat, we were just getting started," Dad said.

"So Tess, why don't you tell us about this shop where you work."

"Ok," she said. I could tell she was trying not to be nervous.

"Un, like Aidan said earlier, I work at a shop called Exquisite Antiques down near Jackson Square. It's a small shop, we carry mostly old jewelry, some artwork, and some old books. There is also some small furniture items, nothing too fancy. The owner has warehouse where he keeps larger items, especially furniture. I've been working there about ten months."

"The man that attacked you and Aidan, had you ever seen him before?" Dad asked.

"Aidan asked me the same question and originally I didn't think so. But after I thought about it more I did remember a man that looked something like him. Only this man was very well dressed. He came into the store a couple of weeks ago. All I remember is that he asked about our jewelry collection. Like I told Aidan, he left before we had a chance to talk. I was busy with a prior customer and I thought he just didn't want to wait. I think he took one of my cards."

"I have some photographs I would like for you to look at and see if you recognize anything."

"Sure," she said. Dad got up and moved to one of the tables. The materials we had gathered so far in the case were spread out. He pulled several of the photos out. One of them was the one that had a picture of the Shadow in it.

He pointed to the photos. "You recognize any of these pieces?"

Tess looked down and studied it for a minute. "Yes," she said nodding, pointing to the picture of the Shadow. "I've seen one that looks like that."

Dad looked up at Julian.

"What color was it?" Julian asked.

"The center stone was a deep red crystal. It was embedded in a disk that had gold and silver swirls around it. "

Dad nodded. "You're sure?"

"Yes, that's the piece. It would be hard to forget. The owner was very particular about it, I know because I packed it for him before he left."

Dad had an alarmed look on his face, "You touched it?"

"Yes, when I was packing it. He had to go back to the warehouse and asked me to pack his travel satchel. You know it's weird, my memory of it is a little foggy. I do remember the owner told me to be very careful, that it was very old and and fragile. He told me to just leave it in the plastic case it was in. He said that piece had a history of bringing terrible luck to it's owners. He thought it had a curse on it. I thought he was just being dramatic."

She paused a minute remembering, a far off look in her eyes.

"I went into the store room to get several pieces to pack but when I turned around I dropped the case and the piece fell out so I picked it up."

She paused again a minute just staring into space. It was like she was in a trance.

Her hand went cold. "Tess," I said.

"What," she said startled.

I looked at Dad and Julian, beginning to get worried.

"You feel ok? You were talking about the jewelry," I asked.

"Yes, uh funny I remember picking it up and the next thing I remember I was in the front of the store. When I checked on it, it was in its case in his satchel. I don't remember how it got there."

Dad reached over and took her hand. "Tess, I think this is the artifact we have been seeking all this time. It would be very helpful for us to know what happened. I would like to go into your mind for just a minute and look at your memory. You won't feel a thing, would that be alright?"

She hesitated just a minute.

Dad smiled, "I promise, I won't look at any other memories."

She blushed a minute and said, "Ok, not sure what you'll find in there."

"Don't worry I have done this many times before," he said.

"What do I have to do ?" she asked.

"Just sit back and relax"

She sat back and he took both her hands in his. She sat very still and silent.

He leaned in slightly and was quiet as he started then suddenly he took a sharp in take of breath. At that moment Tess's face took on a look of fear. Her hand began to shake just a little and she began to turn her head. "No," she said.

"Dad," I said.

"Wait Aidan, she is in no danger," he said.

"No, No, it's cold, it's cold," she said. Her body began to twist.

"Dad stop, this is hurting her," I said.

"Wait I see it," he said.

"No, it's cold, it hurts," she said.

Her eyes flew open but they were not looking at us, they were unfocused, distant, seeing something in her mind. She shuddered then let out a terrified scream. "NO!" and then she fainted.

Dad let go and I immediately took her in my arms.

"I told you to let go. What did you do to her," I yelled.

Dad was breathing hard. "It wasn't me son. It was her memory. This is much worse than I thought."

He looked up, "Rachel go get Sophie. I wish Grace were here but Sophie can help."

"Right away Marcus," she said running from the room.

Tess was still mumbling as I held her, "Cold, cold" was all she kept saying.

My mind was racing. "What happened to her, is she going to be ok?" I asked.

"Yes just give her a few minutes. The memory shocked her. It was Magnus, I felt his presence," Dad said.

"Dad, how is that possible? He's been dead for centuries."

"Remember Aidan, the Shadow holds his essence. His power its still trapped in that crystal."

He looked at Julian shaking his head.

"I'm sorry Aidan. When Tess touched that crystal, the essence of Magnus, his spirit that is trapped in there fed on her. He drained her of some of her life force. That's why I was concerned when she said she touched it. These kinds of artifacts are cursed and for good reason, oftentimes the victim doesn't survive the encounter. She is very lucky Aidan."

"Is she going to be alright?" I asked pain in my voice.

"Yes, she should be fine. There was no lasting damage. Sophie will give her something that will ease the trauma and help her to sleep. There should be no long term effect, but she needs to rest."

Julian put his hand on Dad's shoulder. "Are you alright Marcus?"

"Yes," he said shaking his head. "In the memory, I saw her pick up the crystal. It came alive when she touched it, its inner light red and glowing. A dark fog flowed out of it. I could see his dark tendrils swirl about her as he fed on her. Her aura still has wounds from his claw marks embedded in it. This is a vile and evil thing, Julian and it has gotten more so over the years. We have to find this thing and and cleanse it once and for all."

"Aidan, there is one thing," Dad said.

"What's that?" I asked.

"Tess now has a connection to the Shadow, a link that we could potentially use."

I shook my head, "No, absolutely not. I am not having her exposed to any more of this. She has had enough. I won't allow it. She has nothing to do with this."

"Alright son. You're right, no more."

Tess stirred, "No, I want to help," she said in a small voice, her eyes beginning to open.

A wave of relief washed over me. "You feel ok?" I asked.

"Yes, what happened?"

"You fainted," I said as she tried to pull away and get up.

Dad reached down and took her arm, "Hold on Tess, take it easy, go slow."

She sat up. "Oh crap, not again. I always seem to be fainting around you Aidan," she said.

"She fainted before?" Dad asked.

I nodded, "Yes, the night with the werewolf, Tess hit her head and fainted. I had to take her to the hospital."

"Why didn't you call me?"," Dad asked.

"I didn't know what to do," I confessed.

I put my arm around her, "But Dad's right. You need to gather your strength. Can I get you anything?"

She snuggled up against me, still a little groggy, "I could go for one of those donuts now, and a big cup of coffee to warm up," she said trying to smile.

"I'll get you a dozen," Julian said.

At that point Rachel and Mom came in. "Tess, Rachel told me you fainted. Let's get you upstairs"

"I'll take her," I said.

I carried her upstairs and laid her in her bed. Everyone crowded in her room. Even Stefan seemed worried about her. Mom mixed up some herbs from some of Grace's jars and gave her a drink.

"Uh, thats pretty awful Mrs Croft," Tess said taking a sip.

"I know sweetie but it will help you," Mom said.

"Go on, drink it," I said.

She squished up her nose but finally finished it. She blinked her eyes, "I feel a little sleepy," she said.

Mom smiled, "You go on to sleep, dear. It'll give you sweet dreams."

Tess fell fast asleep. Dad came over and placed his hand on her head. He closed his eyes. He stood like that for several moments.

He opened his eyes. "I placed a protective spell around the memory and I put a healing spell on her wounds. She's young Aidan and quite strong. She has a very vibrant spirit, it will heal in no time."

"Thank You," I said.

He put his hand on my arm, "She's part of the family now Aidan."

I tucked her in as they started to leave. "I'll watch her," I said sitting on the bed.

My emotions were raging all over. I was furious at what had happened to her, mad at myself for bringing her into all this, elated that she was going to be ok, pissed off at my Dad for waking her memories but grateful that he healed her. I would have to talk her out of any more encounters like that one. I didn't want her anywhere near that evil artifact again.

She slept for two hours. Mom and Dad checked on her a couple of times. Julian and Mora got back with a dozen donuts. At one point Rachel was pacing in the room.

"Rachel, please go down stairs, you are making me nervous," I said gruffly.

"You know for once you bring something good into this house and first thing you and your dad have to do is knock her out. I don't know who is more stupid, you or him. I could crown you both."

She stopped and said, "I'm worried about her too Aidan."

I could see I was being unfair. I softened my voice, "I'm sorry Rachel. Come sit with us." I patted the bed next to Tess.

She smiled and sat on the other side of her.

We sat there for about five minutes just watching her.

"She really is something, isn't she Rachel?"

"That she is Aidan. She's good for you, I'm glad to see you happy." At that point Tess started to wake up.

"Hey beautiful," I said as she opened her eyes.

"Hey you," she said back yawing. I reached down and gave her a quick kiss.

"How you feel," I asked.

"Like sleeping beauty being kissed by Prince Charming," she said.

"He's no prince," Rachel said laughing, "More like the toad."

"Hi Rachel," Tess said sitting up. "How long was I out?"

"About three hours," she said.

"Wow, what did your Mom give me?"

"A sleeping potion, what else," I said smiling.

Tess rubbed her eyes. "I'm starving," she said.

"Good, thats a good sign," Rachel said nodding. "Come on lets go downstairs. Julian went out and got you a whole dozen donuts and Sophie made some soup."

"Oh that sounds wonderful," Tess said.

"You want me to carry you down?" I asked.

"No, I'm ok. I'm not quite ready for you to carry me over a threshold," she said.

Now it was my turn to be embarrassed.

"Just kidding I can make it on my own."

She stood up a little wobbly.

"Boy, that was some powerful stuff your mom gave me," Tess said rubbing her head.

"Well she is a witch," I said.

"Right," Tess said slowly.

We headed down stairs and straight into the kitchen.

"You feeling better Tess?" Mom asked.

"Much better thank you, Mrs Croft."

"Hungry?" Mom asked. "Yes a little," she replied.

"I just made some soup, how about a bowl?" Mom asked.

"I would love some," Tess said.

She sat at the bar and Mom gave her a big bowl of chicken noodle soup. The smell filled the kitchen. It brought back memories for me. It was my favorite growing up. I could see that Tess loved it as much as I did back then.

"It's good to see you up and eating, Tess," Dad said.

"Thank you Marcus, I feel much better now."

"Tess I am very sorry about what happened. I didn't intend for anything to hurt you," Dad said.

"It's ok. I know that's not what you intended but I don't understand what I saw. I just remember being very,very cold."

"When I looked at your memory, you relived it. It must have been very frightening for you."

"Yes, it was. So what actually happened to me?" she asked with some hesitation in her voice.

Dad looked at me "It's ok go on and tell her," I said.

"I am not sure what Aidan has told you about our past but years ago there was a very powerful and evil sorcerer named Magnus. Years before we met him, he found a crystal that we think our ancestors created. He corrupted the crystal and transformed it into a very evil instrument. He projected part of his power into this crystal, we call it his shadow. In a very real way a part of him is still in that crystal. When you picked up the artifact, that shadowy presence woke and it stole some of your energy. Th cold you felt was its touch."

"Will I be alright?" she asked, her voice shaking just a bit.

"Yes you should be fine. It's healing, it'll just take a little time. I wove some additional healing magic around where it touched you. I'll also have Grace check when she gets back. But there should be no long term effects."

She got up and hugged Dad. "Thank you so much Marcus."

He smiled and said, "I was happy to do it, Tess."

She let go of him and turned around "Thank you too Mrs. Croft. The soup was wonderful."

"I am glad you enjoyed Tess. But please call me Sophie."

"How about some dessert?" Julian asked.

"I guess I could have a little," Tess said.

"Great! I couldn't wait to get into the donuts," Julian said jumping up and heading to the cabinet. He came back with a large box.

Mom poured Tess a cup of coffee and Rachel, Julian and Tess each had one.

"Nothing like em," Julian said licking his fingers.

"They are good, thank you very much Julian. As good as the ones Aidan gave me," Tess said winking at me.

She took another sip of coffee. "Marcus, you know I meant what I said," Tess said looking at Dad.

"I want to help. I'll do whatever is necessary so that thing never hurts anyone else again."

"Tess, that's a very gracious offer but I think you need to rest. We can talk about that in the morning," I said.

"Aidan's right, we can discuss all this in the morning. Its been a long day for you, Tess. How about tonight we all just relax."

"Hey how about a movie," I said.

"Great idea," Dad said. So after cleaning up we all walked down to the entertainment room.

I scanned through the movies we could rent. After a few minutes Tess stopped me at 'The Proposal'.

"Have you see this one?" she asked.

"No, not exactly my genera," I said.

"It's wonderful, just what he needs," Rachel said.

"The Proposal it is then," Julian said.

Tess snuggled up next to me and all of us watched the movie.

As it played and everyone laughed, I felt then that life was perfect, that for this one moment everything I loved was safe and happy.

At the end of the movie we all got up to leave.

"Thank you again, Marcus, Sophie. I can't express how grateful I am for both of you taking such good care of me," Tess said.

"You are part of the family now Tess. Sleep well," Mom said.

"I will you too," she said.

Everyone else said good night and she and I went up stairs.

I followed her up the stairs and into her room. I laid down on her bed.

"What are you doing, Aidan?" she asked one eyebrow raised.

"After today, I'm not letting you out of my sight. I am going to stay right here."

I patted the bed next to me.

"Shh," said said in a whisper, "What will your parents think?"

"I don't care what anybody thinks, I am not leaving you alone."

"Ok," she said heading into the bathroom. In a few minutes she came back out wearing a pair of pajama bottoms and a tank top. She laid down and I put a blanket over her. She put her head on my shoulder.

"I'm glad your here. That was very scary today," she said.

"I'm so sorry Tess. I had no idea that would happen. Believe me, I am never going to let you near anything like that again."

"Aidan it's not your fault. I was just I was so cold and I couldn't get away. I felt so helpless. It was worse than the werewolf."

"I know, I felt helpless too."

She raised up. "You know, what's incredible? I was up to my neck in this stuff all along and didn't even know it. I just can't get over it, that all this was happening and I was blind to it. It's just crazy."

She laughed a minute, "Of course if someone had told me that I would be watching a movie with three vampires and four witches, I would think they were the crazy one."

"Well I would agree that that's just a little out there."

She laid back against my chest.

"Thanks for staying with me, Aidan. I don't know what I would do without you."

"I am always going to be here Tess. As long as you want me, I'll be here."

She fell fast asleep in my arms.

Chapter 11

I want to help

Croft Home, Muir Woods

Breakfast started with an argument. Tess and I were sitting on the verandah next to the pool. She had gotten up about six and after a run on the treadmill and a shower had grabbed a bagel and a cup of coffee and met me outside.

It was quiet, the morning dew still on the plants.

"Did you sleep ok?" I asked.

"Wonderful, especially next to you," she said.

I smiled, "So what would you like to do today? I am sure Rachel would jump at the chance to take you shopping."

She put down her coffee cup.

"Maybe later but first I promised to help your Dad."

"Tess listen, I don't want you involved in any more of this. I know you want to help but Dad and Julian can handle it."

"What, you don't think they need my help or that a mere human could help them?"

I frowned, "No that's not it at all."

"Well that's what it sounds like to me," she said.

"But that's not what I meant. You're twisting my words." I could see I was being out maneuvered and quickly.

"Then what did you mean?"

"Tess I just don't want you exposed to any more of this. That episode last night completely freaked me out. I just don't want anything to happen to you. I am not putting you in any more danger."

"Aidan listen, I know you are just looking out for me, that you are trying to protect me. I know you do it because you care for me, that you don't want me involved."

She hesitated a moment. "But I am involved in this, I'm involved up to my neck in it. I have to see this thing to the end. I want to stop this, this thing before it hurts anyone else."

She took another sip of coffee.

She took my hand, "I might not be a magical being like you. But I'm determined and I know a few things. I think I could really help out here. So for once, just once, let me do something for you ok? Let me help out. It's important to me. I really need to do this. Your family has been so wonderful to me, I want to help them."

She smiled and took a bite of bagel. "Besides, I'll just get Rachel to help me if you don't."

"You are stubborn and devious," I said with a slight smile on my lips.

"So does this mean you will let me help out ?"

I took a deep breath. "Well it doesn't look like I can stop you, especially if you get Rachel involved. But no more trances or mind reading. You can talk all you want but nothing that will put you in any real danger."

"Real danger, got it," she said.

She reached over and kissed me.

"Thank you, this means a lot to me," she said smiling taking another sip of coffee.

"Did I over hear something about shopping ?" a voice asked.

It was Rachel at the door. She had a cup of coffee in one hand and a basket of rolls in another.

"How long have you been there?" I asked.

"Long enough to see you trapped and bagged," she said laughing. I was definitely getting the raw end of the deal here.

"I was not bagged!," I started to say.

"Whatever," Rachel said.

Tess reached over and took my hand, "Yes we would love to go shopping later," she said winking at me. "Come on join us for breakfast. The view is wonderful."

Rachel sat down.

"Thank you Tess. I can never get Mr. grumpy pants here to go anywhere," Rachel said pointing at me, "And we would have so much fun."

"Sounds like a great time," Tess said smiling taking another bite of bagel.

Rachel dropped her smile, "I am sorry about yesterday, Tess. That must have been very frightening. I can't imagine how you must have felt."

Tess was very quiet. "Yes it was very frightening. I felt so helpless. But I think the worst part is that I didn't remember it until now. I had all this inside of me and just didn't know it. That's what I can't seem to get out of my mind."

Rachel nodded and reached over and patted her arm. "Well we are all here for you now Tess. Now that we know, we can deal with it. Believe me, I can relate to having something inside that you don't understand."

Tess nodded, "Your transformation? Aidan said it was unusual."

Rachel sat back in her chair, "Yes, it happened so long ago and yet it seems like yesterday."

"How was it, if you don't mind me asking," Tess said.

"There is nothing to compare it to," Rachel said shaking her head as she looked off into the distance.

"It was the summer of eighteen ninety five. I remember it was hot and humid that summer in Baltimore. I was barely seventeen, the only daughter in our family. We lived in a huge estate that my grandfather had built. He had made a fortune in banking and my father had carried on the business. I remember being so sheltered there, behind the beautifully manicured grounds."

Rachel smiled, "Looking back, I know the changes really started in the spring of that year, in little things, things I saw, things I heard. Doors and windows that opened on their own, lamps that flamed with no effort. By that summer, objects in my room were beginning to move by themselves. And the visions; I was beginning to have visions of far away events. Some were beautiful but many were very violent. I saw terrible crimes as they were committed. The visions would wake me screaming at night."

"By then, by summer, they were beginning to be afraid, my family I mean. The didn't understand but they knew instinctively that something was wrong, that I was changing. They began to avoid me and I grew more reserved. I stopped leaving the house and stayed in my room. My only friend was my brother, David who was next in age to me. We had always been close and he never seemed to care about the odd happenings. I think he just over looked them. If it wasn't for him, I probably would have hanged myself."

She stopped and sipped her coffee. "While my friends were attending balls and looking for husbands, I was at home with my books and my secrets. My mother of course was beside herself. I was such an embarrassment to her. She had come from one of Baltimore's oldest and most socially connected families. All her friend's daughters were either newly married, engaged or had great prospects."

"But her poor, odd Rachel. No prospects; what husband would want such a strange girl. Mother grew resentful, angry and her anger drove me to my own. The final straw was the voices. I could read the minds of those around me. I saw their fear and her disappointment. One night after a bout of drinking, she came into my room screaming. She had received the wedding invitation of yet another of her friends's daughters. She yelled and screamed, threw the invitation in my face, said how embarrassed she was. Said I was ungrateful, that I would never live up to my breeding. I screamed back and my father came in yelling in her defense."

"As he raved at me, I saw in his mind that he was being unfaithful to my mother and with that very friend. I screamed the sordid details at both of them. I told them I would tell everyone and then we would see who was the social embarrassment. David came in and tried to defend me, to protect me. Father struck him and in that moment of rage my power came into its own. I levitated my father, held him in the center of the room. Then I threw him up against my mother's prize china. All I remember was the horrified look on David's face as he fled."

"That very night they came took me. My father and some of his friends came with guns. They had the servants tie me up and hide me in a coach. Father told them that I had gone insane and attacked him.

They took me straight away to an institution outside of town. That night I cried to go home, that I was sorry, that I would never do it again but no one came. The next few days, David tried several times to see me but they would not let him in."

"I was there three weeks. In the third week, an orderly tried to rape me. I knew it when he came into my room, I saw the intention in his mind. When he tried to grab me, I used my mind to throw him against the wall. I reached into his mind and compelled him to take me out of the ward. I had him find me clothes and take me to the front of the building, near the gate. When I was ready, I had him walk to the third floor balcony and jump off. He screamed as he fell and broke his leg. In the confusion that followed, I simply walked out. No one paid me any attention."

"I went by my house but David was not there. I read the minds of the servants. My mother had told everyone that I was dead, that I had hanged myself in my cell. When David heard the story, he and father had a terrible fight. Father threw him out and he left town."

"I thought about many things that night, of revenge, of finding David. But I knew then that my life there was over. I knew I was different, that no one would understand. It was painful but I realized that it was better that David thought that I was dead. That night, I broke in and stole some money from my fathers bank. I took the next train headed north and I never looked back."

"It was hard at first but I survived and found ways to make money with my talents. I could locate objects for people, recover stolen jewelry. I gave advice to gamblers for part of their earnings. Over the next few years, I gathered my own wealth and soon I had my own establishment. One night after staying behind to count the money, I left work alone. I remember it was cold and the moon was very full. I locked up and walked down an alley to the road that led to my small house."

She took another sip. "As I walked I felt an odd presence. I stopped and turned around but there was nothing there. I turned and had walked just a bit little farther when I felt the presence again. I could not see it but I felt its mind and in that mind I saw only one thing; an overwhelming thirst, an insatiable desire for blood. Then I saw him as he flowed down the side of a building like a shadow. I had never seen such a creature, pale as the moon light. I was frightened but I couldn't move. When he reached the street, he stood up and walked towards me."

She smiled, "Of course, he was not expecting what happened next nor was I. When he reached for me, I used my power to fling him back against the building but because I was so intent on the vampire, I had not felt the other presence tracking him. Julian was just turning the corner when I let released my power so I ended up throwing the vampire right into him. Stefan was right behind him."

"Quite a fight broke out. I thought at first that they were just fighting over me, over who was going to devour me. I started to turn and run but when I touched Julian's mind, I saw it was just like mine. I realized that I was not alone, that there were others like me. I discovered that he was simply trying to rescue me. Julian and Stefan fought the vampire and he finally ran off. After I calmed down, Julian took me to meet Marcus. The coven took me in and I have been with them ever since."

Tess wiped the corner of her eye, "My god Rachel. How did you survive all of that?"

"I had no other choice. It was move forward or go insane and I was too stubborn to go mad so I survived. The coven became my family and in that I regained everything I lost. So in the end it worked out for me."

Rachel took another sip of coffee.

"Well enough about me, how about you Tess. Do you have a family?"

Tess told her about her upbringing and her brothers. She told her about Nick and Karen and Austin.

Rachel said, "Let me get this right. Aidan was a babysitter for your young nephew?"

"Yes, Austin loves him. He plays with him all the time."

"This man, right here, probably the strongest vampire I have ever seen he's a baby sitter."

"Thats the one."

"Well I guess hell can freeze over now because I have seen everything, Aidan playing with a human child."

"Aidan can be quite sweet when he wants to," Tess said.

"Come on Tess, you are ruining the image," I said with a wink.

At that point, Julian came outside.

"What's going on?" he asked.

"Rachel was just telling us how you two met," Tess said.

"Oh you mean how she tried to kill me with a vampire," he said as he sat down.

"I did not," Rachel said, "You were just too stupid to get out of the way."

She reached over and gave him a kiss, "But you did rescue me."

"Smartest thing I've ever done, tangling with that vampire," Julian said.

"You have big plans for today Tess?" Julian asked as he reached over and picked up a roll.

"I think the girls are going into the city to shop," I said.

Tess said, "After I talk to your Dad."

"Tess, really do you have to do that this morning?" I asked.

"Yes, we went through that earlier and you agreed."

"So there's going to be no talking you out of this, is there?"

"Not today," she said smiling.

"Alright, let's go on and get it over with. When you're finished, we'll go find him" I said.

They finished up their breakfast and all four of us walked into Dad's office as he was studying the book we found.

He looked up, "Didn't remember calling for the calvary," he said smiling.

"Tess insisted on helping out this morning," I said.

"Well given the progress I am making, I could use her help."

"Anything I can do Marcus?" Tess said.

"Please everyone come in and sit down. Coffee?" he asked.

Tess nodded yes. He smiled and poured her and himself another cup.

"So Tess, tell me some more about the shop and the owner. We didn't get much chance to discuss that last night," he asked.

"It's a small shop. Like I said, the owner deals mostly with jewelry, books, small items. Nothing fancy."

"Who's the owner ?"

"He's a older gentleman named Peter Moreau. He told me he came to the US from France about 20 years ago. Quiet, generally keeps to himself, speaks perfect English. I've never met anyone in his family, I think they are all back in France. I believe he lives alone here. He travels back about three times a year. Returns with new items for the store. Very nice man, always brings the staff back a present. Like I told Aidan, he's gone back now."

"Do you think he had any idea what he had?"

"Uh, hard to say. I don't think so. There was nothing strange about him, just kept to himself. Had a very dry sense of humor. "

"Did he say anything unusual when he left?"

Tess thought a minute. "Now that you ask, one thing he said was a little odd. He said he was going to right an old wrong. He said that he was taking something home, back to where it belonged. I thought he meant he was taking something from the store to his house but I suppose it could have had another meaning. I thought at the time he was a little sad."

"Do you know where in France he was going?"

"No he never told me."

"Did he leave a forwarding address?"

"No, he wanted respect for his privacy. He would call sometimes."

"Did he leave a number?"

She shook her head, "Sorry all my answers seem to be no but no, he never left his number."

"Thats fine. When did he leave?"

"About three days ago."

Dad looked at Julian, "Lets run some checks on him, use our Paris contacts. Let's see if we can track down his calling address. Julian perhaps we should use some of your shipping contacts and see if we can find out where his flight took him."

"Good idea Marcus."

"Thank you Tess, you have been very helpful."

"Marcus can I ask you a question?"

"Of course, anything."

She pointed to the items on the table. "Can you explain what all of this is?"

"Dad," I said.

"Aidan I just asked your Dad a question, no danger in that."

I let out a long sigh, I could see that it was a losing battle.

"Alright but just the facts. I don't want her messing with anything."

"I promise I won't mess with anything. Please go on Dr. Croft, I mean Marcus," she said shooting me an irritated look.

He took her over to the table. "Up to now we have have found four pieces of evidence."

'We have a recovered journal that gives us some facts but is partially encoded. Second, we have a scrap of the same journal that Julian recovered from a friend. We have some photographs which I showed you last night and we have a far seeing mirror. Our chore is to put all of this together."

"Is that the Journal?"

"Yes"

"May I see it?"

"Tess," I said.

"I'm not messing with it, I just want to look at it. Maybe you should just go for a walk or something."

She was so stubborn. "No, I'll just sit here. Somebody has to watch you."

Dad had a smile on his face as he opened the Journal to the end and handed it to her. "See the numbers. There are several pages of them, followed by the torn page that Julian found and then more numbers."

"So you need both pieces to read the code."

"Exactly, but we have not been able to decipher it."

She turned back to the beginning of the encoding. There was just a series of numbers. Periodically the rows of numbers were broken by a diagram.

"I'm not an expert but I think I might know what this code is, at least partially."

"What?" I said.

"My Father, when he was in the army, served in military intelligence before he went to medical school. One summer he got me interested in cryptography and we took a class. One of the cyphers we studied looked like this. It was a long series of numbers and to decode it you translated the numbers into letters"

Dad nodded, "We've tried several different combinations without success. I even had some of Julian's people look at it. They thought there was some type of enhanced encryption involved. They did a pretty deep analysis and there did not seem to be any patterns."

Tess nodded, "In some cyphers you have to have a key. One we studied used a text as the key. I don't remember the name of the cypher but basically you use a number as an index into some random piece of text. The text gives you a word or character. Thats how you translate it."

Tess handed the book back to Dad.

Julian said, "We didn't try that Marcus, we were looking for something more sophisticated."

Tess said, "The key can be any text. A book, a poem, a letter. For books, the series of numbers represent a chapter, a page, a line, and a letter on that line, so each four numbers represent a letter. But you have to have to have the text, otherwise there is no way to translate the code."

Dad thought a moment. "Julian when Jakob handed you the fragment, what exactly did he say."

"He pushed the fragment into my hand then rambled some gibberish."

"I mean his exact words."

"He said find the twins, that we were in grave danger. He said that only together was it strong enough. Then he rambled something about an old book."

"Could it mean something else, could you have have misunderstood him?" Dad asked.

"What do you mean?"

"Is it possible he was giving you a message, trying to tell you something?"

"I don't think so, but we should ask Stefan, I was a little preoccupied, perhaps he heard something different. He was standing right next to us," Julian said.

I said, "I'll go up and get him."

I ran upstairs and got Stefan and Mora. When we got back we all sat around the table in Dad's office.

"Stefan what exactly did Jakob say when he gave Julian the fragment?"

"I was standing next to him but it was very faint. I remember he whispered Old Book. It seemed like gibberish to me.'"

Dad thought for a moment, "Julian you knew Jakob the best. Could this be a reference to something else?"

"No, nothing that I can think of," Julian said shaking his head but he paused a minute and said, "Jakob was a well known translator as well as an architect and mathematician."

Dad thought a minute. "He said the phrase old book?"

"Yes, he said old book but in German. I thought he was hallucinating and speaking in his original language but perhaps he meant an old book in German."

"Thats a little odd," Tess said.

"Whats that?" Dad said turning towards her.

"German. Mr Moreau, the owner of the store, he kept a book on his desk. I saw it there once when I was was looking for some shipping labels. It was a beautiful illustrated leather book. He showed it to me and I remember it looked very old but I couldn't read it. He said that was because it was in Old German. He said it was his favorite book, that a very dear friend gave it to him a long time ago."

"Tess can you still get into the store?" Julian asked.

"Yes I have a key. I am supposed to be picking up the mail."

"Wait, wait just a damn minute," I said. "Tess is not going anywhere near that store."

Tess looked at me. "Aidan you're being too cautious. You know that I've been there several times. Besides he took the piece with him remember? There's nothing there that can hurt me."

She took my arm, "Besides, I know you will be there to protect me."

"I don't want you to be in a place where that is necessary," I said.

"We'll you're not going without me. I know where everything is," she said.

"She does have a point, and we will all be there," Mora said.

"Thank you for being reasonable Mora," Tess said.

Again I was out gunned.

"Alright but I am not letting you out of my sight. And I want everyone, Stefan Mora, Rachel and Julian. I want all the protection we can get."

"Are you sure, Aidan?" Dad asked.

"Not really but I don't see that I have much choice," I said nodding towards Tess.

"Just promise me that you won't let anything else happen to her."

Dad nodded, "We'll look after her, don't worry son," Dad said.

"Then what are we waiting for?" Tess said.

"You are impossible," I said shaking my head as we left the room.

The drive back down town went quickly. Tess tried to cheer me up but I wasn't buying it. She could tell that I was upset.

She tried to reassure me. "I promise, we'll just go in and out and I won't leave your side."

"I'll just be happy when this is done and you're back at the house," I said.

Rachel said, "Why don't you put on some of your happy music."

"Happy music?" Tess asked with a quizzical look.

"I got razzed by the happiness police here for listening to some of the music you put on my phone"

"I was not razzing you. I was just surprised by your sudden improved taste in music.," Rachel said smiling.

I smiled a little at that, "See you can smile," Tess said.

"Oh alright," I said and I turned on my iphone. The sound of 'Young Blood' by the Naked and Famous filled the car.

"Now thats more like it," Rachel said.

We pulled up into the small parking lot and everyone got out of the cars. We were quite a sight, a human leading three vampires and three witches. It was a older, victorian style building. Tess quickly went to the front door and opened it and we walked in.

The store appeared bigger once we were inside. There were several glass cases full of jewelry. Bookcases filled with old books were arranged in one corner. Along the other wall were paintings and some small statues. Off to the side was another room with furniture.

"His office is in the back," Tess said.

She opened the wide wooden door and we all walked into a large well decorated office. The walls were paneled with a dark wood and expensive furniture was arranged around the room. Against one wall was a large bookcase with leather bound books. On the far end was a giant wooden desk.

Tess went to the desk, "The book is gone, it's not here," she said.

"Look around a minute, perhaps he moved it", Dad said.

"Lets check the bookcase," I said.

Tess and I looked over the titles.

Behind us, Rachel stood staring at the bookcase.

"There is something behind this wall," she said.

Julian went over. He passed his hands several times over the books.

"Here," he said pulling a book out. Behind it was a latch. He pulled on the latch and part of the bookcase swung out like a door. A dark passageway was behind it.

"Oh my God, I didn't know that was there," Tess said just staring at the door.

Julian said, "we might as well check it out." The opening led to a small flight of circular stairs. I took Tess's hand, "Stay right next to me."

"Don't worry," she said, "I can't believe this is here, as many times as I've been in this room."

We all walked down the stairs which at the bottom let out in into a large dark room.

Rachel stopped just as she entered.

"Marcus," she said.

"I know, I feel it too," he said. He turned on the light. The room was a store room. There were chests and old furniture scattered about.

He continued, "There's definitely something hidden here. Look in the chests or maybe a cabinet."

We went from item to item but found nothing. The chests had some old clothes along with some china. One had some books but not the one we were looking for.

It looked like a dead end.

"I don't see anything here," I said.

Rachel shook her head "Nor do I."

I took Tess's hand and started to move to the stairs. I turned around and saw Dad staring at a huge standing closet. The doors were open but it was empty inside.

"Dad", I said.

"There is something about this cabinet. I think there is something behind it."

"Here, let a thief look," Julian said.

He stepped inside and looked around. He felt the edges. On the front was a small drawer. He pulled the drawer open and put his hand in.

"Ah, here it is," he said.

He pulled on something and the back of the closet swung inward. There was another room behind it.

"Come on," Julian said.

The room seemed to be cut right out of the stone. Symbols were carved into the stone walls. The room was empty except for a door on the other side.

"My God, Marcus", Rachel said as she stepped across the threshold.

Dad nodded, "The whole room is sealed. He was definitely hiding something here."

There was a strange feeling to the room, like an undercurrent of something powerful, something hidden. The room seemed to be charged with electricity.

Dad said, "This room is covered in spells, powerful enchantments. A very powerful witch has been working magic here. We need to be very careful. Don't touch the walls."

We all circled Tess in the center of the room.

Dad opened the door on the far side. A long flight of stairs went straight down. Julian lit some witch flame in his palm and we followed him and the light down.

The stone stairs finally let out into a another much larger room.

Dad gestured with his hand and candles around the room lit up. Stone work lined the walls and in the dim light I could see a circle etched into the floor. To one side was a table that contained small tools and several crystals. A book was lying next to them.

The electric feel to the air was stronger here. The air almost seemed to hum.

Rachel said, "Very powerful magic was practiced here."

Tess pointed, "That's the book, there on the table."

Dad held out his hands and a large book floated over to him. He left it floating right in front of him.

"I'll never get used to that," Tess whispered.

Dad closed his eyes and a blue light swirled around his hands. The light floated over to the book and surrounded it. It swirled for a few seconds then disappeared. Dad opened his eyes and the book floated into his hands.

"It's clean now," he said.

He opened it.

"It's in German, an old book of spells. Jakob's name is at the front."

Julian went over to the table. Next to the tools was a box with a symbol engraved on it's cover. "Arius," Julian said.

Dad walked over looking at the crystals. He pointed to several of them.

"It's Arius alright. He was a master of crystal magic. The best at the academy, the best I have ever seen," Dad said shaking his head. "He was here all this time with the shadow. He certainly cloaked it well."

"You mean Mr Moreau was ...," Tess asked.

Dad nodded, "Yes Tess, the store above us was just a front. Your employer was one of the most powerful witches of all time. He was hiding here all along. I think he took the shadow and fled when he realized Draven's men were close."

"I wonder where he took it?" Julian asked.

Dad shook his head, "We won't know until we decipher the journal. My suspicion is that being fearful of being discovered he took it back to where he thought it would be safe, where he and Jakob hid it long ago."

A cold wind seemed to blow through the room. The candles flickered.

Dad looked around and said, "We probably should leave. We have no idea what other protective spells Arius may have left behind."

A far off sound seemed to come from the walls. It started out low but built to almost a wail. A shadowy image began to form along one wall. The room suddenly seemed to take on a menacing feel, like the walls were watching. I took Tess's hand, "Come on we're getting out of here."

As moved towards the stairs, I pushed Tess ahead of me. The image on the wall started to take on shape, a cloaked figure was forming. A cloaked arm reached out from the wall, a pale hand forming at the end. A screeching wail began to sound, an otherworldly, piecing sound. I picked up Tess and flew up the first set of stairs and then then the other. I ran out the front door. I didn't stop until we were in the parking lot, in the bright sunlight.

Tess reached over and tapped me on the arm, "Aidan, you can put we down now."

"Oh, sorry," I said. As I put her down was Mora and Stefan came out of the door, followed by Julian and Rachel. Dad was the last one out.

"I resealed everything. It was good that we left when we did, we triggered one of his protective spells."

"Is that what was on the wall ?" Tess asked.

"Yes, a guardian spell. I sealed it in behind us," Dad said.

Tess's hand was shaking a little as she took out her key.

"I'll lock up," I said taking the key from her. She nodded.

After I locked up, we all got back in the cars and headed home.

Tess was quiet on the drive back, just staring out the window. Rachel could tell the episode shook her up some. "You ok Tess?" she asked leaning forward.

Tess turned around. "Yea, I'm alright. I mean that was some scary stuff but the real thing is I can't believe that Mr Moreau was involved in all this. He was always such a kind and gentle man. He certainly hid things well. I mean I had no idea at all. That room was down there all the time. It just gives me the creeps."

"Camouflage, its one of the first things we learn," Rachel said. "Sometimes you get so caught up in it that you forget you are doing it. I am sure he never meant you any harm. Sounds like he was completely alone all this time."

"I would have gone completely bananas," Julian said.

"Me too," I added.

"Well you have me, so you'll never be alone again," Tess said taking my hand.

"You too, you old rascal," Rachel said to Julian taking his hand.

"Now aren't you being sweet," Julian said putting his arm around Rachel. "Tess I think your having a positive influence on her."

"Alright, don't push it," Rachel said with a smirk.

"So speaking of influence. Any way I could now get you to listen to me when I say that something is too dangerous," I asked Tess.

"What and miss all this excitement, not on your life," she said.

"Julian come on, help me out here," I said.

"No way I am getting in the middle of that."

"Coward," I said smiling.

"I know a fight I can't win," he said.

"Hey lets just agree to disagree and leave it at that," Tess said with a slight grin.

"I think you should listen to her Aidan," Rachel said.

I just shook my head.

When we got to the house we all went back to Dad's office. He pulled down Jakob's text, the torn page and sat the copy of the old spell book next to it. He pulled down the mirror.

He said, "Now all of the pieces fit. The path to the Shadow's location is encoded in this mirror. But the location is protected by a series of spells. Thats why we can't see anything in it. I think the spells to open the mirror are what is encoded at the end of the journal. I believe after the battle, Jakob and Arius split up. Jakob took the journal, Arius had the key in the book as well as the mirror, which he hid in yet another location. They created this elaborate structure so only someone they trusted could find the shadow."

"But then I think something unexpected occurred. For what ever reason, fear that war in Europe would reveal it or perhaps just curiosity, Arius moved the Shadow from its hiding place and secretly took it to the new world. He setup this elaborate front as an antique jewelry dealer to hide it. Years passed but somehow Draven tracked down Jakob and stole the journal. That's how Tomas got it. But Jakob kept one page safe so the text could not be translated. This one fragment he gave to you Julian."

"I think he notified Arius when the journal was lost and Arius knew he had to run because it would only be a matter of time until Draven found him. I believe Jakob gave us the fragment because he knew that Arius would need our help. He was telling us how to decipher the journal. If Arius is taking the Shadow back to its original hiding place, this will help us find him."

He paused a second, "So let's give Tess's idea a try. Julian read the numbers to me. I'll look them up. Stefan please write the letters down."

Julian opened the journal. He called out the first number. It was a four.

Dad said, "Ok, chapter 4."

Julian read the next three numbers. Dad moved to page, line, then letter.

Dad said, "It's an A."

They went through 20 more letters.

After the last one Stefan shook his head and said, "Marcus this looks wrong. I see no words here, it's just random letters."

Dad said, "Lets try a few more."

They did another fifteen. Stefan shook his head again. "It's just gibberish, I don't see any meaning at all."

Dad took a look. "I am afraid he's righ. It doesn't look like this will decipher the text. We must be missing something."

I looked at the numbers and asked, "Could the numbers need some kind of transformation before they are used?"

"You mean the numbers themselves are encoded somehow?" Dad asked.

"Its possible, we learned in our class that it was not uncommon that multiple ciphers be used," Tess said.

"But what kind of transformation ?" Julian asked.

I looked at the numbers. "I don't know but I know someone who might, someone good with numbers."

Rachel looked at me, "Oh no, Aidan, anyone but him."

"Afraid so. I think its time we talked to Henry."

"So who is Henry?" I asked.

Rachel and Mora just shook their heads.

I went down stairs and walked outside by the garden. As soon as I was outside, I dialed Henry's number.

A high pitched, young voice answered. "Aidan, Man, what's it been like three months. Hows it going?"

"Fine Henry, how are you?"

"Awesome, I just scored this new server, you know high end custom specs, just got it shipped in from Taiwan. It's a real beauty. And speaking of beauty, is Mora still with tall, pale, and boring?"

"Afraid so Henry."

"Too bad."

"Hey listen the reason I called is I have a job for you."

"Well anything for you Aidan. What's up?"

"It's an encryption. Pretty complex. Wonder if you would take a look."

"Sure, just email it to me."

"It's not that kind of encryption. Its actually an old manuscript that has some kind of manual encoding."

"Oh now you are going to make me work for a living. Sure I'll look at it but its going to cost you."

Ah always the deal with Henry.

"Ok, so what's it going to be."

I listened to Henry for a few minutes then said, "Sounds good, Thank you Henry. Meet you then."

The girls were not going to like this, not one bit.

Chapter 12

Assistance

I walked back in the house and when I sat down, Tess asked her question again. "So who is Henry?"

Rachel leaned forward from her seat, "He is the weirdest vampire you will ever meet. I mean strange, really strange. And if it has on a skirt, he is going to chase it. He is like perpetually on the move."

"Oh don't listen to Rachel. Henry is harmless," I said.

"So whats so special about Henry?" Tess asked ignoring Rachel.

"He might be a little odd, I'll give you that but he's also a math genius."

"Sounds like a strange fellow, how did you meet him?" Tess asked.

"We met eight years ago by accident. Late one evening we were down by a local hospital when I noticed a pale shape slipping into a third floor window. Stefan and I followed it and we found Henry stealing blood. We cornered him but instead of fighting he just put his hands up, I thought he was going to cry. Anyway we left the hospital and he told us his sad story."

"Twenty years earlier he had been a very promising student at Yale. He was actually something of a mathematical prodigy there. As it worked out, one of his professors was a vampire who was so impressed with Henry's talents that he wanted to preserve them forever so he changed him. But Henry never took to the vampire life. In the end, he finally fled to get away from the professor."

"When we found him Henry was scared, wretched, living in abandoned buildings and surviving on stolen blood. We took him in and taught him how to live among humans. Now he is very successful computer hacker. We check in on him from time to time. If anybody can figure out those numbers it's Henry."

"The only numbers Henry is interested in is 36-24-26," Rachel said shaking her head.

"Don't listen to her, he's not that bad. Anyway he said he would help us, we just need to do one favor."

"Oh here it comes. What do you mean we?" Rachel said.

I squirmed a minute in my seat. "Well," I paused a minute.

"Come on, spit it out, Aidan," Mora said.

"Henry's going to be at a club at nine tonight. All he wants is for us to meet him there and have a night out, go to a few clubs then he'll help us with the cyphers."

"Oh, Aidan come on, club hoping with Henry," Rachel said.

"Rachel we need his help, besides it's only a few hours."

"A night on the town would be nice," Tess said.

Rachel with a slight smile said, "Well if we have to go on the town, I'll need a new outfit. How about you Tess, Mora ?"

Oh now I see, more shopping. My penance for Henry.

"Shopping would be great, would't it Aidan? Tess said smiling at me. I could tell Rachel was almost giggling.

"Sure, it would," I said a note of resignation in my voice.

As we walked up to the club, I had to admit that the outcome of the shopping while painful was definitely worth it. The girls looked incredible. Now Rachel and Mora always looked fantastic but tonight Tess was stunning in her new red dress.

I took her arm as we got out of the car. "You look beautiful tonight," I said as we walked up to the door. She smiled, "Thanks, you're not too bad yourself" and squeezed my arm as we walked in.

"I give it less than five minutes until he makes a move," Rachel said as we walked in.

Julian said, "I say he'll go for ten."

"100 bucks and you're on," Rachel said

We gave our coats to the attendant and walked through the doors to the club. Immediately, we were greeted by a sea of people and a wall of sound. The dance floor was packed with dancers as a DJ was blaring out music. I looked around and saw at least 6 or seven bars also filled with people. There was a second floor with another set of bars and rooms. Henry said it was a very popular place.

I could see our entrance was noticed. Heads turned as we walked in. The sound of all these hearts beating was like the roar of a waterfall. With so many active humans near, this would could be a difficult place for a vampire to maintain control with the sound and smell of so much human blood.

Tess looked up and said over the blaring music, "Everything ok?"

I smiled and said in her ear, "Yea, there's just a lot of humans here. The sound of all these hearts beating is almost deafening." I motioned to Julian and pointed up, "Take everyone to that bar at the top of the stairs. Just wait there until I find Henry." I told Tess, "Go with Julian and the others, I am going to look for Henry. Just stay with Rachel and Mora and you'll be fine." She nodded and they headed up to the bar.

I made my way around the dance floor. I caught several smiles from women but I just nodded and made my way around. When I got to the far side of the dance floor, I stopped and turned as I caught the scent. Vampire. I followed it along the back wall.

I found Henry around the next turn. He was standing next to a pillar just watching the crowd.

He was dressed in an old blue jacket, jeans, and tennis shoes. He always looked so young to me, tall and lanky. His dark brown hair was flopping in all directions. He smiled a mischievous grin, like a school boy caught with the class cookies. He held out his fist for a knuckle bump. I tapped it then he hugged me.

"Good to see you Henry," I said pulling back.

"Always good to see you Aidan, where's everyone else?"

"At the bar upstairs, come on lets go find them."

We made our way up to the bar. When we got upstairs, everyone was standing at the back. Stefan with his height and white hair made them easy to spot. Henry of course made a bee line for Mora and Rachel. He hugged each one then shook hands with Julian and Stefan. I could see Stefan was not that amused. As he was shaking hands, I stepped back and put my arm around Tess. He turned around and noticed her.

He looked at me with some confusion, "Ah Aidan, what gives, you fall off the wagon or something?"

I laughed a little and said, "No, this is my friend, Tess. Tess meet Henry."

As he reached for her hand he said, "Aidan you've been holding out on me. How long have you known this beautiful creature?"

"Some time now," I said.

"Very pleased to meet you Tess," he said taking her hand.

"Its a pleasure Henry," Tess said. "I've heard many wonderful things about you."

"Well they are all true," he said laughing.

He kept ahold of her hand, "Let's all go down and try out the floor. What about it Miss Independent, would you like to dance?"

She said, "Of course, I would love too"

As we moved towards the stairs, Henry leaned over and asked me, "Does she know?"

I said, "yes, everything."

I heard Rachel lean over to Julian and say, "three minutes, you owe me a hundred."

I just shook my head.

When we got to the dance floor, Tess and Henry headed straight out. The rest of us just waited at one of the lower bars.

I watched them on the floor. My initial impression was right, Tess moved like a dancer, graceful, sinuous. But Henry, well Henry moved like Henry. More jerking and flapping than dancing but Tess seemed to not mind.

Rachel leaned over to Mora and said, "Can you imagine how he must have moved before he was a vampire?"

Mora just laughed.

After a few dances, I cut in. Rachel and Julian joined us. Mora came out on the floor and danced with Henry. Tess raised her arms and we moved across the floor.

After several more dances, Mora finally got Stefan to come out and it was Rachel's turn to dance with Henry. He was all grins and even Rachel was smiling.

We danced on and off for several more hours. Finally, around two even Henry was ready to go. Tess and I were laughing as we headed towards the front of the club.

"Well I have to admit this was really fun tonight even if it cost me a shopping trip," I said.

"Yes it was," Mora said.

"We should do this again," Tess said, "and we should invite Henry."

"She is very persuasive isn't she," Mora asked.

"Yes, yes she is," I said as we got back to our cars and followed Henry to his house.

Henry lived on the top floor of a small renovated warehouse. It was nothing to look at from the outside but it was quite nice on the inside. The entire top floor had been converted into his living area. On one side was a kitchen while the other side held a huge entertainment area.

"You have a wonderful place Henry," Tess said as we came in, hanging our coats.

"It works," he said, "The real office is down stairs. Sorry I don't have much but there are a few drinks in the frig. Grab what you want and meet me downstairs."

Tess said, "I could really use some water."

Everyone else followed Henry down while Tess and I went into the kitchen.

I opened the refrigerator. Inside were several bottles of water, a few soft drinks, and several bags of blood. I quickly pulled out a bottle of water and shut the door so Tess could not see inside.

I shut it so quickly that Tess asked, "Everything alright ?"

"Yes, fine," I said grateful that she didn't see his supply. She had seen quite enough for one day.

The downstairs was filled with computers. They were everywhere. His desk was circled with monitors. Off to one side was a small conference room circled with glass. Everyone was inside waiting.

"Henry are you hunting enough?" I asked.

With a slight look of guilt he said, "Well you know if I am working really hard, days on end," Rachel stopped him injecting, "Or playing video games." He smiled and said "Yes or sometimes playing marathon video games, I don't have time to hunt. Don't' worry it's all legit."

"Whats he's talking about," Tess asked

"Its not important, I'll tell you later," I said.

Turning in his chair Henry asked, "So you said something about encryption."

Julian pulled out copies of the journal we had made along with Arius's book.

"We think these pages are encoded with a cypher that uses this book."

"An Ottendorf cypher. Like in National Treasure."

"What?" I asked.

Henry said, "Never mind."

"He really needs to get out more," Tess remarked smiling.

Henry laughed nodding,

"You have the cypher and you have the text so the problem is?" Henry asked.

"It didn't work, we think the numbers themselves are encoded somehow," I said.

"Let me take a look," Henry said.

He looked over the numbers.

"There's no internal pattern that I can see. Let me scan it in."

He took the copies over to a scanner and scanned them. After a few seconds, they showed up on his open laptop.

"Let me run a few tests," he said. We just sat and watched him type. Tess sipped her water.

Just outside the conference room, was another entertainment area with several game consoles on it. Henry saw me eying them.

"Go on, take a look. Tess will be fine."

I went out and looked around. He had the latest gear, consoles, HD TV's, he even had a set of simulated musical instruments.

"Its Guitar Hero. You should give it try sometime," Henry said.

After a few more minutes, Henry motioned me back in.

"I can't find any internal patterns. It must be something in the book."

He looked at the old German book.

"A leather manuscript?" he asked.

"It's a long story," I said.

He glanced again at the copies of the journal.

"What are these diagrams?" he asked.

There were a series of boxes with horizontal and vertical lines on them. Some of the lines had circles drawn on them.

Henry looked at the boxes and them looked at the device I still had in my hand.

"Very clever," he said.

"What?" I asked.

"You have the key," he said.

"What do you mean I have the key?" I asked. He pointed to the device.

"Music," he said.

"Music?" I said questioning.

"These diagrams, they're a musical notation called tablature. It's a way to describe cords on a stringed instrument without writing the music itself down."

"Jakob was a musician. I can remember him often playing the lute," Julian said.

"Who's Jakob," Henry asked.

"Again, its a long story. Do you think you can use it to translate the numbers."

"Yes, I think so. The cords indicate a transformation. Steps if you will. All we need to do is apply these to the numbers."

He typed a few more minutes then the numbers on the screen changed into a whole new set. He did this for each section separated by one of the boxes. He printed out several sheets.

"Try it now," he said.

I read the numbers and Julian looked up the letters. After a few minutes he nodded. "Its working, the first line is, The path to the Shadow starts in shadow."

I gave Henry a high five. "Henry you are a genius," I said.

"Well if you say so," he said smiling.

Even Rachel looked impressed.

"And see all it cost you was a couple dances," he said smiling.

We gathered the sheets and the books and got ready to go.

"It was very nice meeting you Henry," Tess said as we were leaving.

"You too Tess, stop by anytime," he said. "And Rachel, anytime you want to party I am here," he said with a cat's smile.

She just shook her head.

"Thank you very much Henry. You have been a very big help," I said.

"Anytime, Aidan. Tell your father I said hello and don't be a stranger."

"I won't. How about I call you next week. Do a movie," I said.

"Awesome and bring Tess, she's a blast. You're one lucky man, Aidan."

"Don't I know it."

He gave us all big hugs, especially Tess and we left.

When we got back to the cars Tess said, "I thought he was nice. Not at all what I was expecting. A little odd but friendly. And very smart."

Rachel said, "Well at least we got what we were looking for, thats what's important."

"Oh Rachel, you know you had a good time," I said.

"That she did, come on admit it, Rachel," Julian said taking her arm.

"Alright, alright it was fun and Henry was a part of it. Just don't tell him I said that" she confessed.

Well at least I won one argument today.

It was almost four when we finally got home. Dad was waiting at the door. He, Julian and Stefan took the new cyphers upstairs to translate the last of the journal. The rest of us waited down stairs. Tess and Rachel fell asleep as we tried to watch TV. I threw blankets over them and took a walk with Mora. Finally about seven thirty, Dad called us all back together. This time Lucian joined us and I introduced him to Tess. She was very careful with his name. Rachel and Tess convinced Mom to make a big pot of coffee for all of us and we headed back into Dad's office. As we sat around the table, he pulled out the mirror.

Dad nervously turned it in hands and said, "I fear I was only partially correct in my prior assessment of what happened to the crystal. We were right about Jakob and Arius, they did take the shadow, to hide it from Draven and Malek. But what happened next is almost unbelievable. As I told you, Arius was a master at crystal magic. He and Jakob took the shadow to a secret location and there Arius split the crystal into two halves, one greater, one lesser; two twins."

Julian interjected, "Thats why Jakob told us to find the twins."

Dad nodded, "Yes. The crystal was too important to destroy but infected as it was with Magnus' spirit it was too dangerous to leave intact. So Arius simply divided it, separating its power. The lesser crystal, Arius took with him and it's been with him all this time. The greater crystal Jakob took and hid, even Arius did not know its final hiding place."

Julian said, "This explains something that's bothered me ever sense we saw the photograph of the crystal. I knew there was something wrong with it, I just couldn't put my finger on it. Now I see, the crystal in the photo was too small."

Dad paused a moment. "Yes, it explains many things. It's the lesser crystal that we have been chasing all this time. It's power while still incredibly strong was diminished. I think thats one reason Arius was so successful in hiding it."

He smiled and looked at Tess, "There was another benefit in splitting the shadows power. Tess only encountered the lesser one and we are all grateful for that."

I wrapped my arms tighter around her.

Dad paused a minute and then shook his head. "But I fear Jakob was not warning us about Draven; he was warning us about Arius. He is seeking vengeance after all these years of hiding. He aims to confront and kill Draven with the crystal."

"Tess thats why he told you he was going to right an old wrong, to take care of something he should have done long ago."

"I believe Jakob had a vision of what Arius was planning, that he confronted him but was unsuccessful in stopping him. Jakob then found you Julian and gave you the one item we needed to find the greater crystal. I think Jakob foresaw that Arius was going to put into motion events that will endanger us all and his final request was for us to reunite the two parts of the crystal. That's what Jakob meant by saying that only together will it be strong enough. He saw that only when the full crystal is recreated will we have the power to defeat Draven."

"It is essential that we find Arius and the larger crystal before Draven does. His evil forces have grown very strong. As strong as Arius is, he would never survive such an encounter even with the power of the smaller crystal. This is what Jakob feared, that Arius would fail and that Draven would finally possesses the means to reconstitute the full shadow again and with it he would be unstoppable."

Dad held up the mirror. "The text says that the path to the Shadow starts in shadow. The next line says the shadow is hidden and may only be found by one who has known its power. It says the path is difficult, that the seeker must prove himself worthy by passing through four tests, one for each element."

"The elements?" Tess asked.

"In ancient times, people believed that there were four basic elements, Earth, Air, Fire, and Water. They are common themes in early witchcraft writings. Jakob must have devised four tests , each one relating to one of the elements."

"Now that we have everything, we should try the spell, unlock the mirror" Julian said.

Dad said, "I agree Julian, we have no time to wait."

We all followed Dad back down to the first floor and into the library. Dad reached up and pressed a small button at the back of one of the bookcases. Part of the case swung open and we followed him down a flight of stairs.

Tess just shook her head, "What is it about you guys and bookcases."

I laughed but grabbed her arm and we followed everyone down.

We came into our coven room. As we walked in, Dad lit the candles with a wave of his hand. Like all the others, it was a stone room with a large circle etched in the ground.

Rachel and Julian, Grace and Lucian and Mom and Dad walked into the circle. Tess started to follow them. I put my hand on my shoulder and shook my head, "You should stay back with Stefan, Mora, and I. It's safer that way." She nodded and we stood next to the stone wall.

Dad chanted one tone and the etched circle lit up with a soft blue light.

He said, "Julian hold the text."

Dad took the mirror in his hands and reading the translation, started chanting. Nothing happened. He tried it again. Again nothing happened.

"You've got to be kidding," I said shaking my head.

"Did you chant it correctly ?" Stefan asked.

"Yes," Dad said. "I followed the spell exactly."

Julian said, "It's says the path to shadow starts in shadow. Perhaps you need to intone the word shadow at the beginning of the spell."

Dad tried it again. Again nothing.

"Try it in a shadow," Lucian said.

Dad waved and some of the candles went out. A shadow was cast across the floor. Dad tried it again and still nothing.

Rachel says, "Marcus, when you read us the text it said that the Shadow could only be found by one who has known its power. Did you ever actually use the crystal?"

He shook his head, "No, Magnus was very, very protective of it. He lectured about it, and sometimes would show it but no one actually held it but Magnus."

"Julian"

"No never. Like Marcus I attended several lectures Magnus gave but I only saw it when Magnus was wearing it."

"Stefan, Mora ?"

"No, it was gone before we reached him."

"How about you Lucian, or Grace or Sophie"

Mom shook her head, "No I never came close to that thing."

Lucian and Grace shook their heads.

Dad said, "You may be right Rachel. I think I understand now. Jakob intended that only someone who has the lesser crystal in their possession can find the greater one. Someone who has felt its power."

Julian said, "Then we've hit a wall Marcus. Jakob is dead and Arius is on the run with the lesser twin. So we have no way to activate the the spell."

Dad replied, "Then we'll just have to find Arius."

Lucian said, "That will never work, we'll never find him in time."

A small argument started, loud in the stone room.

In the midst of the argument I heard Tess say softly, "I'll do it."

"What?" I shouted and with that, the argument stopped and everyone turned around.

"I'll do it. I'll hold the mirror. I've touched the shadow remember, I've felt its power."

"Wait Tess, you don't need to do this. We have no idea what could happen," I said a sense of panic rising.

Dad put down the mirror and extinguished the circle. He stepped over next to her and said, "I agree Tess, we just have to find another way. We'll have to find Arius first. This could be very dangerous for you."

"I appreciate all of your concern but you are running out of time. Besides, Mr Moreau , I mean Arius, could be anywhere. You don't have another option. You have to find it first."

Dad was frowning, "Tess, I don't know what would happen if a human should attempt it it, it might not work at all."

I shook my head, "I don't want to put her in any more danger. Tess this is a terrible idea."

"Marcus," Rachel said, shaking her head.

But Tess was adamant, "Please Aidan, it's the only way. Let me try. If I could take the Shadow, I think I can take this."

She was very brave but I just couldn't stand for her to be put in danger again. I shook my head, "Tess"

She said, "You risked everything for me. Please let me do this, let me try?"

She had that look in her eye. And we needed her, this time we all needed her. Against my better judgement, I nodded yes.

Dad nodded and took Tess by the hand back into the circle. He ignited the circle and they were surround by its blue light, he handed Tess the mirror. I stood immediately outside the circle directly behind her. At the first sign of trouble I was going to break through and grab the mirror from her. She stood very still with the mirror held in both her hands.

Dad said, "Ready?" She nodded and Dad chanted the spell. Immediately the symbols on the mirror's edge began to glow blue. Within its silver surface, blue shapes began to swirl. A single low tone emanated from the mirror and a blue light shot straight up. It startled Tess. I thought for a second she was going to drop the mirror but she held it firm.

The light just swirled there floating for a few seconds then it seemed to coalesce. A three dimensional scene appeared floating above the mirror. It was a view of an old red building, with other buildings clustered around it. Water surrounded them on all sides and I saw people walking across bridges. There were boats traveling back and forth under the bridges. The building itself looked ancient, a Janus seal could be seen high on one wall. A loud hum filled the room as the picture turned.

Tess seemed mesmerized at the sight she was seeing.

"Do you recognize it?" I asked Dad over the hum.

He nodded, "Yes, its changed some but I recognize it."

"Where is it?" I asked.

"The first element must be water because the building is in Venice," he said smiling.

Chapter 13

Water and Fire

Venice, Italy

The trip was a whirlwind. Of course, I tried to keep Tess from coming with us but she simply pointed out that she had to go since she was the only one who could work the mirror. So again I lost out. A pattern was developing, one that I was growing increasingly alarmed with. I couldn't stand having her in danger but she somehow seemed destined to be right in the middle of the storm.

And a storm it was. We all rushed to get packed but there was one item we had to take care of first.

Tess was talking to Mora and I about what to pack when Stefan approached us.

"Aidan we will not have time to hunt before we leave. We need to go downstairs now."

I saw a puzzled look on Tess's face.

"Remember the other day when we were at Henry's and you asked me about what he had in his refrigerator?"

She nodded.

"Sometimes we can't hunt so we keep supplies. That's what I didn't want you to see in Henry's refrigerator,; he had blood stored in there."

I paused a second. "Tess why don't you just go upstairs with Rachel and we'll be up in a little while."

"No" she said shaking her head, "I want to come."

I looked at Stefan and Mora. "It's ok by me," Mora said.

"Ok, let's go"

We turned and went towards the kitchen. "There's a down stairs pantry," I said pointing to a door that led off from the kitchen. I turned on the light and we all walked down. Rows of food supplies were on shelves.

"The wine cellar is at the back."

We walked down to the end and there was another set of stairs. We went down those and I opened a door. We stepped into a very cool, climate controlled room.

"Julian is very particular about his wine," I said. Tess just smiled.

At the very back of the wine cellar was a wall filled with bottles. I pulled on the bottle at the upper left. The wall swung open. Another door was behind it.

"You guys have more secret rooms than a fun house," Tess said.

I just shrugged and unlocked the door.

We stepped in to an icy cold room and I turned on a bright overhead light. The room was full of metal drawers. I opened one and let Tess look in. It was neatly filled with bag after bag of blood. I picked up twelve bags and put them in a basket. I shut the drawer, turned off the light, then closed and locked the door. We went back up into the pantry.

A machine was built into the wall on one side of the room. "It heats the blood," I said as I placed the bags into the machine. I pressed a button. The machine made a sound of water running, then a whirling sound came out.

"You sure you want to see this?" I asked.

Tess nodded.

We waited in silence for another minute. The machine made a ringing noise.

"Dinner's ready," I said. Tess had just a bit of a smile.

The face of the machine read 98.9. I pulled out the bags.

Mora pulled three large glasses down from the cabinet. Stefan pulled out his knife and cut a line along the top of three bags. I poured the contents of a bag into each of the glasses. The rich smell of blood filled the room.

I looked at Tess. "I don't think any human has ever seen this."

"Well I am not just any human. Besides, I think this is the first time I've ever seen you drink anything. You've watched me eat so I guess it's my turn."

I nodded. The glasses were stained red. We drank them then repeated the same cycle with the remaining bags.

When we were finished, Tess looked at me then tapped the side of her mouth. I didn't quite understand. She smiled, shook her head and grabbed a paper towel and wiped the side of my mouth.

"Tess, you don't."

"It's ok Aidan, just like with the donuts. It's who you are."

"I guess we're both messy eaters."

Mora had a puzzled look on her face, "Donuts?"

"It's a long story, I'll explain later." I said.

I picked up the empty bags and put them in a special trash container. Tess threw the paper in behind them.

"This gets burned," I said.

She looked intently at my face, "Aidan, your eyes are really, really blue; almost crystal."

I nodded, "It happens when we consume human blood."

She looked at Mora and Stefan.

"You're not too grossed out?" I asked.

She shook her head. "No, my Dad eats really, really rare steaks. So this is just a jump from that right?"

Mora shook her head in disbelief. "You are certainly a most unique human Tess. Even Rachel gets a little squeamish at this."

Tess laughed, "I would believe that."

We went back upstairs and found the house in absolute turmoil.

Everyone was flying out except Mom and Grace. Dad and Lucian wanted them here in case we needed help from home. We were about to go into my room when we met Rachel.

She looked at me, staring at my eyes. "Did you?"

I nodded. She looked at Tess. "Did you?"

She nodded.

"Ugh and you are not puking?"

"No, it was fine," Tess said.

"You never cease to amaze me Tess," Rachel said grabbing her arm. "Come on and help me pick out some clothes for the trip."

Tess smiled and went in with Rachel. I quickly grabbed jeans, shirts and some other stuff and threw them into a suitcase.

I headed over to Rachel's room. Rachel and Julian's room was a wreck. Rachel's clothes were everywhere. Coats, dresses, pants and god knows what else where on the bed, the couch, even the floor. Tess and Rachel were looking at a couple of coats. Julian was nowhere to be seen.

"Rachel", I said. She and Tess looked up

"This is what happens when you shop too much. See it gives you too many choices. We're not going to a fashion show, how hard can it be?"

"You know Aidan, you just have no sense of taste," Rachel said shaking her head then looking at Tess she continued, "Except for girlfriends. That you got right."

Tess just laughed. Rachel continued, "I'm serious Tess, how do you put up with him? He's such a pain."

"He's got his own special charms," Tess said with a smile.

I tapped my watch. "You know as much as I would just love to stand here and have this debate, we have a plane to catch. Tess we need to go. We've got to get your passport and I'm sure you need time to pack. We'll just meet everyone at the airport."

Rachel hugged Tess and said, "Go on, go before he has a fit. We'll just meet you there."

"But", she said as we started to leave, "Since we don't have time to properly pack, we'll just have to shop when we get to Italy."

"Oh that would be great!", Tess said.

Shaking my head, I grabbed Tess's arm and we ran to the garage. Tess and I jumped into the car. When we got to her house, we told them that my father had to go to Italy on business and we had the opportunity to go. Karen was thrilled for Tess and the two of them went upstairs to pack while I played with Austin.

After a couple of reminders from me about the time, they finally came down with her suitcase. There was of course a whole series of tearful goodbyes, promises to bring toys for Austin and then we left. We passed through security and met up with everyone else at the gate.

The flight over was uneventful. Tess and I read for a while, she and Rachel talked at length about some movie they had both seen. We all watched a movie then she fell asleep on my shoulder. We changed planes in Rome flying through customs. Julian was a master at that; he had made a few calls ahead of time. This was followed by a quick flight to Venice.

It was warm as we exited the plane in Venice. The airport was packed; tourists and sightseers roaming everywhere. A mom tried to entertain two children while the father looked over a map. As we stepped out of the exit, a man in a dark suit met us. Julian spoke with him a few minutes in Italian and we followed him out of the terminal. Two more men were waiting for us at baggage claim. They quickly picked up our bags and we walked outside. The sun was bright and a light wind was blowing off the water. Two limousines were waiting for us. We drove down to the dock and boarded a private water taxi.

Tess was all eyes. She had never been to Venice and she was drinking everything in. Venice was one of my favorite cities, beautiful and rich with an abundance of history. Tess was completely enthralled.

The city of course was magnificent and the water beautiful. I was sad that Tess' first visit had to be under these circumstances. I would have loved to steal her away and come here to just relax and enjoy ourselves. We could have spent weeks just discovering the city. But that was not possible now.

The water taxis quickly got us to our hotel, a beautiful site that Mora, Stefan and I had stayed at several times. We stepped off the taxis and porters grabbed our bags.

The hotel was a grand affair. Several stories tall built with classic Venetian architecture. The lobby was ornate with white marble floors and gold trim.

"I still can't believe it," Tess said looking around. "It's just so beautiful here."

"I wish it was under different circumstances Tess. I would have loved to bring you here just the two of us, to get away."

She grabbed my arm. "Well we're here now. That's enough for me."

Dad and Julian checked everyone in and Julian threw me two keys smiling. "I got a room for you and Tess with a balcony. I figured you could use your privacy."

"Thank you Julian," Tess said giving him a quick kiss on the cheek.

"Piacere mio," he said.

We headed up to the room, dropped our bags on the bed and went out on the balcony. The view was spectacular. Venice seemed to flow all around us.

"It's just so beautiful," Tess said. "The water and the city, it's magical."

"It is wonderful. A beautiful place for a beautiful woman. It's just not fair, to have you meet the city like this," I said.

She turned to me and put her arms around me.

"It doesn't matter Aidan. We are here now, let's just enjoy what we have."

"You're right, you're right," I said and we shared a long kiss. We just stood there with the beauty of Venice around us.

After a few minutes there was a knock on the door. It was Stefan so I told him to come in. "Sorry to disturb but Marcus wants to leave in five minutes, he wants to visit the site before we lose the light."

"It's ok, Stefan. We'll be ready," Tess said.

"Time to go to work," I said shaking my head.

"We can always come back Aidan."

"I promise. I'll bring you back and then we'll have all the time we want," I said kissing her again. We grabbed our things and made our way to the lobby.

Dad and Julian were looking at a map when we got there.

"I think the building we are looking for is near here," Dad said pointing to a spot on the map. Julian nodded his head. "Lucian, what do you think?" Dad asked. He nodded. "I think so, you and Julian would know better than I."

Julian called us two water taxis and we were off. We went down canal after canal. It was a twisting and turning trip. We passed under multiple bridges and several churches and old buildings. Tess was completely mesmerized by the view. Finally we arrived at an old set of buildings on an Island that set by itself. We got out of the taxis and Julian paid the fares.

The building was exactly like the one in the mirror. It was old but solid. I could tell the red walls were very thick. It looked like some sort of a fortification that had been turned into a museum. A few tourists were leaving.

I pointed up. There at the top was the Janus figure we had seen. Dad nodded.

"Let me go in and speak to the steward," Julian said.

"The order keeps many of these old buildings as museums, to keep their secrets from prying eyes," Dad said.

"The order?" Tess whispered to me.

"I'll explain it later. It's an organization of covens," I whispered back.

Julian came back out and nodded his head. "They close in about twenty minutes. We can stay and look around. Let's go inside."

We walked into the building. The contrast was striking. While it was warm and bright outside, it was cold, dank and dark inside. A smell of stale air and water was everywhere. We waited at empty tables in a small cafe that was closed. Finally the last of the tourists left.

"We can look around now," Julian said. "The steward left me his key."

We walked through the museum. Various aspects of the cities history were displayed. There were paintings and drawings along with artifacts of daily life. Tess was in heaven. We went from room to room and found ourselves at the back. I was about to turn around when I noticed something. The back wall to this room was particularly gloomy, hidden in shadow. The wall had a faded fresco of Neptune on it. But at the top about three inches down a symbol of wavy lines was cut into the wall.

"Dad over here," I yelled.

Everyone came over. "Look above Neptune at the top of the wall, there is a symbol cut into the stone."

Dad nodded, "It's the symbol for the water element. Good find Aidan."

He and Lucian looked over the wall. "I don't see anything special," Dad said. Lucian stepped back. "Lets try the symbol itself"

The wall was high, almost twelve feet. "I need something to stand on," he said.

I shook my head and climbed right up the wall.

"Show off,' Rachel said.

I just smiled and looked at the symbol. There was nothing fancy but I followed the line of the waves. I could see to the right was a small opening. "There is an opening." I put my hand in the opening and found a latch. I pulled on it. There was the sound of stone scraping and a passage on the wall to the right swung open. I jumped down.

It was dark and smelled wet.

"I'll go first," Dad said.

He held out his hand. A flare of witch fire opened in his palm.

"I wondered why we didn't bring a light," Tess said.

Dad nodded and we all went in. There was a short walk then a flight of stairs. We followed them down. The building sat on a hill. By the time we stopped we must have been at water level.

We came out into a tall narrow room. It must have been twenty feet high. At the very top on one side, small slits let in a small amount of the now fading light. There were a few faded frescos on the walls. A rough map of Venice was drawn on one end and on the other end was a small pool that had a short lip around the edge. It could have been a well at one time. The whole room seemed to be made of rough stone. The walls were damp and shiny.

"What did the next lines of the translation say?" Dad asked.

Julian pulled out his bag and took out the translation.

"It says that only the new man will pass."

"Look around and see if you see any markings," Dad said.

There were carvings in the walls and some recessed openings. We looked for any sort of symbol. We checked the walls and the frescos but nothing stood out. Time had not been kind to the walls. I was afraid that the years and the water had erased any clue that might have been here. The light was beginning to go and Dad finally stopped us. "We must be missing something."

Rachel spoke up. "Julian you said that only the new man will pass."

"Yes that's what it said," Julian replied.

"What are you thinking Rachel?"

"New man, perhaps it needs to be born." She pointed at the pool.

"Brilliant Rachel, of course," Dad said.

We walked back over to the well. It was dark and the water smelled salty.

Stefan said, "I'll go in"

"You're too big, I'll go," I said.

"Aidan wait," Tess said.

"Oh, now that the shoe is on the other foot, now you want to object."

"No it's just I don't want you to get into some kind of trouble in there," Tess said looking down. "The water is very dark."

"Trouble is his middle name," Rachel said.

"We could get men, a diving team," Dad said.

I looked up at the light and shook my head. "We don't have time. We need the crystal. I'll go. It'll be fine."

I took off my shoes, then my shirt and pants. I put my phone and a camera in a plastic bag.

"Just in case," I said.

"Don't worry Tess, I saw him naked as a baby," Rachel said smiling.

I stuck my tongue out at her.

My white skin almost glowed in the gloom. I could tell Tess was worried.

"Don't worry I'll be ok." I kissed her and let my self down into the pool.

It was much deeper than it looked.

I sank down about fifteen feet when I felt my feet hit the bottom. It was dark, the water gloomy. I felt my way around the well. The walls were slippery. On one spot I felt an indentation and inside was lever. I pulled it and immediately the wall behind me opened and a steel grate slid across the top section of the well.

I heard Tess scream and I saw her bend down.

"Aidan!"

"Stefan please, tear it off, tear off the grate. We have to get him out of there, he'll drown," she yelled.

I could just make out Mora talking.

"Don't worry Tess. He'll be alright, remember we don't breathe like humans. He's not going to drown."

I turned and swam through the opening which lead into a small, thin tunnel. I swam down the tunnel thorough the darkness, even my eyes could not make out any light. A current was flowing, moving me forward. The tunnel seemed to go for hundred feet or so until I hit another stone wall. I felt all around it but there was no way to open it. I almost turned around when I felt along the top of the tunnel. There was another indentation and inside another lever. I pulled it down and the stone wall in front of me slid back. The current stopped and I could see light ahead of me. I swam into what seemed like another pool and I followed the light above me until I broke to the surface.

In the gloom I could see that I was in some sort of a cave or grotto. Again there were lights cut into the top of the steep walls. The walls themselves were similar to the other room, rough stone but generally dry. I climbed out of the well and looked around. The room appeared abandoned. Old stone tables were standing along one wall. As I looked around, the room seemed completely empty but in the back on the far wall partially hidden in the shadow I noticed a small symbol that looked like a flame. Under the symbol was a whole series of numbers. I took out the camera and took several pictures. The flash illuminated the entire room. I looked at the pictures to verify that the numbers and symbol were legible.

I looked up and thought about scaling the walls but the holes at the top looked too small and the walls too thick to break so I sealed everything up and went back into the water. I retraced my steps closing the well with the levers behind me. Finally I was back in the first well. This time I pushed instead of pulling on the lever. The metal grate slide back and I kicked my way to the surface. As soon as I broke to the surface, Tess jumped right in with me.

"Oh my god Aidan, I thought you were going to drown. I am so happy you are alright." She put her arms around me gave me a big kiss. Everyone laughed looking down at us.

I smiled and stroked her hair. Now we were both wet.

"I'm fine Tess, its ok, I'm just wet."

She said laughing, holding on to me, "now we're both a mess."

She put one hand on the wall of the well and said, "You scared me to death." Then she splashed me. I splashed her back laughing.

I heard Dad clear his throat.

"Oh, sorry," I said.

Stefan and Mora helped Tess out and I followed her.

We were both sopping wet. Dripping I said "I found another symbol, here are the pictures." I pulled out the plastic bag.

Dad pulled out the camera and took a brief look at the camera.

He nodded, "I think it'll be enough. Let's get back to the hotel."

Rachel brought us some towels from the gift shop. We dried off and got dressed as best we could. We left the building and Julian called for our taxi.

Tess was shivering in the night air so Mora brought over her jacket.

"Put this on Tess, it'll keep you warm."

I put it on her and put my arm around her.

"Thank you Mora," Tess said her teeth chattering.

When the taxi arrived one of the men looked at Tess and I. He asked a question in Italian. Julian replied, "Yes they threw each other in the water; a lovers quarrel." Both men just laughed.

When we got back to the hotel, Dad and Julian took the camera and Tess and I headed back to the room.

When we got back to the room, Tess threw her arms around me.

"I was so worried Aidan, I thought you were going to drown in that well."

"Now you know how I feel," I said.

I just held her for a few minutes.

"I could use a hot shower," I said.

"Me too," she said shaking again.

I smiled and took her hand. "Come on," I said. She smiled and we headed into the next room.

Cleaned and dressed, we met everyone in Mom and Dad's suite. Dad had connected the camera to his laptop and he and Julian were reviewing the pictures.

Dad pointed to the symbol. "That's the symbol for fire so it must be the next element."

"And the codes ?"

"We are translating them now. Give us an hour or so."

"How about a walk around Venice?" I asked Tess.

"Sure, sounds wonderful," she said.

We headed down to the lobby of the hotel and walked out the back onto one of the bridges that led away from the hotel. The night view was spectacular as we watched the water. The ancient city curved around us and we could see what seemed like a river of lights stretching out towards the bay. A light breeze was blowing and the waves made a soft splashing sound against the hulls of the boats anchored in the dark water. Far in the distance a cathedral rose like a mountain into the dark sky.

She held my arm as we walked. Lights from street lamps reflected on the water and we could smell the salt air. A gentle mist rolled between the buildings so I pulled Tess closer. "Are you cold?" I asked. "Not after that shower," she said laughing. I laughed too.

"It's perfect here Aidan, I could stay here with you forever," she said.

"I feel the same way."

We saw another couple a head of us, walking hand in hand.

"I've been thinking about something, Aidan. But I'm not sure how to start."

"What is it? You can ask me anything."

"Today, when you were down in the water, I realized there's no way I could live without you."

"I couldn't live without you either, Tess."

"But we both know that's not true," she said holding me closer.

I stopped and pulling back said, "What do you mean, you know it's true."

"But you will live without me Aidan. One day I'll be old and I'll die and you will be without me."

"I won't live without you Tess."

"But you will, you will have to, unless..."

Then I realized what she was talking about. Transformation.

"Tess," I said.

"You could transform me, make me like you and Mora and Stefan then I could be with you forever. Evenings like this would never have to stop and our life together would never have to end."

I knew that at some point we would have to talk about this subject but I had hoped it would be years away. But Tess, so full of life, was quick to grasp the real nature of things.

"Tess, you don't know what you are asking for. This life, this life of pain and constant struggle, you don't want that. Always on the edge of evil, of battling the thirst, worrying always of becoming something that you hate, of hurting the ones you love. I couldn't do that to you. None of us would do that to you."

"But I'm already in this life, Aidan. I just want to stay with you. I couldn't stand losing you and if that is what it takes to be with you then I would do that."

She held me tighter, her face buried in my chest.

I circled my arms around her.

"Tess, let's not worry about these things now. We have years before we have to deal with this. Listen, we're going to find this crystal and then we're going home and I want you to have a human life, a long, happy life with me."

I put my hand on her face. "Besides, you still have your family; Nick and Karen, and Austin, your parents and friends. I could not stand taking them away from you and believe me that's what would happen. You could not be with them changed into what I am. It would be too dangerous. Tess, you have too much living to do for me to take that away from you. Trust me, we will be together and I will be there every step of the way and when the time comes, we will deal with this."

"But I'll be old and my life spent. How could you possibly love me then?"

Then I realized what she was really talking about, what she was really afraid of.

"Tess I love you now and I'll love you then and we will be together through everything. I'll never leave you, don't fear that. How could I ever not love you."

She looked up, and I wiped tears from her eyes. She nodded. "Ok, we can talk about it later, just promise me that you will think about it. I just can't bear the thought of being without you."

I nodded and held her tight.

"How about something to eat, I bet you're starved.," I asked.

She smiled and nodded. I saw a cafe that was still opened and we went inside. She had a small snack and we walked back to the hotel. Her mood was better on the walk back. She seemed her happy self again. We laughed and kissed the whole way to the hotel.

We went straight back to my parents suite.

"Ah, Aidan, Tess just in time, we just finished the decoding. Can you get the others, I think we are all ready."

Tess and I walked out and gathered the others then everyone sat down in the living area of the suite.

Dad started, "The translation of what you found was pretty straight forward. It was a slightly different. The codes were indexes to words instead of individual letters but we figured it out. Anyway, the text says the path to fire is found by the man of vision. But then it says that only the blind may pass and following that is the location spell. That's all it says."

Julian said, "Tess are you ready?"

Tess nodded and Julian handed her the mirror.

Dad said, "Stefan draw the curtains."

The room turned dark.

Dad began chanting the spell. Again as he chanted, the mirror began to glow. He intoned the spell again and again. Each time the glow increased. Finally he said it one more time and the light leapt from its surface. As before the blue light swirled and formed into a scene. The tone off the mirror seemed to bounce off the walls.

The view was of a wide city with a harbor. A mountain rose in the background and the view seemed to fly towards the mountain. A small Italian city appeared with ancient buildings clustered together, the mountain rising up behind it. The scene continued to move until it stopped in front of a low, brown building. Again there was a Janus symbol high on one wall. Another symbol seemed to float in the air.

Dad terminated the spell and Tess handed him the mirror. As if on cue, the hotel phone rang. Dad answered it. It was the hotel manager. Yes we were alright, No the problem was a faulty computer, nothing with the hotel equipment. We were very sorry for the noise.

"Does anyone recognize the location?" I asked.

Julian nodded. "I know where the building is. Jakob had quite the sense of irony. The city with the harbor is Naples and the mountain is Mount Vesuvius, the volcano. Talk about fire. The location is a small city outside Naples. I believe the building is one of the ancient baths. At one time witches I knew maintained a coven there."

Dad looked at his watch. "It's much too late to get transportation tonight. We'll have to stay the night then leave first thing in the morning. Everyone rest up, it will be a long day tomorrow."

Tess and I left for our room. We cleaned up then turned out the lights. The view on the water was spectacular. We could see the whole city and bay. "Promise me, that when this is all over, you will bring me back here."

"I promise," I said.

She was exhausted falling right to sleep in my arms.

I held her tighter, "I love you Aidan," she said with a sleepy voice. "I love you too, Tess. Go on to sleep. I'll be right here," I said. She snuggled closer to me. I held her but I couldn't get her question off my mind.

She woke up early the next morning and as we lay there, I could see that Tess was worried.

"Something bothering you?" I asked raising up on one arm.

She shook her head, "Just a bad dream, I don't remember much of it, all I remember is seeing flames, shooting flames."

She paused a minute with a frightened look on her face, "Aidan, will it be dangerous, for you? I mean it's fire, right. Fire can hurt you," she asked holding my hand.

I didn't want to lie to her.

"It might be. But everyone will be there and we are a pretty powerful group. I think we can handle anything that comes up but I'll be careful. You just have to trust me and try not to worry."

"I'll try," she said.

We packed quickly and stood for a moment looking at the view.

"I remember my promise," I said squeezing her shoulder.

She put her hand on mine, "Both of them," she said.

I nodded.

We grabbed our bags and headed to the lobby.

Rachel and Julian were in the restaurant. They motioned us to join them.

"Your parents are on their way down. Your father is arranging transportation."

Rachel said, "Come on Tess, we have a few minutes, sit down and eat. The coffee is delicious."

"Go on," I said.

I sat down while Tess pulled a roll and jam from the self serve table and the waiter brought her a cup of coffee.

"It's wonderful," she said taking a sip.

"Never learned to drink the stuff," I said not thinking.

Tess and Rachel looked at me then laughed.

They had just finished when Dad walked in.

"I have booked us on a private jet to Naples and the taxis will be here in twenty minutes. Let's meet down here in fifteen."

The taxis were right on time. I could tell Tess was sad at leaving, the city suited her well. We quickly drove to the airport and were on the plane in no time. I let Tess sit next to the window. She stayed glued to it, watching Venice fade until we passed through the clouds.

The flight was quiet, everyone caught in their own thoughts. Even Rachel was subdued. As we came in, I looked beyond Tess to the outside. Naples was as lovely as I remembered. Julian had lived here for years and had brought me back several times. I could tell he was excited to see the city again.

He tapped Dad on the shoulder. "When we land we should rent cars and drive over ourselves. I think I can find the building." Dad nodded.

The airport at Naples was just as crowded as Venice. Tourists were everywhere jostling to make their way to the exits. We made our way through them and two cars were waiting for us outside. After Julian paid the delivery men, he headed for the first car. "I'll drive the other one," I said jumping in before Stefan could say anything.

"Just try and keep up," Julian said smiling. "We are traveling to Sant'Anastasia. The bath is there."

Tess and I drove with Mora and Stefan. Luckily I was just as fast a driver as Julian. We took the main highway out of the airport and drove east away from Naples towards the mountain, Tess intently watching the view. The sun was up and the weather was perfect. It reminded me of our drive on the California coast. On any other occasion, it would have been an idyllic trip. We passed through towns with narrow streets so tight you could almost reach out and touch the old buildings we passed on the way.

I could tell that Tess was still somber, her mood unchanged from the flight. I reached over and took her hand.

"Its lovely here," she said with a slight smile.

"Yes, yes it is.," I said.

"Have you been here before, Mora," she asked turning around.

Mora could see that she was worried so she smiled and looked out the window. Memory had her.

Both she and Stefan seemed calm and happy.

"Yes, we lived here many years ago, over in Naples. It was wonderful then. Another life." She paused a minute and looked at Tess.

"It's still beautiful though. The light and the water. It's as if time stops. When this is all done, you must make Aidan bring you back." She took Stefan's hand.

"Stefan and I spent many a happy year here."

Stefan smiled, "Yes, we have my darling. Maybe we will travel back with them. Show them how to really enjoy what the city has to offer."

Their warmth seemed to flow through the car and Tess' mood improved. She smiled and said, "Yes, I would like that very much."

She was quiet a moment, "Did you live here with Julian?" Tess asked, "Aidan said that Julian lived here a long time."

Mora laughed shaking her head, "No. Absolutely not. We were all in the city but we lived in different places. In those days it was unheard of for vampires and witches to live together under the same roof. There was still a lot of mistrust between the two races. Besides, this was long before Rachel joined us and Julian, well Julian was something of a scoundrel then. He was always getting himself and your father into some kind of trouble."

"What, I never heard this story," I said as we drove down yet another narrow street.

"Oh yes, the two of them made quite a pair. I thought poor Sophie was going to lose her mind. They were into all sorts of business activities. Now don't get me wrong, they made a lot of money but not everyone was happy with them. Stefan, remember the incident with the pirates?"

Stefan smiled, "Oh yes one of their best."

"Pirates?" I asked.

Stefan said, "Seems Julian had arranged for a shipment of rare artifacts from Egypt. Your father was always buying that stuff and Julian normally brokered the deals. In those days every deal was a little shady but this particular sell was lets say not with the most reputable firm. Come to find out that what they bought had actually been stolen from pirates who themselves had stolen it from yet another band of thieves in Egypt. Well the whole nefarious mob, pirates and all showed up at your fathers warehouse looking for their goods and a huge fight broke out."

"Now of course they couldn't use any witchcraft; they were all trying to keep a low profile. It was quite the fight. The magistrates finally showed up and threw the whole lot of them in jail, Julian and your father included. Your mother made them stay there for three days until she finally sent myself and Lucian to bail them out."

Stefan laughed, "I still remember how they looked coming out of that place. Flea ridden, cut up, bruised. Grace worked on them for days."

Mora continued, "In fact, Julian had to move away for a little while. Out in the countryside. He came back after five years or so once the incident was somewhat forgotten. Aidan, I thought your mother was going to kill him."

She laughed again, "So to answer your question Tess, no we did not live with them."

"I knew they had some business dealings in the past but pirates," I said shaking my head.

"Never judge a book by its cover," Mora said smiling.

The rest of the drive went by quickly. We drove into Sant'Anastasia winding our way through the small cramped streets. Buildings rose around us as Julian weaved from street to street. Once he got lost and we had to turn around but after a few minutes we went down a long road and stopped at the building we saw in the vision.

We got our of our cars. "One of the orders contacts are on the way. The building has been locked up for many years," Julian said.

"You sure they're not pirates," I asked smirking.

"Who told you that?" Julian asked a shocked look on his face.

I heard Mora and Stefan laughing behind me.

I walked around the site. Like the other one, this building sat on a small hill with several other buildings around it. There seemed to be nothing special about it, just a three story brick building. High near the roof was the two sided Janus figure.

Tess was staring at the mountain.

"A penny for your thoughts," I said coming up behind her. I put my arms around her. She placed her hands on mine.

"Thats Vesuvius isn't it. The volcano that destroyed Pompeii."

"Yes, yes it is," I said.

"It seems threatening somehow," she said.

She was still worried about her dream and what could happen here.

"Don't let your imagination get the best of you, Tess. Everything will be alright."

She turned around and put her head on my chest, "I don't know Aidan. This place seems so dangerous. It's not at all what I expected. I have a terrible feeling about this."

I put my arm around her. About that time a car pulled up and three men got out. They were well dressed in suits but no ties. Julian stepped forward as did one of the men. He was older than the others with long grey hair. Julian greeted him warmly in Italian. They shook hands and spoke for several minutes. While they were taking, the two younger men were looking at us. They paid special attention to Stefan and Mora. Then they turned and looked at Tess and I. I heard one of the men whisper "Vampiro" to the other. He called out to the older gentleman. The older man excused himself from Julian and the three men had a very quick exchange. One of the men pointed in our direction.

Their tone became sharper, their speech faster. The two younger men were arguing with the older man. Finally the two younger men stopped talking and turned towards us. They raised their hands and I pushed Tess behind me. Mora, Stefan and I stepped forward ready to defend ourselves.

Julian ran over putting himself between us and the younger men. The older man joined him and put his hand up. The younger men stood still.

The older man had a worried look on his face. He turned and spoke to Julian in English. "You travel with strange companions, my friend."

He looked over at Stefan, Mora, and I. Then he pointed at Tess.

"I trust all is well with your interests here, we don't want any difficulties with the local authorities."

Julian smiled, "Don't be alarmed Enrico, they are all part of the family. No one is in danger here. We wish you no harm. All will be well. We will finish our business then be gone and no one will even know we were here. You have my word."

He nodded and spoke to the younger men. They went back and stood by their car.

The older man walked over and unlocked the front door of the building with a large key. He gave another set to Julian. He put his hand on Julian's shoulder, "I shall keep you to your word Julian." With that he motioned to the other men. They got in their car and drove off.

"What was that?" I asked.

"They were worried about you three, made them nervous so we just did a little business deal. And no they were not pirates," Julian said.

Dad looked a little embarrassed and Stefan and Mora just laughed again.

Julian pushed open the door and we walked inside.

"Enrico gave me a brief history of the building. Like me, it has had many lives," Julian said winking. "For years it was a gathering place for the local coven. That's when I was here. Then it became a school for musicians. After that it was abandoned but during all this time the order has maintained it. I believe what we are looking for is in the second basement."

We walked in and it was clear that the building had set empty for years. There were several rooms some with desks. Musical diagrams hung on several of the walls. One large room had been a library at one time with tables and chairs arranged around a large window. At the back of the library a staircase lead up to a balcony on the second floor. Behind the staircase was a large locked wooden door. Julian took out one the the keys and opened it. A set of stairs went straight down.

We took the stairs down into a hall that lead to another door. Julian opened that one and we were in the ruins of a roman bath. The room was in bad shape. Not much was left of the original structures. Julian motioned to us, "This way."

We came to yet another door. It was a huge oak affair with brass metal bindings. Julian opened it and there was another flight of stairs. This time they went straight into darkness. Julian held out his hand and a flame of witch fire leapt up, illuminating our path.

The stairs opened into a large coven room. A circle was etched in the center and symbols were cut into the walls. "This was a meeting place for a coven, hidden here beneath the bath. As I said, I visited here once many years ago. There should be a clue hidden here somewhere."

We broke into groups looking over the walls. After a few minutes Lucian called out, "I think I've found something here."

There was another fresco on the wall, a picture of Vulcan the roman god of fire striking a hammer. Lucian said, "Look at his other hand, he's pointing." The hand pointed to a series of shelves cut into the stone. The contents were long gone but on one side a symbol was cut into the back of the shelf. It was the same symbol I saw in Venice, the symbol for fire. Lucian pushed the symbol and a door opened in the stone next to the shelf.

Julian said, "This might have been an exit, cut into the rock as a way to escape. The inquisition was never far in those days."

The door lead to yet another set of stairs, long and narrow which ended in a small room. From that room two tunnels led out. Above the one to the left, the same symbol was cut. That tunnel led down on a steep grade for several hundred feet. As we walked, I held Tess's hand. I could tell she was frightened. Finally the tunnel opened into a large cavern. We walked out onto a kind of shelf and beyond the shelf the floor was just stone but cracked with deep fissures. Periodically a rush of steam would shoot out from one of the cracks, while from others a line of flame would erupt.

The cracks seemed to run all over the floor randomly. The smell of sulphur was strong, almost overwhelming.

Lucian threw a stone out onto the floor ahead of us. A large crack opened up and the stone fell into it. The crack seemed to fall into complete darkness.

"How can we possibly get across this. The floor is unstable.," Julian asked.

Stefan looked up and said, "The ceiling is too high and glassy. It would be very hard to climb over it. Besides the steam and flame reach all the way to the top."

"What did the Journal say?" Lucian asked.

"It says that only the blind can pass."

I noticed there was a raised stone out on the floor.

I took Tess's hand and said, "Julian, I want to try something, can you put out the witch flame?"

He nodded and the room was plunged into complete darkness, a darkness so deep that it seemed to press in on us from every-side. Even vampire eyes could not see anything so deep was the darkness. Tess clutched my hand. A flame shot out of one of the cracks against the far wall. The room was filled with a dim orange light. I put my hands on Tess's shoulders and put my forehead against hers.

"I love you," I said and kissing her forehead, I put her hand in Mora's. "Mora watch her."

"Aidan, what are you doing?" Tess asked.

"Trust me," I whispered and as soon as the room went dark again I jumped out onto the fractured floor landing on the raised stone.

"Aidan!" Tess yelled in the darkness.

Stefan heard me land and yelled, "Aidan what are you doing, come back." He started to jump after me.

In the darkness, I saw what I suspected. Once on the floor from the viewpoint of the raised stone, I could see glowing footprints leading across the floor. I yelled back, "I'm alright. There is a path laid out across the floor but you can only see it in the dark. Only the blind can pass."

I stepped down on the floor onto the first of the glowing prints and looked ahead. The prints wound back and forth across the room. I stepped gently on the floor, stepping only where the prints lay. I had taken about three steps when I heard a sound behind me. Even though I could not see him I knew that Stefan was on the stone.

"I am not letting you get all the glory this time," he said.

"Stefan be careful," I heard Mora say.

"Just follow me. Step only where the prints are," I whispered.

Stefan yelled back to the others, "We are alright. Aidan, impetuous as he is, has figured out how to get across."

In the darkness we gently walked across the floor. We had moved about thirty feet when another pillar of fire burst upwards about fifteen feet to our left. The footprints disappeared in the light. As the journal said we could only move when the room was pitch black. I stopped moving and turned around. In the dim orange light I could see concern in everyone's face. Tess was still holding Mora's hand.

We slowly made our way across the floor. The path while snaking near places where steam and fire erupted, kept us a safe enough distance. It was very slow going. We had to stop several times when an eruption occurred and wait for the darkness.

Finally the footprints ended at a small opening at the far wall.

I went in and I heard Stefan come in behind me. We made our way through a tunnel dug into the stone. Here too it was pitch black. The tunnel turned several times but after a few minutes I could just make out a dim light ahead. I followed the light into another room.

A wide fissure ran completely through the center of the room. Far down in the fissure, lava boiled, its light turning the room a blood red color. The sulfur smell was much stronger here and it was much warmer. About ten feet above us, a thin stone arch ran over the fissure to the other side.

"We have to climb over," I said pointing to the arch.

Stefan looked at it, "I wonder how long that has been here?"

I looked around, "I don't know but there's no other way across. I'm just glad Tess can't see this."

"Or Mora," Stefan said.

With that, I jumped up and grabbed the stone of the arch. It was warm. I climbed upside down across the fissure. Luckily there were no flames. On the other side I found a statue carved into the wall, a woman. A symbol was carved next to her and again there were a long series of numbers. I took pictures of everything and we climbed back over.

The trip back was just as tedious as the trip over. We gently retraced our steps and when another flame occurred, we jumped from the stone back onto the shelf. Tess rushed over and wrapped her arms around me. "What am I going to do with you. First I think you're going to drown and then that your going to burn up. I don't think my heart can take much more of this."

God let the next test be easier I thought.

I tried to calm her. "I'm sorry, Tess but we were in no real danger. We just had to stay on the path. It looked more dangerous than it was. We just had to figure it out. You just have to trust me."

"I'm trying," she said but she had an iron grip on my arm.

"We have everything, let's get out of here," I said. Dad nodded and Julian lit our way with witch fire as we made our way back to the coven room.

Once there, Dad looked at the pictures. "These look good. It will take me a few minutes to translate them. Julian will help me?"

"Of course, Marcus."

"I could use some fresh air," I said.

Stefan said, "So could I."

We followed the path back to the main building and from the library we took the stairs up to the balcony. It was already afternoon. From the balcony you could see over to Naples and just beyond the city, the bay. The air was much sweeter here. There was a slight breeze. I was just glad to be above ground. Tess held my hand as we just took in the view. We just stood there for a while. Finally she turned to me and said, "I am sorry I yelled down in the tunnel. I just can't seem to get used to this stuff. It still frightens me."

I smiled and said, "I know Tess just try not to worry. We know what we are doing."

She nodded and leaned against me and we just watched the town below us. People were going on about their business, shops closing and cafe's opening. The people completely unaware of what was under their feet.

After a few minutes, Rachel yelled from down stairs, "They're ready."

We traveled back down to the coven room. Tess was a little shaky but she stood firm. Dad incanted the spell. This time the mirror showed a scene that was in high mountains. You could see snow was on the peaks. Down the mountain on a cliff was a tower and at the base of the mountain was a cave. A Janus figure could be seen carved high above the mouth.

"The symbol, it's the symbol for the element Earth, it looks like a cave," Dad said.

"Do you recognize it?" I asked.

Dad shook his his head no, "I don't place it. I don't think I've been there before." The hum was beginning to build.

"Julian," I asked but he shook his head no.

Stefan stepped forward and looked up at it.

His eyes were cold, almost distant. He said over the hum, "I know this place. It's in the French Alps near Annecy, I remember the cave well."

"How do you know it?" I asked over the hum.

"Because years ago, Draven enslaved me there."

Chapter 14

Earth and Air

Naples, Italy

The coven room was suddenly very quiet and the darkness felt much deeper.

"Stefan I never heard this," Dad said. "How did this happen?"

"I've not thought of that place in years.," Stefan said pushing his white hair back. Then looking at Mora he said, "Lets go upstairs and I'll explain."

We all filed upstairs as Julian locked up behind us. We found chairs in the library and Stefan looked out of the window for a few moments before he spoke.

"Before the conflict that brought Magnus down, Mora and I were in a vampire coven in France. Over a few months time, some of our brothers went missing. We looked for them everywhere but we found no trace; it was if they had vanished into thin air. In our search, we heard whispers of shadows, servants of our enemies, the witches. One night during my search, I followed a young witch who had been pointed out to me as someone involved. I meant to trap him to discover what he knew. Little did I know that it was he who was setting a trap. I followed him down a deserted side street and when he reached the end he simply vanished and out of nowhere dark shadows leapt at me. I'll never forget the screeching sound they made. It was like the sound we heard in Arius's work room that day but much louder and stronger. I tried to escape by crawling up the side of the wall but to no avail. These shadows surrounded me and held me in place while the witches bound me with a set of enchanted chains. In those chains I was powerless."

"They threw me in the back of a wagon. I remember it was a long trip in those chains. Finally we arrived at the cave. I remember the snow piled up against the entrance. Once inside, I found dozens and dozens of vampires imprisoned there. Some the witches just tortured.

Others they transformed into mindless slave; fanged red eyed soldiers. Others like me they kept caged, starved so that when they needed us to drain a human we were their willing instruments. These humans he changed into more vampires, part of his growing army."

"I was imprisoned there for four months. In despair I thought I would never be free again. I lived in fear that I would end up one of his mindless guards. But my Mora would not give up. She searched and searched and finally discovered Magnus' evil lair. One night she and a dozen other vampires broke into the prison. The guards were completely overwhelmed. She saved me, saved all of us. That event is what ultimately brought us into the war."

He turned and looked at us, "So yes I know exactly where the location is."

We left the building. Julian locked the main door and we walked to the cars. I put my hand on Stefan's shoulder, "I'm so sorry Stefan, I had no idea." Dad had a pained look on his face, "I am sorry as well Stefan, its almost unimaginable what you must have suffered."

Stefan said, "It was long ago and those days have long faded. Julian bring me your map and I'll show you the cave's location.'"

Stefan studied the map for a minute then pointed to a spot near the base of the French Alps. "It was here at the end of this valley." Dad looked for the closest city then made a call on his cell. He spoke a few minutes and when he finished the call he said, "It will be about 4 hours before we can take a charter into France. We can either wait at the airport or we can go down into the city for a few hours."

Rachel said, "Lets go into the city. I could use a little distraction."

"That's a wonderful idea," Dad said. "Why don't the rest of you go and Lucian and I will head on to the airport and make our arrangements."

We drove over into Naples.It was a quick trip into the city down winding streets. Mora had us park near the waterfront. The late afternoon sun was warm and the breeze off the water was wonderful. Tess and I walked hand in hand behind Mora and Stefan. Mora motioned to Tess to come up to her. "There is something I want you to see." She pointed to building down the street on the corner.

"Stefan and I once lived there in a very happy time. The building still looks the same after all these years. There was a cafe downstairs and on the roof was a wonderful terrace. You can view the whole bay from that point. Would you like to see it?"

Tess nodded and I said, "Go on, we'll wait on you." She, Rachel and Mora walked down to the corner.

Vendors were selling flowers just down the street. I walked down and bought Tess a single rose. I needed to try and makeup somehow. I guess Stefan had the same idea and so he bought Mora a small bouquet. Julian walked up and said, "I guess I better fall in line or I'll be in deep water". He bought Rachel a bouquet too.

When the girls came back we gave them their flowers. Mora laughed. Tess smiled and winked at me. Rachel grinned and gave Julian a big kiss.

So we all laughed and walked down the street, arm in arm. "Mora's right, its a very beautiful city," Tess said smelling her rose.

"Romantic is the word I would use," Julian said giving Rachel a hug.

"That it is," I said.

We walked for a few more blocks and found a small outdoor cafe with bright yellow umbrellas. We stopped and Julian, Rachel and Tess ordered a late lunch.

"Its times like this I feel bad for you Aidan," Tess said taking a large bite. "The food here is delightful."

"Its ok Tess," Mora said. "We may get a chance to hunt when we get into the mountains so don't feel bad for us."

"Is that true?" Tess asked.

"Perhaps," Stefan said. "There are still some deep forests near there."

I could see the curiosity in Tess's eyes. "No you can't come," I said shaking my head at Tess, "Vampires only."

"Well then I am going to order an expresso," she said.

"And I am going to get a dessert," Julian said.

"And a glass of wine for me," Rachel chimed in.

"Not the same," I said smugly.

They ordered and we just sat, enjoying the light on the water.

I asked Julian about the pirate story. He laughed, "Yes it happened but let me tell you the true story."

He went through an elaborate tale of intrigue. Of course in his version, he and Dad were quite the heroes.

Mora and Stefan just laughed.

After the third glass of wine, Julian finally looked at his watch shaking his head. "Time to go."

Julian paid the bill and we drove back to the airport. Dad and Lucian met us at the gate. We followed them and only waited a few minutes before we boarded and took off to the French Alps.

It was a relatively quick trip. We were not in the air ten minutes until Tess was asleep snuggled next to me.

Mora leaned over and said, "She's very brave, isn't she. Even in the cave she kept it together."

"Yes, too brave I think," I said.

"You know, she loves you very much Aidan."

"I know," I said stroking her hair.

"I worry about her, involved in all this. As soon as this is finished, I'm going to take her someplace safe, where we can put all this behind her. She doesn't deserve this. I am beginning to think I did the wrong thing, bringing her into all this."

"Love has blinded her, so don't be too hard on her. And don't underestimate her. I think there is more to her than meets the eye. There is am inner strength to her. She reminds me of myself when I was her age, so in love with life, the world yet to be explored."

Mora put her hand on my shoulder, "We'll protect her Aidan. I promise no harm will come to her." She paused a moment, "Of course .."

Mora's face took on a look of hardness and she said, "There is one option, we could change her, then there would be no worry."

"No," I said shaking my head, "She's not ready. I am not ready. Like you said she's too in love with life. There is still too much for her to do. One day perhaps but not now. I don't want her to have any regrets. I want her to keep her innocence for as long as she can, there's still time."

Mora face softened and she nodded and said, "You are wise Aidan and I know your love for her is just as deep. Its a wonderful thing this love. Treasure it, and protect it. It's the rarest thing in the world."

The trip went quickly. Tess woke up her eyes full of sleep," I am sorry, I must have fallen asleep. I guess I don't travel as well as you do."

"It's fine." I pointed over to Rachel who was asleep next to Julian. "See everyone is tired."

Julian woke up Rachel and as we left the plane, there were two Range Rovers waiting for us. We packed quickly and drove out of the airport. Soon we were high in the foothills. The cars wound through back roads that cut through the deep forest. We drove for over an hour then pulled down a long narrow road.

It was late afternoon and the sun was golden as we drove up to a large wood and stone house deep in the trees. As we got out, I saw a small lake behind it. Another of Dad's arrangements.

"This is awesome," Tess said as we got out. I nodded and grabbed our bags.

"The cave is not far from here," Dad said pointing up at the ridge to the left of the house. "We should unpack and wait for dark."

I felt it when I got out of the car. Thirst. It was there just below the surface. There was game nearby and I needed to hunt. I could tell Mora and Stefan felt it as well. Stefan said, "Marcus, Mora, Aidan and I would like to take a few hours to hunt. We need to replenish our strength. This may be our last chance for a while."

"Good idea, Stefan," Dad said. "The rest of us should eat and rest as well. I had them stock the house with food. It may be a long night."

I pulled Tess aside, "You going to be alright?"

"Sure, I'll hang out with Rachel and Julian if thats ok."

"Absolutely," Rachel said putting her arm around her.

"We won't be gone long," I said.

I carried the bags up to our room and met Mora and Stefan downstairs. As we started for the forest, I looked back. Tess was on the back porch with Rachel. She waved to me. I waved back then we flew into the forest. Moving like ghosts, we made for the area on the other side of the lake. Luckily for us the forest was full of deer.

We returned to the house about eight and found Dad, Julian, and Lucian looking at a map on Julian's laptop.

"Ah Stefan, Mora glad you're back. We have some questions." He pointed to the map. "We were thinking of parking the cars here and walking to the cave entrance. It's a little open but it doesn't look like we have much choice."

Mora shook her head and pointed up the hill. "The tower is the best way in."

"The tower?" Julian questioned.

"Yes, through much effort, I discovered that there was a tunnel that lead from the base of the tower down into the cave. It was how we surprised Magnus' guards."

She pointed at the map. "There's a path up to the tower from this side of the forest. It appears to still be overgrown and we will be invisible in the darkness."

"How far is the path from here?" Julian asked.

"About ten miles to the north. I checked while we were hunting," Stefan said.

"Let's wait until midnight then we'll start under the cover of darkness," Dad said.

"Where's Tess and Rachel?" I asked.

Julian rolled his eyes, "Watching some god awful Italian fashion show."

"Figures," I said.

I walked back to the family room where Rachel and Tess were sitting.

Tess got up when I walked in. "Feeling better?" she asked.

I kissed her neck, "Yes much."

She laughed, "Aidan, please not in front of Rachel."

I laughed myself, "We have a few hours, Dad wants to leave at midnight then it's just a quick trip through the forest."

"Come sit with us," Tess said sitting back down.

"So whats on?" I asked looking at the TV.

"It's a fashion show."

I listened to a male voice as women in dresses walked down an aisle.

"It's in Italian," I said.

"Rachel is translating for me. So how was your hunt?"

"Better than an Italian fashion show," I teased.

She hit me with a pillow but I settled back to watch.

The show ended about 10:30 and Tess and I walked out on the back porch.

The moon was shining and you could see the snow on the mountains in the background.

"Reminds me of our trip to Tahoe," she said.

"Yes it does," I said.

"You know I watched you that night, from the trees," I said.

"You what?"

"That night at the condo, I stayed outside your window all night. I just couldn't keep my eyes off of you. You were so beautiful."

"Why didn't you tell me the truth when we were on that trip?"

"Would you have believed me?" I asked.

"Probably not. Why did you leave that night? Did Julian or Lucian get hurt?"

"No. There was another attack that night and I had to go home to help out. I'm sorry I lied to you about that."

I paused a minute.

"I didn't want you involved in this Tess, this dark and evil world. I wanted to keep you in the sunlight, safe and free. But now look, my worst fears have happened, you are mired in all this same as I."

I shook my head. "All this danger and darkness. I never wanted any of this for you."

She took my hand, "Aidan it's like I said, I don't care as long as I am with you. Besides I've seen some pretty awesome places on this trip, things I'd never see on my own. I'm here because I want to be here. I made a choice, a choice I would make over and over again. You worry too much."

She stopped a minute, "But just don't do anymore of that superman crap alright? I'll be ok as long as you're ok. Deal?"

I smiled and nodded, "Deal."

We just watched the moon and the lake for a while then went in to get ready to go. We left right at midnight and walked a short distance into a opening in the woods. "It's that way," Stefan said pointing to the left. Everyone turned in that direction when I remembered Tess. I looked at Mora and she nodded.

"Tess I need you to do something for me."

She was still trying to make her way past a downed long when she looked up and said, "Yes, what do you want me to do?"

"I need to carry you. We can run much faster in the darkness that way. Mora will run right behind me. Is that alright?"

"Sure," she said with a little hesitation in her voice.

Stefan looked around at the bright moon light. "Marcus we could use some cover."

Dad nodded and raised his arms. He closed his eyes. Within a minute, wisps of fog began to flow down the hill between the trees. The fog grew thicker and thicker and soon the whole area was covered in the thick mist.

Tess leaned over and whispered, "Is he making the fog?"

I nodded and whispered back,"Yes he's calling it." She just shook her head in disbelief.

When we were completely surrounded, Dad nodded and said, "Ok I think we're ready."

At that moment, Rachel and Julian changed; Rachel into her wolf form and Julian into his jaguar form. When they were done, Dad transformed into his wolf form and Lucian into his bear form. They stood around us, the mist right behind them.

"Oh my god," Tess said her eyes wide, "I see it but I don't believe it."

"Shape shifters," I said.

Rachel came up and nudged her with her nose. Tess instinctively reached out and petted her head. Julian stepped up and put his head between them wanting a scratch. She rubbed him behind his ears, the clearing was full of his purring. Lucian growled.

"Time to go," I said.

In the moonlight, Mora, Stefan and I looked like ghosts, our white skin almost glowing.

'Boy, I'm glad I am on your side," Tess said.

"Come on," I said and pulled her up onto my back. and we all took off running towards the tower.

We were all a blur in the forest. Tess held onto me with all her might. I could hear her heart beating. "Don't be afraid, I won't drop you," I said.

"I know," she said laughing, "This is way better than the roller coaster."

We were at the base of the mountain in minutes. We stopped under a set of trees.

Mora pointed to a trail that led up the side of the mountain. "We have to make our way up here, just around the curve at the top of the hill is the tower."

Rachel and Julian took off leaping from spot to stop along the way up. The rest of us followed them and soon we are at the base of the tower.

We stopped and the others transformed back. I sat Tess down. She went over to Rachel. "Thats the most amazing thing I have ever seen," Tess said. "I just couldn't believe it. Does it hurt ?"

Rachel smiled, "Not at all. A little smelly sometimes but generally wonderful."

"Maybe one day we'll take you camping and," Julian said.

Dad cleared his throat, his signal to focus.

Mora walked around the base of the tower, "There is a door to the left." She said

We got to the door but it was locked.

"We could break it," Lucian said.

Dad shook his head, "I would rather not leave any evidence."

I looked up. The tower was about 100 feet tall.

"Wait here," I said to Tess.

"Aidan," she said but I was already on the wall. I climbed up and over the side. I quickly went down the stairs and opened the door from the inside.

Everyone filled in. "You do know that Spiderman is a super hero just like Superman right ?" Tess said.

"Hey it was a simple climb," I said.

The base of the tower was cut up into several small rooms. Mora pointed, "It's in the back."

Dad held out his hand and from his palm a flame of witch fire sprouted. He followed Mora giving light to everyone. At the far end Mora stopped and looked at the floor. "Here," she said and pulled up on one of the stones that made up the floor. It pulled up easily and a stone staircase lead down. "Its a long walk," she said. She and Stefan went first followed by Dad. I took Tess's hand and Rachel and Julian followed us. Lucian came down last pulling the stone back into place.

It was dark, only Dad's flame illuminating our way. It was a long walk down several stair cases and tunnels. Finally we came to a stone wall. Mora felt over it. "Here's the latch," she said. She pulled and a door swung open. We walked into a large stone room. "It's this way," Stefan said pointing to his right.

As we walked, Rachel asked a question. "There's something I don't understand, why would Jakob put a clue here? I mean it was one of the bases for Magnus."

Dad answered, "I think Jakob and Arius waited several centuries before they created this. By that time Draven and his coven had long fled. They would never come back here. So in a sense, it was a perfect place."

We walked though several dark rooms, iron bars embedded into the walls. "He kept many of us chained here," Stefan said as we passed them. We came to what was some form of a prison. Narrow cells were lined down a long hallway.

"This is where he kept his human and werewolf slaves as well as his vampire prisoners. I was held in enchanted chains in the third cell down." He pointed down the hall way. "The main entrance is this way," he said going down a tunnel to his left.

We came into a large room. "This was the main hall, offices were that way."

"We need to look for a sign," Dad said.

"Rachel do you feel anything," he asked.

She closed her eyes. "There is still some lingering magic here. I see a door, it has the Janus figure above it. One wall is red."

Stefan nodded." I know the room. The taskmaster's office, we feared going there. You never came back from that visit. It's this way."

We followed him through several more turns and stood in front of a large wooden door reenforced with huge iron bars. Stefan pushed it open. Inside was a large room, one wall had a faint red color to it. A door was cut into the wall, the Janus figure above it. Next to it was another symbol.

"The element of earth," Julian said.

Stefan nodded, "this way." The door opened into another long stairway that ended in some sort of storage room. The walls here were rough cut from the stone of the mountain. Three tunnels branched from the room.

"What did the journal say ?" Lucian asked. Dad opened his notebook.

"This one is a real puzzle. It says the earth is a mystery and not easily uncovered. The man who knows his heart will choose wisely. Follow the music of the earth and descend the stones but beware of the false note."

"But which tunnel, they look the same?" Rachel asked.

"Are there any markings, do you see a symbol?" I asked.

Mora looked, "None that I see."

Julian thought a minute, "It says the man who knows his heart will choose wisely. I remember once that Jakob got in a great deal of trouble for dissecting a human heart. Which is the largest vessel leading from the heart?"

"The aorta," Dad said, "It leaves the heart from the left ventricle."

"Let's try the left tunnel," Julian said.

"Very good Julian, very good," Dad said smiling.

Julian bowed.

"We don't know whats down there," I said. "Let Stefan and I go down first."

"You'll need light," Julian said.

I nodded.

"Aidan," Tess said.

"Its ok, we'll be alright. We're just going to see what's down there." I kissed her lightly.

"You come back, old man," Rachel said to Julian. He smiled and kissed her.

Mora and Stefan just put their heads together for an instant. Dad handed Julian the journal and then when Julian started his witch flame, he, Stefan and I headed down the left tunnel.

The tunnel went almost directly down into the earth. It twisted several times then opened into a large room. In the center was a strange opening, almost like a spiral stair case.

"It's a vertical maze. The stones must be hinged somehow. My guess is that it goes round and round, level by level. You must have to step on the stones in exactly the right spot."

"That's what the journal said, descend the stones."

"It also said to beware of the false note," Stefan said. He started toward the maze.

I took his arm shaking my head, "You're too tall Stefan."

Julian started towards the first step. "Don't even think about it Julian."

We looked over the stones. "They all look the same," I said.

Julian said, "It said to follow the music of the earth but beware of the false note."

Julian pulled out the journal and thought a moment. "See the diagrams, the ones you used to translate. There are 7 musical notes drawn there. I think we need to follow them in the correct sequence. "

"Can you call them to me?"

"Yes," Julian said.

"What's the first one?"

"In the diagram, from middle C, it's three steps."

I walked out on the third stone and it tipped down and locked into place. I followed it down into another chamber.

I yelled back at them, "Its working, give me the next note."

"Its six steps above middle C."

I stepped on the sixth stone and again it swung down into another smaller room.

I carefully walked down the seven maze rooms. At the very end it opened into a final small room. On the far side was the Janus symbol again and another sequence of numbers. Cut into the wall was the symbol for air, the last element. I took pictures again then retraced my steps. The stones snapped back into place as I moved back up.

Everything was perfect until I got back to the top. I was just coming up the ramp when something no one expected happened. A large rat ran across the room. It startled Julian and when he went to move out of its way, he frightened it. It jumped onto one of the stones. The stone moved slightly and when it did the stone I was standing on tilted back. I heard a click above me and a short spear with a long metal blade shot down from the ceiling. It buried itself in my upper chest to the left. I cried out putting my hand around it. Dark blue vampire blood began to well out around it.

Stefan yanked me out of the maze and laid me down.

Julian looked at the spear. "We need to let Marcus look at it before we try and remove it."

The pain was searing. Stefan said, "Can you walk?"

I nodded. They grabbed me by the arms and we started back.

We made our way back up the tunnel, a long line of blood trailing behind us. We finally came out into the main room.

"Aidan," Tess screamed as we came in. They laid me down on the stone ground. Blood began to pool around me.

"I think the blade may be enchanted," Julian said.

Dad said, "We have to remove it and bind the wound. Aidan I'm going to pull it out. Hold still son."

He chanted just a second and I screamed when he grabbed the the spear right above the blade. When he pulled it out, the blade was covered in blood. I could see glowing red symbols etched all over it. A gaping three inch gash was cut into my chest and blood was still pouring from the wound.

Dad sat down the blade then placed his hand over the wound. "He's still bleeding. You're right Julian, the blade's enchanted and the spell is still working. I have some herbs in my bag back at the chalet that will stop it."

Tess knelt down and took my hand, "I am here," she said.

"I know," I said trying to smile. The pain was blinding.

Dad ripped his shirt and made a bandage.

He looked down the tunnel, "He's lost a lot of blood. This will stop it a little but we have to get him back to the house and fast."

"I'll carry him," Stefan said. "and we are going out the front, screw anyone that sees us."

"I'll take Tess," Mora said.

Stefan picked me up and we made for the front of the cave. Stefan did not even stop when we got to the front, he kicked the main door open and we all flew out. I vaguely remember seeing Tess on Mora's back..

When we got back to the house, Stefan ran me upstairs and laid me down on the bed. Dad pulled the bandage off. It was soaked in dark blue vampire blood. The room was beginning to spin.

Dad cleaned the wound and made a paste from some herbs. He pressed them all over the wound as he chanted.The pain eased off.

"It's a very strong spell, it's going to take a while for my spell to counteract it."

I could see blood was still seeping from the wound.

Stefan looked up at Dad and said, "He's lost too much blood Marcus and he's still bleeding. He needs blood, human blood. That's the only way he will heal."

Julian said, "There's a hospital about 30 miles from here. I saw it coming in."

"I'll go," Stefan said.

"I'll come with you," Julian said.

"Alright but hurry," Dad said.

Time seemed to stop and the room began to get dark. I heard Mora say, "He's slipping Marcus, we have to do something quickly. I could get a deer from the forest."

"Use me," I heard Tess say.

"No," I cried trying to sit up, "She doesn't understand the danger."

Dad put his hand on arm, "Aidan, you have to be still."

Tess said, "I've given blood lots of time before."

The room got darker, it was hard to see.

I could just hear Dad say, "Tess there is a danger, you could go into transformation. I can arrange the equipment so that shouldn't happen but there is a risk."

"I don't care just do it" she yelled.

"Alright, just lie here next to him and I'll setup."

I was barely conscious but I could tell Tess was lying next to me. I could hear her heart beat then I smelled blood, human blood, her blood. It was the most wonderful scent I had ever smelled. I felt a slight prick on my arm then Dad chanted a few words and I fell asleep, something I had not done for decades.

I don't know how long I was out but I heard Tess's voice.

"Aidan, Aidan, wake up," she said. At first I didn't want to wake. I was dreaming of Tess, her warmth next to me. I knew she gave me something but I couldn't remember what it was. Finally I opened my eyes.

Tess and Mora stood over me. "You had us all scared there kiddo," Mora said.

"How long, how long did I sleep?" I asked seeing that it was light outside.

"About six hours," Dad said.

"What hit me," I said. "I've never felt anything like that."

"It was a spear. The blade at the end was enchanted. Quite a wicked one, looks like Jakob was taking no chances. It seems to have been crafted especially for vampires. You lost a great deal of blood son. The enchantment prevented you from healing."

Then I smelled it. Blood. A bag was suspended above my head and an IV was running directly into my arm.

Julian walked in, "You are very lucky, that hospital ran a blood bank. Stefan and I made a rather large withdrawal."

I could see Stefan behind him, tearing into packages, filling up a cup.

I turned and that's when I noticed Tess's arm. A bandage was wrapped around it.

Panicking I asked, "Tess what did you do?"

Then I remember what happened right at the end.

"She did what she needed to do," Mora said standing next to Dad. "Be grateful, she kept you alive until Julian and Stefan returned."

I was frantic with worry, "Dad is she alright, she wasn't exposed was she?"

I tried to get up.

"Whoa not so fast," Dad said helping me sit up.

"She's fine son. There's no danger of contamination or transfer. I arranged the equipment so there would be no cross over. We just took enough to get you through until Stefan and Julian got back."

I nodded and said, "Tess I am so sorry I don't know what to say. I never dreamed that something like this would happen."

She came and sat next to me, "Don't say anything. It was my choice and I was happy to do it. Anyway, it's no big deal, all I had to do is give you a little donation."

She laughed a little and said, "I know you've got a thing for my blood, just next time try not to get shot, Ok superman?"

I laughed too, "Ok, I promise. I'm just so happy you are alright. "

Dad put his hand on hers, "We're all very grateful Tess. You are a very brave young lady. Now you need to get some rest and some fluids in you too, Doctor's orders."

She nodded.

Dad looked back at me, "So how's the arm?"

"Sore, but better," I said.

"Let me look," Dad said. He pulled the bandage off. The wound was no longer bleeding and it was beginning to heal. Mora leaned down.

"It will heal in another six to ten hours," she said, "But he has to drink more, lots more."

Dad said, "Let me get that IV out first. I had to use an enchantment to get it in."

Once he had it out, Stefan brought over the cup.

"Ugh," Rachel said, "I am going back down stairs."

"Tess why don't you go down too.," I said wanting to spare her.

"No way, not happening," she said shaking her head.

"Alright," I said and Mora handed me the cup.

"Just chug it baby," Tess said with a slight smile.

I nodded and started drinking.

In a few minutes, Mora brought up some tea for Tess and we rested a bit. Later Dad came and got Tess to do the next reading. She didn't want to go but I insisted. While they were gone, I kept on drinking.

Mora was right on the time, the wound was all healed in seven hours.

Dad took a final look, "How's it feel now?"

I rotated my arm. "Like it never happened."

Tess looked down at where the wound was. The skin was clear, not even a scratch visible.

"Thats just amazing, how did he heal so fast?"

"Vampires," Rachel said shaking her head.

I finished dressing and we loaded the cars. Stefan, Julian and I burned all the blood packages and we left.

"Where are we going?" I asked as I put on my seatbelt realizing I didn't know our next destination.

"Switzerland, the alps. The last element is air," Julian said.

We drove back to the airport and caught another charter flight.

"How you feeling ?" Mora asked.

"Fine, good as new," I said.

Tess and I had just snuggled and rested on the flight. I felt good now, energized by all the blood.

"I've never seen eyes so blue," Tess said looking at me as we stepped into the late afternoon light.

"Only for you," I said.

"Down boy," Rachel said as we got off the plane.

Two black Mercedes were waiting for us.

Dad said, "It's about a three hour drive up the mountain and it'll be dark when we arrive. I have arranged for a chalet so we can spend the night. I think Aidan could use a bit more rest. I'll take the first car, Julian just follow me in the next."

I had no idea where we were going.

Once we were on the road I asked Julian, "Where are we going exactly?"

"It's the element air so it's a cave high in the Swiss Alps."

"Great, another cave," I said.

Tess was glued to the view out the window.

"Spectacular, isn't it ?"

She nodded.

The sun was setting as we arrived. We drove up a long road, snow still on the shoulders. The chalet was magnificent, the sun reflecting on the mountains behind it. It was cold when we got out.

"Let me get your coat," I said to Tess.

"No just let me enjoy it," Tess said taking a deep breath of the mountain air.

"Ok nature girl, lets get inside, I'm freezing," Rachel said.

We walked inside. The place was huge, a giant fireplace in one corner. Dad smiled and waved his hand as he walked in and flames shot up.

"Thanks Dr Croft," Tess said warming herself in front of the fire. I think she was finally getting used to witchcraft.

"Anytime my dear."

After she had time to warm up I said, "Come on" and we went upstairs and unpacked.

"How does your Dad find these places?" Tess asked

"He has unbelievable contacts," I said.

The room was nice; clean and airy. There was a balcony so I stepped outside. The view was incredible, the high alps in all their glory. Tess came outside, the air misting with her breath. "It's quite a sight," she said.

"We going up there?" she pointed

I nodded, "I think so at least part of the way."

She took my hand, "Promise me Aidan that you will be careful tomorrow."

I smiled, "I promise besides Stefan made it painfully clear that I am to take no more chances and believe me, I listen when Stefan talks."

Tess was shivering.

"Come on we have to get you inside. Tomorrow, we're going to buy you a better coat." She nodded her teeth chattering.

We had just closed the balcony door when Rachel popped her head in the door.

"Hey, I'm starving and so is Julian. There is a pizza place down in the village, want to come?"

"Sure," I said, "but we have to get Tess something warmer to wear."

"I think I can arrange that," Rachel said.

Rachel brought Tess a coat, a big furry thing.

"Looks better on you anyway," Rachel said.

The four of us drove down into the village. It was quaint, with Swiss style buildings. The pizza parlor seemed somewhat out of place but it was warm and the people friendly. There were only a couple of other people in the whole place.

They ordered pizzas and beer. They also put in an order for Dad and Lucian. I made my usual excuses.

"So did Aidan tell you about our ski trip? This place reminds me of Tahoe," Tess asked.

"No, Aidan skiing, really?" Rachel said taking a piece of bread.

"Not just skiing, snowboarding. He is very, very good," Tess said.

"Really, Aidan, I am impressed," Rachel said. "Of course you would have never done that without Tess."

"True, very true," I said nodding.

"He never did anything until you showed up," Rachel said.

"That trip, that's when I became suspicious that there was something very different about Aidan," Tess said.

"Different, now I would agree with that term," Rachel said laughing.

"No I mean different in a good way. He was so poised, I'd never seen anyone move the way he moved down the mountain. I could tell he was holding back too and a couple of times I thought he fell on purpose. There was something about him I could't figure out."

"I still can't figure him out," Rachel said.

"So how did you two really meet ?" Julian asked.

"Well I embarrassed her in front of class and she tried to trick me," I said.

We went through the whole story for them. I could tell that there was a real bond developing between Rachel and Tess. When the pizza arrived, they finished it and another round of beer and we left.

Everyone said goodnight and when we got back to our room Tess said, "Your father seems nervous."

"Tomorrow is going to be a big day for him. He's spent centuries looking for that crystal. He told me once that all of our history is in this thing, answers to our most basic questions, who we are are, where we came from, why we're here."

"And you, are you as curious as he is?"

I shook my head, "No not really. I'm much more interested in the future than the past. I worry about it though. They went to such great lengths to hide it all these years, maybe it will tell us things we don't want to know. Dad believes he can purify it, remove the taint of Magnus from it but I'm not so sure."

When she was in my arms next to me I kissed her and stroked her hair and said, "I never really thanked you for today. What you did was very brave but foolish. It was a very dangerous thing Tess. What if the blood had mixed? You would be in the agony of the transformation now only to become a monster like me. I just could't do that to you. You didn't need to take that risk."

"Oh yes I did Aidan. Seeing you lying there. Seeing how much blood you lost, I just couldn't stand it. I was afraid they wouldn't get back in time. I was frantic. I would have done anything for you."

She turned around and kissed me again, "Besides you are no monster."

"You don't know Tess," I stared to explain but she put her fingers to my lips.

I kissed her again and she fell asleep in my arms.

The morning was bright and the air crisp when we walked out of the chalet. After breakfast we packed the cars and the girls bought warmer clothes then we left. It was going to be a long drive. Again Tess was transfigured by the scenery. We stopped once to verify the directions then we came to a small village high in the mountains. We parked the cars on the outskirts and got out.

Julian had been near here once before so he lead the way. Our destination was a cave about a mile away. Now how a cave would fit into the looking for something that had to do with the element of air, I had no idea but we followed Julian.

The trail led higher into the mountain. We began to see more snow. After several twists and turns the trail straightened and I could see a small opening in the side of the mountain. It was more of a large crack in the face of the mountain than a cave. High above the crack the symbol for air was etched into the stone.

We walked into the crack and Julian lit the way with witch fire, its blue flame throwing shadows on the wall.

The rough stone path gave way to a more polished tunnel. We followed the tunnel for what seemed like a half a mile and came out onto a large shelf on the side of the mountain. It was like a crack had opened within the mountain itself, steep vertical walls surrounded us from behind and high above us I could just make out a band of blue sky. Ahead of us, not more than fifty feet away the shelf just ended and a great chasm opened up. I walked over, the drop down seemed to go on for thousands of feet. I could not even see the bottom. Far across the chasm I could see another shelf. I looked around but there was no way across.

The wind was howling around us. Now I understood why Jakob had chosen this spot for air. It seemed we were suspended in it, thousands of feet above the ground.

"There doesn't appear to be anyway across," I yelled at Julian.

"What did journal say," Julian yelled at Dad.

"It says that only the man that doubts his sight can cross. The humble man will see victory and the end of his quest. Seek the way of light and let the wind be your ally."

"That's all it says?" I asked.

"Yes, thats all it says," he replied.

The wind was howling even louder now. It seemed to blow directly down the side of the cliff.

"It said let the wind be your ally. It seems to blow down and over toward the right," I yelled.

"He's right," Julian yelled back. I pointed to Rachel and Tess, trying to stay out of the wind next to the tunnel. "Rachel you, Mora, and Tess should go back into the tunnel. The winds are picking up." I pointed to the tunnel.

Tess shook her head, "I'm not leaving you," she yelled.

I went over to her, "Tess, I promise I won't do anything foolish but I can't look for clues worrying that you will fall or be blown off the side. Please go inside with Rachel, I promise I won't do anything stupid."

Rachel grabbed her arm and yelled, "Come on Tess, we need to let them work."

Finally she agreed and she, Rachel, and Mora went back into the tunnel.

The rest of us headed towards the right. The wind seemed to pick up here and blow even harder.

Dad said, "It says the humble man will see victory." He got down on his hands and knees. We followed suite, crawling around on the shelf floor. I moved farther to the right but did not see anything. I was about to turn around when something glimmered ahead of me. I crawled over. A piece of quartz was embedded in the floor. I looked up and one small shaft of light seemed to fall down on it. You would only see it if you were here on the ground. I motioned to everyone. "Over here," I yelled.

They came over. "Bend down," I said. They did too. "See the quartz, from this angle the light hits it just right. The light is pointing in that direction," I pointed to a spot at the edge of the shelf. We walked over to the side. The wind had all but died out here.

There right on the edge of the cliff was another piece of quartz. It pointed out across the chasm.

"I don't understand, it looks like it points off into space," Julian said.

Dad said, "Only the man that doubts his sight can cross."

"What does that mean ?" I asked.

With that Dad jumped off the side of the shelf. I screamed and went to grab him but instead of falling he seemed to just float in space.

"Its an optical illusion. There is a bridge here. It just looks the same as the rest of the mountain, that's why you can't see it. From down here I see that it crosses the chasm and there's no wind. Julian come with me, the rest of you stay put."

Julian shook his head and squinted his eyes but stepped out. Like Dad he appeared to be floating in space. He waved and followed Dad out across the bridge. They got to the shelf on the other side and went into what appeared to be another tunnel. After a few minutes they emerged. Dad had a box in his hand. He waved and held it up above his head.

He had found it, the crystal he had searched centuries for, he finally had it.

They came back over the bridge. Stefan and I helped them up.

Dad was all smiles, "We found it, we finally found it."

I patted him on the back, "I can't believe you finally have it, after all these years," I said.

We went back into the tunnel. Tess was relieved to see that I had not done anything dangerous.

"Did you find it?" she asked.

Dad nodded, "Yes, yes we found it," he said beaming.

Tess grabbed him and gave him a big hug. He smiled and hugged her back.

"A lot of the credit goes to you, young lady. This would have never happened without you. I am eternally grateful to you and Aidan."

"I was just glad to be a part of it."

He smiled and hugged her again.

"Let's get out of here," he said.

Tess said, "I'm ready."

"So am I," said Rachel.

As we started walking, Dad put his arm around me and said, "Aidan when we get back down the mountain, I want you to take Tess home. She has been away long enough and both of you need some rest. Julian and I are going to take the crystal to the house in London. The rest of us can start our search for Arius there. Once I have purified and opened the crystal, I may be able to use it to find him especially if he has the lesser twin with him."

I nodded.

We walked back through the tunnel, Julian leading the way with his witch flame.

We were almost to the end, walking through one of the larger passages when his light suddenly went out.

I heard a screech, like the sound we heard in Arius's office, and following that was a metallic sound like metal on metal.

Then everything went dark.

Chapter 15

A Battle for the Soul

French Alps

When I came to I was in a prison with my feet chained and a gag tied around my mouth. My hands were chained as well and pulled up over my head. I looked up and saw that the chain was bolted into the stone wall. I pulled but the chains would not give. Enchanted, the same kind that kept Stefan imprisoned. I tried again but the chain held.

There were openings high in the wall above me. I heard sounds, voices coming from them. I was still coming to but I tried to make out the voices. Finally my head cleared and I could tell who was speaking. It was Malek, same sneering voice I remembered from New York.

"Well look at the mighty Marcus now. Tied up like the little bug you are. You and your precious little coven."

I could just make out Dad's voice, "Where's my son?"

"Oh we have much planned for your son, Marcus. He is very rare, too rare to destroy. Draven has great plans for him. He wants to examine him himself. Perhaps we will convert him, or perhaps we'll just dissect him. We'll have to see what Draven's mood is."

"Don't touch him," I heard a voice say. Tess. My heart sank. They had all of us. Any hope I had that she had escaped was gone. I had to get out of here. I pulled on the chain again.

"Ah and you brought us a human, how charming. One of your little pets no doubt. Actually this is quite fortunate as we are going to need a human to expedite the spell. You saved me the trouble of securing one."

I heard him walking, "Pity, you are quite beautiful."

"Don't touch me you pig," I heard her say.

"Oh you will be begging me to touch you soon enough my dear. But we have bigger plans for you than just my amusement."

I pulled against the chains with all my might. I tried and tried, but I was powerless. The spell on the chain was too strong.

I heard footsteps again.

"You see Marcus, we are going to complete what that fool Jakob and Arius interrupted centuries ago. I saw to it that Jakob got his reward and Arius ..." I heard a sound like witch lightening followed by a low moan. "Well Arius will get his reward as soon as Draven is ready."

"Where is your master?" I heard Dad say.

"Oh he is coming and then you will see his transformation. When he is revived and we have the full power of the Shadow in our grasp, you and all of your family will die."

"You see, thanks to these cretins, my master Draven has spent centuries locked in a failing body. That imbecile Jakob interrupted the transfer spell when he and Arius stole the Shadow. Draven's essence was transferred to his new body but the transfer was incomplete. Only a portion of his power transferred. He has spent centuries, captive in a body decaying around him. Only with the darkest of arts have we been able to keep him alive."

"But now you have done us this great service Marcus. You found the larger twin and this worm brought us the lesser one so now we have them both. In the coming ceremony, when Draven arrives and the moon is full, I will rejoin the halves and with this new Shadow, my master will transfer into a new, whole body. Then the world will be ours."

He paused a moment.

"Poor Marcus, now you are beginning to realize the magnitude of your folly. Who do you think organized the army, made the vampires our servants? Magnus? Magnus was too arrogant to deal with those details, to get his hands dirty in the actual fighting. He was too caught up in his visions, his knowledge, his lofty plans. So he left all the real work to us."

"So it was Draven and I who made the armies; armies loyal to us. With the forces under our control, all we needed was the Shadow to overthrow him. But to steal it, we needed a diversion and that's where you came in. When the time was right we disclosed to you the truth about Magnus and then you played your part perfectly. Pool fool, you never saw what was coming. We were ready and then you killed the only one who could have stood in our way."

"Everything was perfect until this worthless maggot uncovered our true plans. He and Jakob interrupted the transformation and stole the Shadow. His treachery sentenced my master to centuries of agony while his body aged and rotted around him."

I heard another shot of witch lightening.

There was a slight pause then Malek continued.

"But all be remedied tonight. When my master arrives, I will perform the spell myself. There will be no interruption. Your pet's blood will be the catalyst along with that witches blood. When both have been drained and the shadow is full of their life, my master will transfer in whole to his hew host. Their life will enable his transfer and they will feed his new body."

"So you were our tool then and you are our tool now. Who do you think provided you all these clues? Who sent you Tomas? Draven and I knew you would be compelled to find the Shadow. When Arius showed up with the lesser crystal, we set our plan in motion. Our agent in Venice called us as soon as you arrived. We knew you would find it, we just had to wait."

"So you see Marcus, you have been our willing instrument all along. But tonight once your women have fed him, once Draven is whole and powerful in his new body, then you will have one more task to perform. You are going to watch as Draven kills the rest of your coven one by one, one more service you will render to your true master."

Malek's laughter filled the room above me. I yanked harder and harder on the chains. I had to get out, somehow I had to escape. I must have struggled for another twenty minutes but there was no way to break free. I could hear Tess crying. Rachel too. I thought I was going to lose my mind. I tried to yell but the gag was tight and the chains had me completely in their power.

It was quiet after a while. I could tell the sun was set and the moon would be rising soon. Lights were lit down the hall from me. I heard movement and a voice down the hall say "The master is arriving."

I pulled against the chains again.

Everything grew still. I knew it was the end, everything I loved was going to die and there was nothing I could do about it. I cried in despair.

I heard voices above me. Things were being moved around the room. I heard Tess cry out then her voice was cut short. I thought I heard Mora hiss.

I began to hear chanting. It droned on and on.

I had all but given up hope when something moved down the hall. Wind. It was strange, a wind was blowing inside the building. I could see it blowing dust. It spun like a dust devil, whirling in the shadows. As it got closer, I could see lights in the dust, shimmering.

Then the lights and the dust began to take on shape. I could see a form materializing in the wind. The lights got brighter then they merged together and in the center of the whirl wind stood a woman, her long black hair blowing. The wind stopped and she stepped forward. She was very pale, her skin almost glowing in the dim light. I recognized her, the pale form I had seen in LA. that night.

I tried to cry out but my voice was muffled; she raised one hand and the gag fell off.

"Help me get lose. I have to save my family!," I pleaded as I pulled against the chains again.

She walked up to me. Her face was timeless, her eyes blue like the sky. She smiled and gently reached out and ran her fingers through my hair. Then she spoke, her voice melodic, like the wind.

"I have followed you for many years Aidan and there are many things I should tell you now, but we have no time. One day you will understand the truth Aidan; you are the promise."

Her eyes became harder, "But now you must stop Draven. He must not possess the crystal. But warn your father, there is door in that crystal he must not open; remember that, he must not open that door. It must remain sealed."

"I don't understand," I said shaking my head.

"You will and he will at the right time."

She looked up the hall that ran by my cell. "I'm sorry but I have run out of time. In a minute, an acolyte witch will come down this hall to retrieve the crystal. Take his place and when the time is right use the crystal. Free the wind Aidan."

She reached out and waved her hand. The chains fell off my feet and wrists.

She smiled again and stepped back. The wind began to blow around her.

I held out my hand, "Wait, I still don't understand."

Her smile brightened and she said, "One day."

The lights around her grew bright and the wind began to swirl tighter around her. Then just as she came, she was gone. All that was left was a dust devil spinning down the hall.

I kicked the chains out of the way and moved into the darkness.

The chanting increased in volume as I heard many voices join in.

Then down the hall I heard footsteps and so I jumped up, waiting in the darkness on the ceiling.

A young man in a robe and hood ran by me. I followed him as he went into a room down the hall. I dropped down and slipped in behind him as he pulled a box from a cabinet. It was a smaller version of the box Dad found.

As he turned, a look of surprise came over his face. I backhanded him and he flew into the brick wall. I took his robe, bound him and stuffed him into a closet. I locked it and grabbed the box. As I ran out I put on the robe and pulled the hood over my head.

I followed the path that the acolyte had taken down. It led to a long, dark hall then to a wide set of stairs.

The stairs opened up into a large circular room. We were high in a stone tower with glass windows surrounding it on all sides. Some were clear but some were covered with red stained glass. Moonlight poured in from them. As I looked out of the windows I saw that the tower sat high on a cliff, its walls falling straight down into darkness.

To the right of the stairs, Dad, Lucian, Julian, Mora, and Stefan were bound with enchanted chains. Stefan and Mora were pulling to get free, their teeth bared. Several of the fanged vampires stood watch next to them. Dad, Julian and Lucian were now gagged, no doubt to keep them silent during the ceremony. Each of them had been struck multiple times; Dad had a long gash on one cheek. They were exhausted hanging down against their chains.

Farther down another man was chained, Arius no doubt. He was in significantly worse shape; very badly beaten, eyes swollen with blood caked on one side of his face. Across his body I could see several burns from witch lightening.

My heart turned cold when I looked to the center of the room. A witches circle was etched on the floor. I had never seen one like this. It felt wrong somehow. Strange symbols were etched around it and the circle itself was glowing a dark orange light.

Four stone tables had been pulled into the circle making a cross shaped altar. Tess was chained on one; her arms bound above her head, her wrists exposed. Rachel was likewise bound. A young man was on the third table. He was naked, symbols painted all over his body. His eyes were open but he just stared ahead as if he might have been drugged.

Something hideous was stretched out on the fourth table. A small, frail form lay there, the body thin and emaciated. The skin was brown almost moldy in spots. The hair was gone, even the eyebrows. But the eyes were bright, full of malice and hatred. They looked hungry.

The tables were arranged so that the young man's head was vertically across from Draven's wretched body, their two scalps almost touching. Flanking them on either side were Tess and Rachel. Each had one wrist bound to Draven's table and the other bound to the young host.

The spell had already started. Several witches stood next to the tables chanting. A cut had been made on each of Tess's wrists. A small trickle of blood flowed down onto Dravens's table as well as the young hosts. A knife lay next to her arm. A similar one was next to Rachel's outstretched wrists.

The larger crystal was already engaged. It sat in the center of the altar. A dark shadow, almost a mist emanated from it swirling from Draven to the young man.

All they needed was the lesser crystal that I had in the box to complete the spell.

I knew what I had to do.

When I reached the top of the stairs I walked out onto the stone floor and threw back the hood of my robe.

Vampire guards, their fangs showing stooped down to attack.

Malek held up his hand and stopped the chant.

"Wait," he said.

"I see you are more resourceful than we thought, young man."

I didn't say anything, all I did was open the box and pull out the crystal, holding it by its chain.

Malek sneered, "Let me guess, you want to trade your family for the crystal."

I said nothing.

He pointed to Dad and the others.

"You want to save them, these liars? Your whole life they have told you we are an abomination, that we are unnatural, evil. But you see it is they that are the abomination, they are the ones that are unnatural. They have twisted their true nature into something that is weak and corrupt."

"Even you are corrupted Aidan. You, a vampire, born to feast on the blood of humans, pity them, console them, fight for them. You are the unnatural abomination."

Then he pointed to Tess and smiled, a wicked smile.

"I can see into you Aidan, I see your inner struggle."

"You smell it don't you. Her blood. I feel it in you. You want nothing more than to sink your teeth into her delicious flesh and drink from that warm and flowing fountain, to feast on her life. That's what makes you strong, that's what makes you a vampire, that is your true self."

Then he pointed at my family. "But these worms, these charlatans have twisted you, corrupted you from your true form. You see, we are the rightful rulers of this world. These lesser creatures, these humans, exist only to serve us. We are their masters. They are nothing but our servants and our food. That is the true order of things. The world exists only for those that are strong, that can seize it and can drain it of its life and grow stronger."

He laughed. "Look inside yourself Aidan, feel your thirst. You know this to be true. Trust your thirst. It is the one true constant you have. The rest of this, all this that they have told you, is a lie."

"Join us. Follow your thirst and take your prey. Drink this beautiful woman dry, have her life and I promise you that you will have an inexhaustible supply. We will teach you your true nature. Draven can awaken your witch powers. Help me save him. Help me finish this and the three of us will be unstoppable. We will take our rightful places as the true rulers of this world."

I looked at Dad. He was tired, drained. So were the rest. Only Mora and Stefan's eyes smoldered with anger.

I looked down at Tess. She was beautiful and her blood was delicious. The smell of it filled the room.

I held up the crystal and I took it in my hand.

I felt the thirst flow, it sang in my ears. My throat was on fire. Then the power, the witchcraft that had eluded me all these years flowed with it. The two flowed together and a strength I had never felt before filled me. Witch and Vampire became one and in that instant they worked together, no longer at war each holding the other back but now merged together.

I looked into the crystal and I called to the shadow living there. A dark form began to flow out. It flowed and mixed with the thirst and power that was already flowing through me. I pulled that last remnant of Magnus from the crystal into myself. He was hungry, very hungry. He flowed around me. I called to his hunger and he answered.

Freed of Magnus, the crystal was now clear, its beauty shimmering in the air.

I looked at Malek. He was smiling and I said.

"You're right, I will follow my thirst."

I looked back into the crystal and in my mind, I saw it. A wind. Freed of Magnus, a wind was swirling in the crystal, howling in it, an elemental power straining to be released. I remembered what the pale woman said. I looked deep into crystal and there in the midst of that whirlwind was the stillness. At that moment, knew what I had to do. I thought of my love for Tess and I opened myself to the stillness. I let the surge of that trapped power flow through me. I freed the wind.

It streamed out blowing like a hurricane in the room. It howled as it swirled out across the room, dancing like it was alive. I directed it towards the chains that held my family. The chains sang as they burst, the wind flinging the links across the room. It picked up the witches standing next to the altar and flung them like toys into the walls.

I felt Magnus' hunger flowing around me. It swirled in the wind like a dark cloak about me, mixing with my own thirst.

The crystal was still glowing in my hand as I looked down at Rachel. The wind had freed her and there was rage in her eyes. I threw the crystal to her.

"Save Tess," I yelled over the wind and jumping across the room, I grabbed Malek, holding him in a tight embrace. I gave myself over to the thirst, sinking my teeth deep into his neck. I could feel Magnus' hunger swirling about both of us.

I knew what I had to do to save Tess. Wrapping my arms tighter around Malek, I jumped. Pulling the wind to my back, we exploded through the stain glass window, the wind howling behind us. The red glass shattered following us as we tumbled out of the tower and down the steep cliff. Falling I could feel Magnus feeding.

The last sound I heard was Tess screaming my name.

A darkness took me.

Chapter 16

A New Beginning

Croft Home

Muir Woods

It surprised me that I was still alive. Everything was dark but I knew that I was, somewhere. It was like the transformation but without the pain. In fact I didn't feel anything at all. I was just floating in the dark. I dreamed of wind, howling wind. In the darkness, I felt detached, almost peaceful though a hurricane was swirling around me. But something was wrong. I was missing something.

Then the wind stopped and there was a sound. Not the tap, tap sound of a butterfly's wings but a slow thump, a rhythm; not the howling of the hurricane but the steady, simple beat of of a heart. I simply listened to it for a while. It was beautiful, like a symphony. It seemed to call to me so I followed the sound.

As I followed the sound of the heart, I felt pain. Not the burning of the transformation but an aching all over. Oh yes, I was definitely still alive. I couldn't move but I felt pain. Even with the pain, I followed the heartbeat.

Following the beating sound, I struggled back into my body. Finally something seemed to click and I knew I was lying down and something soft and warm was in my hand. It held it tightly. For a while I just rested there. I was very tired after the struggle but I knew I had to get to that heartbeat. After a bit, I could see light behind my eyelids. It was difficult but I finally opened my eyes.

I looked up. It was Tess. Her face looking down at me. It was the most beautiful sight I had ever seen. It was her hand I felt, her heartbeat I heard.

"Hey beautiful," I whispered.

She smiled and said, "Hey you."

Then her mouth began to tremble, a tear fell down her cheek.

She put her head down on my chest and began to cry.

I tried to lift my arm but I couldn't.

I looked up and saw Rachel and Mora. Rachel was crying and Mora had a single blue tear flowing down her porcelain cheek.

I tired to smile but it hurt. The slightest movement was difficult. My bones felt like broken glass.

Tess felt me trying to stir and sat up.

"Aidan be still, your still healing," she said.

Dad stood behind her, "Listen to her son. You have a ways to go."

I could just nod my head, what felt like glass in my neck was breaking with the movement.

I could just make out my Dads's voice, "Son you're going to sleep now."

A rush of calm swept over me and I slept.

Next thing I remember was hearing that heartbeat again. This time it was a little farther away. I opened my eyes. I was groggy but I could move, a little. I was sore, really sore but at least I did not feel like I was made of glass. My eyes followed the sound of the heartbeat.

Tess was sitting in a chair, reading. I was in my room at home, the bright morning sun streaming in. She heard me turn my head and she rushed over.

She took my hand as she sat on my bed next to me, "Aidan. Oh my God, you're awake. You're finally awake."

"I missed you," I said trying to smile.

She put her forehead down on mine, "I missed you too. I love you, Aidan," she whispered.

"I love you too, Tess"

I felt a tear hit my face.

"I promised, I promised Mora I was not going to cry."

I lifted my arm and put my hand on her head and just held her a few minutes.

There were a few more tears.

She raised up and said, "How do you feel?"

"Sore, really, really sore. Let me try and sit up," I said.

"Wait, wait, let me get Marcus and Stefan," she said and ran from the room.

I tried to raise up on one arm. Thats when I noticed the other one. It had scars on it, blue welts that were still healing.

About that time Dad and Stefan came in.

Dad reached down and kissed me on the head.

"We were so worried about you son."

"Here I'll help you sit up," Stefan said, relief on his face.

"See I told you he has more lives than a cat," I heard Rachel say behind them.

Stefan got me up and I sat on the side of the bed.

I smiled at Rachel and said, "I think this cat got scalped."

I tried to laugh but I was too sore.

"What happened?" I asked.

Dad said, "You saved us, Aidan. We would not have escaped without you son."

Stefan sat beside me and put his hand on my shoulder. "This is true, we would all be dead without you Aidan."

I put my hand on his arm and smiling said, "You don't have to say anything Stefan. None of you do. You saved me long before that."

I took a long breath, "I really want to get up and walk around."

"You sure about that," Dad asked.

"Yea, I'm sure, Just help me up."

Stefan helped me stand up. He had me by one arm.

"I remember this from once before," I said smiling.

"You were just as stubborn then," Stefan said with a slight grin.

"Can you walk?" he asked.

I nodded and took a few steps. It was hard and I was really sore but it felt so good to be up and walking. It reminded me of how I felt when I was human and was sore from a really long run.

Stefan pointed to the chair. I shook my head. "I'd like to go downstairs."

He frowned. "Marcus?"

"It would do him good to walk if he can do it."

"Let's go then," he said.

I saw my reflection in the mirror. "Damn, I do look like something the cat dragged in. Let me clean up a minute."

Stefan nodded and took me into the bathroom.

I looked terrible. My face was gaunt, deep circles under my eyes. There were scars on my face too, one a long gash that went from my left eye to my cheek. My eyes were grey.

I washed up and looked at my arms. Scars down both of them. I wanted to know so I lifted up my tank top.

The scars were much worse here. There were bite marks from Magnus all over my chest. Around them were big ugly bruises and I had a bandage on my left side. It was stained dark with blue vampire blood.

"You ok in there?" I heard Tess ask.

"Yea, I'm coming." I put my shirt down, splashed my face again. The water felt wonderful. I combed it through my long black hair.

I opened the door.

"You look downright handsome now," Tess said.

"Right," I said.

Stefan took my arm and we headed out the door.

The stairs were quite an adventure, each step painful. My legs were in rebellion but we made it although very slow.

Stefan took me into the family room and sat me in one of the big double chairs. I was exhausted but felt better.

"How you feel?" Rachel asked.

"Tired but better," I said.

I looked at Stefan, "and thirsty."

"I'll get it," Stefan said.

As he left, Mora came in.

"So how are you doing kiddo?" she asked.

"I've been better," I said with a smile.

The smile left her face and she took my hand.

"We all thought we'd lost you, Aidan," she said.

I looked at my scars, "Looks like it was close."

Everyone was at the door. I motioned for them to come in. It was a good thing that it was a big room. Mom kissed me and sat down next to me. She put her head next to mine. We all just sat there for a while.

Finally she motioned to Tess to come and sit next to me. Mom got up and kissed me on the forehead as Stefan showed up with a big stone mug.

"Sorry," I said looking at Rachel.

"Go on, you need it," Rachel said. I drank it all.

Just like years ago, Mora gave me a cloth and I wiped my mouth. Rachel had a sour look on her face.

"Want some," I asked lifting the cup, teasing. She turned up her nose and I laughed a little then a fit of coughing took over. Dad came over but I stopped, "I'm ok, it just hurts to laugh."

"You have a pretty bad cut on your side son. It still needs time to heal."

I nodded then asked the question.

"How long was I out?"

"Five weeks, it's been five weeks."

I was stunned. How could it have been so long?

"That's not possible," I said.

Tess took my hand, "Yes, it's been that long Aidan."

"I was asleep all that time?"

I looked around and didn't see Julian. "Where's Julian and Lucian?"

"They are traveling back from Europe. We had many lose ends to tie up."

"How did you get me home, what happened to Draven," I said. I struggled to lean forward.

Dad said, "Take it easy son, you need to rest. Drink some more and rest and we'll explain everything."

I was exhausted. Stefan got me another mug which I drank and he, Mora and Tess helped me back upstairs. I sat down on the bed and Tess came and sat next to me. I took her hands in mine, there were two small scars on her wrists, gifts from Draven. Anger surged through me at the thought. I lightly brushed them with my finger.

"I'm so sorry Tess, so sorry that I pulled you into this terrible mess."

She put a finger to my lips and shook her head.

"We're in this together. Rest now, just rest Aidan."

I laid down and she laid next to me. We held hands and I went into trance.

The sun was just setting as I woke. Tess was already up, standing at the window looking out at the garden.

"Tess," I said. She turned around.

"Hey, you're up. How you feeling?"

I felt much better, my strength was returning.

I nodded, "Better, much better. I'd like to get a shower and get dressed."

"Let me get your father, he wants to change the dressing on your side."

I laid back down and soon she and my father were back.

I pulled off my shirt. Tess looked at me.

"I know its not pretty," I said.

"I think you're beautiful," she said.

I just shook my head and said "Love is blind you know."

Dad just smiled.

He pulled off the bandage. The wound was almost closed up and it was healing. It had stopped bleeding.

Replacing the bandage, he said, "His natural healing is working. Another day and this bandage can come off."

"He wants to get a shower," Tess said.

"Thats fine, just don't get it wet," he said.

He gathered his supplies and said with a slight smile on his face, "I'll leave you two alone."

Tess smiled a guilty smile and when he left I said, "Race you."

"Your on" and she laughed as I shuffled and we headed for the shower.

It was so good to be clean again. Tess checked my bandage and helped me get my shirt on. We left my room but stopped at the stairs.

"Want me to get Stefan?"

"No I can make it."

It was much easier to get down this time.

Mom was cooking, I could smell it as we got downstairs.

"You hungry?" I asked Tess.

"Starving," she said.

"You two go sit with the others," Mom said.

We sat down at the big table and Mom brought in a big roast.

I saw Stefan at the door, "Here," he said handing me the big cup again.

"Stefan I don't know," I said looking at Tess and Rachel.

Rachel just waved her hands, "Oh go on," she said.

"Tess," I asked.

"Not going to bother me," she said grabbing a large piece and some potatoes.

I nodded and Stefan sat it in front of me. It smelled delicious. I took a large drink.

"Do you realize Aidan, this is the first time we have ever had a meal together?" Tess said.

"Well that deserves a toast," Dad said. They all lifted their glasses and for the first time I did too.

They were about half way done with their meal when I heard the door shut. Julian and Lucian walked in. Julian came right up and hugged me. "Oh my boy its so good to see you up." Even Lucian came over and hugged me. I don't ever remember him doing that. He stepped back and mussed my hair a little.

"Thank you," he said.

"It's ok," I said, "Come sit down."

"I am starving, I hate that food they give you on the plane," Julian said getting a big plate and a full glass of wine.

"The affairs?" Dad asked.

"Spotless but there was no trace," Julian said shaking his head.

"What was that?" I asked.

"Let's all finish then I'll tell you everything," Dad said.

After everyone ate their fill and grabbed coffee or wine we all went into the library. Stefan brought me yet another cup. I found the most comfortable seat groaning a little as I sat down.

When I was finally situated I asked, "So what happened?"

"I could ask you the same question," Dad said.

I thought a minute and said.

"I remember being in the tunnel, then I heard a screech and the sound of chains. I blacked out after that."

"Wraiths. You heard the wraiths, Draven's shadow servants. Malek was waiting for us in the tunnel. He conjured the wraiths and when they had us trapped, he bound us with the chains."

"Just like what happened to Stefan before?"

Stefan nodded.

"I woke up chained to the wall," Dad said, "but where were you?"

"I was in a room below you, chained as well."

"How did you escape the chains?" Julian asked. "Their enchantment was irreversible."

"I didn't, I was freed," I said.

"Who let you go?" Dad asked.

"A woman, a pale witch."

"Who?" Rachel asked.

"I was chained to the wall and I could hear you but I was gagged. I tried and tried to break free but it was no use. Then I heard Malek speaking. I thought I was going to go out of my mind when I heard what he said."

I paused a minute, remembering.

"Then the chanting started and I thought it was all over. That's when I saw a strange sight, a wind started blowing down the hall where I was chained, like a dust devil. It moved towards me and when it got close I saw it had lights swirling around in it. Then a form shaped in it and next thing I see is a pale woman with black hair. Her voice was strange, melodic."

"Anyway, she released the chains and said someone would come for the crystal, and I was to take their place. Then she vanished in the wind."

I thought a minute, "She told me to give you a message."

"A message?" Dad asked.

"She said there is a door in the crystal that you must not open. It's sealed for a reason."

"Is that all she said ," he asked.

"Yes, she said there was more to tell but that there was no time. Do any of you know who she was?"

"I don't have a clue," Julian said.

Dad was caught in thought.

"An elder," he whispered.

"Thats just a myth," Julian said.

"Elder?" Tess asked.

"Our ancestors. The myth says that we are descended from an ancient race, a powerful race of witches that disappeared long ago. They were called the Elders."

"So what happened after you were freed," Rachel asked.

"Just as she told me, someone came for the crystal and I took their place. You saw what happened next."

"Yea you kicked that bad mothers ass," Rachel said.

Everyone laughed.

Tess squeezed my hand, "Why did you jump, Aidan?"

I paused a minute, remembering. "I had to do it. I knew the only way I could destroy Malek was with Magnus. So I pulled Magnus from the crystal and I grabbed Malek. Magnus began to feed on both of us but I knew his guards would intervene so I had only one option left."

"You almost killed yourself," Julian said.

I nodded, "I had to do it, there was no other way."

The room grew very quiet.

"So what happened after I jumped?" I asked.

"Oh the place went to hell in a hand basket," Rachel said. "After the chains blew off and you threw the crystal to me, I grabbed Tess and threw the crystal to Marcus and then a real fight broke out."

"Mora and I circled and protected Tess while everyone else fought the witches and the vampire guard."

"It was quite a maelstrom with the wind, flying stones, and witch lightening."

"Stefan broke several of the guards necks," Mora said.

Stefan continued, "The guards put up quite a fight but without Malek they were disorganized and soon fled."

"Especially after we fried some of them," Rachel said smiling.

"And Draven, what happened to Draven?"

Dad shook his head.

"Enough of the transfer completed that he entered his new host but the transformation itself didn't complete. He was left unconscious. The dark witches rescued him along with several of the guard and we finished off the rest."

"And Arius?"

Julian shook his head, "The minute he was free he grabbed the larger crystal and disappeared. We never saw him after that."

I shook my head, "And the other one, the lesser twin?"

"Upstairs in my study. It's very intricate, it will take some studying to open it. You might be able to help me with that."

"So we are almost back to where we started, Draven still on the loose and Arius no where to be found."

Dad nodded, "Afraid so son, although Malek is gone and we have the lesser crystal. Draven will be weakened for a while, it will take time for him to regain his power and fully control his new body."

He smiled, "Just give me some time Aidan. I'll decipher the crystal and we'll find Arius. We just have to be patient. I for one am grateful, profoundly grateful, for how things turned out."

He was right, I was grateful.

"So how did you find me?" I asked.

Stefan frowned and said, "As soon as the battle was over, we started looking for you. Mora and I scaled the cliff walls. It took us a bit but we finally found you hanging from a rock on the side of the cliff."

Dad put his arm on Tess, "And once we found you, Tess never left your side. She wouldn't leave you. Even when you were in the earth."

"What, what about being in the earth?" I asked.

"Go on, tell him," Dad said to Tess.

"I couldn't believe it myself, Aidan but it somehow worked."

"What worked?"

"You tell him Mora, he'll believe you," Tess said shaking her head. "I still have trouble believing it myself."

Mora's face was pained as she started, "Aidan, you were almost dead when we found you. Somehow in the fall you released Malek, we never found his body. But you fell a great distance, many hundreds of feet below the tower and what damage the fall didn't do to you, the feeding of Magnus did. You were covered with bite marks and you had lost a great deal of blood. His feeding made the effects of the fall much worse."

"When we carried you back up the cliff, Marcus was beside himself. He and Julian tried spell after spell but nothing was working. You were slipping away so Stefan and I convinced Marcus to try something. Years ago he and I ran across an ancient vampire and his young apprentice who were fighting a coven of witches. We stopped the fight and saved the old vampire but the young one, like you was very close to death. The ancient said we had to put the apprentice into the earth. He said when injured and buried in the ground, vampires go into a dreamless sleep their life suspended. In that state he said the young one would heal. He was adamant that we had to bury him in the earth and wait a full cycle of the moon. He said the earth would heal him. So we followed his instruction and wrapped the young one in a sheet and placed him in the ground. It worked and the young vampire recovered. It took a while but he recovered."

"There was nothing else we could do. We could either watch you die or try the same thing so that's what we did. You were in the earth for over a month."

"How did you get me back to San Francisco?" I asked.

Stefan smiled, "Another old vampire trick although it caused Tess and Rachel some heartache. We put you in a coffin and filled it with earth. We flew it back to the states. Of course Julian had to pull some strings with customs."

I looked at Tess, she shook her head, "It was terrible, just like in the old movies."

Rachel nodded, "Oh, it gave me the creeps."

"What did you do when we got back here?"

"We planted you in the garden, next to the rose bush," Rachel said smiling.

"Really?" I asked the sound of disbelief in my voice.

"Yea, I wanted to cover you with manure but Julian wouldn't let me."

At first I was stunned then I laughed, really, really laughed. I just couldn't stop and so did everyone else.

When we had all composed ourselves I said, "When did you dig me up?"

"Three days ago," Dad said. "We had to wait for the full moon cycle. I didn't believe it but it worked. You woke for just a minute but I put you back to sleep to heal a little more."

I asked Julian, "So while I was out, you two were searching the whole time?"

He and Lucian nodded.

"Did you find any trace of them?" I asked.

Julian answered, "Like I said, Arius just disappeared, he and the larger crystal. He's vanished again like a ghost. We have a few leads but nothing is firm."

"And Draven?"

Lucian shook his head, "Gone too. Like your father said, it will take time for him to adapt to his new host but I'm sure he will return and will be in desperate need of the crystal. We've not seen the last of him and his kind."

I rubbed my arm, one of the healing scars.

Dad said, "They will heal son. It's just going to take time."

Mora put her hand on my arm, "You should get some rest Aidan."

She helped me get up and and when we got to the door I stopped. Tess had me by the other arm.

"Have you really been here the whole time?"

She nodded. "I went home for a few hours at a time but I always came back."

"What about Karen and Nick?"

"I told them that you were in a bad skiing accident, that you were in a coma. Of course I left out the part about you being in the ground. When you woke up I called them and told them that you were recovering."

I smiled, "Tess, you should go home. Spend some time with them. Play with Austin. If you have been here five weeks, you need a break."

"Not going to happen. I'm not leaving you, not while you are still recovering."

"Dad?"

"We tried son, several times. She won't leave. She's quite stubborn when it comes to you."

Tess smiled and said, "How about this. I'll take you for a walk in the morning and afterwards, I'll drive home for a while?"

I could tell there was going to be no reasoning with her so I agreed. Secretly I was glad she stayed.

I drank another cup and Stefan helped me to my room. We cleaned up and Tess curled up next to me. She kissed me and said, "Rest Aidan, rest." She smiled and closed my eyes. I lost myself in trance.

Tess woke up bright and early the next morning.

Rachel, Julian, she and I sat in the back next to the garden. They had coffee and donuts, of course. I just enjoyed the sun.

"How about that walk?" she said.

I groaned but nodded ok

We took a slow stroll around the garden. We stopped next to the roses. Adjacent to them a section of the grass was cut back and the red ground was turned up.

"I was really in there for a month?"

She nodded. I could tell the memory was painful.

"And you came here everyday?"

"Yes, I came and sat next to you on the grass. Finally, Stefan brought me out a chair. I cried a lot at the beginning, talked to you while you were asleep. After the second day Mora came out. She sat on the ground next to me and told me not to worry that she could hear you, that you would be fine. She really helped me. I wouldn't have go through it without her. Henry came a couple of times as well. He was very sweet."

As we stood there, she took my hand and said, "I thought I'd lost you forever." A tear rolled down her cheek. I looked at the small patch of dirt.

"I did it to save you, Tess. It was the only way I could save you."

She really started to cry then. I put my arm around her. I think the stress of everything finally hit her. She put her head on my should and sobbed.

"Hey," I said after a few minutes. "Lets take a drive, get out of here. You'll have to drive but I would love to get out of the house for for a while."

"Really," she said wiping her eyes.

"Yea, just me and you."

"Will you Dad let you go?"

"Oh, I think we can convince him. He's no better at saying no to you than I am."

She smiled and said, "Ok, I'll get my keys."

We told Dad where we were going, he was not crazy about it but said ok.

Like I said, Tess could be very convincing.

I got gingerly into her car and we took off. We just drove along the Pacific Coast Highway.

"Turn off there," I pointed. She pulled off. It was the same park where I first told her the truth.

"Lets get out," I said.

"Aidan, I don't know, are you ready?"

"I am tired of being cooped up. I can do it."

"Alright"

She helped me get out of the car and we made our way to that same overlook and sat on the bench. I looked at the tree I had jumped into.

"No way I could do that now," I said pointing.

"Give it some time, superman. That's some some pretty rough Kryptonite you had."

I laughed and took her hand, "I'm glad Lois Lane stayed."

"Lois is never leaving," Tess said smiling.

"You regret your decision, after all of this?"

"Not for a second," she said.

We sat there for a while just looking at the view.

After a bit she said, "Ok enough for today. I'm taking you back home."

She took me back and made me drink yet another cup. We spent the rest of the day just watching movies. She never made it home like she said she would.

Devious, definitely devious.

Thats how it went for a week or so. We would do something during the day and stay home at night. Everyday I got stronger. The bandage came off and the scars slowly faded. They were not all gone but it was much better. I also finally got Tess to go home. Nick and Karen were glad to have her back and so was Austin.

One afternoon, after our morning walk, I asked her to come up to my room. I had a secret to share. "I want to show you something," I said. She had a puzzled look on her eyes but she followed me.

"Here, sit on my bed," I said. I retrieved the box of crystals from my desk and sat them next to her. As I sat on the bed, I pulled three crystals out and laid them in the palm of my hand.

"Watch," I said.

I felt the stillness flow and the three crystals floated up in the air.

"That's amazing Aidan, Your powers.."

I nodded. They crystals began to spin around like small planets.

"My powers are finally beginning to develop. For the first time I'm able to control them a little. I guess being in the ground healed more than my body."

We watched them just spin a second and I said, "Of course I have a long way to go."

"Have you told your father?" she asked

I shook my head, "No. Right now it's our little secret. I want to make a little more progress."

"Of course some revving might help the process along," I said with a smile.

They crystals fell on the bed and we laughing after them.

After two weeks, Dad said I could hunt again. I was ecstatic. Stefan said we would go the next evening. I was finally beginning to feel like my old self.

Tess showed up late that afternoon. She looked as beautiful as ever. I gave her a big kiss when she walked in the door.

"My you're sure feeling better!," she said.

I told her Dad had released me to hunt the next night. "Thats good because I'm sure you're sick of drinking out of a sippy cup."

"Yea I'm starting to feel like Austin," I said.

"He misses you by the way, asks about you all the time. Karen and Nick too."

"How about we see them day after tomorrow."

"That would be wonderful. They would love to see you."

"I'd really like to see them too."

I noticed she seemed a little quiet, not her self. She looked tired. I asked her, "Tess, you feeling alright?"

She rubbed her eyes. "Yea, just feeling a little odd today. Haven't slept too well the last few nights. That's why I was late. I'm a little nauseous too. I think maybe I'm coming down with something."

"You want Dad to take a look?" I asked.

"No, no. It's not that bad. I'm sure I'm just having an off day. I'll be fine. No worries."

"Ok, if you're sure."

Maybe all the stress was finally taking it toll. She really needed some down time. She could see the concern in my eyes. She shook her head, her beautiful hair blowing about and smiled saying, "Don't worry, I'm fine. So where do you want to drive today? Want to go down south towards Carmel?"

I shook my head, "Nope, today I want to take you somewhere."

"Really," she said. That seemed to perk her up.

I pointed out into the garden.

"Lets go to our spot in the forest," I said.

A big smile grew on her face. "That would be awesome."

I walked out and made sure no one was looking then picked her up and bounded over the fence. We flew through the forest. I felt alive again, like all that darkness was finally behind us. We came to the outcropping and I climbed it easily. When we got to the top, I sat her down. It was beautiful, the sun just starting to set. The whole forest was covered in its golden light. A light warm wind was blowing.

We both sat with our legs dangling over the side for a while.

"I really missed this," I said.

"Me too," she said.

She got up, "I'm going to check on the flowers."

"Ok, I'm just going to sit here a minute," I said.

"Take your time."

She walked back to the flowers at the base of the hill.

I looked out across the forest and thought about the past two months. It had been rough but things were definitely improving. I was almost healed and for once I was really making progress on my witchcraft. Tess was just like a member of the family now; she and Rachel like best friends. Dad was making progress on the crystal.

But I was mentally tired and so was Tess. All the events had taken their toll. I knew I needed a break, some time to just be with her. And Tess, I knew she needed a break too. She had been through a lot, more than I could ever ask.

She needed time to be human again.

"The flowers, they smell wonderful," she said.

"I bet they do."

I took a deep breath and just enjoyed the sun.

"Tess," I said.

"Yea," she said behind me.

"I've been thinking. We should get out of here for a while. I promised I would take you back to Venice. We should go next week, then see Naples. And after that."

I hesitated a minute, not sure how she would react, "I want to take you off somewhere just you and me. For a couple of months. Away from all this witchcraft and vampire stuff. We need time off, time to just be ourselves. I was thinking about New York. We could rent an apartment in the city. Somewhere we can relax, just the two of us. Someplace you don't have to worry about this dark world I have pulled you into."

"Aidan"

"Yes," I said turning. She was still facing the hill behind us, where the vines and blue flowers bloomed. She seemed to be studying something.

I got up and with her back to me she spoke, "I'll go anywhere with you but I don't think we have to worry about me being in your world."

"Why's that," I asked smiling.

She turned around and looked up at me with those beautiful eyes and there in the palm of her outstretched hand, glimmering in the fading light, danced a small blue flame of witchfire.

www.ingramcontent.com/pod-product-compliance
Lightning Source LLC
Chambersburg PA
CBHW060512180626
46817CB00002B/348